All That Withers

stories

foreword by Lisa Morton

afterword by Gene O'Neill

John Palisano

All That Withers

John Palisano

CYCATRIX
PRESS

All That WiThers

Collection © 2016 by John Palisano

Trade Softcover (MSRP $19.95)
ISBN: 978-0-9841676-8-5

E-book (MSRP $7.95)
ISBN: N/A

FALL, 2016
First Edition

Book Design/Layout by JaSunni Productions, LLC
Printed/Bound in the United States of America.
No animals were harmed in the making of these books. Go veg!

Published by
Cycatrix Press

http://www.JaSunni.com
Email/Contact: JaSunni@jasunni.com

JaSunni Productions, LLC
16420 SE McGillivray Blvd.
Ste 103-1010
Vancouver, WA
98683
USA

"**Secret Sea**": original to this collection.

"**Eternal Valley**": originally appeared in *Cemetery Riots*,
ed. T. C. Bennett & Tracy L. Carbone (Awol From Elysium Press, 2016).

"**The Curious Banks of the Wabash River**": original to this collection.

"**The Tennatrick**": originally appeared in *Midnight Walk*,
ed. Lisa Morton (Darkhouse Publishing, 2009).

"**Vampiro**": originally appeared in *Evil Jester Digest, Volume 2*,
ed. Peter Giglio (Evil Jester Press, 2012).

"**X is for Xyx**": originally appeared in *M is for Monster*,
comp. by John Prescott (John Prescott Press, 2010).

"**Sunset Beach**": originally appeared in *Famous Monsters* online,
ed. Peter Schwotzer (Literary Mayhem, 2014).

"**I Know This World**": originally appeared in *I Will Rise: Special Edition*,
ed. Benjamin Kane Ethridge (Darkfuse Press, 2012).

"**Forever**": originally appeared in *After Death*,
ed. Eric J. Guignard (Dark Moon Books, 2013).

"**Gaia Ungaia**": originally appeared in *Chiral Mad*,
ed. Michael Bailey (Written Backwards, 2012).

"**Perrollo's Ladder**": originally appeared in *Tales from the Lake Vol. 2*,
ed. Emma Audsley, RJ Cavender, and Joe Mynhardt (Crystal Lake Publishing, 2016).

Dedication

For Pop and for Leo, both of you on either side of me, all of us facing the sea of creativity, each of us casting our lines, ready to report back what we discover. For Mom and Michael, just down the shore a bit, doing the same. We will always be together watching the waves.

Table of Contents

Foreword
by Lisa Morton
13

Preface
15

Happy Joe's Rest Stop
18

Splinterette
32

The Geminis
41

Available Light
56

Long Walk Home
69

My Darkness Travels on Sunshine
81

The Haven
103

To the Stars That Fooled You
108

Mother You Can Watch
123

Outlaws of Hill County
125

Welcome to the Jungle
142

Wings for Wheels
156

Secret Sea
165

Eternal Valley
175

The Curious Banks of the Wabash River
188

The Tennatrick
199

Vampiro
213

X is for Xyx
224

Sunset Beach
234

I Know This World
245

Forever
249

Gaia Ungaia
253

Perrollo's Ladder
266

Afterword
by Gene O'Neill
282

Story Notes
285

About the Author
293

FOREWORD

I think it's now been about a dozen years since Del Howison, co-owner of the horror bookstore Dark Delicacies and a fine writer and editor, hit me with the idea of forming a writers group. At his store, Del has a lot of new writers passing through, and he had enough that we thought we could assemble our own little writing version of The Avengers.

We did. The Dark Delicacies Writing Group met in the flesh once a month, and spent much of the rest of the time online in a private forum, sharing work and exchanging tips. Because Del and I had hand-picked the members, we had a solid circle of authors who were already quite gifted; some had published, others just needed a little polish or encouragement.

I read a lot of great work from that group, but one story made me say, "Holy crap, who *is* this guy?" The story was called "Secret Sea", and I thought it was one of the most original horror stories I'd read since I'd discovered Bentley Little, but even that comparison seemed specious. This story had a voice the like of which I'd never read. It was still a little raw and needed some work, but it gave me a charge that readers have gotten for centuries when they've discovered a new writer they know will become a favorite.

I soon got to know the story's author, John Palisano, and found I liked him every bit as much as I liked his fiction. John was quirky and funny and thoughtful and passionate — just like "Secret Sea" — and, as an added plus, he was hard-working and enthusiastic and gifted in multiple areas (this guy is also a killer musician and filmmaker).

As the Dark Delicacies Writing Group grew, so did John's body of work. He began to sell more and more; apparently, I wasn't alone in finding his work unique, heartfelt, weird in the best kind of way. He began to rack up rave reviews and award nominations. He moved onto novels, and has now published his third, *Ghost Heart*. He's also made (and provided music for) dozens of book trailers (including several for me!), and currently serves as Vice President of the Horror Writers

Association. He's a proud father (no surprise that his son, Leo, is already an award-winning filmmaker before even hitting his teens), and a very good friend.

Most of you are probably reading the greater percentage of these stories for the first time; some will look forward to revisiting these stories after originally encountering them elsewhere; and others may even be getting their first taste of John Palisano's incredible work. I especially envy those in the last group, who will be gifted with that delicious experience of a finding a new author to cherish. John's no longer a new author to me, but I look forward to every new work he produces now, and I'm sure that, after reading this collection, you all will, too.

—Lisa Morton
Los Angeles, California

PREFACE

Looking back on over a decade of published work, I was shocked at just how many stories I've had out there at this point. The idea to put these all in one place dates back at least five years now, and at the time, I thought it'd be more of a complete works kind of thing. As it stands today, *All That Withers* serves as a best-of, or a sort of greatest hits.

Early on we have three Bram Stoker Award nominees, and one that won: "Happy Joe's Rest Stop" (the winner), "Splinterette," "The Geminis," and "Available Light." In no order, other offerings such as "I Know This World" was originally published as a tribute to my late friend Michael Louis Calvillo, as a kind of meta-sequel to his debut novel, *I Will Rise*. It bridges his world with mine. In "Forever" we glimpse an old friend just after we pass. In "Gaia Ungaia," many questions from several of my stories are answered, including one central to my novel *Nerves*. Then there's "Perrollo's Ladder," about a man who is building a ladder to heaven.

Along the way, come inside "The Haven" where a young man finds his home covered through and through with his mother's flesh, and "To the Stars That Fooled You," a riff about wandering New York City as a kid and stumbling into a pair of doomed stars. We go to the Hollywood underground in "Welcome to the Jungle," and then to the Jersey Shore for the "Thunder Road"-inspired "Wings for Wheels".

Later, we discover a "Secret Sea" which brings the dead back to life, and then a pair of stories featuring a mysterious lake, each told decades apart: "Eternal Valley," and "The Curious Banks of the Wabash River."

From there, you'll find some of my metaphysical horror tales mixed alongside fun, old-fashioned monster mayhem in stories like "The Tennatrick" and "Sunset Beach." Like any greatest hits, there are a few new pieces only available here: "My Darkness Travels on Sunshine" and "Secret Sea" among them.

There were many published stories that aren't included. Some I felt weren't among my favorites. Others were one-offs in anthologies where they lost impact without the context of the theme or were part of a larger narrative. A few just haven't aged well.

Having these stories under one roof feels like a great reunion. Many old friends I forgot how much I loved. Many new faces I hope will stick around.

I'm glad you've come to the party, as well. I sure hope you enjoy these stories as much as I had creating them.

Thanks times a million.

—John Palisano
Los Angeles, California

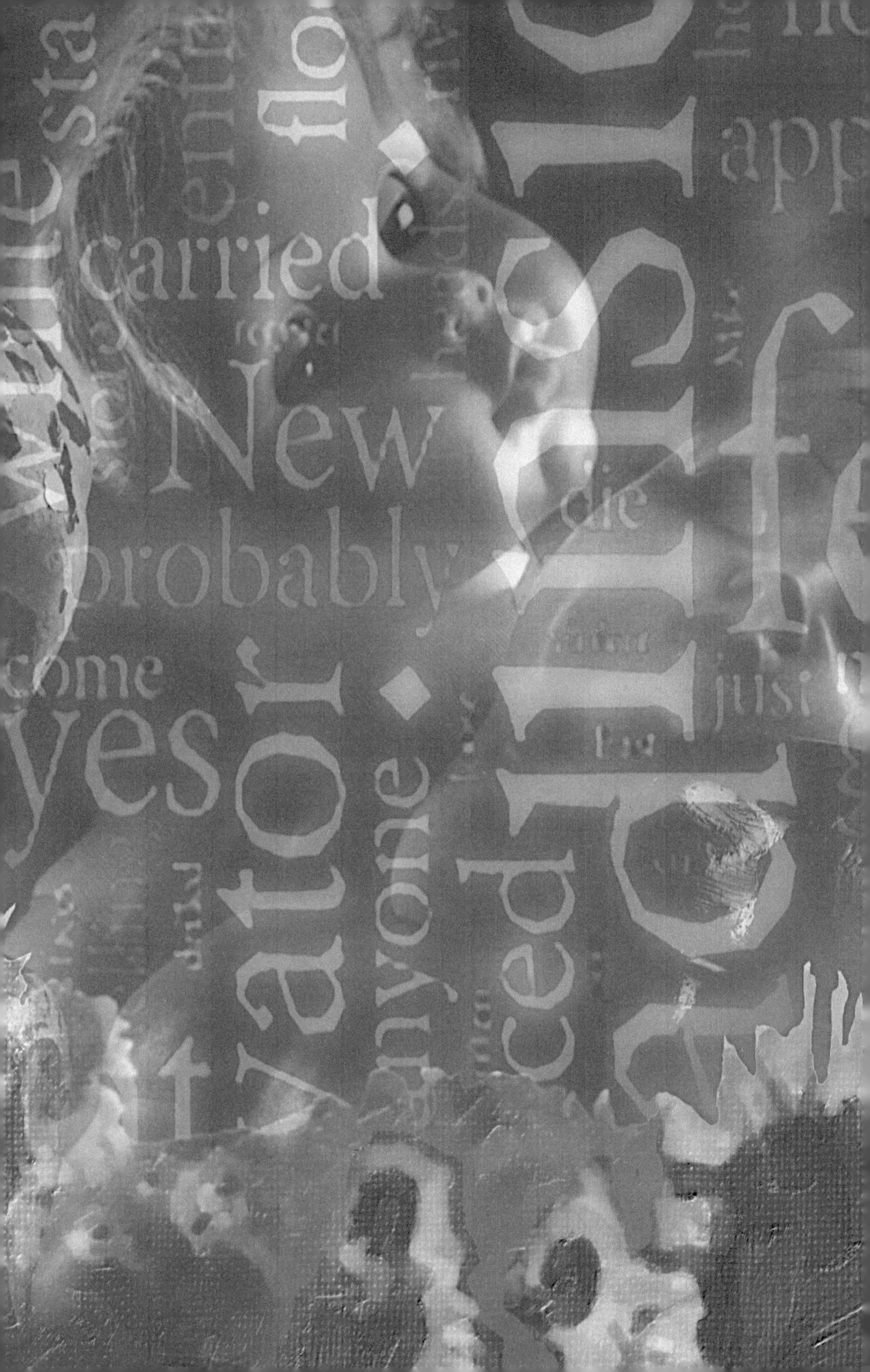

Happy Joe's
Rest Stop

"After you." The man in the white cowboy hat stepped aside and smiled with his mouth closed. The smell of cooking hot dogs came through the doorway. Greg was hungry, and one of those Big'Uns sounded perfect. He'd get right to it, probably round it up with a big sweet tea and some chips. His Papa would be right behind him, once he finished filling up. His dad was going to have to park the rig just outside the stop on account of all the truck parking spaces having already been filled.

Greg was more worried about getting a drink and a snack than his dad's long walk inside. "Thank you," he said. The man smelled funny, kind of like a wet dog that'd recently been flea dipped.

He hurried past and found himself right in the middle of the frenzy unique to a Happy Joe's. The shop was not set up all in a line, like most stores. Instead, there were several stations all around where people could do a variety of things, including checking out. You didn't have to wait for someone to take your money. Some people happily filled their own sodas. Others topped hot dogs. Some shopped for magazines. Greg stopped for a moment at the magazine rack and pretended he was checking out the monster truck magazines, but his eyes really lingered on the fashion magazines with the pretty, half-naked girls on them.

"Mister Fisher, your stall is ready." That was the PA, and the voice of a lady with a Southern Accent. Greg thought it was slightly strange to hear one, because they were in Nevada. It felt right, though, because there were Happy Joe's all through the southern United States. Greg just figured she'd probably been transferred from another location.

He made a beeline for the hot dog station. Dad would be along soon enough, he knew. Of course he would. Where else would he go? Greg looked around the shop and made his way first to the drink stations where, unbeknownst to him, his father had been only minutes before. His father always told him to get the drinks first and then grab any food or snacks he wanted. "That way," he'd said, "if you get to the bottom of your drink while you're grabbing other stuff, you can go back for a refill."

Once he found a medium cup, Greg went to the middle of the machine. There was a big guy with a long gray beard filling one of those monstrous jugs the size of a two-liter. "Be out of your way in a sec," the fellow said.

"No problem," Greg said. "Of course. I'm probably going to get some root beer, anyway. I don't like diet stuff."

The guy gruffed, finished, and stuck a lid on his drink. Then he was off. Greg noticed he was wearing a T-shirt with an eagle cartoon on the front. He always liked how the guys and gals on his dad's routes always seemed to love the country. It made Greg feel like they were all together, and working for the same goals.

He found his root beer and filled his cup.

That's when the lights went.

Not only the lights—the whole place seemed to just turn off. The people turned off, too. Everyone froze for a moment. Greg thought maybe he was having some kind of episode, that maybe it was him. A moment later, he saw people moving. *I bet they all just froze from the shock of losing all their light,* he thought.

One fellow in a cap that read "This Flag Don't Run" looked around and made eye contact with Greg. He nodded slightly. They were both thinking it was only a temporary thing and the power would go back on any second, and they'd be back to the Big'Uns and the 64-ouncers, and then be on their way.

"Welcome." The voice was soft, but because it was so quiet, everyone could hear it. Greg turned and saw the man in the white cowboy hat from the door, only he wasn't standing; his feet were a good two feet off the floor.

Greg looked toward the front door hoping he'd see his dad, but all he saw were plumes of black smoke completely covering the glass.

Something exploded outside. Everything shook. There was little he could do other than stand his ground.

There was a brief moment of silence before everything returned to normal. Turning around, Greg saw everyone looking every which way, trying to figure out what had happened. The

Man in White was out of sight. The music still played. He heard fizzing; a man at the soda station had kept his cup under the nozzle too long. Soda ran over the cup and fizzed into the main drain.

What was the bang? What had happened? Maybe a rig had hit the side of the building? Maybe it was an earthquake. He wasn't sure, but Greg knew he'd have to find his dad as soon as possible. This was way not cool. Not cool at all.

A second larger boom rocked the rest stop.

Greg crashed into a display of audiobooks and barely kept himself upright. Others weren't so lucky. He spotted the guy with the eagle shirt and gray beard lying flat on his belly, his giant drink spreading across the floor in front of him.

What in hell was happening? Earthquakes? What else could happen so fast?

Terrorists. That had to be it. They were under attack. They'd hit the heartland. Why Happy Joe's? They were in the middle of the desert with no one famous or notable—no one powerful enough to justify such an event. Could one of the truckers have been transporting something or someone no one knew about? He supposed it was possible.

"Dad?" he said, making his way through Happy Joe's. There were people lying all over the place. Most were trying to sit up and recover. Greg didn't see his dad amongst them, though. He wasn't even sure if his dad had made it inside. He made to step toward the window, but there was a boom so loud he instinctively covered his ears with his hands.

"Dad!"

Nothing.

The rest stop jolted, and Greg swore it went up instead of back and forth, as if a whale had head-butted it from below.

Where the hell is Dad? Why am I in here all by myself?

None of the other adults even looked his way. He was surprised. Didn't they notice a kid standing there alone? Well, he reasoned, he was big for his age. He was almost thirteen, but most people thought he was almost eighteen. He'd gotten what his mama'd called his father's "football figure," and by that she meant he was big boned, strong, and hearty. He didn't look soft one bit. Still didn't mean he wasn't worried about his dad. Or himself. Why wouldn't he be? It sounded like the world was falling apart just outside Happy Joe's.

He spotted that fellow—the one he swore had hovered—the Man in White. He stood near the front of the store, still sporting that big grin across his face. Greg knew there was something wrong with the guy. Who'd be smiling during what was going on all around them? What the heck? None of it made any sense.

Greg made his way to the front of the store, toward the Man in White. When he neared the front, the Man in White said, "Where do you think you're going?"

"I think my dad's out there." Greg pointed to the window.

"Son?" said the Man in White. "I don't think anything's out there right now."

The Man in White was right: The area outside the rest stop seemed to have vanished, replaced by pure inky black.

"What the . . . ?" Greg said. "Where's . . . ?"

The Man in White shrugged. "Beats me," he said. "It was here a few minutes ago." He hadn't lost his smile the entire time.

"You don't seem . . . concerned," Greg said.

The Man in White said, "Should I be?" He laughed and gestured toward the darkness outside. "This is what I wanted."

"What is it?" Greg asked.

"Nothing and everything," the Man in White said.

Glowing orbs the size of baseballs hovered near the window. On each, wing-like things fanned from four of their sides, matching their phosphorescent bodies. Their tips looked sharp. One came toward the glass and dragged its razor tip downward, making a scraping sound.

Greg stood back. "My father's out there," he said.

The Man in White said, "He's probably gone now. Left under a parade of the Isogul."

"Iso-what? What did you call them? Is that what those things are outside?" Greg said. "Where'd they come from?"

The Man in White said, "It's all magic, my boy."

"My dad," Greg said. "He's out there with those things." He thought: *Who talks like that? My boy? Is he from England or something?*

"Do you want to go out there with them?" he said.

Greg said, "No."

"That's good," said the Man in White. "Because they're coming inside."

- 21 -

Without further prompting, one of the Isogul put its colorful wings against the glass and moved it in an S-shaped pattern. Other Isoguls followed suit.

"What the hell are those things?" a man next to Greg said. "What's going on? Where'd the world go?"

"We better move," Greg said. "If the glass breaks, they'll be in here. On us."

People stared at him.

"Come on," he said. "We need to find places to hide."

"Where is there to hide?" the Man in White said. "They can get through anything."

"Guess we'll just find out," Greg said. "Won't we?" He turned and hurried toward the back of Happy Joe's.

Two Isoguls broke inside the rest stop. One flew right into some poor guy's head, splitting open his face right down the middle. The guy, a big bear of a fellow, cried out just before his face broke apart, revealing the workings inside. Greg saw white and yellow shapes that quickly turned red. Blood streamed out. The fellow's hands were up and at the Isogul, but it was useless. The thing had nailed him. He dropped to his knees and the Isogul made its way inside his head. He fell facedown. The Isogul burrowed its way out from the back of his head and flew into the air, coated in a slick layer of blood and bile. A small proboscis slithered out from a small slit that Greg thought might have been a mouth. It licked some of the gore before slipping back inside the top part of the Isogul.

The second Isogul headed right for Greg. He ducked, but the damn thing found him. His heart raced a million miles a second. *This is it. I'm done. I'm a goner,* he thought.

Greg gulped; the Isogul hovered right in front of his nose. He tried to get a good look at the thing, but it spun around on itself so quickly he couldn't really pin down any single feature, other than it was as dark as night. The Isogul lunged. Greg ducked, half expecting the thing to catch him in the face, just like it had for the big guy.

It did not.

Instead, it hovered in front of him for a few moments before it flew past.

He turned, looked, and saw the Man in White, his arms outstretched in either direction, his palms up, an Isogul hovering over each. He'd been controlling them—Greg knew it was the Man in White who'd been the catalyst.

Greg didn't know what to say or do. He just wanted his dad.

The Man in White turned his gaze on Greg. His smile faded. His chin lowered. Then he turned dark. It was as if his skin had grown see-through, only not with light, but with dark. Greg's heart sank, in the same way it had just before he went over the first hill on a roller coaster, or when he stumbled upon a dead dog, or when he knew he'd done something wrong and was waiting for his dad to come home. Dread. That was what he was feeling.

The Man in White turned, his eyes like two spinning dark holes. His mouth opened, revealing an endless chasm as far and deep as Greg could imagine.

If he gets closer, he's going to swallow me up and I'll never be seen again.

Get out.

Of here.

Now.

Or else.

Dad.

Got to see Dad.

Got to find him.

Get us out of here.

The Man in White went even darker. He was nothing. He was everything. The

Isoguls gathered round. Happy Joe's Rest Stop faded in places. People were on the ground, spread out. The very earth beneath their feet rocked to and fro. Greg felt like he was on a boat, if a boat could somehow be anchored in the middle of the desert. Pieces of the floor fell out. In them, there was the same endless darkness as in the Man in White's empty face.

A woman wearing a baseball cap with a piece of Wisconsin cheese embroidered on it slipped near one of the holes. A man reached out, grabbed her forearm. "Babe!" he yelled. "I gotcha." But he only did for a few more moments. Two Isoguls flew in, hovered, and then dipped down. In a blink, the man's forearm slipped apart from the rest of his body. They'd cut him so clean and quick, reminding Greg of when he cut a piece of ice cream cake for his cousin's birthday using a knife they'd dipped in hot water. He saw a circular shape in the middle of the arm, right before it and the lady wearing the Wisconsin Cheese hat slipped into the black hole. She didn't scream. She didn't seem to react at all. One of the Isoguls followed her inside. The fellow who'd tried to save her yelled—he made a sound like he'd been kicked in the gut. Greg saw him staring at the stump of his arm left behind, right before the Man in White appeared behind him. With one fast kick, the Man in White sent the man with the severed arm over and into the black hole. An Isogul chased him, too.

"What the hell is happening?" Greg didn't know where the voice had come from, but the Man in White with the missing face turned in his direction. A hole appeared where his mouth would have been and opened like the unhinged jaw of a snake about to swallow its prey. Black tendrils rolled outward, like fifteen-foot snakes, and slithered around the parts of Happy Joe's that hadn't turned into black holes.

A guy with a big Steelers shirt jumped up behind the Man in White. He had something in his hands: a huge hammer, the horns pointed toward the Man in White.

The hammer hit the Man in White square in the back of the head.

Dark light, for lack of a better description, exploded out the back. The hammer-wielder ducked a bit, shielded his face with his arm, but the damage had been done. The black light burned hundreds of little holes wherever it'd touched. Greg thought it looked like he'd gotten nailed with buckshot. . . buckshot from hell. The poor guy screamed. Half his face was littered with little holes. They bled, but only for a few moments.

Gray smoke drifted out from the holes. The man shook. He cried out, but then then was silent as his head slowly caved in. First his eyes went blank, and then he collapsed, as if the darkness that had shot inside him ate him from the inside out like an evil batch of otherworldly termites. Then the rest of him flattened, caved, and dropped, his remains a pile of steaming flesh and burned clothes. He was gone in maybe thirty seconds.

Greg froze. What the hell am I supposed to do now? He didn't know, but he felt he had to do something or else it was only a matter of time until the Man in White turned his gaze on him once more. Then what? He'd have to find a way out. But he knew the Man in White could see and sense him. It didn't stop him in any way, shape, or form. *It's like he's toying with me,* Greg thought. *He wants me to see all of this.*

The Isoguls flew through Happy Joe's. They found people hiding behind chip stands, they broke through doors to get into the bathrooms and the showers, and in each place, people begged, people screamed, but people always went quiet. This kept up until there were no more people anywhere Greg could see. He crawled toward the end of the aisle, where there were piles of smashed sunglasses, bags of Doritos, large remnants of a mirrored display, and tons of blood. The only thing untouched was the Happy Joe's theme song, still playing over the house speakers.

Where you gonna go when you've got to go . . . Get refilled. (Killed.)

Happy Joe's. Happy Joe's.
Fill up your tank (skank)
Get a drank (drink)
At Happy Joe's. Happy Joe's.

Greg kept to his place through most of the carnage, unsure of what to do. He thought if he moved the Isoguls would be drawn to him. The entire time he hoped against hope his dad hadn't been in the bathroom, or hidden inside a closet, when the Isoguls searched and slaughtered, sliced and diced.

Where are you, Dad?

The dark black holes spread, swallowing several pools of red gore. The folks were all gone, though, sucked into the endless nowhere the Man in White Without a Face had brought. Greg crawled on the floor, but he didn't get far. The Man in White stood at the

end of the aisle, all the Isoguls spinning around him.

He had no face, but he spoke, and the Man in White used Greg's father's voice to do so.

"I'll eat your fear. Saved the best for last, kid. Made you the most scared. Sweetens the meat."

Greg looked around. He didn't see any way out. The Man in White Without a Face stepped toward him. The ground under his feet faded and turned dark, revealing the great nothingness beneath. Even his feet faded; several green tendrils slid out where his feet had been, their tips like razor-sharp knives.

Crawling back, Greg nearly lost his breath.

"Come on, Kiddo. One last walk. You won't feel a thing."

Don't look up. Don't listen. It's not Dad. It's a trap. Just get the hell out of here. Somehow.

"Kiddo. You won't hurt anymore."

I'm not hurting now. What the heck?

"One last walk."

Greg felt burning on his skin, as though someone were shining a flashlight filled with pain at him. He grimaced, but did his best to avert his eyes and ears.

The Man in White's voice changed. It still used his dad's, but whatever his native voice was, that blended in, too.

"C-come on, K-Kiddo. O. O. O."

It sounded like his dad, but it didn't sound like his dad, too.

"K. Kid. Do. Doh."

There were weird noises mixed in, too: sounds unlike anything Greg had ever heard.

His arm hurt so badly. His forehead did, too.

Need something to protect myself with. Something to hide behind.

He pictured his dad then, and hoped against hope he was all right. If he was here, what the heck would he be able to do against these things, anyway? Then, he knew. Dad's smart. He always has a way to fix things and make things okay, no matter what.

No matter what.

He turned away, twisting around. Saw the pieces of broken mirror in the debris. Reached for a bigger piece. Spun around with it, still keeping his head down. Did his best to aim it back at the Man in White Without a Face.

Like when we used to aim the rearview mirror back at jerks that'd tailgate us with their high beams.

Give it back to them.

Give it back to him.

Greg held up the mirror, catching the Man in White Without a Face in its reflection. Everything the Man in White Without a Face had given—all his dark energy—every bit of it—shot right back at him. It happened before he knew it, and before he could turn away.

The Man in White Without a Face made the loudest, worst noises Greg ever heard. Even worse than when his cousin played him that grind core metal stuff he'd found on YouTube. That was funny. The Man in White Without a Face was anything but.

He's trying to burn me out like he did the others. Trying to take me.

He held the mirror higher.

Then he peeked, just a little.

Greg looked into darkness so vast and hopeless—so empty and bleak—he wanted to give in. *Fall inside. There's nothing here worth living for. Everything is hopeless. Everything is for nothing. Just dust floating in a cosmos that's collapsing into nothing. There is no meaning. There is no being. No consciousness. Be one with the universe. End your suffering. End the pointlessness.*

No. I don't believe it.

"There's that 'I' again. Always this meaningless self-preservation. Always this arrogance and belief that you matter."

We do. I do.

"Tell me why? There is only this."

Greg's face hurt as though he'd been stung by a million bees. Same with his arm. *This is what a tattoo feels like. Just a tattoo. You'll look cool. You'll be grown up. The riders are going to think you're okay now. A man.*

Greg knew what he had to do. He raised the mirror shard upward and tilted it until it caught the Man in White Without a Face. Then the Man in White Without a Face stepped back, clutching at the amorphous black that stood in for his head.

There were spots of darkness . . . sub-darkness . . . growing on him. His own projections had reflected back and erased parts.

He stumbled back.

A tendril reached out, flapped around, and went for Greg. He slammed the edge of the mirror down on it, severing the tip. The Man in White Without a Face let loose a horrendous screeching noise. He stepped back again. His head expanded and contracted in several places; its shape and movement were otherworldly and complex, as though made from a dense, stringy cloud. Quickly, his entire body turned into the same. The scream turned into several voices, then more, countless more, until there sounded a hellish choir of trapped souls. The voices slid through several chords, notes changing, somehow drawing a sick feeling deep inside Greg's gut.

In a flash, the dark remnant of the Man in White Without a Face rose and then rolled itself out and away, going through one of the black holes it'd opened inside Happy Joe's.

It was gone. Greg stood. The piece of tendril it'd left behind had shriveled and darkened. When Greg kicked it, intending to send it into the abyss, it crumpled into black dust. That, too, blew away until there wasn't a trace.

There was a path to the front door, to the outside. He hurried over, past the simmering dark holes, piles of debris, and moist human remains.

At the door he saw the pumps. Saw the cars at the pumps. Saw the rigs. When he made it outside, he saw something else: his dad.

Greg rushed out the front doors.

His dad smiled. Spread his arms. Greg couldn't believe it.

"Hey, kiddo," he said. "Long time."

"Dad," Greg said. "So glad you're safe."

He ran toward his dad, but thought: *Weird. Dad never hugs me like that. Hasn't called me "kiddo" in years. What the heck?*

Greg glanced down. He did, as he ran forth, and saw his father's feet weren't quite there. They were cloudy—ghostly—and something moved where they should have been. Something unnatural. When Greg looked up, his father's eyes were empty, replaced with the same endless chasm he'd seen in the Man in White's face.

It wasn't his dad. Not the one he knew.

"C'mere, Kiddo. Gimme a great big hug."

He tried to run past, but something caught him—phony dad's arm. Handless, the fleshy tip ended in what Greg thought might be a snake's tail. It wrapped around him in a millisecond, squeezing him like an anaconda.

"Great big hug."

The Dad Imposter glitched. The outside melted in places, revealing the same dark cloud he'd seen take over the Man in White.

It'd crawled into one hole and came out another, mimicking his dad.

As Greg remembered his dad, so, too, did it. He pictured his dad in his jeans, a black T-shirt, and his favorite red Peterbilt baseball cap. The thing mirrored the picture in Greg's head. He switched it up, trying to recall his dad swimming with him on their trip to Lake Eerie. He'd worn those new, long hip-hop-inspired trunks, and Greg had been shocked at what good shape his dad had been in. While he did, the thing did its best to pull together, appearing just as Greg had remembered his dad. It squeezed tighter.

"Just a hug."

There was no way Greg would get out of its grasp.

He had an idea.

An image.

His dad, leaning over him. Immeasurably sad. Greg lost his breath and faded. His dad looked on as he passed. Sadness filled him tip to toe. He cradled his son's body. Greg's vision went. He slipped away. It was the only way.

Dad. Worse off than any person could possibly be. Dad. Standing over me. Lifts his hands to his head. Lets me go. He has something in his hand. Raises it to his face. Looks at it. I can't see too clearly. Everything's going black. Then there is a loud boom. A white flash. And I am falling . . . drifting away from his grasp.

Its grasp.

Only a moment.

Get up and run. Don't wait until your eyes work again. Go for it.

Greg ran.

He never looked back.

The thing screamed. He knew it was rushing after him. Felt it opening black holes. Knew it was coming.

He didn't look back. Wouldn't. If their eyes met . . .

A sound like the earth cracking.

Don't look. Ignore it. Run.

He made it just past the pumps, and to the small fence at the end of the parking lot. There was their big old red Peterbilt cab. It was fuzzy. He ran as fast as he could. When he made it past the fences, everything cleared.

He made it to the cab, and looked around. "Dad?" he said several times.

At one point, he looked behind, back at Happy Joe's Rest Stop, and saw nothing. A big pit of darkness had swallowed the whole thing, or so it appeared. There seemed to be some kind of vapor surrounding the area. He couldn't place what it was. He heard screams. Some sounded human. Some sounded formerly human. Some sounded like they were from hell.

"Hey?"

Someone touched his shoulder.

He turned.

His dad. It was really him.

"Dad?"

"Uh-huh," he said. "Ain't you a sight for sore eyes?"

"Where'd you go?" Greg studied him, not entirely convinced he was real.

"Came out to the rig real quick. Got a message we have to get to Memphis three hours earlier," he said. "But when I went back to get you . . . I couldn't get in."

"What's happening, Dad?" Greg asked. He couldn't believe his dad had just been standing there. It seemed too easy. He always was pretty matter-of-fact and reserved, so Greg wasn't expecting him to be doing a dance or anything more than he had. And that was another reason he knew it was really him, and not an imposter.

"I don't know," his dad said. "But let's get the hell out of here. I'm glad you're okay."

"Not sure I even saw what I saw," Greg said. He ran through the events in his head. None of it seemed real now that he was with his dad. It felt like it had to be a bad dream, or a movie.

"You're right about this not seeming real. Can't say how glad I am you're safe. Climb in. You can tell me what happened on the road," his dad said. "Just promise me one thing?"

"Shoot."

"Don't tell your mom. I don't know what to make of this. I can't believe it's even real. But I do know that we've got a load to deliver. There are people that are counting on us. You good with that?"

Greg smiled. "How far is Memphis?"

"About six hours," his dad said, clamping a hand on his son's shoulder.

"Great," Greg said. "So long as we don't have to make any more pit stops, we should make it."

"Nope," his dad said. "No more damn pit stops."

"Those places are hell."

They spoke like everything was normal, but Greg knew, just underneath, they were both still rattled. His dad, as always, was a rock.

As they drove away, Greg looked at the dark chasm

that'd once been Happy Joe's, and wondered what others would make of it if they found it. Would it make the news? Would it be swept under the rug? Would someone figure it out?

"That they are," his dad said, and they pulled up the on ramp and headed south on the highway, toward Memphis. There were tons of trucks and cars, with long, dark shadows, and strips of orange light stretching in every direction—a more comforting sight than either of them could imagine.

SPLINTERETTE

The Great Beyond is white. Millions of snowflakes swirl, hiding my memorized world under a pale bright blanket. Lost and losing warmth, I found shelter beneath the branches of an unfamiliar oak. It wasn't much, but at least it partially blocked the punishing snow. The whiteout came out of nowhere. Within minutes, the backwoods I'd learned by heart were erased. Both my sense of direction and my pocket gizmos failed me.

Alone, and with no clear way home, walking blind could be fatal. A steep cliff loomed less than a quarter mile from my back door, dropping off hundreds of feet toward bare boulders. Picturing myself stepping out, and twirling toward certain death, staying put seemed best. Storms that came on fast could leave just as quickly, I reasoned. If I could just wait it out, I'd be fine.

As I hunched down and rubbed my arms for warmth, someone's shadow came forth through the blizzard—a figure as fair as the storm around her. At first I thought it was Sabrina, my wife. The figure moved just like her. This, though, was different: Splinterette's fingers were long and tapered into sharp, needle-like tips. That was how I came to name her.

Her large, dark eyes blinked, meeting my gaze.

I must have died, I thought, for that was the only explanation for what could only be a hallucination. There was no way I was really seeing what I was seeing. Impossible. Her body changed with each step, the outside darkening. Her face formed—her features smoothed and polished until she glistened. Her eyes were alive, reflecting a shade of winter-themed light blue.

I'd gotten lost—impossibly lost. In this age of smart phones with maps, the world, being so built up and over developed, all it took was a pure whiteout of a storm to become a castaway. The phone lost service. I'd walked around aimlessly looking for a signal, but had gotten myself deeper in trouble. With no roads, how would it have guided me, anyway? At the very least, I'd reasoned, I'd be able to make a call. Home. Sabrina. At least she'd be able to find me, or find someone who could. To top it off, I'd only been a few dozen steps from my own back yard when the storm had hit. I'd known it was coming and had ventured out to see if I could grab some firewood. An old-fashioned, romantic notion had turned out to be a tremendous mistake.

What else could I do other than freeze and wait for the storm to lighten up. Usually, I could see my place for miles, no matter where I ventured inside the Calistoga Woods. At that moment? All I saw was blinding white anything more than a few yards away. My nose felt like it might break off at any moment. The only thing I could smell was the icy smell—that sharp, cutting scent specific to the freezing snow. Very strange.

I'd rested down by a tree. I'd cleared away the snow and put a few of the small logs on the ground to keep my hind warm. My eyes were shut for several minutes when Splinterette came forth. Now you know how and why I felt like I was hallucinating. Maybe I'd slept and the image formed strictly from my imagination—this thing coming toward me—and I couldn't move—I was frozen in thought and movement. There I was, all alone. Or so I thought.

Strange as it sounds, her figure was curved and feminine, reminiscent of a woman, but Splinterette was also tree-like, with her limbs splitting off like branches.

I wondered if I should get up and run away from her. Maybe there were sinister intentions behind Splinterette coming to investigate me. Maybe she smelled blood. Maybe she sensed my death was imminent and had come to feed.

She moved faster than I thought possible. Her arms outstretched above her, the branches that made her arms shook slightly in the wind. There were smaller, sub-branches, too, just like a real live tree. Only she was moving and alive in a way sedentary trees were not. She moved with a grace I couldn't quite comprehend. It reminded me of a spider. It was off-putting, while at the same time? I couldn't keep my eyes off her. She was transfixing, mesmerizing, captivating, and absolutely horrifying, because every part of me knew . . . just knew . . . she meant me harm.

Splinterette bent down in front of me. Her light blue eyes examined me and I at once felt like an animal in a zoo, or the subject of an alien autopsy. Her arms stretched outward, the branch-like limbs making stuttering sounds in the air, as puffs of snow shook off. The storm had gotten worse.

For a moment, she stood. She turned her head and back to me, but still looked over her shoulder at me. She was ready. She seemed to be calling for me to follow her into the cold and snow. I couldn't move. Maybe it was just my mind that was frozen, but my body wouldn't budge from where I sat at the base of the tree, even though I tried my best to will myself up.

Splinterette blinked several times. It was like she knew that I was stuck. She came back to me then—her body moving and arriving in front of me in a blink.

The snow blew around her aquiline face. It made me wish to fall upwards into the snow and vanish into the whiteness. My fear had subsided and a calm serenity filled my soul. Splinterette curled her arms and reached toward me, going first for my underarms. The ends of her branch-like arms slipped over my shoulders and curved back round, under my armpits, and lifted. I saw the sharp, needle-like tips. Splinterette's branch tips slithered up my arm like a boa constrictor, crushing prey, although her touch was anything but harmful. At least at first, she felt warm, slick and strong. I was reassured in that moment. She was there to take care of me and to shelter me, and Angel made from trees come to life in the snow.

Her tips reached my wrists. When they made it to the flesh under my gloves, they followed the same direction as my veins. My flesh split, and for a moment, all I saw were my own pale insides.

Two snowflakes fell and instantly dissolved on the hot, exposed flesh. The blood seeped in, filling the wound like saltwater filling a trench dug deep on a beach. The blood overflowed, trickling over my wrists at first, until it poured much too terribly fast.

Her hands, or branches, then wrapped inside mine, and I grabbed them like handles. Splinterette lifted me, and I immediately felt her strength. She held me like an infant. I curled up in her arms. I looked up and saw her face, and the ring of white sky overhead, snow falling quickly and seemingly from nothingness.

The cold had known me, although the slices to my wrists burned. I couldn't tell if I was still bleeding. I wondered: how deep are the cuts? Would I need stitches? I could die. Had she known that she had hurt me? Could she have realize just how much pain she'd caused me? How close to death I might actually be?

Our house became visible area just some small details. The chimney, its gray bricks. The shutters. Reddish brown. Glimpses. My shelter in the storm. My nose felt clocked. My head hurt; the temples pulsed and there was an aching pressure where the back of my head met my neck. My stomach hurt badly, two. That all paled in comparison to my chest, which hurt worse than anything else I'd ever felt in my life.

I figured it out—I must have been losing a lot of blood.

We arrived at the back door. Splinterette knew where I lived, somehow. I had a vision of her looking in on. Perhaps maybe she was what I said so I looked into the darkness, and felt that special pull that made my hair raise and my belly feel hollow. She watched me. My dark Angel. My savior from doom. My Splinterette.

The back door took only the lightest touch open. How could the storm got not have opened it? I really left it unlocked? Yes. I thought I'd go outside for just a few moments. Our backyard was completely fenced in, except where it met Calistoga Forest. I'd been secure in thinking it had been safe to leave the back door unlocked.

The snow blowing around us, we passed the wooden shoe rack and I noticed Sabrina's shoes were gone. Where did she go in the store? My heart sank—she must have been out looking for me in the storm when I hadn't come back. Picturing her out in the storm, lost like I had been, scared me to my core. Then I looked to Splinterette, initially to try and tell her, but as soon as I did, I once again fell silent. My mouth wouldn't form the words. She had some unnatural spell on me.

We approached the stairs that led up toward the bedroom. Splinterette whispered to me, saying, "recover", and carried me in her arms. She spoke more, but it was as if I were underwater. Even though I couldn't make out her words, I somehow knew what she was telling me. I'd need bandages for the wounds and Tylenol for the pain. Would she be able to help? How would I do these things myself? Would I soon die?

I looked at the paintings while we made our way up— scenes of the world me and Sabrina had collected. Near the top, one was missing. Sabrina's favorite—the two foxes drinking from a river. She always said that they were she and I. All that was left was a rectangular outline of old dust.

We turned the corner and Splinterette lifted my head to

make it through the doorway. I felt drunk and incapacitated, and completely controlled by her every movement.

There was something wrong. More things were out of place. Sabrina's nightstand was empty. Not even her beloved knock-off Tiffany lamp was there. Had someone broken in and robbed us? Had she been kidnapped? Where'd she gone? I didn't see any signs of a struggle. No blood. No resistance.

Splinterette put a branch to her lips, and I somehow felt her hushing my thoughts. She placed me on the bed, and as I fell gently on my back, I remembered everything.

Sabrina yelling when I found the pictures on her phone. Wearing her favorite white, lacey top I'd given her for her birthday. Her favorite jeans and ankle boots.

My shoe slipped off and fell to the floor.

Only a traitor would look on my phone and through my pictures, she'd said.

My shirt opened—a cut from Splinterette's branches did the job, while cutting me underneath. The tingling warmth of her incision filled me.

We can work it out. I know we can. True love will prevail, I'd begged.

More cuts as Splinterette cut through my clothes. She was on top of me. Her pure, dark form caressing me—I held her sap on my skin, streaming from open holes where her branches connected. So sticky, and it soon hardened and pulled my skin, making it raw. True love. Pure as the new virgin landscape outside. My eyes caught a glimpse outside our window, to look at Calistoga Woods, past our backyard, where a trail of red was visible. Bright red. My blood—tracked toward our back door. Our back door? Was it even ours anymore?

Who is he?

It doesn't matter.

Splinterette's arms and legs cut me. Her tips were inside of me, like little fingers, like little fiery worms, like prodding needles.

The new pain took away the old pain. I could feel the hurt instead of just thinking. The release made me hungrier.

More. More. Touch me more.

I had to know it's . . . her . . . name. A whisper in my ear as she bent down.

Splinterette.

And that's how I knew who she was.

I said her name to make it real, so I wouldn't forget.

Splinterette. Splinterette. Splinterette.

One of her branches broke inside me. I knew then that she was of the forest, of the trees, and being inside was doing to her what being outside had done to me.

I heard a knock downstairs, then someone calling my name. Who could it be? Sabrina? Had she come home, after all? Maybe the storm had brought her back and somehow brought her to her senses?

Come home my darling.

I am home.

Splinterette's branches broke. Her face started to lose its life. Her hands and her body trembled.

There were cuts all over me. My wrists, my stomach, my chest—all crossed with long ripped marks. Blood stained everywhere.

More knocking. Someone calling hello—calling my name. Was it a man or woman? I couldn't tell.

Splinterette. I called her name, but she seemed lost to me. The blue light seen in her eyes went out.

Her body crumbled, it's pieces crashing around me. Her head was the last to fall, and it did—directly on my chest.

I couldn't believe it. She was gone, so quickly, and with such little fanfare. There were pieces of her around me. I held onto the two of her branches, one in each hand. The tips of the roots were pointed, sharp, and glistened with some sort of moisture. Her head, on my chest, looked just like any other piece of wood, broken or fallen from a tree. The once refined and exquisite features had turned rough and bumpy. Undistinguished.

Footsteps. Someone came up my stairs. "Hello?"

Was it my Sabrina?

No. It was a man's voice. I saw him poke his head around the corner.

It couldn't have looked good. Not one bit. I held two sharp sticks, and bled heavily from several places around my body: my wrists, my stomach, and my chest.

"You okay?" the man said. I saw frost in his beard. "There was so much blood outside." He paused, looked me over, and said, "Oh my God."

I did not wake in the hospital, or startle from a dream in an asylum, all with a hurried gasp like you see in the movies. Instead I woke slowly and realized I was stuck inside the prison of my own hell—created out of the home I'd shared with Sabrina. Memories were my keepers. So many memories. Gone. All that mattered was lost.

All is now empty. Sabrina's gone. Splinterette is gone, too.

My new friend Phil, a neighbor from two houses away, looks after me. He binds my wounds, cleans my bed, and makes sure my trying something so stupid is never going to cross my mind again. That's what he says, at least. I do my best to make him believe.

Of course, I agree, because soon spring will come.

New snow erased the trail of blood. Then the spring rain will wash away any final clues. Summer will bake the ground and new grass will grow. Leaves will once again turn, and the air will chill. Next winter, I will venture into the snowfield once again, calling, searching, and finding my Splinterette. When I do, I'll hold her hand, and together we'll walk into the pale of the Calistoga woods and disappear into the great white nothing.

THE GEMINIS

I know love. It whispers in my ear at night. In a dream she steals a kiss. Her voice on my phone. I feel her against me, if only in my thoughts. Her arms and body wrap around me. Her belly on mine. Her mouth hangs slightly open. Her face twisted in pleasure. Her lips move slightly askew. I have not felt this way in ages—thought my heart cold and cynical and forever gone. Why is it always the unexpected ones?

When I see her I feel light.

When I leave, I am hollow and my heart feels drawn back. My blood curves inside, going left then right like the snake-shaped roads leading to her house.

This is good enough. To know I can feel again. To know my heart can stretch. To know I've finally healed. It's plentitude. But, wow, did it take time. Of course, I'm deeply involved with another, as is she. And so what? A gentle word, a small touch, gives me enough. Our love will not be ruined through familiarity. Our love remains true and unbroken. Love has awoke. Life will follow.

I know her and she knows me. She has luscious dark and wavy hair. A soft face, similar to mine. We were even born close together: her on the 13th of June, and I, the day after. Same year. Hours apart. Both in New York City, although we've met decades later in San Diego. Lia was drawn west like me. The call. The bug. The creative pull. Neither of us have seen our original, youthful dreams through, but we've managed more appropriate dreams. Her a designer. My filmmaking. Now our music. Such cascades of sound. Rhythm. Bass. Counterpoint. Such beautiful melodies. Our voices blend. Her piano. My electric guitar.

It drives away the darkness.

In this sunshine, in the shadows under the greens, hate filled things linger. They burrow inside your mind. They push you toward the edge, and then shove you over.

Take you.

Take yourself.

That's what they say inside my head. They're trying to draw me into their abyss, but I won't go quietly.

What is it that causes love? The years of attraction we program into our thoughts? The way someone looks? The beauty of another human being? Are we attracted to those who are not like our parents? Those unlike those our parents like?

Lia looked up at me from behind her keyboard. "That's a neat riff," she said. "Very catchy. I think we're on to something."

"Sure," I said. It was all I could muster. The jam had felt good. My entire life I've been searching for someone who clicked perfectly with me. So many false starts in all those bands, and all those partners, trying to make films. Nothing was ever a hundred percent. It was always compromised. That's the big problem I've always had. Nothing was easy. The collaborations were forced, most out of necessity. There weren't a lot of options. That, and I didn't always believe in myself or have the confidence to step up and take charge, nor did I have the heart to tell people when they, or I, weren't working. The one time I asked a singer to leave a band, as he never hit the right notes, well, that turned into a disaster. The other members rebelled against me, and I found myself out of the band I'd started. They carried on gallantly, but never found much success. I ventured into obscurity.

This does not make me bitter. Not anymore. Finding Lia has made me realize it was all for a reason, and a bigger plan was laid out in front of me. One I could never imagine or predict.

My white Stratocaster caught some gleaming sunlight. It was a new instrument, which I found necessary. I'd needed to separate from my past in order to start something new without the baggage I'd gathered on my older guitars.

"Do you think we should check the recording?" I said.

She nodded. "Yes. Great idea. I don't want to forget what we just did." She winked. "Shut your eyes and remember, though, just in case it didn't take."

I did.

The high B echoed throughout her living room, plucked by me on the A string. Simple, and the repeating pattern soon caught on. Lia joined in, adding a diminished chord from her keyboard. She filled it in with a droning bass pattern with her left hand.

Expression.

Channeling.

Connecting.

My memory of the jam blended with the recording, which she played through her phone and her keyboard's external speakers.

She was my other half. Not a perfect mirror, mind you, but the other side of me. Where I flew, she came. If her improvisational choices went too far, I caught her. If mine were too safe, she urged me outside my comfort zone. We did this without talking, without looking, and only through the spirituality inside our playing.

Harmony.

Synchronicity.

The sound and movement of Love and Spirit flowing.

And were we only doing it for ourselves?

No.

We didn't know so.

Not until later.

Sexuality is the curve of a body. The feel. The body has limits. We all look similar. How many variations? Hairstyles? Grooming? Body types? Orgasms are centered in thoughts. So why is it only expressed physically? Can people love without touch? Does it always need to become primal. There's little of that left inside me. I cannot express myself solely through sexuality. Bonding through music feels more intimate, more inside . . . sex is only on the outside . . .

The top of Arrowhead road blossomed out into several smaller mountain streets. The houses got bigger. The gates became taller. The roads more rarified. My daily walk with Charlie, her pit, always brought me great inspiration. We were high up off the valley basin. The air was cool and fresh, even in the summer heat waves. There was a lot less traffic, and a lot less people, which I preferred. I liked the relative solitude it brought. Charlie enjoyed the scents.

I saw a pattern.

In the side of the mountain there seemed to be a dark edge running from the bottom of the crest, near to the top. This jagged line was nearly a foot wide at its fullest, but often shrunk down to only a few inches. It ran behind the houses and picked up on the un-built spaces between.

At first I believed it was only a natural sediment layer, naked and revealed. On top of Arrowhead, despite the many houses, most of nature was untouched. There weren't gardeners pruning and planting the area into joyless sameness. No. You could still see nature the way nature grew. No imported grass. No extra plants. No palm trees. Just raw earth.

On my third day of recognizing the pattern, I decided I'd go up for a better look. Why not? Maybe I'd see some kind of fossil. I was kidding myself in that regard, but my curiosity bested me.

"Come on, Charlie," I said, as we veered off the edge of the road and made our way between two sand-colored houses. There was a particularly good and thick section. The closer we got, the more detail I made out. Small granules glistened. They appeared organic to the layer. When we made it only a few feet from the strip, it moved, expanding horizontally, top and bottom, by a foot.

For a moment I believed it'd been some kind of optical illusion or trick of sunlight moving across it.

The strip expanded again and it moved outward toward me. "You see this?" I said to Charlie, but he was looking elsewhere and not interested in the slightest.

Small rocks and sandy soot fell. The strip widened. There was a low rumble, and I swear I heard voices.

I shoved back.

More sandy soot and rocks poured down.

"Come on," I said to Charlie.

It had to be an earthquake. I'd had terrible timing. Scanning the street, I didn't see anywhere perfect to go. If the houses came down, me and Charlie would be right in the crossfire. There were other hazards on the street.

The ground shook.

Charlie whimpered.

Strangely, everything appeared blurry to me. That must have been my adrenaline.

We made it to the middle of the street.

As we ran, I heard a horn.

A white van slammed its brakes.

I pulled Charlie back as fast as I could. Both of us looked toward the van.

The driver, a stout Latin man, said, "What's wrong with you?"

"Quake," I said, and realized it'd stopped.

He regarded me for a moment, shook his head a little, and drove on up Arrowhead.

"That could've been bad," I said to Charlie.

As we walked away, I looked back at the strip. It'd widened considerably. In one place, I swear I saw an obsidian eye.

Sleep came easy. My trusted eye pillow cushioned my eyelids, a gift from Lia. Colors swirled like a million galaxies in my dreams. Dread filled my gut. The worries of my waking life seeped through. Money was always an issue, as was my heart. Both were always on the verge of collapse. This was entirely due to a genetic predilection against normal work and normal people. Why dedicate over forty hours a week to tasks I could do in a few hours? Only for money. Commerce. Why spend time with someone you don't love? These philosophies led me to near ruin. Instead of settling for a decent job and a comfortable wife with her own cozy job, I wanted more. Explore the outer reaches. Bask in creation. Live for the unraveling. But this unmade me. Had it not been for Lia's generosity, I'd be in serious trouble. As it were, the worst was feeling guilty.

That dream, though, unleashed something else. A deep, fatalistic melancholy that infused my heart. I felt guilty for being alive. Humanity held promise, but ultimately failed. Why did I choose to be born as man?

Choose.

There weren't voices in my head, per se, but thoughts delivered. These weren't of my own imagination. I felt them arrive as clearly as someone knocking on the door. They were coming from somewhere.

The colors turned darker and darker until it was an

enormous spinning black mass of organic matter. I travelled toward it, its vastness and freezing temperature slowly overtaking me. This was my destiny. Purpose. Chosen way.

And I remembered the eye looking out at me from the obsidian strip between the houses.

Hundreds of small yellow orbs floating through the air. Where they go they bring death to every living thing. Nothing escapes. I see them pour from the slit in the mountain.

I woke with tears dried to my face.

Lia opened the glass bay doors. Outside, the canyon stretched for miles in every direction. It looked like a sea of green. There were a few houses below, but the steepness and sandstone made developing most of the canyon too treacherous to develop.

"I want to hear our music sing to nature," she said.

We'd already positioned our amps and speakers so they faced outside.

This I knew would be good.

I plugged in my Stratocaster and set the dials on my amp. It didn't take me long to find my sweet spot. Lia tuned up her keyboard. She found the patches she liked and started playing. I followed along. This time in A minor. The notes cascaded throughout her vast living room. I pictured them as colors ringing off the walls and flowing slowly outside. I felt transformed into an otherworldly conduit. There's something surely magical about making music. It's the closest thing you can get to finding God on earth. That's what I've always believed. No other art forms I've practiced have gotten that close. Perhaps writing, when in the zone. Music forces the listener to be in the moment. It's very difficult not to be.

It's hard to say how long the song went on. I didn't slight to the rhythm. My fingers didn't feel like they were my own, but guided by other hands. Nothing else mattered. I felt Electric and pure.

Our spirits melded together. It was as if we had joined somehow in the ether. The music echoed outside of the house and we could hear it flowing into the canyon. This was a new audience for us. Even if there were no people there were other things listening to what we were creating.

Something made me look out across the canyon to the top of the other hell. Something primal inside.

About three quarters of the way to the top of the adjacent hell I swear I saw trees and vegetation moving. It was as if the mountain were about to split. What was I seeing? Was this another earthquake? Wind? My instinct told me it was something else.

I shut my eyes and played.

Other than my hands, I barely moved. I felt hypnotized.

Don't stop.

Almost there.

Feels so right.

When I first became friends with Lia, I felt a pull inside I thought I'd never feel again. I thought I was too old to fall madly in love. We didn't even have to say much to one another. There was a magical connection. I'd drive away down the curving mountain roads and could barely hold my breath. My head spun, hands shook. I could barely focus on the road. I played love songs on the iPod through the stereo. It hurt; I hurt, in that most magnificent and wonderful way.

Back home I had to go through the motions. I wasn't in love with Theresa. I cared for her. Deeply. I loved her. But I wasn't in love. Not like I was with Lia. Many counseled me. Mature love doesn't have to come on strong, they'd say. It's better if it doesn't. It'll be stronger. I didn't believe them, despite my nods, despite my thanks. No. Especially not after my feelings for Lia erupted.

Love is more important than it may seem. Love kept me going back. Love guided me to Lia. Love drove the music. The music drove away the darkness.

Our thoughts meet—our souls embrace and our inside worlds run free creating shades and colors and sounds our bodies on autopilot transcribing what they can through their hands and bodies—does it make it through and sound true—who can know for sure—blue is everywhere like a tinted glass then orange then purple then everything sounds like a million voices.

I can't play it safe anymore. Not if I think I can really get off. I need things to be new. Different. Taboo situations. My brain has to be charged. On fire. Sex is so damn mental. You just know what people are doing. The same old rhythms. Tricks. Positions. Bathroom mouth. Not clever or sexy. It's often ruined with National Geographic like close-ups of anatomy. Why? It's all inside. The eyes. Kissing. The sexiest part. The touching. Feeling someone close to you. It's not all about the genitals. Those are only one means of expression of love. And it's been reduced to something about as attractive as going to the bathroom. It's not sexy seeing girls being abused or their faces used as targets. It's gross. Sickening. Who wants to see that? Romance is a dying art. Pornography is killing it. Broad daylight. Aerobics with body fluids. No fun. Not romantic. Not special. Let's not even cross that line.

Let's just let it melt away until there is only spirit. Let the sounds free us from our bodies. Let the husks fade to dust. Only the humming of our souls, like a drum hit that doesn't decay or fade, but stays on for several minutes.

That's when the soul hums.

That is how it sounds.

They spoke to me, their voices like discordant bursts through the music. I looked down at the amp, convinced something had gone wrong. Lia didn't notice. She was still in a trance, her chin up, eyes closed, dark hair cascading.

What was it, then?

Klaat somi Dow / Klaat somi Dey

The exotic, unfamiliar words came through, bundled in static and volume.

Who spoke them? What did they mean? Why me?

A vision, then:

The mountaintop breaks open. Obsidian limbs find purchase. Their lengths lined with orifii, tasting the air. Protective layers peel away. Small round things are freed.

They'd been cradled within the limbs. Babies? They roll, then crawl, then roll, like smooth, black baseballs. Rows of small thorns circle their diameters. They give off a sweet smell, which I instinctively know is poisonous. They roll toward the houses. I see people—everyone, in fact—on the ground. Everyone paralyzed by the scent. Still alive. Still conscious. Still feeling when the orbs unfold and their thorns grow outward, hungry for the kill. No one can scream when the orbs rip into them. Blood. Tissue. Shredding. Slowly. Painfully. Above, a shadowed thing blocks the sun. The dying see glimpses through their bay windows and sunlight.

Klaat somi Dow / Klaat somi Dey

The city will pay. This city will pay. These people will pay.

And this will only be the beginning.

"That was wonderful," Lia said. "We keep getting better and better. I wish I knew you back in New York when I was just starting out. We both would have probably been much further along. It just feels like I've known you forever. We just click. Where've you been all my life?"

"I don't know," I said. "Wasting my time with other people?"

I turned the volume down on my guitar so we didn't have to hear the 60-cycle hum.

Lia nodded. "I know what you mean. How long do you think we were playing?"

I shook my head. "Ten minutes?" I said.

"Try close to half an hour," Lia said. "I can't believe we lasted that long."

"Wow. Me, neither. That's crazy."

She said, "Want to go again?" and smirked.

"How can I say no?"

"How about we do D minor this time?" she said.

"Sounds good to me. Just make sure that recorder is going."

Lia pressed a button. "Rolling," she said.

Words. Devastating, cruel. It's what drove me forward. The other one insisted on devolving into abuse. When we first met, she loved me. Her eyes lit. Her face lit. But like so many relationships, things went south. Her sloth became overbearing. Her tongue grew critical and sharp. She found faults where once she found redemption. I became litmus for her to get back at all the men who'd done her wrong. She became so cold she literally turned her back on me when my kidney disease flared. Instead of loving me, she picked a fight, accusing me of terrible things. I was the stand-in for her to say and act toward those who'd hurt her, unfair as it seems.

This is so you know what I realized. A larger current pushed me. I may never have become close to Lia otherwise. I'd never have asked her to play music. I needed escape. We needed to come together. Only pure connection . . . pure spiritual love . . . would have been enough. Faking it wouldn't work. It had to be authentic beyond any doubt.

The thing inside the mountain would know.

The house shook. My head felt suddenly filled with small holes, like a piece of corral. Inside these gaps I felt fluid swoosh in and out. It didn't hurt, although it was extremely uncomfortable.

Lia looked uncomfortable, more so than me. She stood from her keyboard and made it to her couch.

The house shook again. It threw me off.

"Quake," I said.

Lia didn't notice. She was stretched out across her white sectional, an elbow over her eye. I ran to her with my guitar.

"What's going on?" I said. "Lia?"

The guitar came off; I rested it against the couch.

Her eyes didn't look right.

There was an odd, smoky smell that overtook the house. The air seemed cloudy. My throat went dry. "Something's going on," I said. "I think there's a fire."

Lia barely registered what I'd said through her tears.

Then she looked to me.

"It's horrible," she said. "The thing in the mountain."

My mind raced.

"I saw it just now," she said. "In my thoughts. Very dark. Eyes everywhere. Mouths."

As she saw, I saw. Pictures formed in my mind. She, my other half, trembled.

"It has long legs with holes in them. Lots of little holes. They all move, too. And it's inside at the top of the mountain. It wants to kill us all. It's just waiting. Extinction. The little black orbs it releases . . . they give off some kind of smoke . . ."

We both looked up

Several orbs were on the ceiling.

That was where the strange smell came from.

Ringing sounds and indistinct words.

Klaat somi Dow / Klaat somi Dey

I heard not through my ears, but somehow through vibrations in my bones. Unlike anything I'd ever sensed. Cacophony. Noise. Disjointed. Not rhythmic at all.

The orbs tore into the ceiling, causing cracks. Their sounds became worse.

Lia screamed.

That, too, made their noises worse.

"I know what we have to do. There's only one way we can get out of this."

I'm not sure what made me think of it. But I knew she wasn't able to walk to the booth. And I didn't have the strength to carry her. Somehow my instinct took over. I hurried to the keyboard, found the box, and pressed the red triangle on top.

Our music filled the room. It blended with the noises coming from the orbs. We realized it all fit together.

Feels like static electricity inside, curling around like waves. Currents carry us, intermix us, our energies move in and out if one another like two cloudy mists, only they're not mists, but countless atoms circling.

It didn't make sense at first but their terrifying notes and sounds blended perfectly and systematically with the music we had been creating. We'd channeled them and without realizing it.

All those memories and experiences turned off. Gone. The world inside fades to nothing. It can't all be for nothing. How can we have this consciousness evolved from nothing? There is meaning. There is reason. There must be a place where all this ends up.

Tears streamed down Lia's face. She gave a slow nod. At that moment my heart broke into a million pieces. I don't know how it had come to this. I loved her so much, but there was very little I knew I'd be willing to do to express that. Many times I thought through a possible relationship with her. I had scanned all the milestones. First date. First kiss. Love making. The proposal. Settling into a routine. Then twins. A boy and a girl. Their hair and make sure of ours. My blond and her dark hair mixing together. I saw the happy faces. I almost heard their names.

But then I looked down at her and wasn't sure it would ever happen. She'd know me from this now. From these things. And our music was magic. What our love made together was some sort of shield against the thing inside the mountain. I knew it in my heart. We needed the passion. We needed our truest feelings. Yet passion and feelings fade over time, even with lovers who are crazy about each other. We couldn't risk that happening.

"I see these things," she said. "There's another across from us, too. Maybe more." She gestured out the bay doors.

She was right.

The top of the mountain moved. There was another thing living inside. We must've woken them. Stark limbs pushed through dirt and rock, setting aside trees and vegetation.

"They won't stop with us," Lia said.

The orbs on the ceiling rolled toward the door. Within moments they left. Their part of the music faded. We waited, our eyes trained on the hell across from us. When the recording stopped, it appeared that the things in the mountain faded back within their hiding place.

No trace of the orbs. A faint smell lingered. I found the courage to sit on the couch next to Lia. I put out my hand, and she held it. Where would we go from here?

"What now?" she said. "What are we supposed to do? Staying in this room forever? Are we supposed to play new music forever, or do we play the recording over and over and over again?"

"I think we'll have to follow our instincts."

"How are we going to know when they come back? How are we supposed to live our lives now? Are we supposed to wait here?"

"Yes. I think one of us is always going to have to be here, waiting. Just in case. If we're not here when they come calling, that could be bad."

My throat hurt. My head ached. I wanted to sleep. To forget all I knew and saw. To forget what had happened.

"What if we're hallucinating?" she said. "What if none of this is real?"

"I've been thinking the same thing. Second-guessing myself. This can't be real. Things in the mountain. Black orbs in the neighborhoods killing people. Doesn't make any sense."

"I was hoping for so much more," she said. "I knew there was something special when I met you. But I thought it was something else. I thought they were something personal."

"This is personal," I said. "You're the left hand and I'm the right. We need each other to be whole. We need each other to make the music. Treble clef and bass clef. We're each playing half the melody. You play phrase and I play a phrase."

"That's it then. We found our destiny. Each other. And those things. Those things in the mountain. They'll be listening."

"Forever."

"Forever."

AVAILABLE LIGHT

The thing that fell from the sky
Also returned
Also went back.

By my sixth birthday I'd become the neighborhood monstrosity. This, in no small part, had to do with the red blotches dotting my pale skin, the aftermath of my aunt June having allowed me to play unsupervised with my cousins for too long. She didn't believe my parents after they told her about my rare disorder. Sunlight could sicken, weaken, and kill me. Aunt June thought it was something they'd made up.

"It's not real," cousin Antonio said. "It's all inside your head. We're going to find out right now. A test!"

He lifted the blind a peak and the sliver-sized sun ray grazed my wrist, burning yellow splotches onto my skin.

"No!" I yelled, cowering away from the sunlight.

Aunt June slammed the door open and found us. I expected her to help. She grabbed Antonio by the arm and pulled him away. "This is ridiculous," she said. "How can they expect me to watch a child that needs such attention!"

When she came back for me, she pulled me up by my arm, which stung terribly. She wrinkled her pointy nose as she rolled my sleeves over my arms.

They left with such a fuss, made so much noise that all the neighborhood children heard their curses and judgments as they hurried away from our house. I was no longer a person in their minds, but a horrible tragedy they could brag about during one of their dress-up martini parties. Antonio and Aunt June would never again visit us. My parents immediately went about boarding up and sealing our house.

My mother's ears seemed as allergic to sound as my skin was to light. Mamma Agatha could hear the tenderest footstep.

If I so much as stepped from my bed after nine o'clock, she would send my father to check after me. If I asked about my mother, he'd quickly dismiss my questions.

"She's fine," he'd say. "Just under the weather."

"I'm glad," I told him.

Then he unscrewed the little brown bottle with the extra sweet syrup inside.

"Your mother keeps this for you for when you can't sleep," he said.

Every window shade and curtain needed to be checked and rechecked. There was no rest without making sure light couldn't leak inside. The edges of the doors had to be sealed off. The windows in the hallways leading to the bathroom were similarly prepared. In our home nothing escaped scrutiny. My parents were always extra careful.

"Sunlight could kill you," my father said. "You need to believe that. At the very least it will burn your tender skin and might bring on a painful allergy attack. Longer exposure can be fatal."

I pictured myself with my eyes pinched closed and my throat swollen so small I'd barely be able to breathe. My extremities would bloat and my brain would swell dangerously. If my body absorbed enough of the happy yellow rays I would die.

Just before the first drizzles of rain appeared my temples throbbed. My body usually felt any change in weather long before anything was visible. I was happy. Rain meant freedom. No sunlight. If the storm lasted. I did not want to find myself outside if the storm clouds broke. Waiting until late afternoon seemed smarter. If the storm passed and the clouds blew back, night would have already come and there'd be nothing to worry about.

Where would I go? Two places. First I would go to Charlie's convenience store before they closed. I might pick out a treat for myself and a chocolate bar for Cassia. He loved them, of course. Not once could I risk telling our parents about giving them to him. They'd probably die. The goodies stayed our secret.

Second place I opted to visit was always Grand Comics, which was only a five-minute walk from my house, and Nils kept late hours, meaning I could visit after dark. The other local stores closed early. There wasn't strong enough business to keep them open past six in Whistleville, so I always looked forward to my visits.

Rarely was anyone else in the store besides me, and those folks never seemed to buy anything. I noticed many of them left with their own bags, though. One man, close to Nils in age, always left carrying a big blue gym bag. The thing must have weighed a ton judging the way he carried it. I imagine he must have been up to something no good. He sure wasn't making a living from ringing up my occasional books. There had to be something else.

"You got this one?" That was the first thing he said to me when I walked in. Nils held up a paperback. He stood behind the glass display counter, near his register. A stick of patchouli incense burned on the shelf behind Nils, but anyone walking inside would still smell the dry paper from the old books and comics.

"No." I hurried toward him.

Most of the items Nils carried were well-loved, so I was especially intrigued when he handed me what appeared to be a brand-new paperback.

There was a painting of a woman with long red hair on the cover.

Dark moon.

Simon Hughes.

Having never heard of Simon Hughes, I turned the book around in my hands to see if there was a picture. There wasn't. I recognized the publisher, and saw that they'd classified it as Action on the spine. I didn't recall owning, or ever having seen, a book categorized that way—I had to have it.

After paying Nils the dollar he said, "More where those came from," he said. "Got plenty if you want to read them."

"Cool," I said. "This'll keep me up through the night."

"How's your mom and dad doing up there? You know I can see your house when I go out back? See the top of it poking right over the trees."

"Really?"

"Sure. You could wave to me if you ever needed to. I never see any lights on after a certain time, though."

"Well," I said. "My mom's got that condition, after all."

"It's time you meet your brother."

Which was why I found myself staring at what I believed to be the skull of a small animal. Only it was much more than just its head: the entire rest of the thing's devastated body was still attached, and the thing still had enough life in it to turn its head and move its legs.

"We'd like for you to take care of him, now," my father said. "You're mature enough to handle the responsibility."

"Wasn't I old enough before?" I asked.

"Maybe," he said. "The time is right." My father always came off as so cold and brittle when he spoke. It was always business, business, business with him.

"What about you two? Aren't you going to help? I don't even know what to do? None of this seems real to me."

My mother knelt down, touched my wrist, and placed a second hand on Cassia. "I'm here for you," she said. "Of course." Her breath smelled sour and sick. Something was wrong with her. Not one, but two dark puffs circled her eyes.

Cassia looked up at me. The poor weak creature could barely lift his head. I wanted to help.

"What is he? He doesn't look like a person." I asked my father. The thing's yellowed, mottled skin intrigued me because it appeared either plucked clean, or slightly boiled.

"Your brother," he said.

I locked eyes with the creature.

"I don't have a brother!" I said. "I'm thirteen-years-old, so don't you think I'd know if I had a brother?"

My mother came into the doorway of my room, her fingertips touching together in front of her belly. "It's true, Walter. This is him. Cassia." She looked over to my father, and then back to me. "That's what happens when one of you are left in the light. That's why we need to keep you in the low available light of the night, instead."

"Sunlight did this?" I asked.

My mother hesitated before shaking her head.

The thing . . . Cassia . . . My brother . . . Pressed one of his limbs toward me, petting my side. The touch was gentle and slow. Watching his face, Cassia's eyes were the same bluish-gray as mine and my parents.

So what were we supposed to do? I didn't know how to take care of such a dreamlike creature as Cassia, and I imagine he was much more used to the level of attention our parents must have given him.

"Why are you making me do this?" I asked

My mother tightened her jaw. "There are just some things we have to do in life that we don't want to do. Realize it's just the way of the world. Better you find out now, rather than later."

My father chimed in. "We wouldn't want you to get spoiled. Nothing good can come of a boy who grows too used to always getting things served to him in a silver plate."

"What am I going to get out of this other than that?"

Cassia watched me, his eyes wet and curious. Did he know me? Could he have realized that he was in his brother's arms? There was a strange connection, and there was certainly no doubt in my mind that he'd made the connection.

The thing that fell from the sky
Also returned
Also went back

Many things can change when you're thinking of someone else first. Tears of selfish sorrow no longer dried on my skinny cheeks. Instead, I spent endless days and nights caring for Cassia. He needed constant concierge. I was his watchman, nurse, and soon memorized every delicate inch of his being.

Cassia couldn't rest unless his head was propped. There was no going to the bathroom like normal people. His biology was distilled to its very essence.

Several odd appendages lingered from his low quarters, each expelling its own noxious fluids. My mother explained to me what each meant, but I was soon too tired to remember or care.

There is a large ship on the sky that sounds like gray thunder.

Cassia looked as though he'd soon pass on. How could they inflict him onto me when our time together would be so short? They must have known what they were doing. Maybe they wished for his last weeks to be spent with someone who hadn't grown weary of his complete dependence. Another guess—nursing him through death may have been too much for them. The last possibility, and one very much wished for by myself, had Cassia healing and strengthening, due in no small part to my detailed attention and regimen.

There were several weeks where I no longer went down to the comic book shop. I missed Nils and his strange recommendations. I read the Shade book three times cover to cover. Each night, once Cassia fell asleep, I was able to escape into the comforting world inside those pages.

Quickly, I found myself drawn to the main character, Samuel, and had developed some vivid thoughts about what his girlfriend Luna may have looked like. I wished I was as cool as Samuel with the quick-witted comebacks, and the way he kept a few steps ahead of everyone else. If only I were as clever.

As allergic as my body happened to be from light, so my own mother seemed to be from noise. She'd gone great lengths to block as much sound from the house as she could. "Noise distracts me," she'd complain. "And brings on migraines severe enough I might die." Her cold, thin hands would grasp mine, her eyes would search me for the right signs of sympathy. I'd always found it curious that her liquors never seemed to bring on the migraines, but rather, she claimed they loosed her blood and allowed her to relax.

My mother purchased special curtains with extra padding. "They'll block out the light for you," she said. "And mute the traffic and screaming. This neighborhood has changed into a zoo."

When she had one of her spells, we all learned to walk silently, and to lower our whispers. Reading was an ideal entertainment for me. Silent on the outside, but inside there were rocket launches, gun battles, racing cars, fistfights . . . All read with whatever light available to me. Sometimes my eyes felt super-charged, highly sensitive, and sting tears would water my face.

Conditioned to live in low light caused my complexion to lighten considerably. Often my thoughts turned to my memories. My cousins and I used to gather each Sunday at our grandparent's house on Court Street. We'd all sit underneath a canopy of grapevines. Us kids had our own small table while the adults were up on the large green wooden table. Keeping track of which story belonged to whom became trying. So many shared experiences caused details to bleed together. Even the voices merged inside my head. It'd been such a long time since I'd last seen everyone and I'd been very small when I had. That was before sunlight was poison. My mother told me once of how such a tragic allergy got me.

"You almost died on your fourth birthday," she'd said. "The doctors and nurses tried everything to revive you. You had shellfish . . . lobster . . . and your throat swelled up. Your eyes. You went black and blue on me. Then white." I had no recollection of the event, but by the way my mother wrung her hands and kept having to catch her breath, I could tell it still affected her deeply. "They used a new drug on you. Untested. Nobody knew if it would work. Nobody knew what it could do as far as side effects. We found out, after you pulled through, of course. You were at the beach with us and your skin broke out in red hives. We brought you to the emergency room. We thought you got stung by a horseshoe crab or a water snake or maybe some kind of insect bite. We weren't sure. They gave you a hydrocortisone shot but the hives grew. We opened the windows in the room and the way you reacted . . ."

She told me about the priests that came in and tried to bless me. They thought I'd been possessed because I'd screamed to get away from the light. But none of them were right for the longest time.

"It was your father who looked at you and commented that you were sweating so much and that your skin looked shiny like it was sunburned. You sweat and glistened even in the moonlight. We shut the shades so you could sleep. We kept them closed the next day and you improved for the first time in weeks. From then on, that was the last we ever let the shades open."

I pictured that moonlight streaming through my hospital window. I imagine that moment even though I don't remember it. And I wish i'd never gotten that vaccine. I'd do anything to change that moment.

Was Cassia with me during that time? Had I blocked him out? Was he, too, changed from the vaccines? No one would tell me the truth. My father would just sing me the same riddle. "The thing that fell from the sky will also go back." Again and again he'd repeat that. To me his song made no sense whatsoever. If he was referring to Cassia, then the idea of Cassia somehow floating up toward the sun was impossible! If he'd had the same allergy as me, then surely rising toward the sun would quickly kill him. And what did he mean by something falling from the sky? Was it some kind of metaphor, like a fairy tale? Because that's precisely what I imagined it to be.

Discomfort and pain couldn't dissuade me. Grand Comics helped me find myself. I always thought that there were places better than where we lived. The comics and books Nils suggested each had elements lurking just underneath their text if you looked carefully enough. That, of course, took time. I didn't have a whole bunch to spare, not with caring for Cassia. Once my parents found out how good I was at taking care of my brother they left his care almost entirely to me.

Soon thereafter, I had very little time to spare for reading anything.

The storm was a shelter. It was as if God had grasped the world like a baseball, and wherever his fingers landed, huge indentations occurred. Ocean rushed in to fill the gaps, and the newly minted landscape seemed at once both fresh and broken.

The high pitched songs of the late summer insects played between the rumbling thunder. Even after several cracks came uncomfortably close, and the sky gurgled, they sang I wondered about where they might go, other than outside. I imagined them marching under my house, inside my basement through some unknown hidden mini passage.

I yawned and kneeled over toward Cassia. He slept soundly, and he did not know what was happening.

Whooshing sounds swirled around us. Our house shook against pummeling winds. "Hold on, Cassia," I said. "It's going to pass." My promise was broken moments later when a large section of our roof peeled away as though it were made of paper. Up above us, the large spinning gray funnel fed the asphalt tiles from our roof to the sky. Near the center, hovering barely within sight, the large gray, bulbous ship I'd seen earlier.

Holding Cassia with all my might against the winds now invading our room, I pointed up. "Do you see that up there?" I said, my voice disappearing into the noise. Cassia would not raise his head from my arm. There had to be a connection to the ship and Cassia. Something was much too odd. We did not get tornadoes. We did not have weather like what we were seeing. They'd come to find Cassia. They wanted her back.

The rain blanketed down but did not come inside. How this was possible, I can't be sure. Most of our roof had gone, and a spinning funnel hovered directly above us. Everything should have been soaked and destroyed.

An inhuman retch sounded over all the other noise. Cassia wiggled in my arms. His body had changed. The rotten, molting skin smoldered in a heap on Mama's prized carpet. Mamma lay out on the neighbor's lawn; I thought none of her worry about fancy floors, paint colors, and what her acquaintances might think, meant anything. She could have spent her last days doing just about anything else other than worrying. Looking at her spent, dead body, the only thing I could think of was that life wasn't going to pass me by—that I was going to live every second as best and full as could be.

Then Cassia wiggled towards me, spouting flames and fire from his mouth and nose like a dragon made from hell's inferno. His hair had gone, but he had new hair down the side of his head that covered from his temples, past his ears, and down. The immediate top of his head was clean, and his skin had turned the same color as muscle.

The thing that fell from the sky
Also returned
Also went back

My skin itched and burned. Standing away from Cassia, scared and frightened, my back touched the hallway wall. My eyes only left my brother for a moment, because as I scratched my palms, wetness coated my fingertips and nails. Blood? No. Cloudy plasma oozed from minute cracks in my skin. Maybe Cassia dripped on me while still in my arms. Wiping my hands together, sharp paper-cut stings filled my hands. What could this new sensation be? Where was this thing coming from?

Above us the vehicle I'd seen earlier hovered nearer, so that I was then able to see details more clearly. Unlike most flying machines I'd ever seen, this vehicle's very shape moved and changed. Watching it closely for a moment, every instinct told me that the thing was somehow alive. What I'd believed to be a kind of metallic skin was, for all appearances, some type of alien skin. Possibly this substance was a building material unknown to mankind, but common with wherever the vehicle originated.

Cassia inched closer to the middle of the hallway and let out a guttural yelp. His deformed mouth opened as wide as it would go, and every inch of me seemed to remember the endless feedings. My senses remembered exactly how his mealy flesh had felt, and how spongy his lips felt with a spoon gently delivering him his soup. It was possible and probable that I would never again experience that sensation, and that this was his ride come to fetch him to his true home.

Looking down at my arms, my very skin oozed and melted away from me. Drooping stringlets of colored flesh, blood and nerve wavered in the whirlwind. The shape reminded me very much of dripping candle wax, although the source was my own body.

And where would the flame be, and how could I extinguish it? What else would the following moments have waiting for me?

And there was Nils standing in the doorway, drenched and holding a soaking wet book.

This material world brings no relief from death.

It is a sad world where we spread our amber spotlights only for the monstrous, to gaze upon the unfamiliar flesh. Monsters are the normal — man is cold and heartless. We become rich so we can tune it all out.

All That Withers

My precious . . .

Wish Baby . . .

Cassia stood and I immediately could see something was different with him. The yellow shade I'd grown so used to darkened. *He's burning,* I thought. But Cassia stood and for the first time before me, stretched out his arms. The skin between his arms and body appeared connected. As he raised his arms toward the storm, the wrinkled folds spread out. He turned to look at me, which was a miracle, as he could hardly have moved his own head before.

Meanwhile each and every movement I attempted felt more and more labored. All my strength faded. The sun robbed me of it!

Our fractured existence . . .

Xeroderma pigmentosum. The enzymes in my skin can't fix the damage done to my DNA by ultraviolet light. That's the way the doctors put things. Photosensitivity. Like Cassia.

Spotty red bumps erupt on the tops of my arms and hands. My body will always wear the scars. My skin will always tell my story. If it doesn't dry and burn and turn to ash.

Persistant Light Reactivity.

I have to react. I cannot change things, despite trying, despite wishing, despite believing every positive thing possible. Nope. The blisters rise in the sun, the rays toxic to the proteins in my epidermis.

The world turned dark. People changed. Everywhere around me, screaming and hollering echoed. Loud music bumped through my walls. Selfishness and arrogance are worn on people as if they were courageous. Their smug smiles, and quick-witted use of put-downs and insults for every interaction made me wonder if we've always been this way.

What would the world be known for, now? What would it be? What could it be?

Broad spectrum light testing. Mommy brought me in for this, where they took small little swatches of light on the tops of my hands to see what my body would do. It did the same thing then as it did now. Blistered. Burned. Itched and hurt. And I think of how the two moments are connected. First I had no choice but to go to the doctor with Mommy and see what caused my pain. Now, nobody's idea but my own. No one to blame. Should know better. Should think twice, think things through. Can't. Not always. Not usually. Hardly ever.

Our fractured existence inherited through generations of manipulated abuses within our family. All of it adds toward madness. Every willing moment.

Through our opened roof overflowing with sunlight, as my skin spotted, Cassia carried me, towards the light, unafraid, willing, changing, and new. His body strengthened, born again in the bright rays as much as my own was weakened. I swear it took all the strength I had to just keep my eyes open. I looked up to Cassia, who smiled down at me. The gaunt, tired face I'd grown so used to was now changed. The deathly pale blue eyes had brightened. His thin lips were full, his features extraordinary. His arms felt strong and firm as he carried me. I knew I was now becoming the very thing Cassia once was to me—something that would need tending, something that would need constant care. *Maybe,* I thought, *wherever we're going, he may be able to cure me.*

Where will the light catch?

On rays of floating yellow beams.

In dreams of cloudy panes we watch . . .

Syrupy things drip down off me from around and on top.

My eyes wide open.

A willing heart to let it all happen. My new beginning.

All That Withers

The thing that fell from the sky . . .

I will return.

I will go back.

LONG WALK HOME

Our world falls. Black ash blows from the sea and sticks to cars and houses like sticky toxic kudzu. Swirling pastel-tinted clouds streak across Ocean City's gray skies. Ozone flavored rain wets my lips and moistens my cheeks. Gold-tinted memories loop inside my head. Danielle smiling. Danielle laughing. Her son Andy wiggling in his high chair. The little guy giggles, dangling his plastic green spoon over his head, with me nearby never looking more at home. There's still hope left in finding them, but it's fleeting.

The chemicals that'd mixed with the seawater had brewed a toxic soup unlike anything FEMA had previously seen. Not only had our allies turned on us near the end of the war, they'd been our worst enemy, unleashing toxic germs into our water supply. On top of everything, they'd gotten a lucky natural sucker punch. Hurricane George hit the East coast three days later with 120 mile per hour winds. Our little peninsula took the brunt. Poison penetrated everywhere. Sewers overflowed. Safe water became scarce. Food supplies quickly diminished. Those who didn't die from the initial exposure soon fell ill from what we nicknamed the Sludge. The National Guard cut us off while the government seemed to be waiting for us to die. No more work down the pier for me. No endless music. No faithful friends. Everyone that meant something to me vanished.

Right before the phones and lights stopped working, we heard whispers. *Get out of Ocean City if you can. Head to the Meadowlands. There'll be convoys and trucks and National Guard to tell you what to do. You'll be safe at the arena. It's just off the Jersey Turnpike.* I didn't trust it: too easy, with too many people in one place. If I were looking . . . if I were responsible for the attack . . . it'd be perfect. Take everyone out at once. Wipe your hands clean.

That's why choosing to stay behind felt right. It isn't just me, either. There were other people: Lurkers. Looking. Like sharks smelling blood from miles away. You can feel it—your nerves fire and your guts know a Lurker's close.

The Sludge leaked onto our beautiful island beach, turning the shore red and black. The sand stained my white shoes with oxblood splotches. *Get out of this stuff. Walk faster*, I thought. *Danielle's place is just a few blocks up on Waterway Road. You'll be safe.*

Danielle Ross wandered onto the pier one warm August night and waved a flier toward me. "What time do the bands start?"

"Tonight?" I told her. "The openers come on about eight o'clock."

She squinted and pointed at me. "Didn't you go to Martin College? Evan Stevenson, right?"

"That's right."

"Danielle Ross." She put out her hand. I recognized her name and her bright blue eyes. We went to high school together. Danielle told me she was married, well, married until recently, and she had a three-year old boy named Andy to show for it. "We're right on Waterway. The Clubhouse Lagoon's in back of me. You can see the Harbor." There was a southern accent in her voice I didn't remember. She explained how she'd moved down to North Carolina right after elementary school, went to college at University of Tennessee, and decided to move back close to her parents who were still in Freehold.

The entire time we talked I couldn't look away. Magic fire oozed from my fingertips. My throat tightened. Instinctively I knew things would move forward with her and she'd be okay with it. I asked for her number, and called her once my shift ended. "I know I should have waited a few days, or whatever that rule is, but I really wanted to talk to you more and I didn't want to wait." She laughed and agreed. "It was really good timing running into you. Who knew?"

It started with a couple of beers at her place. We kissed that first night soon after Andy went to bed. Things became hot and heavy over the next two weeks. Then she pulled back, freaked out, got nervous. Didn't want to jump back into something serious again.

"What's the big deal? Big deal's me. I'm not ready." The trace of Southern accent in her voice gets thick. She wouldn't look me in the eye. She wouldn't turn her head up. "Is it over? No. Let's just put 'us' on hold."

"Did I do something?"

"No. No. No. Really. I just want to slow down because I like you. Like you a lot." She turned her head up, finally, gracefully, and smiled.

Maybe there was more to it than that, I hope. What did she mean? She had to be developing serious feelings. That was it. That was the last night before the first morning of . . .

The Atlantic turns jet black at night, especially with no ambient artificial light. The full moon overhead glows through toxic clouds hanging over our sky, and blankets the streets with diffused orange hues. You can smell the light saltwater breeze mixed with a sickly sweet industrial, crude oil-like stench. The Sludge is everywhere. Leftover poison lingers in the air and tickles the back of your throat.

The civilized world only exists in pockets around the perimeter of the island, and you don't want to get caught alone by any Lurkers. I sweat heavily and pull the armpits of my shirt out and find my own smell and filth hard to take. My black jeans feel tight and sticky in all the worst places. If only I could take a shower and change into something clean, then I'd be good. All the utilities in the area shut down after the accidents. No running water. No oil. No gas. No nothing: just candlelight and survival. Itching at the facial hair on my neck, I thought I'd try to shave at Danielle's place. She always kept tons of bottled water for her workouts. There wasn't a good way to heat the water safely without electricity or gas. Even at room temperature, I could do a passable job.

Danielle's house sits about two miles away from my one bedroom on Central Avenue near the War Memorial, between 4th and 5th. She's up in the 40s. It only took me an hour walk. There was no one in sight and all the homes I passed were empty.

The dark, ominous sinking feeling in my guts intensifies. Here I stand, waiting, hoping, and praying Danielle stayed home. Water kisses the shores of the harbor in back of her house. From my vantage point, everything looks just as it always had, save for the towering, colorful plumes reaching up like huge bonfires. *Please be home. Don't leave me out here all by myself. Without you there is nothing left.*

Carefully, I stepped up onto the porch and pressed the handle on the screen door. I opened it and took a breath before I knocked three times. There was no answer. I waited a moment and knocked again. She still didn't come to the door. I looked to my right and left to catch any other signs of life. Nothing. Then I stepped back and stepped away. Both curtains in front of her living room window were open. I pressed my face against the glass and peered inside but couldn't see any lights on.

Danielle kept a spare key under a plant on her porch. The first time she showed me, I told her I thought it was dangerous. Someone could easily get in. She laughed it off. "I don't have anything worth stealing."

I told her it wasn't what someone might steal that concerned me. She shrugged off my fears. "I'm a tough girl."

Tilting the flowerpot backward, I immediately spotted the worn brass key. When I stood, my stomach knotted tighter. I felt a hundred eyes watching me. I wasn't supposed to be doing this. What if she was home and just sleeping? What if she just had her iPod on and couldn't hear me? What if she was just out? She'd think I was stalking her and smothering her, and Jesus, breaking into her house.

I had to follow my instinct, though. Too many things could be wrong. She could be hurt. A thug might be holding her captive. She might be sick from all the awful things blowing around the island.

Hurrying to the front door, I inserted the key, unlocked the door, slipped in, and turned to slide the door back in place gracefully. Once inside, I re-locked the deadbolt and headed to the foyer. "Danielle? Hello? You here?" She didn't answer, and my instinct immediately told me I was alone in the house.

I craned my head up the stairs to see if I could hear anything or see any lights. Maybe hear a radio. Nothing.

Then I made it to the living room. Everything looked recently lived-in: there was a stack of half-opened mail on the coffee table. Her remote controls were side-by-side. Nothing looked tousled. It didn't look like there'd been any kind of struggle, which was good.

In the kitchen, the stove was cool, as well. No pilot light. No gas smell. I opened the broiler and looked for the light. I couldn't see anything, as the moonlight wasn't strong enough to see into the stove. I used the small pen light on my keychain to investigate. Didn't look lit to me.

Something distracted me. Danielle's jean jacket with the embroidered rose hung from the back of her dining room chair. Chills rose up my body as I reached out to it as though it was her, grabbing the arms, and wishing it really was her. Was she there? Was she close by? Had she been hurt? I reached into the pockets on the inside and found them empty, which was good. Danielle liked to carry everything she'd need in those pockets instead of carrying a purse. I heard her voice in my head. "I've left my purse too many places too many times. It's easier." I remember asking her what she did when the weather became too hot to wear a jean jacket, to which she asked, "When is it ever too hot to wear a jean jacket?"

I stood up. It was only then I noticed the folded piece of paper on the dining room table. One corner had been tucked under the salt-and-pepper shakers.

EVAN

The handwriting was flowery, as if she were passing me a note in middle school. She'd put a line to the right side and crossed it vertically in the middle. I opened it.

Hey Evan,

I bet you're wondering why I'd think to put this letter on the dining room table instead of on my door. Well, I asked myself what you'd do and I remembered you knew where my key was. I couldn't call you. All the lines are dead. Even my cell won't work. There was a group of National Guard men that have come and told us we have to go. There are buses coming for everyone tomorrow night. Not sure where they're taking us, but it's off this island. They're picking us up at the route 52 causeway. I think you know where the bridge is. I really hope you find this and I can see you hold Andy again real soon. I'm sorry about everything, by the way. These things make people look at the big picture, don't they? Maybe I was too hasty.

Love,
Danielle

She put a smiley face under her name with a heart next to it. Above that, she put a question mark. I reread the letter to make sure I got everything. The paper felt moist, like it'd been left out on the porch overnight and had been covered in dew. Then again, so did everything. I folded the letter and slipped it inside my jacket pocket. At least she was alive, and so was Andy, and she'd mentioned us.

Oh, please, God, make it true. She loves me after all. Where is she?

As I went to turn around, though, I wasn't alone. An older woman stood at the opposite side of the kitchen. Unsure at first how she'd gotten inside and hid from me, the broken glass at her feet and the missing window-pane in back of her answered one question. "Hello?" I said. "I'm friends with Danielle. The lady who lives here."

The woman didn't move. My gaze dropped toward her arm, which she'd wrapped with multiple layers of toilet paper. Dry, dark, red blood clotted and stuck the makeshift bandages onto her skin. Small ridges of deep yellow bumps had broken out just above her bandaged arm and continued all the way up her neck and the side of her face. She had to have been really close to the site of the accident and that meant she was extremely contagious.

"I'm not going to hurt you." I backed up.

Her mouth opened twice and she let out a gasping, dry sound. She was trying to speak. There was nothing anyone could do for her now.

I touched many things in the house. The door handles. The cable-box. Shit! Was I contagious, too? Was I infected? Damn it all.

Well, having made it as far as I had without getting sick,

the thought occurred to me that maybe some folks didn't get sick and that maybe some of us would be okay, despite Ocean City being toxic enough to have instantly killed everyone. Maybe that was the problem.

Then I thought maybe there were things . . . bigger things . . . just happening beyond my control, you know? There I was, face to face with someone who should have been normal. Because of situations beyond her power, the poor woman was dying a painful death.

A horrid screeching sound broke the quiet.

Danielle?

The screech came again and I listened so I could tell where it was coming from. Upstairs.

I hurried backwards down the hall, put my hand along the banister and raced up.

The third step creaked just as I expected. The old house certainly had personality. I sensed someone was upstairs, but I couldn't be sure. I went slowly, thinking for a moment that if someone was hiding and I scared them, well, they could panic and if they had a gun, they'd shoot me, and . . . I stopped myself from overthinking and went forward. Who knew, after all, what might have been going on in Danielle's house after she'd left.

Splashing sounds came from the bathroom. I stopped, nervous. Was it Danielle? What could she be doing in the bathroom? Hadn't she left me a note telling me she'd gone?

At the top of the stairs, you're able to see right into the bathroom. The door was open a crack. The dripping sound increased with each step, becoming louder and faster. Someone inside breathed heavily, as though they had emphysema. With my right hand, I carefully inched open the door.

The room smelled like Iodine and urine and bad breath. A person was in the tub. At first I only registered the big puff of erratically shaped white hair. The texture reminded me of nylon pillowcase stuffing. It didn't look like human hair at all. She sat in the tub and was looking at something floating in the water between her knees. Her arms were mostly black and had withered away—the flesh gone to rot and had tightened and shrunk over her bones. How could she even move? It looked physically impossible.

Then she noticed me and turned. One half of her face was missing. Her lidless stare met my own. They'd gone almost completely white with cataracts and both sockets were ringed with red circles. In an instant, I saw what she was looking at in the tub. It was what was left of her face. She'd been examining it, looking at it, probably wondering what it was. She'd been exposed early and was close to dying. I was sure she was a squatter who'd wandered in looking for some kind of shelter. Maybe she'd come with the person downstairs. That'd explain it. Probably came in together. One infecting the other. The disintegrating person in the tub was someone's mother, someone's wife, someone's childhood sweetheart, now reduced to a half-blind creature swimming in her own decaying juices.

She sniffed the air: her nostrils big and full, her nose swollen and infected like the worst case of skin cancer you ever saw.

"Ha. Ha. Ha. Ha." With every labored gasp, a fresh wave of her rotten, putrid breath overcame the room. It was as though she was rotting from the inside-out.

I was frozen solid. I stared—hypnotized by my own repulsed curiosity.

A cold hand touched my arm.

"Don't . . . hurt . . . her." The woman from downstairs snuck up on me.

Then the victim in the tub splashed again. "Da! Da! Da!" I swear she was trying to say, "Dawn" or "daughter" or some such thing, but I couldn't tell exactly.

"You aren't going to hurt her, are you?" Her raspy voice smelled eerily similar to that of the tub victim. My hand instinctively covered my mouth. Couldn't help myself.

"No," I said. "Just looking for my friend. She lives here. It's her house."

The woman looked around sheepishly. "We just need a place until the soldiers come and help us," she said. "We're not doing anything wrong." She stepped closer, looked me right in the eye. Spooked me because her eyes were all wet and shimmery.

"I know. I understand. It's okay."

Then, with all I had, I pushed past her and raced down the stairs in a flash. Had to get out of there. Away from them. Had to find Danielle. If she wasn't there, why should I stick around? I didn't even bother shutting the door behind me.

Outside, the air was cool and welcoming. Whatever

made people sick, well, hadn't got me and wasn't contagious person-to-person. So we believed.

The moon lit the large yellowish clouds as they hung in the night sky. Would they ever blow away? Would Ocean City ever return to normal?

Shoving my hand into my pocket, I felt Danielle's letter still there. The train. Had to get to the train. Things would be better, then. Things would be all right.

Once I made it off the porch, I curved around back. There was a shortcut back there. If I cut through . . .

The Sludge was within a few feet of the back of Danielle's house and moved like a river of toxic lava. When I first arrived at the house, I hadn't seen it. I'm certainly sure I would have noticed it.

That meant no shortcut for me. I looked to the left, past the row of houses, and to the cross street down the way. The Sludge had cut right across. I felt trapped and quickly tried to think of any alternate ways to escape. To the right, I might be able to beat the Sludge to the other side and get back up onto Main Street.

Hurrying as fast as I could, I darted away.

There'd been so many daydreams about Danielle's house. Me moving in there with her, taking care of Andy, having my toothbrush there, sharing her bed, waking up next to her every morning. Now, with the Sludge inching nearer and nearer, best case would be just getting out of the neighborhood alive and safe. Even without the Sludge, who knew what kind of mess the two rotting women would have left behind for us to clean?

A woman and her son watched me from their porch. It was dusk and hard to see, but they were there and not just figments of my imagination.

Then I noticed two men crouched down just behind a bush. At first they looked normal, but I quickly figured them for infected. They probably knew both women inside Danielle's house. They probably thought I'd done something terrible to the women.

They inched closer.

"I'm just looking for a friend," I called. "Danielle Ross. Do you know her?"

They closed in. Metal glinted near one man's side. He

also had the telltale bumps down one-side of his face. He'd gotten infected.

My instinct kicked in and I ran like Holy Hell. Bearing left, I passed several houses. There were people there, infected, sick people, watching. Where'd they come from? Why was no one here when I first walked up Main Street? Who tipped them off? Did they go into hiding? Did they think I was a threat?

In back of me, the two thugs didn't run after me. I slowed down and tried to catch my breath. A part of me was afraid that someone might hurry off their porch and intercept me for them. I hoped the crowd would be too scared to get involved.

One of the thugs limped. Good sign. The other thug kept in step. Most the folks on the porches were sick. Why hadn't they fled Ocean City and looked for medical help? Why stay behind? Was it because they were standing in the homes they knew, where they grew up and raised their families? Maybe they didn't want to die in some strange, uncomfortable, overcrowded coliseum. If that were true, who could blame them. Had it not been for Danielle, I would have holed up in my studio let the whole nightmare pass me by. I had to find her, had to know where she was, had to say one last long goodbye to her before . . . well . . . hopefully this would all be over in a few days. Hopefully the cavalry would soon be on its way.

I rushed away. Best to be out of sight and out of mind. Despite the two thugs falling way behind me, I turned left onto Bay Street and booked it into a full run. *Get out of here.* I was relieved and happy to find that there were no homes near me. I hurried past Saul's Grocery, and the diner. They'd covered the windows with planks and spray-painted, 'gone' over them just like they always did during hurricane alerts.

Now, there was no one to watch me, no one to watch dying in front of me, and no one left to fear a stranger. I ran to the end of the island, to where the buses waited at the Route 52 causeway bridge, just like Danielle wrote.

Soldiers in gas masks and protective gloves lined people up. Beside them, I could see other people placing something on people's heads. Most people were waved forward. Some were pulled from the line. Then it became obvious. They were checking for fever. A fever like the one I had, except mine hadn't come from their enemy's poisons or from the hurricane's toxic river. Nope. I'm betting mine is just a good old-fashioned flu bug, or stress, or maybe it's just from being overtly tired. Maybe a combination of all three. I put my hand in my pocket to make sure Danielle's letter was still there.

There was murmuring. It reminded me of a summer Boardwalk crowd, only more tired, more scared, and more anxious. Everyone was shuffling. There. I went closer, but not so close as to blend in with them. I fell back and watched them from a safe distance. No one seemed to notice me. Why didn't they use the airport? We had our own, the Ocean City Municipal. Small, but heck, it would have gotten a lot more people out faster. When I thought of it, I had my answer. They didn't want us leaving in a hurry.

To the right side of the street, I could see the flag flying high over our courthouse. On my fourteenth birthday, my Father and me walked down to the same square for a Christmas tree lighting ceremony. He pointed to the flag and told me how beautiful our town was, how lucky, and how fortunate we were to have both been born in Ocean City. Standing alone, I'm glad he didn't live to see what has happened here. It would have broken his heart.

I know that I'm just going to have to wait . . . wait for the fever to pass. Wait until I'm better. There's no way they're going to let me through when I'm running this hot.

That bus is about to leave and maybe little Andy's on there with Danielle.

Don't leave me out here all by myself, Danielle. Without you there is nothing left.

Just wondering if they're getting out safe tonight and wondering if I'm ever going to get the chance to see them again on the other side

What is there left for me without you? My home is gone— my world has been taken. Together we can start again somewhere, somehow. I can't do it alone.

I need you now.

As I took her letter from my pocket, I felt a sharp pain in my fingers. When I took my hand out I saw blood. *A papercut?* Little blotches of reddish moisture bloomed on the places where I'd touched her letter.

Don't leave me alone.

My fingertips looked bruised instead of cut. The skin was soft, and tender, and moist.

What is there left for me? Of me?

I remembered her smile and the way she looked that night at the Pier.

The bus pulled away and my stomach sunk.

Don't leave . . .

My fingers hurt. My hands hurt. An aching fire-like sensation crawled through the nerves from my wrist right up to my head. It was starting and I was sick. I'd always been so damn careful. Where did I go wrong? What did it? How did I finally catch the bug?

I shut my eyes and knew.

The letter.

MY DARKNESS TRAVELS ON SUNSHINE

Dana watched the shadows dance across the ridges of bumpy snow. Even in the middle of winter the sun would come out in the middle of the day. That's when Emma held court. She'd find the same bench right in the middle of the Boston Common and she'd just shine. Folks were struck by her. At first they noticed her long blonde braids, and then her pale pretty eyes. Her caramel skin appeared impossibly perfect. Mostly they'd get pulled in by her questions—the cadence of her voice, and the surety of her intent.

"I know your story." She looked Dana dead on, blinked once, her smile falling away. "You're running from the dark that's eating you inside."

How could she know?

How could she see?

The crowd seemed to part. Dana hadn't wanted to be singled out. Professor Beltran's first class was scheduled to start in twenty minutes. If she didn't get a move on, she'd be late. That meant she'd miss the entire reason she'd gone to the school. Everyone knew the first half-hour of Professor Beltran's first class was what all the famous filmmakers talked about. He laid out their entire careers, they'd claimed. But no one said exactly what. For that? You had to be there. No one leaked the details, although many speculated.

"I'm running because I'm going to be late to class," she said.

Emma's smile faded. "If you don't listen the darkness will catch you."

Dana felt her face redden. Everything seemed heightened—the slightly peeling sections of paint on the bench behind Emma, the smell of the azalea, the floral pattern on the shirt of a woman standing close by.

She remembered years of putdowns. Very few people believed she could go to school and become a filmmaker. Most everyone told her she should stay put managing uncle Isaac's restaurant. She was useful. People loved her. She wouldn't have to worry.

No one understood the pull. She had to go. There were stories to tell that only she could bring to the world. She knew it with every part of her soul.

"I don't know what you're talking about," she said. The small group looked back and forth between them. "I really have to go."

"You have to go," Emma said. "Of course you do. Come back when you're ready to talk about the darkness, sunshine."

Dana hurried away.

She heard Emma in back of her, pinpointing someone new. "I know your story."

It was though she were looking ahead on a sunlit path when a flock of crows fluttered in front, shutting out the light. But it wasn't crows that'd changed her view, it was tears. Her darkness returned, awakened so easily from a few words from a stranger.

Dana made her way through the Garden through rote memory. The routine of the walk was her savior. She felt blinded, and had no idea if anyone even noticed her state. Unlikely, she knew. They'd probably all been staring at their phones while they walked. If anyone noticed they'd probably look away just as soon as they could.

She saw the familiar crux of benches and buildings that made up her school. Drying her face with her sleeve, she too in a deep breath of the frigid wind. "This is your day. This is what you've worked so hard to get to. Don't let anything stop you now. Nothing." She had more time than she'd expected—a small reassurance.

Beltran's class overflowed. Dana found a seat in the very back, and just in time, as several people right behind her had to stand in back of crowd the doorway.

He looked more like a boxer than an intellectual, she thought. He reminded her of her uncle Isaac; strong, stout, and tough as concrete.

He half sat on the desk at the head of the class and half-smiled. "Just so you all know? Most of you are going to fail in the business. No matter what. If one person in this class makes it, that'll be beating the odds."

No one said anything.

"And if you think you can do anything else, get the hell out of here now. You'll fail."

People looked at one another nervously. Was this the talk he gave all the power players? Was this what they were referring to?

He went right into it. "I don't give a rat's balls what you read in books and magazines about me and this class. It's all crap now. Everything's changed. There's no rules. The gatekeepers have retreated. It was hard before. Now it's impossible. Literally. They used to let one or two lucky bastards in once in a while. That's over now. The best you'll be able to do is make your own movie and get it out on the Internet. Hope someone sees it. Hope you make a name. Hollywood ain't doing nothing for no one."

Dana thought he had the cadence of a thug. Her stomach sank and twisted. Had she just worked in vain to make it to film school? Had it been another dead end? It couldn't be. Her face flushed.

"Most of you would do better to take your tuition money and sink it into a film. It's not rocket science, making these things, you know. Everything you need to know is online. Videos. Books. PDFs. Editing software."

Dana raised her hand. She couldn't help herself.

Beltran stared at her, his gray eyes like a wolf's. "You've got to be kidding me. Someone's already interrupting me? This is the big moment. Are you all going to just let her take your time?"

"No." It was all Dana could think to say.

"No, what?" Beltran asked.

"No in that I don't think that's all there is. No I didn't sacrifice everything to get here just to be told to go home. I can't believe it." She would've bet her face was purple. But she thought of how much her father had given her, and how much he believed in her.

"Oh, really?" Beltran said. "Tell me, young lady: Why are you here, then? What's your story?" His eyes, like Emma's, seemed to catch the flicker behind her own.

"I have to do this," she said, unblinking. "No matter what. I have to make this work. That's my story."

Beltran slammed his fist on the table. "She might have a

shot. The rest of you probably don't have a chance in hell."

He got up from the table and paced. "There's one secret to all of this, and all art, and all success. That's finding the truth, d'ya hear me? The truth. It's the simplest thing. And it's the hardest damn thing. Seems easy. But there's a lot riding on that. You've got to be willing to gut yourself. Spill it onto your stuff. So that's the trick. That's the class. It's up to you to deliver a movie that's true on the last class. One minute to twenty minutes long. I don't care about format. Shoot it in 35 or shoot it on your phone. Doesn't matter. Deliver it or fail. If it's false, you fail. I'll be here every week. We'll talk. We'll watch stuff. You can pick my brain. I'm your consultant. Your classmates are your consultants. I don't take attendance. Coming is optional. I'll have office hours. So think about it. Half of you are going to drop out halfway through. It isn't for everyone. And that's fine. And that's it. I'm closing up shop today. If anyone's late, too bad. They missed out. So have a good day. See you all in a week."

He walked out without another word.

People chattered.

Dana grinned. She would be able to make the film she needed.

As Dana made her way back to her studio on Beacon Hill, she felt everything inside her sink. Her blood went heavy. Her heart pumped slow. It seemed like hot blood was leaking inside the top of her skull and covering the tops of her eyes. She went dizzy and sat on a stone wall. The lines in the bench seemed to bloom and blur. Migraine.

It was the sunlight. That was what was bothering her. She put her sunglasses on—her Buggies. She'd heard the stories: light from the sun was supposed to have natural Lithium. It had a natural lift. But it also came with consequences. Indulge too much, and you might eventually find raised melanomas on your skin. Even a little overdose could hurt, as Dana's migraine proved. She was happier in the dark—felt comfort and security within it. That, too, came at a cost. Spend too much time in the dark and it could burrow its way inside and consume you.

This is what my film will be about. The darkness. My darkness.

It would have to be. Her secrets were what had driven her. The world had enough make-believe and fill-in-the-blanks storytelling. Beltran had said as much.

Then she thought: *How?*

Her original idea was for a completely different project. Without a change shortly after she going acceptance. She never thought she'd be able to make the person a movie that she wanted. Dana had gone in thinking she have to make something subpar. She was so happy that wouldn't be the case. The only question was how she was going to convince the woman that she saw every morning in the Boston Common, to participate.

I'll have to offer her something. People need something in order to be convinced. Nothings for free. There has to be some kind of an exchange. But what?

She got up and started home. People, and they all flashed by her, without her even realizing the single detail about any of them. They could've been anybody. Boston look cozy, but it suddenly struck Dana that there could be danger lurking inside any person she passed. Her heart and insides felt hollow.

And there was. That'll darkness come knocking. It always came to claim her. The anxiety always lurking just below the surface, right Beneath her smiles and put together exterior.

It could happen again. It would happen again. If she let it. If she didn't pay attention. If she got soft. If she shut her eyes for too long. It would find her. The incident followed her around like a scarlet letter front and center in her brain. It colored all her thoughts. It made even the happiest moments seem blighted.

She'd made it to the top of the Garden and leaned against the railing of the steps right across the street from the State House. A flare of sunlight reflected off the golden dome— it seemed to have come down and targeted her. The star shaped flare blinded her for a moment. And inside her blindness, against the endless white, she saw death caused by her hands. So many deaths.

Please no. Not again. I've come so far. I've healed. I've come to . . .

The small divots in the big plastic steering wheel grazed the back of her fingers. She'd driven the truck what felt like a million times. It was all routine. Georgie and Paul had loaded it up. She just had to drive it back to the restaurant. No big deal.

Sayer street wasn't particularly packed. A normal

Tuesday afternoon. She wasn't distracted. No phone. No iPod. No radio. She'd looked ahead.

She remembered the sun glaring in her eyes. She put her hand to her forehead to shield and to block and see. She pulled down the visor. The truck jerked forward as though she'd stepped on the pedal. She hadn't. Not that she could recall.

Instinctively, she'd stepped on the brakes and pulled the emergency brake lever. It'd only been a few seconds.

All she'd seen was the sunlight, blinding her.

She'd hit something. A car in front of her. She'd turned off the engine and hopped out. It'd be okay. Just a small accident

Red everywhere. It stood in great contrast to the ice and slush.

People. Several people. A child. Still. Stopped.

Dana went to them.

Please get up. Please move.

My God. No.

This can't be happening. Let me go back and do this again. I can fix it.

Others crowded around and tried to help.

The scene was worse the more she looked. She still couldn't think about the details. She'd repressed them immediately. She'd go insane if she didn't.

Then the pressure built behind her eyes and on top of the inside of her skull. She was back in Boston—back fighting another mega-migraine.

The memories of the accident blurred into what she saw around her. The edges were still fuzzy. She had to make it to her apartment. Bowdoin street wasn't far away. Just around the corner. She made it to the top of the steps, her head pounding in rhythmic bursts of ache. She did her best to look like nothing was happening; she imagined that was what drunks looked like when they were trying not to look drunk.

Every sound was amplified into an excruciating noise. A passing Duck Tour boat's wheezing and whining drilled into her head. It felt like there was fluid bleeding from her sponge-like brain inside her, pooling in her stomach, and making it turn sour.

She crossed the street as soon as it was clear. She could see the steps of her building. Almost there. Almost safe.

Dana needed the dark.

The light was going to kill her. She was convinced of it.

The lines of the street and of the sidewalk shifted. Her brain was playing a trick on her. She reached her door and found her keys. Once she was inside the tiny hallway it only took a step to reach the equally miniscule elevator. She pressed the button, sounding the machine to cry in loud protest.

My eye pillow. Earplugs. Three Ibuprofen. Water. Stillness. Yes. Stillness.

The elevator came. Inside, she leaned against the back wall. She'd normally make the six-story climb to the top via the stairs, but she didn't have it in her.

On the way she imagined the walls of the elevator were open. She rose up past the building, into the New England sky. The city burned in hellfire around her as large beings laid siege. She might escape. But where? The cosmos? Some sort of spacecraft? She wouldn't know. The being ruining the city spotted her—the entire vision was so clear and true!—and it reached out its enormous, three-fingered hand and grasped the elevator. It crushed the elevator, with her inside, slowly. The metal bound in around her, searing her skin, breaking her bones. Blood flowed from numerous wounds.

The thing's eyes met hers. It had so many. Several? It reminded her of a child squeezing an insect. No remorse. No care. Just a slight curiosity about what would happen. Her death was meaningless. Her existence meant nothing.

The elevator banged at the top floor—hers. The horrific vision stopped, but she still felt the fear in her stomach. How could such a thing have even come to her mind? It had to have been the headache, it jarring loose all sort of strange images from deep within its archives.

There were only three small apartments per floor. Here was to the back. She made it inside, where it was blissfully cool and dark. In the bathroom she found the ibuprofen. After she downed three with water cupped from the sink, she stripped and pulled down the shades. Collapsing on her bed, she grabbed her eye pillow from the nightstand. She knew the ritual by heart.

She exhaled heavily. Soon the headache would be gone, leaving her head tingling. It might take two hours, and it might take several. She never knew.

I've got one class tomorrow. And I need to get food. But I can get by if I can't get out. Missing Film History won't be the end of the world. Far from it. I can get the notes online. I can easily catch up. Good to know. I can be off tomorrow if I need to be.

I can think.

Yes. I can think.

She drifted into a strange place where, if she kept still, the pain seemed to hover just above her body rather than throughout her—as if it were somehow orbiting her.

Dana pictured the woman from the Garden she'd seen on the way to Beltran's class. She'd said to come back when she wanted to talk about the darkness. She'd called her sunshine.

She knows about the headaches. Knows about the accident. Knows it all. Damn it. How is that possible?

This is my film. I'll find out what happened. It'll start with her. I'll come to terms with it all. Finally confront it.

Warmth spread through her. For a moment she believed it had to be her innards melting and dying, but then she thought it was something much better: peace.

So she slept. The theater of her mind remained dark. There were no dreams or plays. Only black. Rest came.

Many hours later, though, against the abyss-like state she drifted inside, an eye opened. It was the same eye of the beast Dana had seen in her vision inside the elevator. As large as a whale's, it watched her. She felt it's grasp around her again, squeezing. She couldn't wiggle free. It hurt. Tighter and tighter it closed in, like a massive vice. She tried to scream but her lungs were too compressed.

She woke. Realizing it was a horrible dream, it took her a few moments to come to terms. When she did, Dana felt tender around her middle. When she touched her sides and belly, she was frightened to find her body covered in bruises. She turned on the light and examined herself. Sure enough, there were red marks all over.

There was nothing on the bed that could've caused it.

Did I do this to myself? Did I hug myself so tightly I caused them? If not, then what? How?

She felt a circular thought pattern emerge.

This is how people go insane, isn't it? This is how it starts.

She went to the bathroom mirror to see better and gasped.

It looks like I was squished. They're all around my middle.

Some bruises had turned blue and yellow. Dana felt sick to her stomach.

How do I make these feel better? Do I put antiseptic on them? Wash them?

It all sounded excruciating.

I can't lay on them again. I'll go out. Find breakfast. Go to my class. Get the day together. Maybe I can see if Beltran has office hours. Pitch my idea. Pick his brain.

She picked out an outfit.

Then realized it was quarter to four in the morning. She'd have a long wait until anything opened.

When Dana shut her eyes, she saw fluorescent green blue shapes. Organic in form, their edges seemed lit in a way reminiscent of lightning flashing from within. a cloud. They started as flat, but as she felt her spirit body rise, they took on a third dimension until she floated through them, and all of them housed in a deep corner of the cosmos. She was seen, but through shut eyes, her presence acknowledged and tracked, but not enough to fully awaken the slumbering dark and unfathomable God like beings nearby.

"You're on the right track," Beltran said. He leaned forward in his chair, his hands grasping the sides of the office chair like he'd never been in one before.

"I'm not sure how to make this into a film," she said. "It sounds like a series of interviews. It could be boring."

"That's up to you to not make it boring," he said. "Every documentary should tell a story. It should have a goal . . . a persuasion. It should have a beginning, middle, and end. A good guy and a bad guy."

Dana thought for a moment. "What if I'm the bad guy?" She'd just spilled her guts to him—the accident, the meltdown, the loss of her lifestyle—everything.

"So what if you are? Isn't that what you're going for?"

"Yes," she said tentatively. "I guess I'll go and check out a video camera and get started."

He almost stood up. "Are you in video school?"

"What?"

"Did you come here to shoot video? Or make a film?" He was agitated. "I thought you were the real deal."

"Filmmaker," she said, barely convincing herself.

"Then shoot film. It's a chemical reaction, not an electronic one. If you really want to capture something extraordinary, well, nothing sees like film. Nothing. And don't be fooled by the 24-frame video garbage. It does not capture what real motion picture film captures."

All she could blurt out was a small, "huh" before looking away from him again.

"I'm going to give you an address and a name," he said, taking a piece of scrap paper from the top of the desk. He scrawled something on it and handed it over. "Don't be frugal. Get what you need. Tell him what you're shooting. He'll make sure you're taken care of."

The Green Line was nearly empty, which made Dana grateful. She took the time to look through her Cinematography manual. It was alien to her. The book was pocket-sized, but extremely thick. There were tons of diagrams with equations, many color pictures, and lots of charts. She found a section on film speeds and dove in. It was fascinating. *This is like National Geographic, or something. It's amazing. I can do this. This will be something special. I just know it will be.*

Even the loud banging of the train car didn't jar her focus. She loved every bit of reading about the details of cinematography. She pictured herself holding an Arriflex. She felt the film in her hands. She imagined turning the focus ring and the f-stop rings. It seemed like pure magic—a modern evolution of alchemy. Her thoughts spun, playing through the things she'd read over and over. The world outside blurred. All that mattered was film—her film.

She unraveled the scrap paper Beltran had given her for the thousandth time.

Warren Marsh. Silver Key Films. Buckton, Massachusetts. Just outside of Boston proper.

This person, she knew, would be a key to opening the gateway.

"What are you trying to capture?" Warren Marsh sat across from her. His eyes were intense and very much reminded her of those of an octopus she'd once seen at the Boston Aquarium. Like the creature, his eyes seemed to look through.

"To be honest? I'm looking to do some interviews. I was involved in an accident and I want to get to the bottom of it." That was the best way she could think to phrase it.

"Are you shooting the interviews yourself?" he asked.

"Yes." The hairs on her arms stood up as though an electrical current had entered the room. She couldn't place why she was feeling so strange.

"Beltran called me. Said you were a special case. Said that you needed film stock that'd be a good fit to capture what you're looking for. Some stock is good for making entertainments. Others are right for showing an agenda. Only one can see past that and expose what's not usually visible to the naked eye."

She leaned in. "That's why I'm here instead of just ordering online."

"Right," he said. "Film is a special medium. Nothing compares."

He was up and gone before she knew it. His movements were fast and graceful, which she wasn't expecting from a middle-aged man. When he returned, he had four reels of film in yellow boxes. She was surprised to see that he wore form-fitting black gloves. She thought it must be due to his handling film chemicals all day.

"Kodak makes it?" she asked, surprised.

"Just the boxes I had," he said.

"Where does it come from?" She didn't know why she was curious.

Marsh nodded. "There is a small outlet in Middlecot, Rhode Island. The emulsion is created by hand. There is a special silver halide crystal that is mined by hand just off shore there. Claude wades out and finds the correct rocks. It's said it was made over countless years by the Atlantic and the light of the moon."

"They do all that?"

"They do," he said. "The silver halide in this film is unique to that part of the world. It sees differently. It feels different. The film has what's best described as its own perspective. We run it through our own final wet bath once it's here, as well, to solidify it."

She shook her head a little. "Wow. That's extensive. Crazy."

"Crazy?"

"Just an expression. I mean that this entire situation blows me away." She looked at the stack. "Do you think that will be enough?"

"You'll have enough to shoot for about forty minutes. That seems luxurious to me," he said.

"I trust you," she said. "Where do I have it developed?"

"Bring it back to me," he said. "That's all included in the cost."

"Is there a video screener included?"

He shut his eyes for a long moment. "I'm going to pretend I didn't hear that question."

Damn it. She really wanted a video copy she could watch in her apartment. She had thought it through and knew she could always tape it with her iPhone, need be. "I do have to ask how much it is, because I'm really limited, and I know film can get pricey, and I'm a student, and . . ."

He waved his hand. "This is not about money. We can work out what we need to in that regard. What can you afford?"

She thought. "A few hundred dollars. That's pushing it."

He stood. "I can do it for two, with the promise of an invite to your screening." He put out his hand.

Dana stood, smiled, and gladly shook his hand. It felt odd—reminded her of when she shook hands with a sea lion as a child.

Now the hard part. I have to go see her. I have to convince her, Dana thought as the train carried her back. Dana found Emma not in the park, but in the small Beacon Hill grocery store. She couldn't believe her luck.

Should I go up and say something to her? Should I wait?
No. Don't wait. Go.

She did.

Emma stopped examining cans and turned. "It's you." She said. "Ready to take on the darkness?"

Dana nodded. "Yes. I do want that." She steeled herself. *Ask her, you chicken!*

"Do you think it'd be okay if I filmed it?"

Dana was surprised when Emma smiled broadly. "I thought you'd never get the courage to ask, even though I knew this was inevitable."

"How?"

"I live only a few blocks from here. By the Charles. Can you meet me there?"

"When?"

"Whenever you'd like. The sooner the greater."

"Is have to get a camera. I haven't even used one yet."

"I have faith in you."

And that was enough.

Emma's apartment smelled of frankincense. She'd draped scarves over the lamps, and seemingly, on everything else, as well. Everything looked hand placed. The sun had peaked and was just about to start its descent.

Emma sat in a large black chair and drew pictures inside a sketchbook. Dana couldn't figure out what they were, although she was much more focused on her own tasks.

Dana had trouble threading the hand-held Arriflex camera. She followed the directions and managed it. There was a certain low end rumble that began just outside. Someone in a car with a loud stereo. She felt it inside her skull for a moment, the frequencies bouncing around. For a moment her head hurt and she was back again—back at the accident—back on that road. She shut her eyes and shook it off. Her mind would try and trip her up, she knew. It was inevitable. *Power through this. Don't get triggered. Focus here. Save it for the scene.*

"You okay?" Emma stopped sketching.

Dana nodded. "I'm okay," she lied.

"Get that camera going," Emma said. "The clouds are only going to be parted for a bit."

Dana pointed the camera upward, toward the window, and engaged the shutter. It rolled a few feet of film. "Looks good," she said. "That sounded amazing."

Emma nodded. Dana setup the digital Nagra recorder

and microphone. That was much more straightforward. She mounted the Arriflex on the tripod. Aimed. Focused. Then she pressed record on the Nagra. "Ready?" she said.

Emma smiled. "I am."

Dana engaged the shutter release. "Action," she said, unsure if that was the right thing to say for a documentary.

"I want to talk about darkness."

"Ask me," Emma said.

"Well, I met you in the park. The Boston Common. And you seemed to know about me. You have a gift. Is that something you were born with?"

"I was but I didn't know about it for many years, until I was an adult. Then I just saw people. Saw the colors around them. Felt them. Knew them."

"Everyone."

"Not everyone. No."

"Only some people?"

"Right."

"Like me. You saw me."

Emma leaned closer and stared at Dana. Light bloomed around her, nearly obscuring her. Dana couldn't help but think the shot was ruined. She pressed on. Maybe it could be salvaged? Maybe it wouldn't be a big deal.

"I saw everything that happened to you in a blink. I knew who you were. I knew that the darkness had infused itself to your soul. That was pretty obvious from the get-go. You have to talk about it. But you don't want to talk about it. Because it won't go away. Even if you do talk about it, you it's going to keep driving around your mind like a little mini roller coaster inside your skull."

Dana felt like Emma was just going through the paces. She thought Emma was just making generalizations. Was this all fake? Had she put too much weight into this person? Was that it?

She looked over to the camera and saw that it was still running. The meters on the Nagra were going. Emma went on about nothing, it seemed.

"You said you saw the darkness in me. That could mean anything. What exactly were you referring to?"

"Does it matter?"

"It does."

"Darkness touches people and they cannot escape its grasp."

Dana was feeling had. She wanted to get up and turn off the camera. She was wasting film. It was expensive. Maybe she should have gone back home to Worcester and interviewed her family — the families of the people that were hurt and lost. She'd had it all wrong.

Emma screamed.

A sound came forth that could not have been made by a person. It sounded too deep — too loud — with overtones human vocal chords couldn't produce.

She's possessed.

Or she's making it up.

But how?

The sound kept going.

The meters on the Nagra were peaking so hot that they'd turned solid red. The Arriflex seemed to have sped up. Impossible. The meter was running as if she'd overcranked it tenfold.

This is not the answer I was looking for.

As it began, it stopped. In a blink.

Emma collapsed into the chair. Dana called for her but she didn't respond. The camera had gone back to shooting at normal speed. The Nagra's levels were normal. She turned them off.

A moment later Emma came to.

"You need to go," she said, her voice raspy and torn. "Please. The darkness has infused in you much too deeply. I don't want it here."

"What does that even mean?" Dana said. "How do I know you're not just making this all up."

At that Emma's lip curled like an angry dog's. "You have no idea, do you? You are just a carrier. But I don't want it here. None of it. I have no answers for you other than to leave me be."

"I mean, I'm sorry and all. I just don't know what to do anymore. This is all too much for me, I think."

"What do you think I should do? About this darkness? How can I get rid of it?"

"I don't know," Emma said. "Watch the film."

The entire episode felt off and weird. Dana was sorely disappointed. She wasn't sure how to proceed. The next day she took the Arriflex out on the T and got several beauty shots of the city, all with the sun shining. If she shot during the day she wouldn't have to worry about lighting. "Let the Gods take care of that much for you," Beltran had advised. She'd listened. He was right. She'd captured spectacular shots of the Prudential Building, Fenway Park, Park Street Church, the State House, and Faneuil Hall. Boston was small compared to other cities, and she was able to get everywhere relatively quickly using her T pass. She'd blown through two rolls of film, leaving her one. She'd have ten minutes to tell her story.

The film came back. Dana rushed to get it from Warren Marsh, again taking the long train ride out to Buckton. When she arrived, she found no one in the facility at the front to greet her. She called out, but no one answered. Her reels were on the front desk with her name on them. Examining them, there seemed to be nothing telling about them out of the ordinary.

Clanging sounds echoed from the back, followed by noises of water. She hadn't noticed during her first trip that the facility had been right on the river.

The water sounds like it's inside.

After several minutes of the clangings becoming louder she stood from the waiting chair and peaked through the small plastic window of the doors. There she spotted Warren. He leaned over a pool-like area made of dark brick and stone. There was a strap around his head and he wore large gloves. There seemed to be endless shelves that reached as far back as she could see.

Go on in.

She didn't want to, but she had to. She needed to pay for her film and she was anxious to get back to the school to screen what she had captured. Very gingerly she went through the doors and stepped toward Marsh. The room smelled strongly of vinegar and of the sea. As she approached him, she could see over his shoulder. He ran a long roll of film through a primitive bath; each hand worked a circular crank, with the film rolling from one side to the other. He'd stop every so often and guide the film through the water. To his left, before it rolled onto the secondary reel, there was a roller it ran through that squeezed the water off its surface. She saw small luminescent fish swimming about in the bath. They reminded her of dust that'd caught light against a window, they were so small.

"Don't you need to be in a darkroom to do that?" she asked.

He didn't turn; Marsh wasn't surprised like she'd thought he'd be. Instead, she saw a smile rise on the side of his face. "This is the final bath. This is our special way to bring out all the subtleties."

"Seawater?"

"The only kind with this chemical makeup anywhere in the world. That's why we are built specifically here." The reel rolled out and he placed a piece of paper tape of the end before he slid it off the crank.

"Did my film go through the same process?"

"Of course." He slipped the reel he'd been working on into a box and put it on a shelf. He took off his gloves. The area between his fingers looked connected. She tried not to look.

Did I not notice that before? I shook his hand last time I was here. How could I have not seen something like that?

Marsh didn't seem to notice her spotting his hands. He made his way toward the front of the facility, toward the doors that led to the front desk and her film. She glanced one last time at the bath. The creatures inside had retreated to the bottom and didn't glow as much as they had when the film was being treated. *They must do something to the film to make it look strange. That's probably key to making the film unique. That's must be what it is. Got to be.*

In the front, Marsh kept behind the counter and she made her way back around. "Sorry if I went inside without asking. It's just that . . ."

"I understand," he said. "Don't fret. Now you know one of our secrets."

"Does everybody?"

"Those that need to do."

"Okay. Well, I owe you some money."

"That's right. And don't forget my invite. That's most important."

Dana took a business card from a holder by the register. "This you?"

"Certainly."

He rung her up. She paid with ten twenty-dollar bills.

She opened the box just a bit. She couldn't wait until she got to the school's projection rooms. Threading out from the reel, Dana pulled the film's leader from the spool. She realized she'd have to substantially unspool the reel to see any exposed frames, so she carefully rewound the piece she'd pulled out.

Damn it. Why can't this stuff just be as fast as video? Why am I going through all this just for some sit-down interviews? I could've shot this on my damn iPhone and had the same thing. I just wasted all this time and money, didn't I?

Dana knew she hadn't. It wasn't logical why. Something instinctual kicked in. She felt like she was carrying something special. *This is how drug smugglers feel during a transport, isn't it?*

At least they'd synced the sound for her and put it on as an optical track on the film. She'd be able to screen it with sound straight away.

There were other students in Beltran's classroom when she arrived. She was surprised at finding them. Most were chit chatting and just hanging out. Dana went to the back of the room where she saw Beltran himself speaking to a student. He waved at her, spotted the reels under her arms, and pointed. "You've got film," he said. His face lit.

"Just back from seeing Mr. Marsh."

"Are we going to screen it?"

"I'm hoping."

"Do you know how to thread the projector?"

"I will know very quickly."

He made a clicking sound with his mouth and made a mock-gun out of his hand and shot her. "You've got what it takes," he said. "Lots of chutzpah."

Dana watched him thread the first reel. It was the interview with Emma. "Go sit down in there," he said. "I want you to see this all the way through. Every frame. Turn off the lights."

She did, announcing to the few who were there: "Screening some dailies. So if you'll please bear with us as we turn off the lights."

Everyone went quiet. She'd been the first person to have dailies. Beltran locked eyes with her and she nodded. He turned the knob on the projector and it came to life.

Blinding white light lit the screen at the front of the room. That was followed by pitch black as the leader rolled through.

A small ache presented in her upper right temple. Stress. Anxiety that she's got the shot. Her top right eyelid twitched.

Oh no. Not a migraine. Not now.

The ache bloomed as the film unspooled, stretching to the left side of her head and down into the sinuses behind her eyes. She shut them for a moment, and the act seemed to trigger the pain to spread, as though it were water breaching a levee.

The light came on the screen: the shot when she aimed the camera out the window when she first started shooting Emma.

"*I want to talk about darkness.*"
"*Ask me,*" *Emma said.*

As the image flashed, stabbing sensations pinned the corners of her eyes. Dana was convinced she was about to pass out, but she held herself upright.

It was all too much uncovering.

Something about the sunlight woke her darkness.

Her heart felt hollow and her guts tightened—the same feeling she'd had when she jumped out of the cab the day of the accident and saw the blood everywhere and the bodies on the street.

Emma's image was on-screen. She spoke, but it was the exposure from the sunlight that had remained imprinted on Dana's vision. The intensity of the light had flash-blinded her. Large obelisks of white floated in her vision. She saw colored orbs drifting in her eyesight, too. Remnants of the light.

The orbs became smaller until they were the size of pinpricks.

Stars.

Dana could not truly feel her body around her.

She felt suspended.

A crackling sensation filled inside her head, and she imagined there was a large piece of tinfoil inside her skull being crushed by a pair of alien hands. That was the best way she could compare it to anything she knew.

There were large clusters of colored gas. She drifted toward one. Inside she saw a misshapen figure, coiled and bent into a natal pose. As she neared it moved. The being was larger than she'd expected, perhaps as big as an ocean liner.

How is it just out here without any kind of craft? It is just drifting through . . . space? Is that where this is?

One of its eyes opened halfway. She heard its voice in her head—its intricate language using frequencies she knew she wouldn't normally be able to hear. That would be the only way she had to know that something was wrong.

I know this world. I've seen this before.

It'd been during her vision in the elevator. Dana suffered a similar headache then, as well. What was the connection? Had the headaches been driving the visions? Were they real?

She felt moisture on her lip.

Somewhere, in the background, she heard Emma talking. Her words had a hidden voice. She heard them. It had sounded like she was saying generic phrases, but underneath, masked by her earthly speaking voice, hid the language of the beast. Emma shared a bloodline with the being. Dana knew it. Her instincts were on fire.

The fluid on her lips was warm and tickled out in larger quantities. She reached up to touch it just as the great being in front of her unfurled an arm and a hand, its three massive fingers grasping toward her.

She didn't have to look to know it was blood—hers from inside her head, oozing from her nose.

My brain is melting. Not at off it. Some of it. This thing is flattening it inside my head. That's the sound I heard.

Shut your eyes.

Go back.

Quickly. Before it has its thoughts wrapped around yours, squeezing them dead.

She heard screams and hollers.

The classroom. Something was happening there.

In a flash she returned. Her hands were covered in blood. Her own?

People stood above her. Some had blood on their faces and hands. She saw Beltran looking down at her. "Keep her stable," he said. "Make her comfortable." Their voices were echoes and their images seemed to smear and blur and leave trails. Behind them, the screen where her film had been projected was blank. The projector had been turned off and the room lights were on.

From a window the sun shined in. She put a hand to her eyes to shield them.

It'd found her again.

Then she passed out.

"If you hadn't passed out, we never would have found it," said Doctor Designol.

"Tumor?" Her voice was barely more than a whisper still.

He nodded. "Wrapped around your wiring pretty good up there. We froze it and were able to break it away. You'll be sensitive to light for many years to come."

I already am, she wanted to say, but couldn't find the strength. "Froze?" was all she managed to blurt out.

"In a manner of speaking. We have a special bath we use that can isolate the tumor. It kills it and stops it from growing. It expels naturally after that." He was an affable man, with snow white hair and beard, wearing a big happy smile. "You're lucky we found it. These usually don't present themselves until it's much too late."

"Bath?" she said, thinking of Marsh. Could it be the same material? She pictured the little luminescent fish that had swam around her film. Were they inside her head, eating the tumor? Miniature deatheaters.

Death. Had she really very nearly escaped it?

The tumor was growing when the accident happened. It was eating me alive. It made my mind trip up. It made me . . . less than I

could be . . . but it opened other doors for me. I would have never have made it to college. Thank God it presented itself with the nosebleed and the blackout. I wouldn't be here if it'd been somewhere else.

She'd returned to her family's home in Worcester to recover. School would have to wait a semester. Or two.

Beltran had called her mother shortly after. Her film had burned in the projector, but he'd managed to save a few feet of it, which he'd framed and sent along to her. He'd inscribed the back:

Movies can save lives! See you soon!

—*Peter Beltran*

Most importantly, though, when she removed the glass front of the frame and looked closely at the emulsion side—she had to touch it with her hands—if she turned the piece just so in sunlight, she could make out what appeared to be strange characters from an unknown language, burned into the silver halide crystals. The first time she'd seen them, her headache had returned almost instantly, and she found her mind wandering into the murky great beyond, where the dark god waited and spoke to her in its alien tongue, calling her forth.

She'd put it away after that, mostly, and rested in her childhood bedroom on her childhood bed, drawing the curtains closed each sunrise, because blessed be the night when the darkness couldn't come.

THE HAVEN

Hugh ran two fingers across the flesh-covered wall. It pulsed under his touch, releasing warm, wheat-scented moisture. He didn't expect his mother to respond. *She's everywhere now,* he thought.

On his way to the bathroom he spotted a nick in the wall near the corner—his brother caused it rushing a guitar amp around the corner. Dennis had long since abandoned them in favor living a fantasy life on the West Coast with a tall European actress. Which left Hugh nursing their mother.

The creepy Kudzu-like flesh was slowly eating their past. Looking back at the wall, he wondered how many other marks lay underneath.

Hugh opened the bathroom door and found she'd trespassed there, as well. He lifted the toilet seat with the side of his foot. A puffy mound of flesh covered the back well of the toilet, preventing the seat from fully rising. A thin layer of skin covered its top. He'd have to do something about that, he supposed, but wasn't sure exactly what.

While he emptied his bladder, Hugh saw brown strands of her skin bleed up and over the sides of the bowl, spiraling together near the bottom. She's watching me. Even in here. Her flesh reached too far—Hugh needed some sense of privacy and normalcy.

She's left nothing alone, he thought. *My room is the only place I can go to escape. How long until she gets in there?* He flushed and watched the soiled water twirl away. He smelled his own acrid stench and tried not to gag. The lingering smell mixed with the smoky, mealy odor given off by her flesh.

Turning to the sink, Hugh was relieved to find it had not been overtaken. He grasped the cool, hard metal handle. At least there was something still made of wood or steel. The water felt clean. He washed his face and drank a double handful. As he wiped his hands, the hanging towel stuck against the wall. Peeling it from its hanging loop, Hugh saw the unmistakable mound of flesh behind.

He leaned down and rubbed his face on the towel until he was dry. Then he straightened up, wiped his hands on his pants and went back into the hallway. To his left was Dennis's room. It was exactly as his brother had left it years ago, when he first moved out to go to college.

The last time Hugh remembered Dennis visiting their childhood home, he remarked at how shocking it was to see the disrepair and neglect. But that was before her flesh escaped her room. Before the house had turned into a prison for Hugh.

"There's something weird here," His brother said. "This isn't the same place I grew up in." Hugh hung his head while watching his brother pack. Dennis moved to a hotel for the remainder of the vacation. That had been the last time Dennis set foot inside his childhood home.

As Hugh hurried down the hall, he heard something hit the side of the windows. Oh, no. They're back again.

"Freak!" someone yelled from outside. "Come on out and play with us!"

"What are you doing in there with her?" He heard a second voice.

Hugh put his hands over his ears. How had they found out where he lived? During High School, discovering his address would

have been simple enough. But they'd graduated years ago. Why had they remembered him? Had they Googled their old classmates and come across his name? Had they wanted to pick up where they left off, with their jokes and punches? What did they want from him? Why couldn't they just go away and leave him to his bloated, rotten life? Hadn't they already had enough of him?

His nerves buzzed. Hugh didn't want to be like her and hide in his bedroom amid stacks of second-hand magazines and mounds of thrift store clothes, did he? He didn't want to peer out, afraid of seeing them strolling up the hill or even standing inside his front yard. Oh, no. Not him. He couldn't let himself become devoured by fear.

"Pervert!" someone yelled. "What're you doing? Fucking your mom again?"

The mall. Hugh could almost smell his favorite squishy red fish. I need to get up there. Get a game or a magazine. Still, Hugh couldn't ignore their taunts.

Safe in his own room and free from the taunts and ever-invading flesh, Hugh sank into his bed with his favorite deck of cards. He thumbed through them nervously, recognizing each stroke and color. He'd won the cards playing Skeeball on Cape May. It'd been a proud moment. "Those games," his father later said. "Guess they can pay off sometimes, eh?" Hugh grinned and held the cards, the same lucky deck, as tightly as he could.

"Hugh? Come out and play."

He turned on the air conditioner. It would be louder than them, he knew. He wondered how he might drown out their noise permanently? He wished Dennis still lived in the room next to him. Dennis always knew what to do. Especially when there was trouble.

Maybe I should go and talk to her? he thought. *Make sure she's alright. Make sure she's okay.* He sighed. He always told himself that he'd be stronger the next time things happened. He swore to himself that one day, well, one day enough would be enough and he'd walk out on her. She could have the house she was slowly eating all to herself. You only have one mother, don't you? You don't want to lose that, no matter what.

Hugh hopped off his old bed. One of the old springs made a strange, buoyant sound. He'd slept on it so long, he knew where the dead spots were and weren't. *Damn,* he thought. *She'll hear me coming.*

He looked around the bedroom and waited to hear her call him. Usually, once she heard him get up, she'd call for him to come and bring her food, or a glass of milk, or a cigarette, or her mail.

She remained silent. Weird. That's funny.

Hugh opened his bedroom door and rushed back towards the hallway. There, he slipped on something squishy on the floor. When he looked down, he spotted more flesh that had spilling from the walls. Oh, no. His gut wrenched. Hugh made it round the corner and rushed into his mother's room near the end of the house.

"Mother?" he said. He'd never grown past addressing her with a stilted, frightened tone. "Is everything okay?" As soon as he opened the door Hugh realized that, no, everything was not okay. He gagged from the acrid stench coming from her ballooning out- sides. The entire room was filled as she'd melted off the bed and onto the floor.

"Mother?"

He could not see her breathing. Some of the fleshy mounds pulsed.

He missed her face: it did not light up when Hugh entered. Her big black eyes did not pop open and blink. Her mouth did not move. Her entire essence sunk into the bed. Her head leaned towards one side and he barely recognized her face. Most of it had slipped away.

"Mother?"

Moving closer to the bed, he felt the flesh squish and slide under his feet. "No," he said. "Can't be."

All that was left was her creeping, gooey flesh. Her head had been reduced to bone. It reminded him of the lamb's heads the butcher's counter displayed. But it was no lamb's head. It was his mother.

He stood. She's gone and I'm alone now. He stared at her skull, its jaw hanging open. Should I go over and nudge her? He stepped closer and reached out a finger.

"Mother?"

He poked her skull.

It rolled back and forth and toppled down into the gooey flesh. He saw the cavity of her neck. He saw the bone sticking out. He rushed out of the room before he had a chance to see more. He couldn't be in the house—not with her dead, and not with her dying flesh covering everything.

When Hugh rushed away, he realized his Mother was alive.

The walls pulsed. She'd gotten thicker and covered the ceilings, too.

Get out of here now, he thought. Her flesh was knee deep and it clutched Hugh. *Don't think about it. Just go.*

The walls closed in more as he tried to walk. The flesh grew quicker and more sudden. Transparent, sticky goo bubbled to the surface, which stuck to his elbows and arms.

Toward the end of the hall, Hugh felt her flesh on the ceiling touch down and graze his scalp. *She's not going to let me get out,* he thought. *I'm trapped.*

He remembered his room and all the things he'd kept that reminded him of his childhood. Hugh pictured his cigarettes and his ashtray and really wanted just one last smoke before she swallowed him.

He couldn't move. Below her flesh, her muscle had developed and Hugh found himself no match. He shut his eyes as it closed in. He felt its moist, slippery, salty substance on his eyelids and lips. He could no longer feel. She's got some kind of numbing fluid on me.

Hugh passed out and woke. He had no idea how long he'd passed out for, but he hadn't dreamt or thought of anything. It was as if the time had passed in the blink of an eye. Around him, he saw darkness and skin. He heard the rushing sound of blood and fluid around him. He saw veins and muscles and he felt the flesh around him cradle him and curl him. Hugh tried to stretch, but found he could not.

How am I breathing? he thought. He could not figure it out. He realized that around him, his clothes were gone and his skin itched and burned. Am I dead? Please, God, tell me I'm dead.

But he was alive. The itching and burning became much more uncomfortable. To his right, he made out the open door to Dennis's old room and he saw inside. There, inside, sitting on a bed, he saw his brother. Dennis did not look up to see his brother pass him in the hallway. Instead, Dennis faded.

Hugh felt the flesh moving him along. I'm upstairs, still in the hallway. She's trapped me in her skin. Then he tried to speak.

"Where are you, Mother?"

His lips wouldn't move. Nothing would move. So he thought as hard as he could.

Mother? Where are you?

She didn't answer him.

Light trickled ahead from the doorway. That's what it looks like when it's open. Hugh hoped and prayed he'd be delivered safely outside as his Mother's flesh moved him slowly towards the light.

To the Stars That Fooled You

And from her blood came demons. Small puddles congealed and formed wax-like shapes. Alex saw little nubs stretch out, morphing into small arms and legs which moved on their own. At their tips, three prongs poked forward, wiggling and sensing the Earth's air for the very first time. A reheated, rotten smell blossomed, reminding Alex of the stench fuming from the bums on Brooklyn Avenue.

Alex stepped closer. *These things are what John had been after,* he thought. These little monsters were what made up his Nancy and had driven him over the edge. She'd be free now, Alex knew. She'd also been unable to be saved; John knew that there was no repairing her. The demons had eaten far too much of Nancy for her to ever recover. There was only quiet inside her. There was only quiet.

"What time are you coming back tonight?" Alex looked to his father, who busily stashed pens and a sketchbook inside his courier bag.

"Probably around eight," said his father, who didn't turn around. "Maybe sooner. Who knows? You going to be okay?"

Alex nodded. "Sure," he said. "I was going to go to the movies today."

"Movies? Who needs to go to the movies when you're living here at Hotel Chelsea?"

Alex sat down in a chair, and as he did, he could smell the musty odor of the ashtray on the table near him. His father was silhouetted against the window. The sun was too bright for Alex to see anything outside the window. "I don't know," he said. "I like going outside sometimes, too."

"Of course. I get that. But the movies aren't outside. They're inside. I used to love just sitting in Washington Square and people-watching."

"I'll probably pass through there," he said. "But that place is getting filled with druggies."

His father grunted and zipped his bag. "Well, I'm sure you'll find something to keep you busy." He hurried up to his son, curled an arm around his neck, and planted his lips on top of his head. "All right," he said. "See you tonight."

Alex waved and stared at the door after his father had closed it. His guts felt tied up in knots. His eyes watered. Things were never going to be the same. For some reason, he knew that. For every reason he was glad his father was gone. He's vulnerable. If he stuck around today, he'd be in trouble. What's coming today is no good. What's coming today is the worst kind of trouble.

There was Pop, walking out the door to go to work. He's always at work—never at home. That's why Mom left him and we all split up. They're living in Ocean City, New Jersey, her and my brother. I'm in the city with a father who's never around. I feel like an orphan. I feel alone and underground, like a part of me has already died.

I dream of the big trees and the chorus of chirping birds where I could ride my bike around the neighborhood, along the sidewalks and in the streets. The cul-de-sac is still perfectly safe.

Back in Ocean City, the worst trouble came from the older neighborhood kids. He'd just turned thirteen, but they were eighteen. Not here, though. Not in this place that always smells of heat and motor oil and gas and crowds. The streets were nowhere near as crowded as they would become later in the afternoon.

New York ran faster and faster all the time, it seemed. People didn't look up when they were hurrying along; they stared straight ahead at invisible pinpoints several blocks away. None of them even see me hovering among them, going to school, going out in search of food, going downtown to the record stores to look through the endless bins of cardboard and vinyl. Alex smelled the slightly burned pretzel smoke drifting across the street. It reminded him of the stories his father told him of how he first came to New York and attended the Institute of Art and how he'd go up on the rooftop with the girls and kiss them. Whenever Alex passed the school he always stopped, looked up and tried to picture his father as a young man in his leather jacket and long hair, up there with some hippie chick gazing out over the nighttime New York skyline.

Sometimes he wandered inside the guitar stores on music row and thought he might pick one up and give it a try. One day. He'd use all the knowledge of records and *Creem* and *Rolling Stone* so that it'd all add up.

He passed 7th and made it to 6th without stopping. He knew he didn't have far to go to make it over to the Village. His stomach rumbled but he forgot about it, even as he passed his favorite Italian place by Saint Mark's. *Maybe one day I'll bring someone there*, he thought. *Maybe when I'm older and I'm in college or have my own money. That'll be cool.*

He passed the Bottom Line club, and remembered it from a few years back when his father and uncle had set lounge chairs on top of their garage, drank beer, and listened to a live broadcast from the club featuring Bruce Springsteen. He liked that the band sang some of the oldies his mother liked, but played them louder. Up until then he'd really just liked Kiss and the Partridge Family. Bruce changed that, and opened a door toward other artists like Bob Dylan, Woody Guthrie, and Neil Young. Walking past the club he smiled, remembering that night.

He was off to discover more diamonds amongst the stacks of LPs. Bleeker Street was the gateway. Crossing through Washington Square Park, he saw an old man strum an acoustic guitar. He was sloppy, and could barely play. Alex stared at the man and imagined what he'd look like younger. He fantasized that maybe one day he'd stumble upon some forgotten legend playing alone in just such a way, and that he would be friends with him and, well, he just better be ready for when that day came, because if he wasn't ready he'd miss out.

And that wasn't the half of it. Those were the kinds of thoughts that always seemed to race through Alex's mind whenever he walked through the city. Thinking back to his childhood, he remembered how, growing up in the suburbs, he had been devoid of any such thoughts. Instead, he would think about building a ramp to jump with his bike, or how high he'd be able to climb a tree before it wouldn't be able to support his weight. But there was something magnetic and inspiring to him about New York: The electricity he often heard mentioned by his older friends surged through him. That was what living in the heart of New York City gave Alex.

A plume of sweet, dry, toxic diesel smoke enveloped him and he covered his mouth with his hand. The sharp smell stayed high in his nose for several minutes and made his temples ache. *Man,* he thought. *What kind of crap are we breathing in? Why don't we just get rid of all the cars and make this city walking only? That'd be really cool.* All the transportation moved underground, which it already was anyway. *Science fiction,* he thought, *but if enough people stuck together, it could happen.*

Rounding the corner, he saw a familiar row of stores and coffee shops. I can never remember what all the streets are called. Maybe I will after a few more months of living here. Then he was struck by an image of his mother and brother standing with him in the same spot a year earlier, and her giving them both ten dollars. That was before they hated him, because he had chosen his father's side in the fight.

"You would turn your back on your mother," she'd said.

And his brother scowled from behind her, wouldn't step forward. Nodding. Yes. Alex was the traitor. Wrong words were exchanged and a great divide carved between them.

But you cheated, mommy. You took the policeman home and we both heard what you were doing in there with him. We're old enough now to know. And the look on Pop's face when he came home early and put down his shoulder bag and went upstairs and I wanted to stop him so he wouldn't be hurt but he had to know just what you were up to. I could have distracted him and showed him something outside so you could hear him and Georgie sweet Georgie the cop you called him could sneak out the back door where the dogs go out and do their business. Just like you had to do your business, right mommy? You had to do it! Something inside compelled you. An itch you had to scratch that pop couldn't give you—wouldn't give you.

And there Alex stood, looking for something in the music that might take him away and make him remember the good times and forget the awful things. He listened to promises, and believed the dream.

There were never the same people behind the counters at the record stores. It wasn't that bad because he could be anonymous.

He went right to the middle of the stacks and flipped, stopping if he recognized a name or saw an intriguing album cover, especially if he spotted pretty girls, although he tried not to stop too long at those. He didn't want anyone making fun of him, or catching him . He made it to the 'S' category and found a Springsteen record in a plastic sleeve. The cover looked to have been handmade on a copy machine. He withdrew it and couldn't believe what he saw written on it: The Bottom Line 8/15/75. The same one he'd listened to with his father. He'd be able to relive that night forever. It was thirty dollars. He didn't have anywhere near that, but he tucked the LPs under his arm. How would he be able to get it? He didn't bring the emergency MasterCard his father gave him, either, because he was too scared he'd lose it.

"Hey, Buddy? Any way you hold things for people?"

The fellow behind the counter looked at Alex for a second before checking the store for other customers. "Depends what you want held," he said. "Let me see what you've got." He nodded once.

Alex produced the bootleg and the fellow's left cheek twinged. Alex didn't think the guy would approve. He had a safety pin stuck in his leather jacket, which probably meant he was a fashion punk. The name tag sewn into his shirt said his name was Phil.

"Aw, come on. Really? You're into that guy, too? What's everyone see in him?" asked Phil the Punk. Alex didn't understand why he was still wearing his Getty gas station shirt if he worked in the record store. Maybe he had two jobs.

"He's cool. And I heard this on the radio with my dad."

"You think your dad's cool?"

Alex hesitated. "Yeah. I do. He's a painter. Does movie posters and stuff."

"My Dad's an asshole." Phil looked away. "Why do you want me to hold it? Why don't you just buy it? Doesn't your dad give you dough?"

"Not since we moved out from Mom."

"Oh. Got it. How much do you have?"

"Ten bucks."

Phil flipped the bootleg around. "Says it's thirty bucks." He reached under the counter and stole a sip on a Coca Cola.

"I can give you a deposit."

Shaking his head, Phil said, "I can't. Sorry. We don't do that here." Alex felt crestfallen as Phil looked away. Without looking, he said, "Just give me the ten and take it." He slipped it inside a brown bag and faced Alex. He pointed a finger right at his nose and lowered his voice. "But don't hang around. I don't want Bob seeing you leave with this."

Alex slipped the money from his pocket as fast as he could, slipping it on the table. "Here."

Phil handed him the bootleg. "Enjoy. And go have some fun." He stood and shook his hand. As he did Alex noticed him putting the ten into his own pocket. "What?" he asked,

"Nothing."

"Damn right it's nothing," Phil said. "We got to do what we got to do, right? Cheap old Bob could afford to pay me a lot more anyway."

Alex felt simultaneously flush and pale. Was he stealing? If this Bob guy showed up, would he be caught and get in trouble?

"Okay," he said. "I appreciate it."

"Whatever." Phil turned away and Alex scurried out of the record store into the warm October air. His stomach hurt from both being hungry and nervous. He'd spent his last dollar on the record.

It was getting dark out much earlier and Alex really wanted to be done with everything he had to do before night fell. Not only that, but being able to beat his father home would be perfect. He pictured himself plopping the first side of the bootleg record on his little portable battery-operated player. His father would come home, open the door, and would hopefully enjoy the music once again. But first, he spotted a smallish box of LPs near the front door of a record store across the street. Someone had written 'FREE' in magic marker on a piece of cardboard and laid it on top of the records.

Kneeling in front of the box with the bootleg resting against him, Alex flipped through the discs. Most of them were educational, or sound effects, or in foreign languages. But near the back he discovered a Sinatra LP so worn that the black cover looked gray. Instinctively, Alex slipped the vinyl from the cardboard. There was no sleeve, but the vinyl seemed to be in decent shape. *Probably very playable,* he thought. He returned it to its cover and stood, looking around for a moment. He was sure there had to be some catch to it. After several seconds of no one chasing him away, or even looking twice his way, Alex walked away with his free record. He'd scored well and didn't want to push his luck. His head did hurt though, and he knew he needed food. Luckily for him, when he straightened his legs he felt the unmistakable poke of loose change in his pocket. He couldn't figure out why he'd gotten so lucky, but he bought a Reggie bar and a Coke and made it all the way home.

When Alex walked through the lobby he felt a chill in his gut. The baby hairs on his forearms stood up and his eyes watered. There was nothing he could see, and the room was empty. Regardless, he had to wipe tears from face. From the edges of the room, he imagined unseen things sizing him up. *Something bad,* he thought. Some kind of sticky darkness painted the room. Dangerous vibes stopped him cold.

Follow your gut. If something seems wrong, then it probably is. That was his father's advice he heard in his head.

But where else could I go?

He stepped closer to the front stairway. His stomach tightened and his ears warmed up. Another set of voices echoed downward.

"You can't possibly need more," someone said. "I've been here four times in the past two days and it's just the two of you." The new voice sounded hyper—angry. This was not a person Alex wanted to know.

Don't go up there. Stay away. Come back later. There's bad stuff going down.

Despite himself, Alex approached the top landing of the stairs. The group spoke loudly. At first he couldn't place the accents, but soon recognized one of the men as Russian. Alex slinked down and Alex did his best to stay out of their line of sight

A second voice, this time, a high-pitched woman. "Don't say that, Rocket. We lost a whole bit of it when Stevie came by. He took a lot of it."

"Forget it, Nancy," Rocket said. "There's no way I'm going to have either of you two bringing me down with you. See you later."

A man's voice, British, each word slow and slurred. "Shut up! You're a wanker! You'll be back!" He nearly spit the last word.

The people sounded like they were on his floor. Just what he was trying to avoid. Alex ascended the staircase. Maybe if I hurry they won't see me and I can . . .

"Hey, kid! You're here just in time to meet your new neighbors."

Alex couldn't believe his bad luck. Jack waved him closer. For a second Alex wished he could turn around and run out of the Hotel Chelsea, unseen.

"You're going to love these two."

"Really?"

"Yeah." He gestured to Alex. "This kid knows more about music than I do for cryin' out loud."

Alex finally got to see who was speaking when a lanky pale fellow with spiked black hair leaned out from a doorway. His eyes were bloodshot, but kind. Cigarette smoke poured out of the bedroom behind him.

"Hey Sid? Who's the kid?"

Sid looked back into the room then to Alex. "What's your name, Mate?"

Alex told him, and gave him a good firm shake.

Sid pulled his hand back. "Ah man, come on. Imagine I'm going to need that now, aren't I?"

Clutching his albums close to his chest, all Alex could think of was lifting the lid on his record player and listening to his new music.

"What you got with you there? That what I think it is. Um. No. Probably not. Can't be."

Sid reached out and grabbed the records. He glanced over the Sinatra record, even turning it around to read the songs.

He studied the Springsteen bootleg for a few moments.

"What are you doing? Sid? What're you looking at? " Nancy asked.

"This is a strange record."

"Yup."

"Why don't you all come inside here? I'm lonely."

Something was wrong. Alex sensed it in Nancy's voice. She sounded like she'd been hurt or injured. Without even seeing her, Alex pictured her thin and tired face.

"This is some ancient music for a little guy to be listening to."

"I don't know," Alex said. "A good song's a good song. Don't matter who sings it."

"Sid?"

He looked at Alex a minute, seemed as though he were really pondering what he'd heard. "Maybe. But once in a while things are about a lot more than just the song."

Then it was Alex's turn to stare. Sid toyed with what looked like a dog collar around his neck, clamped shut with a small padlock.

What does that mean? Alex thought. *Is he like a dog? An animal that needs to be leashed? He doesn't look strong. He doesn't care if he gets hurt. Doesn't care if he bleeds. Likes pain. Enjoys bleeding.*

Alex nodded. "Yeah, I get it."

"Sid? Sid? Sid?"

His smiled slid from the center of his mouth to one corner, folding his face in a snarl. Can I borrow this? He showed Alex the Sinatra LP.

"Okay." Alex didn't think he'd ever see it again.

Sid nodded and crept around.

"Sid?"

"We got some music to listen to."

Alex kept still. He didn't want to turn his back to them and Sid had gone inside his apartment without shutting the door.

"How are we going to listen to that? We don't even have a record player."

"Ah, whatever. Well borrow one." Alex heard kissing sounds and groans. Before he got any more involved he rushed away to his room.

Blood dribbles from her mouth. A bloom of orange light descends inside the building. The Angel Gabriel calls, just like his mother used to warn him. Angel Gabriel comes for everyone when it's your turn to go to the Promised Land. Tonight he travels through the rooms and the halls following the scent of spilled whiskey and thinned bowels, of empty, hungry souls. Blood rolls across fingers. Sticky, watery, tainted yellow. Fingers that once caressed and made a heart open where it was once closed, the orange light pilots them to open her with the pocket knife.

She won't feel it. She can't feel anything, anyway. He hears the whispers. It's not you. Nancy needs this. Start things over for her. Wish Baby. Someone's little girl grown too fast like a bundle of ripe grapes too early in the season. Be the sun that dries them and lets them fall. There will be unthinkable pain to come if you don't and you wouldn't want that, would you?

The top of his thumb presses against her belly and he can't see the hilt of the knife underneath. He can't feel it anymore. He remembers how the fine baby hairs on her stomach felt—how clean and salty her skin tasted. This would be their last touch and he felt cold and detached. He looks in the mirror to check if he is crying because he can't tell—none of his nerves are working.

A stranger looks back at him from the mirror. The man has black skin, dark as the underground. He blinks and the man looks like Jet. Behind Jet he can see Steve sitting on the bed strumming his white Les Paul. That already happened. This already happened. He looks down and she's crawled away from him under the sink. There's no one in the mirror except Sid. No one. He's sad. Never more alone.

"Don't want to leave a mess for you, Sid," she mumbles. "There's water in here. I can clean everything up. No big deal. Just let me sleep. I'm tired, Sid. He gave us some bad shit, is all."

He finds himself standing back several feet away and looking in on the bathroom, where his Baby, his Angel Girl, rests. The knife is on the ground and he checks his hand. It is clean and her blood is not there. He is clean. She is clean. He hears something behind him and sees a face in the hallway he recognizes but just can't place. The face is in darkness and shade. Is it the Italian? The Iranian? The Puerto Rican? Or is it the shade making their skin darker? Gabriel is leaving, his duty fulfilled.

Where's the boy?

Sid screams his name.

The Hotel Chelsea vibrated and Alex sat straight up, believing he heard someone yelling his name. What the heck is that? He looked around his room and expected to see his father. Then he remembered that his father said he wasn't coming home and asked if he'd be all right. He was going to spend the night at Judy's place. Judy—the new woman. She was prettier than his mother, and nowhere near as mean. Not yet, at least. His father told him that they all get old and mean eventually. And what about Nancy? He wanted to ask his father. She's already old and mean. What does that mean?

Someone was playing music loudly. He could barely tell what the song was it was so distorted, but he focused and figured it out.

Frank Sinatra. "My Way."

Am I going to get in trouble for this? I gave him that record. The last thing he wanted to do was to jeopardize them having a place to live. Not that he believed the Hotel Chelsea was perfect, but his father loved the Hotel.

He kept waiting for someone to yell to turn it down, but no one did. The song was almost over as Alex crept from his bed and inched towards his front door. Just as it ended Alex perked up and put his ear against the door.

The record player was so loud he could hear the needle dropping on the grooves. He waited for someone to holler and scold Sid. Instead, the song started again.

He stood from the door and went to the bathroom. It was almost noon and he couldn't believe he'd slept so late. Alex was supposed to meet his father—supposed to go to the studios and meet up for lunch. Later they were all supposed to go out for dinner. His mother was coming into the city to try and " . . . figure a few things out." Of course, Alex was skeptical. The last thing he wanted to do was to head face-first back into the abusive, unkind life in Ocean City. Anything was better than that, even listening to someone blast Frank Sinatra records in the hallway.

Alex got in the shower and started getting clean. The song was so loud he was beginning to think it was playing inside his own head.

No. Not that. It's still coming from the outside. Go in and do what you have to do. He's trying to make you crazy on purpose so you will go outside in the hallway and they'll be there.

He pictured them standing there, covered in blood, covered in white, foamy, soap. They were trying to get clean. Wash away the pain with soap and gore. Bleed out and clean out. Bleed away and clean away. That was it. Yes. Yes. Yes. Their eyes were vacant. Their hearts colorless and albino, beating outside emaciated bodies. Sid hands him the records, a smear of blood-tainted mucous left behind from his hand. Alex doesn't want to touch it. Because sometimes it's about more than just the music. He could hear Sid in his head. Alex washed harder and quicker and tried to think if he could go out through the fire escape or one of the other ways. There was nothing he could think of. The Hotel Chelsea just wasn't built that way, not from where they were. Damn. Maybe if I hurry up and get out of here fast enough they won't see me.

The music stopped.

Sirens.

Finally someone had called the police. Alex heard voices. Footsteps filled the hallway. What had taken them so long? New York certainly wasn't like Ocean City, where if you called the police they were there in their squad cars within a few minutes. Maybe that's what everyone meant when they said living in the city was hard and cold. He wanted very badly to run away out into the street, and get on the subway, and to see his father. He'd tell him that they couldn't live there any more, that things had changed, and that bad people had come to lay their hats with them. Not a place for a young boy, nope. Not even a place for most normal people. Yes, he was normal. He wasn't like them and he was fine with that. And so was his father. And so what?

Two knocks.

Was it his door? Was it the one next door?

Alex didn't want to answer. He hopped on his bed, and wrapped the blankets over himself. They probably had heard him in the shower. They probably heard that he was in there. Damn it! He was still wet. There was no knock. Alex grabbed his clothes, which he'd laid out on the foot of his bed, and put them on as fast as he could. Then he got right back into bed, right back under the covers, right back underneath.

What are they going to do? Come in here? This is my fault. I shouldn't have ever let him have that record. I think I spurred him into doing something. It was me that inspired all this. And something bad's happened. Something terrible.

Bam!

The knock nearly sent him flying from his bed it was so loud. He wished his father was with him and hadn't abandoned him by going to work. If only he hadn't been alone through all this.

"Alex?" The voice was familiar. "You home?" His father. "I forgot my keys." Could it really be his father after all? Could it really have been just the right person? "Alex?" his father sounded less patient, and nervous.

He didn't want to answer, afraid that it might be an impostor. It seemed too good to be true. How could his father know he was in trouble? How would he have known while he was a t work?

Then he heard the key jangling and there was some mumbling. "Okay, okay, thanks." The door opened and he saw his father being let in by the building's superintendent.

Stopping for a moment, his father regarded Alex. "You okay?"

Alex didn't see the Superintendent, but heard him." Kid's scared. Look at him."

"Okay, okay," said his father. "Thanks. Let me talk to him."

"Alex?" he said. "I saw something on the news. There's been some bad stuff this morning. We need to go." His father rushed to him and hugged him. "I'm so glad you're okay."

He couldn't say anything back for several minutes. As they walked out from their apartment and down the stairs, he saw the policeman hanging around Sid's room. For a moment he got a glimpse inside. It looked as he'd remembered it, although there was no cigarette smoke. Someone took a picture and he saw blood on the rug. Black, branch—shaped pools of inky spilled chocolate syrup. It was out in the hallway, too. He couldn't help remembering that he'd been standing there only yesterday, in the same spot, where he'd given Sid his free Frank Sinatra record. And now, in a blink, everything had changed. Everything went still. Everything went black, and Alex and his father never looked back.

MOTHER YOU CAN WATCH

The sign glowed Bates Motel.
Hell came tonight, Mother, with the wind and thunder.
Flustered and anxious to hide,
her secrets won't fly away.

Mother can you watch? You can always see,
from your window as the lonely hot desert winds blow.

Smell the sand like the stuffing inside the animals,
everything crumbles in the heat.

A door handle, a belle sings, a bell rings, a belle lies, her
voice! A bird with a broken wing; I'll take her in so she can eat.

Mother, you'll like her.
"Stuff her! Use your glistening little knife!"
I can't,
do it,
can't,
take it.
"Get out of the way! I'll do it for you.
When I'm done you can stuff her!"

Mother can you watch?
These sometimes sure, sometimes trembling hands.
"I can't stand to look at her, like the birds and the
raccoons—the cranes.
Someone will see her car and know she was here."

She'll forget as soon as the hurting stops. Blood clots.
Swirls down the drain.

Maybe I'll just take her head. Do you think it'll be
enough?

Vacancies. Our heirloom sign tempts them off the road.

All That Withers

Can't sleep. You hate her. Hate me. You took her away.

Maybe I'll drive inside the water with her by my side.
I'll lift her lid to see her pretty eye one last time.
The lake will swallow us while I hold her hand.

"What are you doing? My son doesn't love me!
You'll leave me all alone."

Mother you can watch me drown.

Outlaws of Hill County

The night before Halloween, the Long Fellow sucked Jenny Lou Harrison's soul right through her fingers. Bright red strands connected her freshly blackened fingertips to his. She wiggled and cried. I just stood there by that big oak tree outside her room and watched, unable to do a damn thing to stop the Long Fellow's terrible meal.

When he was done he hurried out of her room, out her window, and made it into the crest of the tree above me. I hunkered down; scared it might see me and make me its next meal. It didn't. Instead the Long Fellow bowed his head to me. He had a face with two large gray eyes, a long nose, and a mouth filled with small jagged fangs that reminded me of broken shards of glass.

All the acid in my stomach rose up. My balance went out on me and I buckled down against the trunk, hugging that oak tree with the single ounce of energy I had left. His hot breath blanketed the back of my head and neck. My hands wiggled uncontrollably like the old men at Tully's Tavern who'd courted years of whiskey.

Once I rolled onto the grass my body gave out. My sick hit the dirt. The smell of my own cooked bile made my guts clench.

Above me the Long Fellow climbed the oak tree. Branches moaned and leaves rustled. Several twigs dropped near me. I wanted to get a better look at the Long Fellow—see what kind of being could turn someone sick with its own will—see how such a thing drained the life from poor pretty Jenny using only its Unholy fingertips.

Harvest Hill felt colder that night than any other night I remember, even though it wasn't yet winter. Part of me believes the Long Fellow sucked every ounce of warmth and comfort from the air along with what he stole from Jenny Lou.

My throat felt dry and sore. The few inches I managed to raise myself up made my head spin. *You got to stay awake,* I thought. *The Long Fellow's still here.* My body didn't listen.

As I drifted off I watched Jenny Lou fade away.

I woke late that night. At first I thought I'd fallen from the tree and knocked myself out. Something deep down inside me didn't want to believe the Long Fellow had returned to Harvest Hill. Maybe that's why I dismissed seeing Jenny Lou's still body through her window as just her sleeping.

Hurrying from her house, I did my best to tuck my hair under my leather jacket's collar to try and keep a little warmer. One the benefits of keeping your hair long, I guess. That, and everyone seemed to know where I stood concerning the war. I wasn't one of them, after all. Never thought going to 'Nam was a good idea. We have enough trouble here at home.

I couldn't stop remembering things about Jenny Lou. We went out a few times, but always with a group, never just her and me. I would have loved to, of course, and was working up the courage to ask her. That was before the Long Fellow came and took away any chance of that happening.

"You shouldn't be drinking at your age."

Grandma thought she was doing well, but she didn't understand. "I haven't been drinking," I said. "I'm sick. Caught something."

She met me just outside the bathroom, where'd I'd recently emptied my belly. "You look pale as a ghost, Lew Rogers."

"I feel like it," I said. "And I'm not joking about not drinking. I swear I think I caught something."

"You gone and ate at that girl's house again, haven't you?" Leave it to Grandma to try and place blame on someone for something.

I shook my head. "I haven't eaten anything since lunch at school," I said. "Haven't been able to keep anything down." Trying to walk past her wasn't going to work until she had the final word, so I let her have it.

"Maybe you should take the food I make you and stop eating that garbage."

She wasn't making me feel any better. "Sounds like a good idea. You're right. I need to lie down. My head's spinning."

Grandma smiled just a bit; I could tell she was happy

telling me her two cents worth. "You go to your room," she said, finally moving sideways so I could get past. "Just make sure you sleep on your side. Don't want you throwing up in your sleep and choking on your own vomit."

"Will do," I said.

Once I was in bed I couldn't sleep. My mind raced with images of the Long Fellow. No one would believe what'd gotten me sick. The Long Fellow was something the kids sang about— he wasn't real.

> "When the night gets long
> And the day goes quick,
> You better hide inside,
> Or you might get sick,
> Out come the Long Fellow,
> Playing his tricks,
> Sucking your soul,
> Through your fingertips . . ."

All of us knew the rhyme. We grew up singing and scaring each other with Long Fellow stories. Legend was he down from the mountains on Halloween every year to feed on kids. He'd put out his hands and pull your essence from your fingertips, leaving them black and shriveled. You'd never be the same.

So what was I supposed to do? I knew what I'd seen, but knew no one was going to believe me. *Well,* I thought. *Just keep your mouth shut and forget it.*

I raised my head and body on the pillow. My stomach felt better being elevated. It wasn't as comfortable as being all curled up, but eventually sleep found me.

"We've got some bad news this morning." That was how Mr. Palace started homeroom. Before the bell I spotted him chatting with Mr. Block, our science teacher. Something about the way they were stood with their backs to us made me believe they were sharing secrets.

"Probably cancelling Halloween tonight 'cuz they think you dumb hippies are going to go and protest it." That was Eric Sable, a nasty piece of work who never had a good word concerning anything.

I wanted to say something quick and clever right back, but I'm one of those folks that can't think of anything smart until two days after. Then I've got a million comebacks. I just shook my head.

"Kids?" Mr. Palace said. "There's going to be lots of you talking over the next few days and we didn't want there to be any rumors. You're all old enough to hear the truth."

Get on with it, I thought. *Come on.*

"We lost Jenny Lou Harrison last night." His voice broke saying her name; he lowered his chin and he put a thumb to his forehead before looking back up.

My chest felt numb. How could she be dead? The Long Fellow wasn't supposed to kill you, after all, just leave you an empty, soulless shell. I was there last night. Did anyone see me? Are they going to make the connection and pin me at her house? Are they going to arrest me? What am I going to tell them? That the Long Fellow did it? I felt dizzy. Clutching the sides of my desk, I took a long deep breath.

"She passed away in her sleep. No one's sure exactly why, but we'll let you know as soon as we do." He made himself stand straight and put his hands to his hips like a drill sergeant. "If you feel you need to talk about this please let one of us know or see your guidance counselor. Does anyone have any questions?"

Eric Sable raised his hand. "I do."

"Shoot."

"Does this mean we're going to have to cancel Halloween tonight?"

By the time third period rolled around, I knew I had to sneak out of Harvest High. "I think Steve Woodworth got a visit from the Long Fellow, too." My good friend Jules Shepherd bent my ear while we were switching books at our lockers. "He's got the same black fingers you were telling me Jenny Lou had. I saw him leaning on Mr. Strabb and going inside." He showed me his fingers. "I wonder if the Long Fellow gets me how anyone would know? My fingers are already black!"

I smiled. Jules always tried to make light of things.

"This is too messed up. Kids are getting sick. We've got to cruise down to the nurse's office." Jules wiggled his nose just a bit. It was a habit he had ever since I knew him. When he was scared or excited he tended to punctuate his sentences with a little twitch. "We got to play sick."

Nurse Lorraine wouldn't buy Jules story. "You look just fine to me, Darling," she said—and was right. Even standing still, Jules looked like he might just pounce any second. "But I guess if you want to put your head down it won't hurt. Just in case."

Jules stuttered. "Okay. Great. Good idea. I am dizzy now that you mention it."

She forced a grin. "Last room on the right," she said before looking at me. "And you, Mr. Garner: you look pale as a ghost. What's going on?"

"My stomach," I said. "Been killing me since last night." I placed my hand on my gut. I didn't have to imagine anything.

"Last night?" she said. "That so?"

I nodded. "Yup. Just about nine o'clock."

She reached up and adjusted her green cube-shaped hat. It looked kind of like a military hat worn on the front lines. "Huh," she said. "Not cool. "We all had reason to believe Nurse Lorraine lived two lives: one where she took care of us kids at the school, and the other where she got really into her Mary Jane and Dead records. Maybe it was because she wasn't much older than us.

"I don't think I'm really too sick," I said. "But I just thought I should get checked out in case."

"You look a little green around the gills. Why don't we get you lying down?"

I agreed.

Nurse Lorraine stood. "Come on," she said. "Before you pass out. "She smiled but didn't look me in the eye.

The rear of the nurse's office had several small open rooms, each with its own cot. As we neared the back, I could see Steve Woodworth lying on a cot, his hands by his sides. I slowed down and saw his fingers, black and shriveled. "Jesus," I said.

"Keep going," she said. "Don't look."

"Why?" I asked. "What happened?" Steven had the same affliction as Jenny Lou.

She nudged me and we passed Jules. He was wide-awake and smiled at me. Not the best faker, that's for sure. "You're room's in the back," she said.

From there Nurse Lorraine guided me in, I sat, and she had me lie down. "Put this under your tongue. "She nodded and bent down a bit. As she did, a sliver of tie-dye poked from between the buttons of her nurse's shirt. Nurse Lorraine was cool after all. She was one of us. She suddenly looked a lot prettier to me. Funny.

"Okay, so keep that under your tongue for five minutes. I'll be back to check you out." She nodded and I gave her a thumbs-up. I watched her walk out of my room and did not blink once. I couldn't help but see her differently. Suddenly, her straight, long blond hair and thin body made sense. She didn't have her hair up in a bun. She didn't wear a ton of make-up. She didn't look like my Mom or any of our normal teachers, who all looked stuck in *Leave It to Beaver*. Nah. Nurse Lorraine was a hippie. Peace. Love. I dug her.

I put my hands behind my head and closed my eyes. The first thing I thought about, after Nurse Lorraine's secret other life, was the whole situation with Jenny Lou and Steve. Trying to think that the Long Fellow hadn't come seemed impossible because I had evidence right in front of me. But who would believe me? Who could I go to for help? None of the adults were likely to believe me.

Someone charged through the front door of the nurse's office. "We've got another one Lorraine. "It was Mr. Strabb. "Something bad's going on here. I think we need to call the Capitol or the State Department or someone in the District. I don't know."

Her chair squeaked on the tile and I heard her get up. "Jeff? What happened?"

"Not sure," he said. "I don't feel so hot."

I took the thermometer out, read it, and leaned up on my elbows. I was just over 99 degrees.

"Hey?" It was Jules. "Let's go," he said. "I think we've seen enough around here. Don't you?"

"I didn't even hear you get up," I said. "What're you doing?" He looked toward the Nurse's receiving area just as we both heard Jeff Scranton. "It hurts!" he yelled. "Oh, God! Help!"

Jules shrunk back inside my room.

"My fingers! I can't move my fingers!"

"Calm down, Jeff. We'll figure out . . ."

"No! I need to go to the hospital. We need to call the police. The Long Fellow did this."

Mr. Strabb's voice turned stern and deep. "You've been reading too much Famous Monsters, mister."

"It's not that," he said. "It's real."

Their footsteps became louder. Jules looked to me. "We've got to sneak out," he said, whispering. "Soon as their backs are to us we have to run."

"Okay," I said, putting the thermometer back in my mouth and lying back down. Jules curved around the corner and out of view.

He looked at me for a moment and I shut my eyes. Then I heard them hurry past. "Oh, God, Miss Minerva, it really hurts," Jeff moaned. "Are you going to bring me to the hospital?"

"We'll do everything we can."

They passed and I opened my eyes. Jules waved. "Come on," he said. "Quick." We hustled out of there.

As we made it to the main room I heard Nurse Lorraine. "Lew? Where are you going? Do you have a fever?"

The door was closed and we were around the corner by the time she called again.

"We're going to Rob Cash's place?" Jules didn't sound excited. Then again, most folks weren't too thrilled with my cousin. He ran the local biker gang, The Outlaws of Hill County.

"He'll know what to do," I said. "He's used to dealing with things outside the law."

Jules tugged at my sleeve. "This is outside everything.

What makes you think he's going to believe us that the Long Fellow's here?"

"He'll believe me," I said. "I've never lied to him."

"People lie all the time. "We made it a little ways down Telegraph Hill. "Asking someone to believe there's a monster in their town is a little hard to do, isn't it?"

I nodded. "Sure is," I said. "But you believe the Long Fellow's here, don't you? You ain't seen him in person."

We stopped and our eyes met.

"You saw the Long Fellow?"

"I'm going to wait and tell you and Rob what I saw at the same time," I said. "You still want in? Or do you want to go home and not help out?"

"It's Halloween?"

"So no one's going to think twice about why we're outside late hours. Who else do we have on our side? If Rob says he's not going to help then it'll be just us two. Not sure that's going to do the trick."

We rode our bikes down to Rob's place and found him relaxing on his porch with a beer and his Martin acoustic. "That's one sorry looking excuse for a Halloween costume," Rob said. "I can't believe you're even related to me." He pointed toward my head. "Who's going to believe a black kid and his Hippie friend with long hair who's wearing Army clothes?"

"You?" I said.

Rob took a big sip from his Moosehead before resuming picking at his Martin. "Your hair's long," I said. "And you wear black leather jackets like all the greasers used to in the 50s."

"They were riders, too. Just like me. There's a relationship." He winked. "There's no connection between G.I. Joe and Haight, friend."

I pointed to the peace symbol I'd painted on the breast of the jacket. "Look," I said. "Peace. Love. I'm wearing this as a protest. I can be an Outlaw, too."

"Not really," he said. "You just look confused to me which side you're on."

"I'm a hippie. I don't believe in war. I ain't going."

"You're sixteen. The war will be over by the time you're

old enough to get drafted. It's going to be the '70s in a few months."

Jules said, "We've got to be out of 'Nam soon, right?"

"Hope so," I said. "And, yeah, talking about that, we need to talk about what's going on it town."

"I seen some real messed up shit," Jules said. "The Long Fellow's back."

Taking a moment to register what he'd just heard, Rob just said, "really?" and then kept strumming. It sounded a lot like something Peter, Paul and Mary might play.

"I seen him last night," I said. "Outside Jenny Lou Harrison's house, Rob. I saw that thing sucking the life right out of her. And when he was through with her he climbed the tree over my head and I could smell his breath. Worse thing I ever smelled. Made my stomach hurt awful."

He stopped playing and looked up so that our eyes met. "You shitting me?"

"Uh-uh," I said. "That thing's come back because it's Halloween—knows it'll blend in—knows it can use it to hide with."

"Her fingers looked like she had frostbite on the ends?" Rob asked.

I nodded. "Yup. That's right. Steve Woodworth came in to the Nurse's Office with the same thing. Then Jeff Scranton."

"I don't know," Rob said. "Sounds suspicious."

Jules and I looked at each other. Rob was supposed to believe us.

"Isn't that the same thing that happened with Dave?" Rob looked at me, then Jules. I knew I shouldn't have mentioned his brother, but I was desperate.

Jules shrugged. "Who's Dave?"

Rob charged Jules, grabbed his collar, and snarled. "That thing took him seven years back," he said. "That thing has come knocking around again looking for me now." Rob turned to me. "Is that what you're trying to pull?"

"Hell no," I said. "Not like that. My cousin, Rob's brother, had gone missing under mysterious circumstances. Rob claimed that some fellow with real long, claw-like hands came down and rooted his brother right up from the ground. Claimed there was a way the guy sucked the life out of his brother, leaving him for dead. Rob was the one who had to take the hit on it. His story could never be verified. Judge Robbins gave him involuntary manslaughter for five years. Said they'd probably both been drinking too much and probably Rob had egged him over the edge. I didn't buy it, but the law's the law. Like Creedence sings, you fight the law, they're going to win every time.

"You kids are fucking with me," he said. "I ain't got time for this."

"The Long Fellow's here," I said. "We've got to stop it."

Rob kick-started his gold Harley Davidson motorcycle. The cylinders purred; the engine vibrated. He reached inside his jacket, pulled out a Zippo, and lit up a Camel. Rob squeezed the clutch on the handlebar and rolled the gas with the other. On the shoulder of Rob's leather jacket, I spotted his hand-sewn gold 'Outlaws' patch. "Don't ever bring this up to me again!" he hollered as he rode off, giving us the finger over his shoulder.

"He didn't believe us," Jules said.

"There's got to be someone that can help us."

As we rode our bikes through town we realized Harvest Hill was deserted "It's three o'clock in the afternoon and everyone's missing," Jules said.

"Everyone's getting ready for the Halloween assembly at the school tonight," I said. "They're setting it all up right now, I bet."

"So we have to go back there?"

"Unless you've got a better idea."

As me and Jules pulled inside the Harvest Hill High parking lot, none of the lights were on and all the doors were locked.

"Looks like trouble. "Jules peered into the lobby through the glass doors by cupping his hands against the glass. "This makes no sense."

Grabbing his arm, I pulled him from the window. "I've got to say I'm agreeing with you."

Someone was walking on the roof over our heads.

We both craned our heads trying to see who it could be. "Hello?"

His eyes went wild. "Shut up!" He whispered, but I'll bet he wanted to shout. "We don't know who's up there. We don't want to give ourselves away." He looked me up and down. "What kind of Outlaw you going to make, anyway?"

Not knowing how to act or what to say, I backed away from the doorway.

We both heard skittering again.

Something thumped behind us, like someone had jumped off the roof and onto the sidewalk.

Standing between the two of us and the parking lot, a large fellow pointed at me. The sun was in back of him, so neither of us got a good look.

"Hey, man. We don't want any trouble." Jules stood behind me. "We're just looking for our kin." I squinted and tried making out the fellow's face.

The large fellow pointed his finger toward Jules and hissed. My eyes got used to the light. The thing the fellow gestured with was not a finger at all—it looked much more like a sickle-shaped claw.

The Long Fellow hissed again.

"Jules?" I asked.

Jules pushed past and stood between the Long Fellow and me. "I know, I know," he said. "I see him."

"H-him?"

The Long Fellow jutted forward, bending at the middle. Opening its jaw, I imagined the thing must have been eating rocks to sport so many busted teeth. Some were black and sharp, like edges of broken bottles.

A rancid smell like gasoline and spoiled seafood overtook us. The Long Fellow's breath was poison.

My eyes filled with water and my guts went all tight.

The Long Fellow let out an ungodly sound, which I heard through a daze, like he was on TV in another room.

I hurled on the sidewalk, turning away from Jules. Keep yourself standing unless you want that thing to get you.

From the corner of my eye I spotted Jules huddled on the ground. He'd had his own sick and wasn't moving. My head spun: I'd never felt so dizzy in all my life. I wanted more than anything to fall down and sleep.

Another blast of poison spewed from the Long Fellow's mouth. I tried to turn to see the thing, but the pain was too strong.

I retched again, only this time nothing came out besides a string of sticky spittle. It hurt worse than anything.

What's this thing want?

It should have been eating Jules, or at least taking him away. It should have used its sickle-arm to cut him.

It's probably already eaten half the town.

The Long Fellow spat another blast of poison, missing me. It leapt onto the roof and vanished.

"Jules?" My best friend was lying a few feet away. I stared at his rib cage: it was moving. He grunted. "We've got to go."

Inside the school the halls were dark. Paper jack o' lanterns and scarecrows stared down from the walls. We'd made them to decorate for our Halloween assembly. I leaned my forehead against one of the cold, small rectangular classroom windows. The lights were off. A desk was overturned near the front of the room and appeared covered with thick, dark fluid. Small bits of what appeared to be chewed-up food dotted the floor.

"Someone attacked us." Jules rubbed his head and moaned. "Hit me over the head."

"The Long Fellow," I said. "Come here to fight."

"Yeah, well, my stomach hurts worse than anything. I'm in no condition to fight."

"Mine, too." I reached out my hand. "But we've got to do something."

From the other end of the hall someone threw up. It came from just outside the doors, on the back patio where some of the students hung out between periods.

Something smelled fishy and rancid. We crept toward the back door. He wasn't sure who was out there, or who would actually not be in class at that moment.

Whoever it was made another heaving sound, which was quickly followed with a nasty, large splatter-like thump on the concrete. We could hear him sighing and gasping.

Jules made his way to the far side of the hallway and signaled for me to follow. As we neared the end of the corridor we spied Eric Sable hunched over just outside the back door. A bright red trail of spittle wavered in the air from Eric's lips toward the ground.

Blood. More blood.

More vomiting followed. Eric put an arm out against one of the posts and retched.

Backing out from the rear hallway, we walked away as quickly as possible.

We made it to the gym, where music played inside. As soon as we were through the doors we knew where everyone had gone: to the Harvest High gymnasium for our annual Halloween show. In one corner there was a large tin bucket filled with water and apples. Miss Deloitte was watching the kids try their luck bobbing. To her right there were several small clusters of kids and students mingling and talking. Most importantly, to me, at least, was seeing The Amphibians jamming there right on the floor. Acid rock filled my gym. That was cool. Nurse Lorraine was stage left, nodding her head, sipping something from a straw.

"Quite the party," Jules said. "So what're we going to do?"

We wouldn't be waiting long for our answer. I heard the back door open and saw the Long Fellow walk inside. For a few brief moments no one but Jules and me even noticed.

"Nice costume," someone said.

The Long Fellow lowered his bony head and smiled.

Everyone around him scattered.

With one graceful leap, the Long Fellow made it to the center of the gym. It stared right at us. "Holy Shit, man!" I hollered.

It hopped again, this time landing ten short feet from us. My eyes locked with the creature. My stomach hurt again, just as bad as it had the first time. My arm rose like someone had it on a string. My fingers spread out. So did the Long Fellow's. I noticed that the veins on top of his gray hands pulsed.

He squeezed his fingers as though he were milking an orange.

My life-blood rushed to my own fingers, where it seemed to pool. I couldn't move a muscle. I couldn't even take my eyes off the Long Fellow; no matter how hard I tried.

"No!" Jules said. "Not again."

The crowd hurried toward the back gym door. Something pushed them back. Something loud. Something scared them backwards. At first I thought that it had to be another Long Fellow—a mate. As the crowd spread themselves away from the door a half-ton Harley Davidson rolled right through them. The Outlaws. There's something in the pitch of those engines that sounds just perfect. I don't think I ever loved hearing that sound more than I did that Halloween. I couldn't help, though, but wonder where they heard the Long Fellow had come, or how. I imagined Rob signaled them somehow . . . left them some kind of message.

As the first of the Outlaws rolled in to the gym, spreading the crowd against the walls, the second bike drove inside. It was Rob.

I still couldn't move. My fingertips were turning dark and my stomach wrenched on itself. Any second, I felt like I might fall down.

The band was still playing. Jules was nowhere to be seen. It seemed I was alone, standing inches from the Long Fellow while he drew my life from my hands.

Rob's Harley roared. The bike raced toward us; Rob was hunched down low toward the handlebars, his teeth gritted, his mouth snarling.

The Long Fellow turned in time to see the front wheel lift from the gym floor. The Harley was up on its back wheel. *How the hell is Rob strong enough to pull a wheelie on a Harley?* I thought. *Those bikes weigh half-a-ton.*

But he had, and impossible as it seems, the Harley drove full speed toward the Long Fellow. In a flash the front wheel bashed into the Long Fellow's chest, sending the creature backward dozens of feet, breaking its connection to me.

Two more Harleys raced right behind Rob right as I fell to my knees. Once the connection to the Long Fellow was gone, what little energy I had left wasn't enough to keep me up. My hand tingled like it'd fallen asleep. I tucked it into my shirt without looking at it. I didn't want to know the damage. Not yet.

On the other side of the gym near the band, the Long Fellow was on the ground and Rob was circling behind it. The crowd screamed and gasped. Some of the band members were watching. I guess it was impossible not to notice.

The Outlaw with the red hair drove up near the Long Fellow and swung a massive metal chain around his head. His bike bucked a little; he lost his balance for a second 'cuz he was riding with one hand.

The Long Fellow jerked toward him, its mouth open, its sickle-shaped claws swung. Red flinched, but didn't stop rotating the chain over his head. It was getting faster and faster. On the opposite side of Red, I saw Rob doing the same thing.

Red whipped the chain at the Long Fellow and it wrapped around the creature's middle. Then Rob threw his chain, which made it round its neck.

Screaming and protesting, the Long Fellow threw out its arms. The chains fell off and you could see a big black mark across its chest where Rob's tire had struck. I saw little splotches of blood throughout the wound. *That thing bleeds red just like me,* I thought. *Isn't that funny?* By then I was curled up on the gym floor watching the whole thing sideways.

Red bent down to pick up his chain and the Long Fellow swung. Red dropped and rolled onto his back. It looked like he'd fallen off his bike before and knew how to fall without hurting himself too bad. The Long Fellow swooped down and hit him again with its sickle-claw, slashing Red in the back. His leather jacket split. He stood up, although he was limping a little bit.

The Long Fellow made to strike again, but Rob managed to hoop his metal chain around its neck again. That gave Red time to hop back on his bike and twirl his own metal chain. The third Outlaw, one I never seen before, got chain around the Long Fellow, too.

Toward the back of the gym we spotted several more Outlaws watching the scene, although they seemed to be keeping folks out of the way more than anything.

When I turned around Red was nodding at Rob and the Long Fellow was wiggling like a stuck pig. It tried to jump and Rob jerked upward a little. He pulled his chain tight so that the Long Fellow couldn't raise itself more than a few inches. Red did the same. They nodded and Rob put both feet up and steered for the back door.

The Outlaws guarding the gym raised their arms to keep people back as Rob and Red dragged the Long Fellow across the way. At one point it dug its claws into the varnished wood flooring, scratching long ruts in its wake. It hollered, as if struck, but it was one of its black toenails that'd caught in the ruts. The Outlaws pulled the Long Fellow, breaking the nail off in the process. As soon as it'd passed I spotted Jules run toward the nail, wiggle it free, and put it in his pocket.

The Amphibians kept right on playing. I don't believe they missed a single psychedelic note. "Hey, there?" Nurse Lorraine bent over me, her eyes darting left and right real quick, scanning me.

I showed her my hand, careful to keep my eyes on her and not look at it. "It got me a little," I said. "Hurts."

Held my wrist so that she could see. "We need to get you out of here," she said. "Are you cool otherwise?"

Wobbly on my feet, and doing my best to get up, I said, "I'm cool." She held me by the crook of my arm.

Before she walked me out of the gym, and away from the music, and the scattered crowd, we watched the Long Fellow screech and claw at its chains as the Outlaws rode into the night. I hoped they took the damn thing somewhere far away, and I hoped I never had to see it again, and I hoped they made it pay for Jenny Lou, and for me and my hand, and for everything it'd done to Harvest Hill.

Just outside the gym Jules caught up with me. "So wasn't Rob the guy who gave us the finger earlier?"

"Yup," I said. "Guess he had a change of heart."

"Can't believe that thing's real," he said and produced the nail for me to see. "At least I'll have this to remind me." He put it away.

I showed him my dark fingers. "And I've got these," I said. "And hopefully I won't have anything to remind me. Hope that that thing's going to get lost after tonight. Hopefully we're done with that thing forever."

Once we walked away none of us ever spoke of the Long Fellow again.

"Is that true?" Lew, Jr. asked his father.

His dad smiled and stood from his recliner. "Well we all grew up and the world replaced the Long Fellow with Vietnam, Communists and atom bombs. Heck: getting married and getting a 9-to-5'er seems more frightening." He winked at Lorraine, who'd brought them some cocoa. "But it is Halloween, after all. Never saw what happened to the Long Fellow. Rob never told me. If it's still out there somewhere he might decide he's hungry enough to come on down here again." He stretched his arms. Both his sons' eyes went immediately to their father's left fingers, which were a shade darker and covered with scar tissue.

"You even have the marks still?" Lew, Jr. poked his brother. "It is true. Poppa wouldn't lie to us."

When they turned their parents had gone, leaving them to look out their living room window, out towards their yard, their town, the big oak tree swaying in the wind, and the moon that hung low on the horizon. There was a scratching sound somewhere close by, followed by a faint howl. Then they could both would swear they heard children singing outside, their voices carried on the cold October wind.

> "When the night gets long
> And the day goes quick,
> You better hide inside,
> Or you might get sick,
> Out come the Long Fellow,
> Playing his tricks,
> Sucking your soul,
> Through your fingertips . . ."

Welcome to the Jungle

Michelle remembered the black business card and had a vision it would be her way out of obscurity. "Always follow your gut," she said. She never got in trouble whenever she listened to her instincts.

She'd woken up after another anonymous day as an extra more tired than she'd felt in her entire life. Even her coffee didn't seem to do much to rouse her. She thought about calling Pam and telling her how it went. They'd both moved out to L.A. within weeks of getting out of Palmville, Texas High School. Pam settled in with a good casting company while Michelle beat the boards pursuing an acting career. She went on the occasional audition, but she never landed anything: another blonde in a sea of blondes. How would she ever stand out?

She grabbed the business card and looked it over. Dusty Palace. Jungle Productions. There was a snake-like drawing at the bottom. He'd introduced himself the night before at the Frolic Room, her favorite neighborhood bar. He'd directed two movies she'd actually heard of, The Longfellow and Hounds of Hell. After he left, the bartender, Mike, told her he thought the guy was sleazy. *Aren't they all?* she thought. At least she could call him . . . find out what he was about. So what if it was straight to home video? So what if she had to be in a horror movie? She didn't mind. Whatever the project, at least she might be seen in something that had distribution. She certainly didn't want to pantomime to invisible dance music for fourteen hours a day for the rest of her life.

She looked him up on the net. Everything he said checked out—his company website, his IMDB credits. He was legitimate. "Wow," she said. "This could actually be something."

"So glad you called." Dusty talked warm and slow.

"I just wanted to find out a little bit more about the shoot next week. I mean, what's it pay? How long will you need me for? That sort of thing?" Michelle asked.

He laughed a little. "Now you sound like an actress."

"Well, I came here to act," she said. "Otherwise it's not really worth it to me to be here. I mean, I can make more at an office job back home in Texas, and work a lot less hours. It's not like I'll ever be seen doing extra work, anyway."

"I hear you," he said. "Well, look, I can't offer up too much more than two grand for the day without seeing how you act. I'm sure you'd be good enough for one of the girls in the dungeon scene, though."

"Okay. That sounds better."

"Are you good at being scared? Are you okay with nudity? Being topless? Can you scream?"

There it was. She heard Pam's voice in her head telling her not to call him. Fine. She'd test him. "I'm great at being scared. Honestly? The other stuff? Not really. I'm not sure I want to go there just yet."

"Fair enough," he said. "I've got other girls for that, but you did say that you're okay with being scared, maybe dying on-screen, maybe a love scene, right?"

"Sure! What's a little blood and screaming?" she asked.

"Right. Well, look, we're going to do that scene in two days. Here's the deal. . . "

"Are you nuts?" Pam asked. "You shouldn't be doing sleaze like that. Just stick with the extra work. It'll begin to pay off. Everyone in the industry has long hours. It's a given: The extras, the PAs, the entire crew. Heck, even those of us in the office, we all work long days. I even have to read scripts on the weekends a lot of the time."

"He's offering two grand for one day."

The line was silent.

"Really?"

"Yes."

"Get it up front."

"He's paying me as soon as I get there," Michelle said as she paced her studio. "That's rent and food for an entire month. And I don't have to wait three weeks for the check, either."

"Take it. Just be careful."

Sun Valley felt like an entirely different state. There were farms and horses. Houses spread out more. It reminded her of some of the border towns she'd grown up with in Texas, so she felt immediately at home. She thought: *This is going to be great. This was a good move.* Her little Toyota Yaris pulled onto the side of the road and she patted her GPS. *Best invention ever,* she thought.

The house was larger than she expected. She saw cars lined up and down the street. She wondered where the crew vans were parked? She hadn't seen any. Where was Craft Services? Were the actors being held inside? She saw none of it and just assumed they were in another location. *Ah, so this is what indie film is like,* she thought while she proceeded to the front door. *This feels really small.*

A handmade sign taped to the door read: WELCOME TO THE JUNGLE. The bottom had the same snake logo as Dusty's card. "Cute," Michelle said.

There was a lavender bush growing right next to the door and its smell mixed in with that of stables and horses. It reminded her so much of Texas that she shut her eyes for a moment and imagined she was home again, right on her Daddy's front porch.

The door knob rustled and she got her composure. Then she put on her bravest smile. Again, her stomach was in knots from the nerves. One day, she knew, it would all be familiar to her and she'd walk right into these situations as easy as iced tea.

Of course, it was Dusty who had opened the door. "Michelle!" he said. "My Michelle! Welcome to our little place in paradise city."

The cottage seemed perfectly interior designed with all sorts of traditional southwestern themes. The walls were painted sandy with Aztec blue accents. Every surface looked fussed over. There were people sitting on the couches. One was reading a script. The others joked and laughed.

"You have perfect timing. We need to get you changed and down to set."

"Down?"

"The basement."

"Oh, right. I just don't see where this place would have a basement."

"That's why we chose it. It's rare in L.A. to find a house with any kind of basement."

Michelle met Rebecca, the wardrobe person. She had Michelle keep her jeans, but changed into a white blouse. "The blood will show up better," she said. They both laughed.

"Speaking of that? Where's all the crew trucks and stuff?" Michelle asked.

"These low budgets . . . we have to carry everything in our trunks," Rebecca said. "Craft services is pizza. Dressing rooms are bathrooms. You get the idea. I'm doing lights, too, by the way."

"It's already a lot more fun than the other set I was on this week," Michelle said.

"Let's make it even better." Dusty reached into his pocket and gave her an envelope. She looked inside: Twenty hundred-dollar bills. It was impossible for her not to grin ear-to-ear.

The basement was hot and unfinished, so one could see the exposed rock walls. The floor wasn't much more than a layer of sandy dirt. There was a naked woman chained to the wall. She didn't look up or respond when Michelle and Dusty entered.

"What's the name of this movie?" Michelle asked. "I forgot to ask."

Dusty frowned. "Appetite," he said. "Some poor fellow, played by me by the way, has a monster chained up in his basement and he has to feed it live kill every few days to keep it happy, or else."

He gestured to a huge mound about as high as their shoulders on the far side of the basement. It looked like a giant red crab coiled in on itself. Each of its claws had a shiny dagger affixed.

"That's our special effect," Dusty said and laughed.

"It looks real." Michelle said, stuttering. In fact, it looked very real. There was something about it . . . a presence that touched her instinct. Something about it just wasn't right. She thought that maybe it was a giant puppet, but she couldn't see any wires coming out the back. Maybe there was a guy inside to puppeteer it.

Dusty waved a hand under his nose. "It stinks in here

something fierce," he said. "We better hurry up and shoot this sucker."

Dusty picked up a hand-held video camera off the washer and dryer unit. "That's what we're shooting on?" Michelle asked. Rebecca the wardrobe girl, and grip, apparently, walked closer to the naked woman. There was another set of cuffs hanging near her.

"You can shoot Hi Def with this thing. It's better than what George Lucas used on Star Wars. If it's good enough for George, it's good enough for me."

Michelle was beginning to rethink having called him. Was she just in some terrible exploitation movie? Was this a mistake after all? Maybe she should have listened to Pam. Still, two thousand bucks to be scared of a giant crab monster is still two thousand bucks, she knew, and it'd get distribution.

"We just need you to put your hands up in these cuffs," Rebecca said. "Then we can shoot."

Michelle stepped over to the cuffs and turned backward. She raised her hands, smiled, and said, "These are, like, real chains?" She had a nervous pit in her belly, just like when she rode the rollercoaster at the theme parks growing up.

Rebecca cuffed her. "These are actually cheaper than the prop ones. Don't worry: They're perfectly safe."

Dusty opened his camera, turned it on and walked over to Michelle. "Okay, so here's the scene. She's going to get eaten, and all you have to do is scream and act terrified of big old Red over here."

"Okay!" Michelle said. "But once this is over I've got to see how that thing works." She nodded to the giant crab monster.

"Oh, you mean Red?" he asked, then nodded with a smile. "Sometimes a magician shouldn't reveal his secrets, right?"

"I guess," she said.

"I don't want your performance to suffer. I want this to be real."

"Action!" Dusty called.

Red unfolded slowly and gracefully. Michelle thought it looked like a one of those Transformers toys, or like a blooming onion, only more organic. Dusty held the camera rock solid. Red moved, creeping along the basement floor. It'd gotten almost an entire head taller since it unfolded. Four thin arms on each side closed in on the naked girl like two hands coming together.

"Farrah!" Dusty said. "Wake up! Look who's here to see you! It's Red!"

The naked girl looked up from her daze and saw the monstrous thing in front of her. Then she thrashed in her restraints. "Let me go! Let me out of here! Come on! Please!"

Michelle did her best to keep her face looking as though she were terrified, even though she wasn't. She kept staring at the beast, studying it, recording it in her brain. *The craftsmanship,* she thought, *was outstanding. Who'd need CG when they could make real objects look so life-like?*

Farrah screamed. One of Red's hands slashed her across her belly with one of the knives. A curved slit opened and she bled profusely and quickly.

Michelle wondered how they were pulling off the effect. She thought that maybe Farrah had worn a false stomach pre-loaded with blood. Michelle thought they were quite clever. They could make it look like it was all one continuous take, and by using a hand-held camera, they could tie into the whole reality TV phenomenon.

Red split in half horizontally. His eyes opened at the sides of his head: Even those seemed super realistic. It reminded Michelle of when she once swam with dolphins . . . she could see the intelligence in their eyes, just as she saw the intelligence in Red's. It was some magical trick.

Then Red opened his mouth, which seemed to take up the entire middle of his body. He had rows and rows of shining metal, shark-tooth-like teeth. Something else struck Michelle as funny: The smell. The air around them filled with the most rotten stench, like a hundred dead teeth, mixed with vinegar and spoiled meat. It came from Red.

She wracked her brain. *Maybe they'd made him with animal parts to make him more realistic?* No. She knew that wasn't it.

Red advanced toward Farrah and opened his mouth. The bottom jaw unhinged and fell to the floor. Knife-shaped teeth scraped along the dirt floor until they were just under her feet. She whimpered and screamed. "This can't be happening," she said. "No. Please. No."

In a blink, Red jerked forward and swallowed her entire

bottom section. Some of the teeth gave her little slices.

Then Red clamped his mouth shut, like a giant shark. Farrah screamed and Michelle screamed, too. It was so real-looking!

Please let this be fake, she thought. *Please God let this not be happening.*

Something clicked in Michelle's head. She realized none of it was fake: Not a bit. Farrah's insides drooped from her top half. There was blood everywhere. Her head was slumped and she'd stopped moving. Her skin had gone ashen.

Red chewed on the bottom parts of Farrah. Michelle saw one foot and bit of leg before she turned away. She couldn't take any more. Tears streamed down her face and she shook uncontrollably.

Please let me live through this, she thought. *Please!*

She heard Red chewing for a few moments. *Pretend it's not real. Pretend it's just a big puppet. Don't worry about it. Act!* Then she sensed his warm breath on her. She wouldn't open her eyes . . . she refused to look . . . she refused to do anything other than what she had been hired to do, which was to act scared.

Act scared!

Then the beast's breath was away from her and she heard Dusty. "Here's where I need you most," he said. "Red here wants to copulate with you." He folded the LCD display of the camera down flush, turning it off.

"What? Someone's dead here!"

He smiled. "Is she really dead or is it just a special effect? I'm not telling."

Michelle was speechless. What was he telling her? Was Farrah truly dead? She looked over to the remaining half of the woman. It was too real . . . the smell of the blood was real . . . how could it not be real? She'd seen it in front of her own eyes.

Dusty said, "Come on. You'll be fine. You'll be famous for this. It'll be unforgettable."

Red made a grumpy noise and inched closer.

"Anyone who sees this movie will never be able to forget this scene with you and Red," he said. "What do you say?"

"I . . . don't . . . want to," she said. "I don't do nudity. Is she really dead?"

Dusty got up in her face. "Do you really want to find out if she's dead or not? Why don't you just do the scene, take your money, and go home? I thought you wanted to act! Do whatever you have to do to make this moment happen for me!"

Michelle felt her eyes well up. How could she have gotten herself in such a position? Did Grace Kelly really need to get choked by a telephone cord in order to become famous? "It's not really going to . . . ?"

"We'll just make it look that way. Don't stress." Dusty's voice was very low. "You're just going to have to die in the end."

"Like Farrah?" Michelle felt sick. "I don't want to really die."

Dusty winked. "That's why they call it acting, you know?"

Michelle shut her eyes. *Can I trust him? That thing bit Farrah in half. Who says it won't do the same to me?* Michelle thought.

She said, "Just make it classy, okay?"

He laughed. "Not sure how much class is going to be involved with Red dry-humping you," Dusty said. "But I'll do my best." He unfolded the LCD on his camera and pressed a button. "Here we go. Ready?"

"Okay," she said.

Dusty moved closer toward Michelle. She could see that he had a much longer body than she'd originally thought. For some reason, Red reminded Michelle of a slinky as Red stretched out. He was some kind of horrific snake, she believed, like one of those fabled gigantic anacondas: Only Red was, well, red, and his head was closer to being nothing but mouth, teeth, and the six spindly red, dagger holding arms jutting from the rim of his mouth, three per side.

Dusty moved to her right side and got a different angle. She could almost see what he was shooting on the LCD. She looked at it from the corner of her eye: Michelle didn't want to ruin the shot by looking directly into the lens. The last thing she wanted to do was have to re-shoot the scene.

"Good," he said. "I'm going to be quiet now. I'll move around you two, but just be natural. Remember: pretend you're chained up in this crazy guy's basement and he's trying to feed his pet monster. If he doesn't feed the beast, it will eat him!"

Michelle said, "Okay."

"Okay . . . so . . ." Dusty said. "Action!"

Michelle felt Red's heaviness at her feet as it slowly

crept upward. Red put his arms out. The daggers made a perfect halo shape around her face. Michelle instinctively made a whimpering sound. The daggers were so close, so sharp, and so very real. *Those are the same ones that I just watched cut Farrah. This thing could kill me in an instant.*

She shut her eyes for a moment again. Reaching down deep inside to the core of her training, she knew she had to use any acting tool available to her to make it through.

She searched her memories for something that really scared her. *You need to believe that this thing is fake. Then you need to be scared of something else . . . something from your past.*

What scared Michelle more than anything? A memory of a helicopter trip as a young girl flashed through her mind. She'd been riding in the back with her father. They'd barely lifted off, and the pilot banked them to the right, when her door suddenly swung open. Her father grabbed her with both of his arms, holding her. She'd had on her seatbelt, so her father's reaction was more instinctual than lifesaving, she knew. Michelle, in that moment, looked down onto the river below them, across to the shore side landing area where they'd taken off. She was filled with dread that she was about to slip out and fall to her death. That was the feeling! She played over the helicopter moment in her head again. Her stomach tensed and she felt the exact same numbing fear.

Red slithered up and on top of her. She opened her eyes to find one of his looking right at her. He had to turn his head to his left a bit because his eyes were on the side of his head, like those of a fish. He blinked once.

She knew he was real!

No!

I'm going to fall out! Fall right down to the ground and that's the end of it! That's what I'm scared of happening! Nothing is worse . . . nothing is worse than that!

At her thighs, she felt two nubs hardening. She looked down and saw a pair of thumb-shaped organs pushing into her. Thank God she had her clothes on.

It's all pretend. Nothing's real. Simulated.

"Okay, everyone hold on a sec," Dusty said. She looked up at him and saw Rebecca in the background quietly watching the scene. Her face was cold and expressionless.

Dusty went somewhere behind Red where Michelle couldn't see him. He returned a moment later with a plastic jug. "We'll need some blood for this one," he said.

He worked his way to her middle and poured it on her thighs, hips, and belly. It was warm. *That's human blood. From Farrah, or maybe someone else.* She tried to psych herself out of the thought. *No way. The blood's just been sitting in a hot basement for God knows how long. Maybe he just made it on the stove or something. Don't effects people make their own blood by cooking it with Karo syrup and red food coloring? It's cheaper than buying it from the supply shops, especially if you need a lot, right?*

Only problem was the blood smelled like blood, too.

Dusty said, "I'm ready," and grabbed the camera again. "Rolling."

Red's thumb-things massaged her thighs, searching for the place where they dipped downward between her legs. Michelle clamped her thighs together as hard as she could. No way was this thing going to get that close to her.

She sensed Dusty moving his camera down toward Red's thumb-things. Then he started panning the camera upward. She looked down so she wouldn't look directly in his lens again. She just let it happen without trying to force a scared face. *Maybe if she kept it simple the scene would be scarier? Wasn't that what she was taught? Don't do anything.* That was one of her acting teacher's voices in her head.

Then Dusty panned back down.

The blood had soaked right through her clothes and she felt numbness starting at her hips and going all the way down to her feet. It was what she'd imagined an epidural would be like.

She could still feel the thumb-things working faster and faster, but instead of hurting her, Red's weight was making her tingle. *Probably the blood rushing down from being hanged,* she thought. *There's really just a big special effects monster on top of me. That's all.*

Red moved faster. Dusty moved to the opposite side and panned up and down rapidly.

The thumb-things managed to spread her legs just a little, but not enough to get to any sensitive parts. It seemed to be working harder now that it'd gotten a small break. Michelle writhed on the chains. She wanted the scene over already!

Then the thumb-things managed to get between her legs deeper and Michelle screamed, "No!"

You're going to fall out of the helicopter. That's the only thing that's real. That's the only thing to be scared of. The rest of this is just Hollywood.

The thumb-things moved quicker: It reminded her of when people would flutter their first and second fingers to simulate walking. It did not feel good at all, especially with the blood starting to dry and stick.

She looked down the length of Red's body and could see small ripples moving up and down his sections. As Red's skin moved, the circular bones stretched through. It was as though he were shivering.

Dusty kept shooting.

Then, as quickly as Red's assault started, it stopped. At least it looked that way for a brief moment. Red's face inched back away from hers. Dusty stepped back to get the whole scene.

Red opened his mouth and Michelle swore he was smiling. He moved his head from side to side, checking her out with one eye and then the other. Michelle wondered what Red was doing.

He slashed at her face with one of the daggers. She felt a hot pain flare across her right cheek, stretching from just under her eye to her chin.

She screamed, despite herself.

Red unleashed a rather giant tongue and rolled the tip. He used the tip to lick the slash he'd made top to bottom.

"No," Michelle said.

Red pulled his tongue back inside his head and shut his mouth.

Michelle looked down and could see she was still bleeding heavily. She felt as though she might pass out. *Is this what happened to Farrah right before he bit her in half? Am I about to die? How can I get out of here?*

Red backed away, slithering off her body. Michelle was relieved not to have his weight on her. She could see the nubs near his bottom, now flaccid and pale. She had an idea.

The nubs.

It had to be!

Even though she could barely feel her legs, she tried moving them. They wiggled. Her brain still worked!

Could she strike him?

No. He was too far away.

Dusty said, "All right. Take two!"

Two? Hadn't he gotten what he needed with one? She'd been cut, for real. How would that edit together? Well, she didn't think continuity would be high on Dusty's priority list in the end.

The nightmare started again, with Red bulking his way toward her.

As soon as his little nubs were close enough, Michelle kicked them.

Red raised in the air with all he had. He lifted up and his back touched the ceiling. It was his turn to scream! His voice was hoarse and deep, like a sick sea lion.

"Shit!" Dusty screamed.

Michelle looked down at his nubs. They were no longer pale, but red, and not from being turned on. Michelle kicked them again. The pitch of Red's scream rose. His eyes rolled back and he shoved his arms up toward the ceiling, where he stuck each dagger deep and into the woodwork.

He cried out again, his eyes locking with Michelle.

This is it, she thought. *He's going to kill me for that move.*

Red dropped back down, his arms whipping out from the ceiling. Chips of wood fell all over. He swung them around and violently punched them into a circle around Michelle. They were sharp enough to stick into the rock.

His mouth opened and she could see the little specks of blood in his drool. Had that been her blood?

Then Red tried to pull his daggers free. He couldn't. He pulled several times, but he was totally stuck.

"Cut!" Dusty said. He hurried up toward Red. "It's enough. Stop this!"

Red kept right on yanking with his arms.

Dusty said, "You're going to hurt yourself!" He looked around the basement. "We'll find a way to get you free."

Michelle felt something at her wrists. She jumped! It was only Rebecca with the key to unlock her. She was so busy staring straight ahead; she hadn't even noticed Rebecca rush up to her. In a moment, Michelle was free. Her legs were so numb and she felt incredibly wobbly without the chains to hold onto.

She ducked and bent, feeling some of the blood had

dried to her clothes already. She noticed she was trembling. Her heart was beating fast and her eyes were watering. Overhead, she felt Red's violent jerking ever-so-close.

Standing up on her own, and still only a few feet from Red, Dusty jumped in front of her. "You can't leave! We're not done!"

"*I'm* done!" Michelle pushed past him and made it nearly to the stairs. She hurried. In back of her, she heard Red struggling.

She heard Dusty: "We have to stop her! If she tells anyone . . . she's supposed to die in the end! You shouldn't have let her go!"

Someone grabbed at her shoulder. Michelle spun round and Rebecca cold-cocked her. "We're not through! I need this movie for my IMDB credit!"

It barely registered. Maybe because of her adrenaline, or maybe because she'd grown numb, Michelle was able to shake Rebecca's punch right off. She returned the favor.

Rebecca went right down, holding her jaw, and cowered. "Screw your credits!"

Dusty was right behind her. "You!" he yelled.

"Me!"

Red broke free from the ceiling and dropped back to the floor with a hideous howl. His eyelids were slightly drooped. He turned to face Michelle.

She took the moment, with Dusty standing between them, and shoved him toward Red as hard as she could.

Dusty was surprised, said, "Hey!" and fell toward Red.

Then he stopped moving. It took a second for Michelle to realize Dusty's back had met a handful of Red's daggers.

Dusty looked up and choked up some blood. He reached his hand out. "Please," he said.

"No," she said back, and gave him another kick. The daggers went deeper. Michelle looked down and saw Dusty's feet hovering: his entire weight was carried by Red's daggers. Dusty's eyes shut and Michelle turned and ran toward the stairs.

She didn't look back. She heard slicing sounds. She heard moans. She heard Rebecca scream.

Michelle ran up the stairs.

The scene behind her got extremely quiet.

Don't look back.

She made it through the short foyer and right to the front door. She heard some kind of scraping behind her. She grabbed the front door handle and opened it. She hurried outside. Her car wasn't far.

Do I call the cops? Do I go to the Emergency Room? What?

Michelle made it to her car. Her keys were still in her front pocket, and although they were sticky, they worked. She patted her butt and felt the envelope with her cash still intact. Thank God for small miracles. As she climbed in, she heard a roar coming from the house.

From behind a curtained window, she saw Red. It'd made it up the stairs! It watched her with one of its eyes. Michelle wondered if Red had killed Dusty and Rebecca, and if they'd come after her. Would Red dare come outside and expose itself? She couldn't know, and wouldn't wait to find out. *Always follow your gut,* she thought. *Gut's telling me to get the hell out of here.*

She did see the sign on the door, the hand-printed one that Dusty had made that read: Welcome to the Jungle.

Michelle couldn't drive away fast enough.

Later, Michelle received a text message from Pam. "How'd the shoot go?"

She replied, "I'm retired."

WINGS FOR WHEELS

The Hot Rod Angels called for Mary.

Their blackened Camaro idled out on Thunder Road, several paces from Mary's front porch. She slipped off her headphones, took the needle off the record player, and inched open her bedroom curtain without taking her eyes off the three Angels emerging from the burned car. Tommy and two pale-skinned boys. The paint on the car's hood had splintered into raised brittle bubbles, some of which had split open to reveal the gray steel underneath. Even the white walls on the tires were charred. Mary couldn't imagine how the car could be in such poor condition and still be running.

The familiar sound of Roy Orbison's "Only The Lonely" echoed from the Camaro. Just after their last dance as a couple at the Senior Prom, she had told Tommy that song was her favorite; she imagined that was why he'd chosen to play it now.

On the first step of the walkway, Tommy stood between the two boys. When he turned to one of them, Mary glimpsed a hole in his leather jacket. The gouge stretched from his left shoulder blade down to the middle of his back. From his right shoulder, she saw a second hole where a frayed black wing fanned out.

Tommy twisted round, looked up, and locked eyes with her as she felt her throat go dry. Was she seeing a trick of the moonlight? His eyes had changed into glossy black crystal balls. She saw herself reflected in them, only she'd aged, thinned, and looked ill. Wisps of blood curled down the insides of Tommy's eyes. He blinked and instantly his eyes transformed back to their familiar steely, cold gray.

Mary squeezed her eyes shut and hoped what she'd seen was just because it was late, and she was tired. Moisture from the rain played tricks, was all. She wanted the Angels to get away from her house. Their skin was gray, too, just like Tommy's eyes. Every gesture seemed pained. They're like ghosts. Tommy stared at her from beyond his empty eyes. Her house was small; the second story was no more than twenty feet from the walkway where they stood. It seemed she could reach down and take his hand, if she chose to. . .

The Angel next to Tommy stepped back to the Camaro. Tommy put his hand up. "Not yet." Then he pointed at Mary. "You lied to me." He spread his fingers and put his hand out to her. "I forgive you. Come outside."

Mary recalled what she'd told him: that she'd always love him, and that they'd always have something special between them. Well, it hadn't really been a lie, had it? She still felt good about what they'd shared, and he still mattered to her. And it wasn't as though she had her choice of the boys in town. Regardless, Mary wanted to find out what lay beyond the borders of their sleepy oceanside town after she graduated. Although she really had no idea what she eventually wanted to do with her life, she was sure it would happen somewhere other than The Shore.

Tommy blinked, and his eyes turned back into shiny dark mirrors. "We have Redemption." Mary again saw herself reflected in Tommy's eyes. This time she was hung up on a cross, nails through her wrists, a crown of thorns, her face framed with dark, drying blood. She pictured everyone in town gathered and watching her as if she were on stage. And she was beautiful to them. She saw a black crow on a barren tree above. It eyed her like a merciless devil come to collect her soul.

For a moment, rushing out her front door and going for a ride with the Angels seemed like a great idea. They'd found a way to be known—to be something other than what people in their town ended up being. Then her eyes strayed to the dying bouquet of roses that Tommy had given to her on graduation night, curled blackening petals lying strewn across the top of her dresser. "It's a fine area to live in," Tommy had said that night, talking about how they could build a life there. "I'm going to work at the Belco Steel Mill this summer, and maybe I can hang on after that . . ." But he chose his friends over her. She'd told him she didn't want him racing, that he might eventually get hurt. He hadn't listened.

Mary scooped the drooping roses out of the vase, opened the window, and threw them down onto the sidewalk.

Tommy glared up at her, then he and the Hot Rod Angels climbed back in their Camaro. She watched them screech away from her house, heading out to Highway 9. But she knew they'd be back tomorrow, calling for her, just as they did each night.

Mary quickly hopped back in bed and pulled the quilt up to her neck.

All summer she'd prayed for someone to save her from Tommy, and from the promise she'd made. It didn't matter to him that he'd sold his soul to run with the Hot Rod Angels: Mary was his.

Everything changed the night Mary first laid eyes on The Kid. Johnny. Each night since she'd met him, she'd marked a cross on the back of her bedroom door. She'd made seventy-five of them since May. Some of the drawings were simple, while others were elaborately decorated. It depended on her mood. Still others were circled; those were for the nights she'd seen his band.

I wish he'd come out tonight, Mary thought while curled up on her bed. For the first time in her life she felt old. Her mind raced with what she'd just seen. Tommy. The Hot Rod Angels.

It took her a while, but she eventually slept.

She awoke to the sound of an idling engine; her veins felt filled with ice. They'd come back for her. Tommy's chant rang in her head.

We have Redemption.

At the bottom of the stairs, Mary looked out her open front door. She was scared, imagining the worst. She stared out at the car parked in front of her house. It took her a few seconds to recognize The Kid's '57 hardtop convertible Chevy. His car was the only one she knew that had orange flames painted on the hood. Mary's entire body went cold.

She spotted him behind the wheel, leaning down in his seat enough to have seen her come down the stairs through the open passenger door. How could he have known? He must have heard her praying for him to come.

Mary's white cotton dress fanned out as she hurried across the porch and she clutched at the bottom hem to keep it from rising up. She made it down the three small steps that led off the porch and headed for The Kid's car, stepping over the scattered roses she'd thrown at Tommy.

"Climb in," he said, his voice distinct, smooth, and clear. Mary felt electricity race through her and pool in her fingertips. It seemed impossible that Johnny had found her now, of all nights, of all moments, after a summer of being endlessly bothered by Tommy and the Angels. In the backseat, she saw his blonde Fender Telecaster. Mary had seen him play it dozens of times during his shows.

Mary stopped before getting in, leaning down to see him. "What brings you to my neck of the woods?"

Johnny smiled. "You," he said. "We can make the last ride around the Circuit before the sun comes up if we leave now." The arms of his black leather jacket creaked as he stretched over towards her.

Mary climbed in. "Me?" she said, running her hands over the upholstery. "This is gorgeous." The dashboard glistened; every detail was perfect. The interior smelled of vanilla and the earthiness of his leather jacket.

The Chevy's door was heavier than she thought as she pulled it closed. The sound reminded Mary of the steel mills, The Kid's drummer and a prison door all rolled into one. She turned to Johnny.

"Why'd you come get me, Kid?" she asked. "How'd you know I wanted to go out with you?" At that moment, Mary wanted to tell him all about Tommy and the Hot Rod Angels, about their burned-out car and the blank looks in their eyes. But she thought better of it, not wanting to ruin the moment, afraid he'd think she was crazy.

Johnny tapped the side of his head. "Your light was on and I was just passing by. Figured I'd take a chance."

"But don't you already have Maria? She's the most popular girl in town." Mary looked at her feet. "I don't even come close to looking like her. No one even looks at me when she's around."

He shook his head. "But there's something special about you. I just couldn't talk to her, you know?" He leaned over. "I have something I want to ask you."

The streetlights of the boardwalk glowed just over the horizon. Mary wanted nothing more than to float out past the dashboard, over the hood, and disappear inside their warm, fuzzy colors. The radio played The Ronettes "Be My Baby". Ronnie Spector's otherworldly wails at the end always sent shivers down Mary's spine. There was something magical in the hollow, shambling drums that made her feel comforted and sad, like the sun peeking out during a rainstorm.

Familiar icons of her life rolled past: Max's Hot Dog stand, Arnie's Arcade, Peter's mini-golf course, the Wonder Bar.

She saw a few kids walk between the clubs and the food joints, but no one looked up to see her ride by in The Kid's Chevy the way she hoped they would.

When Johnny spoke, she jumped a little. "Penny for your thoughts?"

"Oh, it's nothing," she said. "I was just looking at the lights and the arcades and the rides and thinking about how much time I've spent down here over the years."

The Kid steered them onto Ocean Avenue, which was four lanes wide. At the corner of First Avenue, they passed the Empress Hotel near the Golddigger.

"Funny, isn't it?" the Kid said. "We spent so much time here waiting to leave, and then, when someone gets a chance, they get nostalgic. Well, that ain't me. I'm not going to be one of those losers. I met this guy last night at The Upstage. He's got tons of connections. Liked what I was playing. Told me I should come down to a party tonight on Tenth Avenue."

Mary looked out at the bars. She could hear the live rock n' soul bands reverberating from inside. "Lots of people like your music. I mean even Terry at the Upstage loves you."

"This is different." The Kid reached into his inside pocket and took out his wallet, handed it to her. It felt thick and heavy. "Look inside." As they talked, they rode Ocean all the way down before they headed west to Kingsley. They passed the Stone Pony and the Palace and finally back to Ocean.

Mary didn't open the wallet, simply held it for an entire lap around The Circuit, saying nothing. Her mind raced—was The Kid going to sell his soul like the Angels? He couldn't. He was different. She was different. She took in a breath—the air smelled charged.

The Kid broke the silence. "Aren't you curious to see what I'm talking about?"

When she opened the wallet, Mary saw the largest wad of cash she'd ever seen. The blood in her veins seemed to freeze; she felt sick to her stomach. "What is this?"

The Kid smirked. "Five grand." They pulled up to Ocean Avenue. "That's just a promise from him that he was serious."

"A promise?"

"He told me to write four or five songs and have them ready to play for the Big Guys tonight. He said that no matter how it turned out, I could keep the money as an advance." He pointed his thumb at the Telecaster in the back seat. "That's why Sandy's with me."

"It seems weird that some record bigwig would just give you money like this." He shook his head. "You never know when your break's going to come. You just need to jump in and be ready."

"It seems dangerous." His wallet suddenly felt tainted and poisoned. He was busy turning the wheel, or she would have handed it right back. "Are you sure you're not doing anything else for him? This isn't a trick of some kind?"

The Kid shook his head. "I trust him. Look behind the money." Mary found a white business card with a big red logo on the front. "CBS Records? John Hammond?" She turned it over and read the address scrawled on the back. "One- Nine-Seven-Five Tenth Avenue. Third floor. Eight O'clock."

"He's a scout," The Kid said. "Do you want to come out with me tonight and be my good luck charm? Find out if it's for real or not? Escape this place once and for all?"

"I don't know. . ." Mary started hesitantly. "Listen." The dials behind the steering wheel became brighter. Mary stared at them for a second before she noticed the light was coming from The Kid's fingertips. They glowed a bright orange, as if little ovens were heating up inside.

He flared the fingers up on his right hand, but kept the butt of his palm on the wheel. "Want to hear that guitar really talk?"

Little sparks shot from his fingertips. They multiplied until they looked like five small volcanoes, then fires rose, stretching along the top of the Chevy's ceiling, rolling back and down onto the Telecaster.

The Chevy filled with his music. She recognized some of the chord progressions from his show, although the sound was different than anything she'd ever heard. Each string lighted up, vibrated, and sounded. There were notes, followed by chords, and finally, songs.

The interior of the car brightened and the windows fogged. The lamps and neon signs of the boardwalk melted and bloomed. Roadside stands blended in psychedelic ooze. The amusement park, the people walking alongside the boardwalk—they all appeared to melt into a pool of yellow and white light. Mary felt a strong summer sun on her forehead and smelled the salt from the ocean. The car seat no longer felt like leather. She didn't know how, or why, but she swore she was sitting on the beach on a hot July day instead of riding in The Kid's car on a chilly night.

Then she realized his music was making her feel this way. His songs changed the world around them. She closed her eyes and the music grew louder; Mary felt it in every pore. She saw him in front of a sea of people, playing, singing, dancing. She saw him turn to her and smile, as if she were standing just off stage. In the crowd she saw people staring at her, and she felt as though she was trespassing. The music and the noise from the crowd blended together until it was one large rumble. Everything turned dark and Mary felt like she was spinning head over heels. She reached back to steady herself and touched the car seat.

As she opened her eyes the boardwalk scenery had returned to normal. They'd nearly pulled up to Kingsley and were about to enter The Circuit.

Mary turned to the Kid. "How . . . how did you do that?"

"A magician never reveals his tricks." They'd nearly pulled up to Kingsley and were about to enter The Circuit again. "So?" he asked. "You think people will dig my new song? Think it might get me a deal?" Before Mary could answer, a deafening mechanical roar came from behind them, followed by a high-pitched wail. Mary turned to see a blackened Camaro race toward them. The Hot Rod Angels swerved, their tires screeching, horn blaring.

The Kid looked away from the rearview mirror and stared straight ahead. "They heard the music," he said, almost to himself. "Or saw the light show." He pulled onto Kingsley, shaking his head just a bit. He looked back up into the rearview, and then quickly away. "They'll want it now that they've heard it."

"Why won't he just leave me alone?" Mary clutched the side bar on the door and looked over at The Kid. Her throat tightened.

The Angels pulled up alongside the Chevy on Mary's side as "Be My Baby" blasted. They'd heard that, too. She saw Tommy behind the wheel. He turned to look at her, ghosts in his eyes. Mary wanted to duck down, but was so scared she couldn't move. When the Camaro passed them, she again spotted that black wing curling out of Tommy's back like a vampire's beckoning finger. The Camaro's engine revved and Mary swore her ears were going to ring for a week.

"What are they, Johnny?"

The Kid didn't turn to her but kept his eyes forward, on the Camaro. "Sometimes Devils have wings," he said. "But us Angels have wheels, baby." It sounded ludicrous, but it didn't seem as though he were joking. Rolling down his window, The Kid put his left hand out and pointed it upwards. Mary heard an incredibly loud wailing noise from the Telecaster, as though it might have been plugged into a wall of Marshall amps a half-mile long. The music lit the air around them with fire.

For a brief second, both the Chevy and the Camaro burned in a violent inferno. Mary threw up her arms to shield her eyes. After a moment, she lowered them and watched as the Camaro raced past. Its tires spat feather-shaped flames. Several panels and doors were missing: burned away, she imagined. Mary wrinkled her nose as the smell of burned rubber, metal, and skin engulfed the Chevy in a plume of sweet-smelling exhaust.

Finally, the Camaro degenerated into countless black embers. The asphalt sucked them in as the street caught fire near the Camaro's final resting place. The Kid rolled right through it.

"Don't be afraid," he said. "They can't hurt you now so long as you're with me." When she turned, Mary found The Kid staring right back. His sunglasses were off. Colorful organic shapes flickered where his pupils should have been. The shapes turned into a cheering crowd. "What's it gonna be?"

Mary shook her head. "It's your dream," she said. "You need make it come true." She knew his life of magic and midnight drives along the boardwalk wasn't hers to share. She'd had the night, and it was beyond her wildest imagination, but she was not meant to be part of his future. The Kid was different than Mary. He needed the attention from playing for people. Mary knew she'd never be comfortable tagging along. In the end, she wanted a better life—freedom instead of fame. With Tommy gone, The Kid had given her back her independence.

The Kid slid his shades back on. "I might not be able to come back after tonight," he said. "This might be the last chance you have to see me. Come with me."

Mary smiled with her lips closed. She looked right into

The Kid's eyes and knew that, soon enough, he'd be gone, and she would not be with him. In some ways, she felt he'd already left without her.

She stood on her porch and watched The Kid pull away. He put his hand out the window and waved. She waved back, but The Kid kept his hand fanned out and pointed at the sky. His fingers glowed a deep orange, five strands of fire burning upwards into the night in a flurry of drifting sparks.

She heard the tremolo and reverb-soaked twang of his guitar, once more the single notes building into scales, chords, songs. His music was so loud it echoed off the inside of her porch. It sounded even better than it had inside the car. Comforting warmth filled her as though she had a hole in the top of her head and he'd poured the sound inside her entire body.

Thunder Road glowed, everything lit with the unreal bloom flowing out from his hands.

Then the Chevy rolled away, slowly, until it picked up speed. Mary watched the light fade away as the taillights became smaller. The Kid raced into the night, to Highway 9, to Tenth Avenue and beyond, for once and most likely forever, away from Thunder Road.

Mary stood a bit longer before she turned and went inside, shutting the door against the night and all the possibilities it had once held, gone now on the wind. And she thought that if by some miracle Tommy and the Angels were to somehow show up tonight, maybe she would take that ride with them.

Just maybe.

Secret Sea

The skulls of the recently dead poked above the water. Major hadn't weighed them down properly, and so the Sunday Brunch crowd found themselves looking out not at dolphins and seagulls and sun rays breaking through cloud cover, as they'd thought they would see, but at dozens of floating bodies bloated by salt and sea.

"Is that a person?" Sharon asked her Aunt Annie, who shared the same short, straight bobbed black haircut and big shining pitch black eyes.

"No," Annie said. "I don't think so. It's probably just kelp or seaweed or something." She looked around the Harpoon House, eager to see if anyone else had spotted the floating lumps. They had.

Most of the diners were up from their seats and rushing toward the windows and doors. "They're moving," someone said. Annie looked over and matched the voice to a single middle-aged woman dressed all in red. "What in God's name is this?"

Out in the calm, cold sea, Major Flynn pulled a white plastic bucket through the knee-high water. He scooped at the bottom and grabbed an equal amount of sand and sea. Quickly, he stomped out of the water. Fizzy seawater splashed over the sides of his rubber pants and coated his jeans.

As soon as he was safely out of the water, he knelt down and peered into the plastic bucket. With a hand on each side, he steered the bucket down deeper into the sand.

"Is it in there?" Bob Balthazar hollered behind him. "Come on, tell me. Is it?" His snorkel dripped on Major's shoulder as he tried to peer over his shoulder.

"I don't know," Major said. He leaned in. "I don't see anything yet." He was looking for any signs of the Elcantrant Fluid they'd so generously poured into the sea.

"Let me look," Balthazar said. He shoved his body up against Major, nearly knocking him down.

Major stood, happy to let his overbearing partner sniff for his own mistakes. "You see it?" he asked.

Balthazar shook his head. "Nothing in there," he said. "They can't pin this one on us. It's all dissolved."

He turned his neck and spotted Major five paces behind him. "Good," Major said. "Let's get out of here, then. Fast. Before anyone sees us. Those things are moving down there."

Balthazar smirked, turned back to the bucket, lifted it and poured it out on the sand. Then he stood and looked out at the writhing bodies. "Have a nice life!" he yelled out at them. "You jerks." He heaved the white bucket out at the bodies. It wiggled in the air like a Ferris wheel cart before it finally landed in the water.

"What do you want to do about the boat?" Major shouted after him.

"Is it tied up to the dock?"

"Yeah."

"Leave it. We'll get it later."

William Webber saw a deep, gut-colored green. He tasted salt. He felt wet and bloated. *Is this where we end up?* he thought. *Is this where we go?* Several months earlier, he'd died in immeasurable agony. The sneaking virus began as a stomachache and developed quickly into the internal revolt of cancer. He lasted a month before he'd finally succumbed.

He breathed salt water and choked. Then Webber lifted himself up from the water and spit. *What am I doing in the sea?* he thought as he looked around. His feet could not touch the sea floor, so he paddled. He noticed others near him. *What are we doing?* he thought. Then he sensed a thick, syrupy film on his face and head. He reached up to touch it. Bringing it in front of his face, he observed the white and oily syrup coat his fingers. *My God*, he thought. *What it this?*

In the water, he noticed several more puddles of the white oil floating on top of the sea all around him. Another person raised his head, also layered with the white oil.

And then Webber heard far off voices. Cries. To his left he saw a structure on the waterfront. He noticed the poles going into the water under the dock foundation. He saw the pastel blue name painted on the side. *Harpoon House*, he thought. Webber paddled towards it and the curious faces staring at him from the pier.

"He's coming towards us," Annie said. "What are we supposed to do?" She held Sharon close in front of her.

"Was there a ship that went down or something?" someone said behind her. "I don't think so." "I don't know." "I didn't see anything."

"What should we do?" Sharon said. "Should we leave?"

Annie clutched Sharon's shoulders. "Stay put for now," she said. "Until we know what's happening."

The help at the restaurant pushed through the crowd. "What's going on?" one of them said.

"There's people washing up out there."

"Washing up?"

"Yes. There's been an accident. A boat or something."

Annie counted at least a dozen bodies struggle to the surface. It seemed they were all coated in a white film of some kind. One of the bodies paddled towards them.

In the cab of his pickup, Balthazar slammed his fists on the seat. "You didn't weigh them down enough," he said to Major. "They were supposed to be out there longer."

Major downshifted to third gear. He looked in the rearview as the familiar site of the beach parking lot vanished with the curve of the road. "I thought I did," Major said. "They were completely tied to the bottom. I'm not sure why they came up."

Balthazar turned forward. "So?" he said. "They came back. It worked."

"Are you surprised that it did?"

"I'm surprised how much better it worked. You should have seen them twitching underwater. Wild." He turned and looked at the buckets and tubes and diving gear in the bed of the truck. "What are we going to do with all this? What would a funeral director have with all this scuba gear, anyway?" he laughed to himself. Major concentrated on the road ahead; he didn't find their situation too funny.

Webber's legs felt heavy as they kicked into the sand. He'd reached shallow water and stopped swimming. He walked a few paces until he was able to reach down and feel his legs.

There was something on them. He bent over and grabbed at his ankles. Iron cuffs wrapped around his shins. *Why do I have restraints on?* His thoughts raced. *Am I a prisoner? Is this a tracking computer on me? Was I damaged? Is this a brace of some kind?* Before his mind could search further, the terrible, crippling pain in his intestines returned. It seethed through him, agonizing him much more than before he'd died. He reached down to touch his stomach.

What's wrong with me? Webber thought. Pressing on his stomach, he learned that there was a lot less of it than he was used to. In fact, there seemed to be very little of it left. He lifted back his shirt and saw that his skin was very different than he once knew. The pliable, supple skin had turned into a thick, wrinkled shell. The small potbelly he'd grown was shriveled and lost. He noticed cracks and tears in the skin. Raising his hands, Webber gasped. They looked like the hands of a skeleton, thinly wrapped and covered in rotten skin and worn away muscle.

He touched his face and found the flesh thin and coarse. *How am I alive again?* he thought. *What's happened to me? Where am I?* Webber felt his thoughts cave in. The world in front of him seemed to topple sideways. He dropped to his knees and gasped for air. *This isn't real,* he thought. *Can't be real.*

He watched a tiny fish swim away, rushing behind him. Then he saw something shiny that caught his attention. A plastic white bucket floated in the sea. He lifted himself up and made for it.

Webber lunged for the bucket and grabbed it by its side. As he lifted it he noticed something written in permanent black marker near the rim. "Balthazar Funeral Home," he said. And then something else caught his eye. Something very faint, and something most people would not have noticed. Webber's mind always went back to his days in college. He'd been one of the best hitters on his team. His technique was to always take in the entire field right as he got to plate, before anything happened. He watched the fielders carefully. Did they step in closer? Did they move out further? Did they speak to one another or did they keep focused on themselves? He looked for players not paying attention. He looked for players that seemed a little off guard. And he'd hit to them when he could.

And so, as Webber held the white bucket in his whittled hands, he spotted Balthazar's pickup off way to the right, nearly a mile away. It could mean nothing, or it could mean something, he knew. Either way, Webber made sure to remember. Just to see if any players were off guard. Just in case he knew he would have had to come up to bat.

"He's carrying a bucket," Sharon said as she tugged at Annie's sleeve. "Why is he doing that?"

"Maybe he was fishing?" Annie looked around at the other diners. Her stomach rumbled.

"It's all right," one of the waiters said. "You can all head back to your tables now." He waved at people to break up. "There's nothing to see. Everyone's fine out there."

Some of the diners turned and headed to their seats. But most of them stayed where they stood. "No! They're not okay," a man with a mustache said. "Look at them. There must have been an accident. Maybe their boat sank?"

"Has anyone called the police or the coast guard?" Sharon said. It seemed everyone turned and looked right at her. No one said anything. "Well?" she said. "Have you?"

The waiter shook his head. Then he looked at another waiter. "Go," he said. "Call them. Now. Hurry."

And then something rattled throughout the restaurant. The diners looked at each other. "Now what?" the waiter said, half-angry and half frightened.

"I've had about enough of this!" the man with the mustache said. "I'm going to get to the bottom of this once and for all, damn it." He rushed out the glass paneled doors and out onto the deck of the restaurant. "Nick!" a pretty redheaded lady called behind him. "Don't leave us here!"

"Don't worry about it," Nick said. "Just stay put for a while, all right?"

Before she could answer, he rushed outside. The sound still came from below and the whole place seemed to shake. He looked over the side of the deck and down at the sea. He saw heavy waves, but not much else. He rushed to the end of the dock, the area that pointed out furthest into the sea. To his surprise he saw a large boat banging against the dock. "Shit!" he said. "Anyone down there?" He stared and listened intensely. He was met with silence.

Webber rushed to the dock and looked up. Cold seawater chilled him. The pain inside his intestines grew with each step. He wished he were still dead. But he clutched the bucket, sure that it meant something, and sure that somehow it would give him peace. Somehow.

Next to him, Webber saw a woman struggling to find her footing in the shallows near the dock. She looked over at him. Her mouth opened and closed, but only faint wisps of sound escaped. "What's . . . ?" he thought he heard her say.

He shrugged and stepped closer to her. "I don't know," he said. "I think we've come back to life somehow." Her skin looked as though she'd spent a hundred years underground. Her eyes blinked, although the pupils were foggy and white. She, too, was coated in the white and oily substance. He approached her. "I have an idea."

Major piloted the pickup towards Balthazar's one level ranch house on Houston Street. "So what just happened?" Major looked over at Balthazar, who seemed confused. "I think there's something we forgot," he said. "The bucket. The white bucket. The boat?"

"So?" Balthazar said. "Who cares about that bucket? We pay to have the boat tied up there. It'd look weird if it wasn't tied up."

"Remember how I had you label all of them?" He looked over at Major. "So we could re-create the mixture in case it worked?"

And then Major got it. He'd made a second mistake. The second error of the day. "But no one's going to know that the reanimate came from us? How could they?" Then he suddenly doubted himself that he'd tied and anchored the boat probably. "Think I forgot the anchor," he said. "When I saw Balthazar come up hollering. Shoot." He went over in his mind what would happen to the boat if it weren't anchored and he imagined it'd smash into the docks.

"Who else sells Elcantrant Tree extract? Anyone you know?"

"Man," Major said. "I don't even know who else has been successful growing them since we found the seeds. Just us." Major smiled, happy with himself, as he remembered when they won the grant to grow the seeds. Only six groups across the country had received the seeds, found deep inside the earth after a California forest fire gutted areas that, until then, had been dense with growth. The botanists were not sure if the Elcantrant trees had lived and populated the forests unknown and undiscovered for decades, or if what they'd found were miraculously preserved seeds.

Then Major looked down a bit. Pictures of the bodies played in his head. Balthazar told him to keep them in the morgue room. He told him to keep them there until there were a dozen. Major thought about their faces. He thought about their bodies, splitting open in places because Balthazar would not embalm them.

In his mind, he remembered the night when they'd gotten twelve, finally, and He and Balthazar carried them into the back of the pick-up truck, drove them to the boat. Then they chained them together, attached weights and doused them with the Elcantrant. Last, they dropped them in the sea. "This isn't going to last long," Balthazar said. "And the sea's going to wash away the Elcantrant." He'd already had on his wet suit when they left the Mortuary. He hopped in the corner with a smug smile on his face.

While Balthazar was underwater, Major drove the boat to the docks on the other side of the Harpoon House. It took him an hour to get back to the other side where Balthazar waited for the secret sea to bring the corpses back to life.

What about the bones? What if the Elcantrant doesn't make the flesh go away after it brings them back? he thought. *What if he's wrong?* Major believed his boss. He had to. If he had refused, or reported what they were up to, then Balthazar promised Major would be next in the sea. And Balthazar's brother was the police chief, Major knew. "Best keep your nose down and do the job best you can," he heard his father's voice over and over in his head.

Major snapped out of his daze and looked at Balthazar. "Hey, man," he said. "There's no way anyone knows that the extract has such big healing properties, right? They just think it's some stupid New Age snake oil, right? That it's just a bunch of Funeral Guys messing around with some money-making thing on the side?"

"Don't' worry about it. It isn't going to take too much longer until they start to decompose from the Elcantrant," Balthazar said. "Not too much longer at all."

"Well, then," Major said. "How are we going to explain how our bucket got out there during all this?"

"We're not," he said. "Forget it. It's not our problem anymore, right? Anyone could have put it there. Besides; there's going to be nothing left of them soon."

Major shoved his tongue inside his upper lip and teeth, pushing his lip out a little. He looked at the side of the road instead of at Balthazar. "I'm not so sure about that."

Annie and Sharon looked down at the wobbly man looking up at them. "Is he saying something?" Sharon asked.

"I don't know," Annie said. "I can't tell."

Webber held up the plastic bucket. It took a lot for him to lift it. His body shrieked in pain. Webber's eyes grew tired and blurred. *I'm slipping away,* he thought. As he lifted his hands up to the little girl and her matching aunt, Webber noticed the white oil dripping from his rotten flesh. Wherever the potion did not cover him, burning pain poked through like steam escaping from the sides of a microwave dinner. He sensed a gravity reach up deep inside him and pull him down to the sea.

Beside Webber, two others just like him fell in heaps into the shallow sea. He turned and watched them. The one closest seemed to dissolve and wither before his eyes.

He looked up as soon as he realized his last moments were upon him for a second time. The little girl looked down at him, her expression, cold, harsh and distant. Above her, Webber saw the blue sky and he remembered his daughter's wedding day on Cape Cod. Gray blue skies. The smell of the cranberry orchards just around the way. Then Webber fell face first into the sea, dead again before his rotten nose touched the water.

"Is he dead?" Sharon asked.

Annie ushered her niece inside. "I think so."

"Am I going to die like that one day?"

"I hope not." She shuffled her niece away. "Come on," she said. "Time to go home."

As the briefly re-animated people fell and crashed into the sea, the diners fled the Harpoon House. They rushed to their cars.

On the dock, Nick stared at the boat banging against the boat until his wife came and ushered him inside. And then he said, "I think I know who did this." He'd seen Balthazar's logo on the side of the boat.

In the sea, the bodies turned into lumps of stringy, dark, wiggling rot. As the coast guard, and police, and sea workers searched the seas, and poked at the piles, they scratched their heads and filled their report cards in. But before any of them collected a single sample, the bodies broke up and washed out deep into the ocean beyond. No one noticed the plastic bucket deep under the pier gently floating against a column.

In his driveway, Balthazar nodded at Major. The men lifted the canisters of Elcantrant into the garage.

"That was a great day," Balthazar said. "Phase Two begins tomorrow. So be ready."

"Uh-huh." Major drove away wondering if anything or anyone would ever discover the source of their awful experiment. He thought about driving the pick-up off the side of Adams Bridge, but he lost his nerve.

That night he dreamt about driving into the water at the beach and vanishing underwater where the bodies of the Elcantrant Re-animates swam to him and smothered him. And as he looked over, he saw Balthazar struggle and protest as the re-animates pulled them deep into the depths of the secret sea.

ETERNAL VALLEY

May we walk this Eternal Valley
May we walk this land in peace
May we find the Place We're looking for
May this Eternal Valley ever be

The railroad men sang as the first cold winds blew across Diamond Creek, carrying smells of earthy grass, leaves, and dirt. Looking out over the sunny valley, past the men working on laying the tracks, my head overflowed with memories of little Jesse and me: us diving and playing up near the mouth of the Wabash River. Mary and me brought him, day before last, us exploring our new Missouri home, the place that would save Jesse's life.

Our place in New York sold high and left us a comfortable cushion. It was more than that, though, that made us move. Our Jesse didn't much do well in the cold or crowded city streets. Hell, none of us did, but reacted unnaturally toxic. His throat closed so tight he couldn't breathe. Probably had something to do with the factories sprouting coal smoke all around us in New York. Doctor Faith said Jesse probably wouldn't make it unless we moved somewhere with lots of space and clean air. Sounded good to me; I harbored no love for the City because it made my son ill. Top of that, my school smarts were not enough to land me inside a brownstone building writing on papers for a living like Mary's daddy. I made my living on the shores of the Hudson with my hands unloading and packing ships. Living off the land would suit me just fine.

Work in Diamond Creek turned out to be fulfilling. Doctor Norton managed his own grape vineyard and I did everything he'd let me. Most my days were spent training the vines and making sure the condition of the fruit remained reasonable. We worried about the grapes catching powdery mildew or black rot, although the good German Doctor earned his name as horticulturist after cross-breeding the varieties so they'd grow more resilient than their European cousins. America turned out to be a harsher environment for grape growing. The seasons, like the people, showed no mercy.

My life was simple. My life was good. My life tore apart in an instant. One moment little Jesse played the part of a healthy six-year-old, running, playing, eating, laughing . . . the next minute his skin turned gray, his lips turned purple, his eyes glossed over. He wouldn't rise. He hardly moved. It took all we had to feed the boy sustenance. We were scared giving him water. Jesse barely swallowed and we were afraid he'd drown.

Jim Longforth, our neighbor to the south, rushed over with his case of potions. He wasn't a doctor, but he was all we had. Rubbing a whitish, oily concoction across Jesse's forehead, he said, "Scott? I think the Devil has captured his soul. This will draw the monster out."

I was skeptical. Mary nodded, said, "Maybe we should bring him to Hermann and see Doctor Wallington—Hermann being the nearest big town."

We cleaned Jesse's head off and tried to move him. He moaned like a hellhound.

"He break something, you think?" asked Jim. "If you move him might make it worse: might even kill him."

Mary looked to me. "I don't know," I said. "He seemed just fine all day."

"He'd just laid down for a nap when this started." She put a hand to her mouth. Her eyes watered. "I don't know what's happening."

"Could be consumption," Jim said. All the color drained from his face as though he'd stumbled across the answer and was embarrassed about it.

I put an arm on his shoulder. "If it is consumption, you best get going. Make sure you ain't around the boy enough for it to rub off."

"What about you and Mary?" he asked.

"We're his parents. We'll do what we have to," I said. We walked to the door where Jim snuck a last long look at Jesse. "Don't stare at him like he's not going to be here next time you come down," I said. "Don't you dare."

After Jim left I sat on Jesse's bed, looked at him until I couldn't look any more. "Was Jim right?"

Mary said, "Where would Jesse catch consumption? He's not coughing."

"There's got to be a treatment for him." I looked out

the window. The valley had grown dark. It'd be hours until the moon was at its highest.

"Tomorrow you can talk to the Good Doctor and see if he might know of something," Mary said.

I shook my head. "He's a doctor of plant life, not people. His skills will be no fit for this."

She said, "Still—he may have recommendations."

I turned my face to Mary's. "I will leave in an hour, soon as there is moonlight to light my way."

"No. It's too dangerous at night." Mary clutched her cross around her neck. "There are demons outside."

"Nothing will bother me," I said.

She shook her head. "The Conner boys over the hill? They hear you coming and don't see you they're ripe to shoot. They might fire just for the game of it."

I stood up. "They don't frighten me and no creature of the night can get in the way of saving our son."

"Won't you be better useful here? What if he needs you?"

I squeezed Jesse's hand; his was limp and cool and barely squeezed mine back. "He won't miss me for a few hours. If he does, you tell him his Daddy went to find him a special medicine that will make him better."

Long purple trails of light stretched across the valley. The grass seemed painted and alive as it swayed from the nighttime wind. I pulled my jacket closer and tightened my scarf. For a late September night, the weather was colder than I remembered.

Far below, stretching across the flat lands, fires from the rail worker's tents glowed. I could make out the long black railroad lines near the camp. It wouldn't be long until the big steamers raced across our valley on their way across Missouri. The peace and tranquility we had known would now be forever broken. Mary and me spoke about the trains coming through. A new century loomed. We were both concerned because we didn't want noise and crowds they'd bring.

"It's like the city is following," Mary had said, and I'd agreed.

There was a rustle near me. I looked round and saw nothing but knee high grass. The nearest trees were still aways off, and there were no big rocks for hiding.

I stopped and listened for a moment. Whatever it was would spot me. I was the tallest thing in the field. My mind raced because I knew some of the railroad workers liked to drink a little too much and wander the hills. I hoped it wasn't one of those boys laid up in the field waiting for something dumb to stumble on by.

"Hello?" I asked, knowing I was taking my chances. If someone were hiding they'd see me.

Something rustled behind me and I turned full on. "Hello?" I called.

Training my eye to where I thought I heard the sound, I saw only the tops of the grass swaying gently in the night wind.

I smelled something burning—reminded me of sweet natural tobacco. *Someone was with me.* Nothing burned all by itself—that's for sure.

Who could it be?

"Who's there? My name's Scott Robertson and I'm just passing through."

"So am I."

A woman's voice—she appeared from nowhere behind me, all slinking and sure of herself like I've never seen a woman before or since. She was striking. Long hair flowed down halfway down her body. Her eyes were dark and glinted in the moonlight. She held a wooden pipe. Smoke trailed from its end. With a hand on her hip, she raised an eyebrow.

"Who are you?"

She smiled. "My name is . . . Mary."

I was taken aback. "You're name can't be Mary," I said. "You're an . . ."

"Indian?"

"Yes. You need to have an Indian name like *Sunwater* or *River*, right?" I asked.

"Says who?"

"Well . . . I don't know. Ain't that just the way it is?"

She shook her head. "Does the name Mary upset you?"

I stepped back. "Why would it?"

Mary shook her head. "You know someone else named Mary?"

"Sure," I said. "That doesn't mean anything. Look: who are you and what are you doing up here? You scared me half-way back to Jesus."

She moved closer, raised the pipe and took a pull. When she was done, she handed it over. I waved it away. "I don't smoke."

She exhaled. "Fine with me," she said. "I already told you."

"Told me what?"

"That I am passing through here," said Mary. "Same as you."

"Ma'am? I don't mean to be rude, but I have a sick child waiting on me and I need . . ."

She put up her hand. "A sick child? Is that what makes you walk alone so late on such a night?"

"Such a night? What the heck you getting at?" I asked. "Tis the same as any other night, maybe a bite colder, might be all."

Mary said, "This is the night when the animals feast."

"Okay? You know what? I don't believe in any of that Indian smoke. I'm a dyed-in-the-wool Christian," I said. "I sure wish there was a church up here. You believe we got a theater for actors, another one for musicians, but we got no church. Not enough people would go. I guess that's what happens when you're in the business of spirits."

Mary nodded. "Business of spirits?"

"We grow grapes," I said. "For wine. Gets you drunk. Kind of like that pipe you've got there." I pointed.

"I know what wine is," she said.

"Good Christians would probably frown upon our livelihood."

Mary looked around. I guessed her smoke was playing its fun little effects on her. "This is a special place," she said. "Don't you think so?" She shut her eyes and breathed as loud as she could. "You can just hear the animals and the spirits around you. It's safe. I could live here forever and never grow tired."

"That so?" I said. "I do need to move along. My son's going to need me to get back real soon." I started walking past her.

"May I walk with you?" she asked. "I wouldn't mind just for a little bit?"

I shook my head and put out my hand. "I don't know," I said. "That probably wouldn't look right. If anyone sees us together it could mean trouble for me."

"I thought none of the Christ-inns cared?" she asked.

"That's different," I said and stopped in my tracks. "They all on the same page so far as God is concerned. They ain't all going to look kindly on a man if he's walking around with another woman while his wife's home tending to his sick child, are they?"

She pulled a hood over her head. "I could wear a disguise," she said, "lower my voice, pretend to be a man." Mary laughed. "What if I were an old woman lost in the fields?" Her face changed before my eyes. "And you were just being a good Christ-Man . . ." Mary looked older and slighter and her hair went gray, all in a blink. "You might be leading me somewhere warm." By the time she'd finished speaking she again looked far too beautiful for her to be safe.

"You blow some of that stuff at me?" I asked. "That what it is? You got a trick up your sleeve? A couple boys hiding somewhere to hit me on the head and rob me?"

Mary laughed again. "You find me very threatening," she said. "I find that touching." She stared me in the eyes, looking back and forth inside mine several times to make sure she had my attention. "I am here to help you, Scott Robertson," she said. "I am here because of Jesse."

All the blood in my body froze.

The only thing I could think to say was, "Your name ain't really Mary, then, ain't it?"

She smiled.

"How am I supposed to know you ain't talk to the Longforth clan before you found me? How do I know this ain't some elaborate trick?"

She shook her head. "I am not asking you for anything," she said. "I have no weapons with me."

"There's still something about this I don't trust," I said. "I'd feel better if I could go talk to Doctor Norton about this. I bet he's got some ideas about what we could do."

"You can do that," she said. "But Jesse is in trouble, is he not? What if it is something much worse than you know? What if he only had hours left?"

"You know something I don't know?"

"I know where we can go to find him something that will take it all away."

Mary looked up and to our left, to where the hill grew steep, to the top of Diamond Creek. "There is a point where the Wabash holds magic and power," she said. "I know of a place we can find his medicine."

"The Wabash River?" I asked. "You want to head on up there at this hour, on this freezing night?" That moment I noticed something peculiar. No longer was I shivering. In fact, the air felt just as warm as a summer evening. "Well damn me—did we hit some kind of hot spot or did the wind stop blowing?"

Mary looked right through me and I just sensed that she was the reason things were a lot more comfortable. How could something like that be unless she was a witch of some kind?

She must have heard what I was thinking because the next thing to escape her mouth was, "you need to let go of some things you're holding close to your heart—at least for the next few hours."

"This ain't natural at all," I said. "It's all going against God."

"Is it?" she asked. "God would not let things happen if they would harm you, would she?"

"God's a man."

"Does it matter?"

"Sure as hell does."

"Your son's life is hanging on by breaths," she said.

Bugs crawled all over me. I felt them crawl up from the grass, up through my pant legs and right up onto my chest. I pulled my shirt away from my stomach and scratched at the little bugs. Only thing is there weren't any. I still felt them crawling. They'd reached my hair, my scalp, and nose. The itching was maddening. "Excuse me, Miss," I said and dropped to the grass and started itching like mad.

"This is the disease that's befallen your son," she said, her tone serious and forceful.

The itching burned; the sensation became more unbearable. I felt what seemed to be spiders crawling all over me, biting me, nipping me, burrowing inside. Once inside I rubbed at my skin to try to free them, but they would not come back out. I fell on my back. As I lay in the grass, I found I could no longer move my limbs. The hand that scratched at my belly froze; my fingers curled into a stiff claw. My sight blurred and the night sky felt like it might fall and smother me.

My heart slowed and I could hear its beats, which sounded to me very much like the easy tides of the Hudson River back in New York City. It sloshed in and out, steadily. With each pull, a new wave of pain surged through my veins, beginning at the soles of my feet, gathering and intensifying inside my head. My stomach tightened and I wanted to throw up, yet, I could not even move. Blinking hurt, believe it or not.

It seemed as though I might die shortly. Jesse was in bad shape if what I was experiencing was the same for him. I was a full-grown man; feeling that horrible as a young child scared me silly.

In my head, I willed Mary to stop what she was doing. *She might be a witch, all right. Maybe she cast this same spell on Jesse when he was outside and made it a trap to catch me.*

"No," Mary said, kneeling down and looking me in the eyes. Her lips were shut but they still formed a smile. "I am not trapping you or your son. You must believe that I was called here to help you and your son."

Another wave washed over me, but it was warm and lessened the pain, as if it were being cleaned from my insides. After several seconds, I was able to move my fingertips. Soon, my hands and arms moved and I was able to lift my head. Blessedly, the itching was gone. All that remained was a numb tingle in my hands and feet. I sat up and rubbed my eyes.

"You have only felt that way for a few minutes," Mary said. "Your son has been feeling that way for much too long already. We have to be quick. There is a point where the body will no longer tolerate pain and will stop."

"What does he have?" I asked.

"The curse of the wind," she said. "Which was what called me."

"Why?"

"You are here in a sacred place," she said. "And not everyone is happy about it."

"He is a child!"

I stood.

She said, "Gods do not discriminate."

"If God has done this than how can we stop it?"

"We will ask."

After we turned left and made it through the prairie, we arrived at the bottom of a steep hill. The hill turned into the base of the mountain. There was a path, carved out by many of the town's folks. We climbed the side of the mountain's trail, me following Mary. "Good thing the moon is high," I said. "We can see our way."

"The Gods work in our favor," said Mary. "It's of great importance. They must know what we are doing."

"I sure hope so," I said.

As scared as I was about my son's well-being, I could not help but find myself deeply intrigued with Mary. Of course, she was beautiful and strong, but she also possessed a kind of magnetic pull. "I don't understand why so many people hated the Indians," I said. "I'm looking at you and you look just like a person to me." Her back was turned to me and I was embarrassed because her curves were quite wonderful and made my thoughts race. Quickly I remembered that she might have somehow been hearing what I was thinking.

"The earliest people who came to this land and met with the Lakota were our friends," she said. "They lived with us. They dined with us. Our women loved their men."

"I can see why," I said, my mouth opening before I could stop it.

She paused, briefly, and kept walking. "You are right in believing all of what makes us people would be the same."

The path steepened. We passed a small tree, no larger than either one of us. I recalled being struck by the same tree when I'd brought Jesse and my Mary to the Wabash's mouth to play only a few days earlier.

"It just seems silly to me that people always seem to want to fight over something," I said. "Especially the color of our skins. I mean, I kind of like all the different ways people look. If we all looked the same it'd be like that field down there all covered with one kind of flower and one kind of tree and nothing else. That seems awfully uninteresting to me."

She stopped. "I believe that may be part of the reason why I was called to you," Mary said. "You see the world not like most of the men around you."

"Come on," I said. "I can't believe I'm the only one who ever thought of that."

She shook her head. "I'm sure many others have. I'm not so sure many others would allow themselves to believe so."

High on the hill, where the grass gives way to the towering granite of the mountain, the Wabash River curls around a bend and forms a large lake right before it all rolls down toward the valley on the other side. The land is flat surrounding the lake, and large enough for several houses. Trees and brush rim the lake. The water swirls gently and slowly round and round.

"I know this place," I said. "We brought Jesse here the other day. He loved it."

Mary stood still, her eyes fixed on the water. "This is where it began," she said. "He caught it here."

I stared at the water, too, searching for some kind of sign. I saw none. "You mean the water's poison? Is that it?"

"Something in it," she said. "Something's living inside."

"A fish?"

She shook her head. "Not quite." Then she turned to me. "You must go inside. You must clear your mind and you must ask for your son to be taken back."

I was confused. "Your son's spirit was taken," she said, her eyes glanced back to the swirling water. "It needs to feed."

Mary handed me her pipe. She reached inside a pocket, found a match, struck it, and as I lifted the tube to my lips she put the flame near the opposite tip.

I inhaled. My mouth filled with smoke, its sweet flavor reminding me of nutmeg and leaves. My lungs opened and warmed. Immediately I felt dizzy. The top of the lake seemed to glisten more than any body of water I'd ever seen. Every reflection bloomed and glittered. Mary took the pipe from me and smoked some herself. We shared her pipe for several minutes. Each pull brought me deeper and deeper under its magic spell.

The earth moved under our feet. I crouched slightly to keep my balance. "What was that?" I asked. My voice sounded as though we were inside a cave. It was difficult to keep my eyes open, despite the shaking ground.

"Look inside the water," she said, and pointed.

The bottom of the lake moved. The edges of the lake grew lighter as the creature curled its sides and revealed the true bed beneath. Its body was as dark and smooth as the night and it floated effortlessly. While the waves rippled, the creature at the bottom seemed to blend in with the water. If I broke my stare for even a second I lost track of where it was and what it was.

"You must go inside," Mary said. "It can only hear you when you're in the water with it."

"It will kill me! It will devour me and have its supper! I'm no fool! Are you sacrificing me to this creature?"

"This is your choice," she said.

My instinct told me I couldn't go in the water. The thing filled nearly the entire lake. I pictured walking into the water and it covering me, smothering me, dragging me underwater with it—bringing my limp body toward its beak-shaped mouth. That had to be its plan.

"It has no mouth," Mary said.

"I don't want to be in this world if Jesse can't be here with me," I said. My mind seemed to flip in on itself. "If this thing took him then I guess I'll have no choice."

What happened next was a blur. As I put one foot in the Wabash Lake, the dark thing in the water moved back. When I'd swum in the lake with Jesse and Mary, the bed was dark. We'd been stepping on this thing the whole time and we hadn't even known it. Damn. Maybe Mary was right. I still was not sure how she came to be or how any of it was happening to me, but I knew, somehow, deep within, that I needed to have faith.

In no time I was up to my waist. The water was warm, which it hadn't been the other day. The air was warm, as well. The thing still moved away from me as I stepped inside. I imagined it was as scared of me as I was of it, although that changed as soon as I ducked my head under. I turned one last time and my eyes met Mary's. She smiled and blinked once. I nodded and lowered myself under the water.

Once I turned around, I saw nothing but darkness. The thing was going for the kill. It was smothering me. I was soon going to die.

Only I didn't. Instead, I took a few steps forward and saw that I was on a ledge. An endless cavern dropped down into the earth as far as I could see, ending in what looked like a bottomless black hole. The thing had covered the hole. I lowered myself into a sitting position so that I wouldn't step over the ledge and drop down. There was a tidal pull I could sense coming from the tunnel and I didn't want to be pulled down inside.

I felt something watching me and looked up. The thing was above me and I met its stare. Two flat gray eyes, each as big as my head, scanned me. Mary was right: I saw no mouth, although I did see two slits just under its eyes. Its movements were graceful and slow. Around its edges, I saw dark nubs like fingertips rolling across its rim—they looked to me a lot like they might be playing piano.

Then I lost my breath. I gasped and swam, but found the water difficult. I looked up and found I was much deeper than I'd thought. When I first stepped inside the lake, it felt as though I were only a few feet under. Somehow, I'd fallen several men deep.

I thought of Jesse sick and in bed and I didn't want to die. *He's going to need me. He needs to get better. He shouldn't be suffering like this. Take me, if that's what it takes. Take me in his place.*

The thing's eyes met mine.

It was just us swimming in here and having a good time. We didn't want any of this. We didn't need any of this. We didn't want to bother you none. Please. Let him be. You can have me if you need something. He'll miss me but he still has the world in front of him. He can do things I'll never be able to do. He can make things better. I can't. I'm just taking up space here now. I'll tell you what? I'll trade you, big guy, and maybe you can hear me the same way she can hear me. So just take me and throw me down that big hole you got there or whatever you need to do, but just let little Jesse free.

My mind raced with memories of my son. I remembered our room in New York where he was born, Mary's parents standing around, our friends. I remembered his first few nights as clear and as real as new. I felt his little fingers curling around my thumb. I heard his baby cries blending into his laughs. The smell of his hair so vivid I swear he was right there with me.

I saw him on the train jumping on the seats to get a better view as we rode from New York and across the plains. I heard his voice asking me if we were going to be okay. "We're always going to be together, right Poppa?" he asked.

"Of course," I told him. "Of course. Ain't nothing going to get in the way of that."

But it had.

Pictures of him racing across the field chasing some creature or another filled my head. It seemed I saw something just like that every day of my life in Diamond Creek as I passed him and went to work for Doctor Norton in the vineyards. Oh, to just have one more day! To have endless days!

I looked upward at the thing floating above me. It lowered itself onto me and as soon as our skin touched, I felt fire and pain worse than anything I can ever tell. My head filled with colors, exploding as if the heavens were on fire. I couldn't help but wiggle and try to break free. No matter. I was stuck in its grasp and nothing I could do would fix that.

When I woke, I was on the shore and I was alone. I sat up and got my bearings. I was soaked through. All my limbs were there. Everything worked. Nothing was out of place. I had a headache from all hell and I was sore, but that came as no surprise.

Mary was gone. I stood and poured out my canteen. Then I went to the edge of the lake. The bed was dark. The water rippled, but the river bottom did not move. I searched for its eyes and could find none, them being on its underside.

Kneeling down, I filled my canteen with water from the lake. I stared at the dark bottom, and when I pulled the canteen from the water, I saw the slightest twitch.

Then I turned and took the first steps back home. Beneath the fading night, the stars shimmered against the deep blue sky.

Far below in the valley I heard the railroad workers singing again.

> *May we walk this Eternal Valley*
> *May we walk this land in peace*
> *May we find the Place We're looking for*
> *May this Eternal Valley ever be*

I pictured Jesse and knew soon I'd raise my canteen to his lips, and knew its lake water would cure him, and soon thereafter I'd hear his laughs and watch him run, and knew one day soon all I'd seen would just be a curious story I'd tell.

THE CURIOUS BANKS OF THE WABASH RIVER

You get used to being the only person when you live in my part of the Wabash River valley. The animals that lived on, in and around the water were my only company. When night fell, the only light came from my house, the stars or the passing train from Salt Lake City. You can sit in my favorite porch chair and wave at the train as it passes on the other side of the river. They can see you, even though they're about a half-mile away.

Once the train passed by twice, it was time to pick up my old friend Grady Michaels, who'd flown all the way in from Burbank. It'd take me about the same amount of time as it would take the train to get to Derlin Township, which was nearly fifteen miles. So I set out.

The ride was uneventful, other than my thinking of a million little things. For instance, what would old Grady think of my humble, hermit-like existence? Would he understand? Would he approve? I wasn't sure, but what always kept us friends, ever since Loyola, was both of our love for the outdoors. We'd kept in touch. With his divorce from Val finally wrapped up, he said he needed a place to unwind.

After I arrived at Derlin Township, I parked at the train station. There, I remembered how the rest of the world worked. It was weird to see more than one person at a time, I mean, hell; it was wild just seeing other people than myself for a change. Seeing them all scattered on the platform and at their cars made me feel like I'd been asleep in a cave.

"Put it more to the center." Those were the first words I'd heard from another person in seven weeks. I looked to my left and watched a couple pouring bottled water on their windshield as their wipers swooshed something gummy and dark back and forth. I stared a little too long because I realized the gummy mound had a beak and a little orange claw coming out of it. Stupid guy was trying to get rid of it with a bottle of water. A folded-up paper would have done the trick faster and given the bird a little dignity.

I heard the whistle as the train approached the platform. I covered my ears because it'd been a long time since I'd heard anything that loud. At least I'd gotten to the station in time to meet Grady at the train platform.

After I got out of the car, I went up on the platform. It was packed with people, which surprised me. I sure hadn't expected it to be that crowded for such a late train. I tried to think if it was a holiday or if anything special was going on in Derlin, but I couldn't think of anything.

When Grady finally approached, it took me a few minutes to recognize him. His face had shrunk down and he had dark moons under his eyes. When he saw me, instead of the smile I was expecting, I got a brief nod and shrug. He struggled with his suitcase—one of those roller jobs with a retractable handle.

"Can I help you with that?" I asked, before I said anything else to him.

"Long time," he said back to me and pushed his suitcase forward. "I'm okay, though. Thanks." He put out his hand so that I could shake it, which I promptly ignored and gave him a hug instead.

As I pulled back away from him, I said, "How you doing, brother? All right?"

"Much better now that I'm here instead of L.A.—that's for sure." He looked around the platform. "God. I mean, even the air's much better. Cleaner." I'd also forgotten how much taller Grady was than me.

"And you couldn't have come on a better night. Absolutely."

"Why so?"

"When there's this many stars out, it brings the fish to the surface. They get excited on nights like this. They come out to play."

"That's great. I could use a little bit of getting-back-to-nature. Especially after the week I've had. Hell, especially after the *year* I've had." He spotted my bumper sticker. "I am the river and the river is me. Interesting."

"It's the philosophy around here. Give back as much as you take. Everything's dependent on something else, you know?

On the ride back to my house on the banks, Grady told me details about how his marriage to Val had unraveled. "First she stopped sleeping with me. Then she started sleeping with everyone else."

"Why would she do that?" I asked.

He rolled down his window and I imagined he'd crawl out head over heels rather than getting into any more of the painful particulars. "That's what happens when you marry young. All the fire of life stays in you and builds up and just burns a hole right through you."

"You didn't marry young?"

"I married her and she's young," he said. "What can you do about it?" He looked up and into the bright night sky by hanging his head out the window a bit. "Tell me about how you moved out here and walked away from it all."

I dipped the tube for the sample into the river and pulled it back up after a few seconds. "So, yeah, all I have to do is take a sample four times a day and keep track of the results. Make sure the things that have to live in the river can still do so."

"And the school lets you stay here just for doing that?"

"Sure," I told him. "But there's more to it than I'm letting on. I have to mix chemicals in my little lab in the front room. I also, kind of, unofficially, take care of this place. Report anything strange or unusual."

"Like what? Fish with two heads?"

"I haven't seen anything with two heads, but there's some really weird things out there." I stopped myself from getting too weird. "But more like take care of the place. Make sure no one comes here who's not supposed to be here. Safe guard the school's property and make sure the grant for the tests keeps coming."

"And you get a free place to live rent free. And they pay you on top of it."

"Yup," I said. "I got rid of my student loans."

"Oh, man," Grady said while we walked to the house with the sample. "They need anyone else out here?"

We laughed, went inside and I showed him the lab, the scope, the centrifuge, the fancy way I looked at the water and what it contained. Once we were done, I grabbed my lawn chairs, my fishing gear and a couple of Guinness's.

Grady carried a bucket to keep what we'd catch. "Should we start the grill?" he asked me as we trotted to the shore.

"Probably a good idea," I said. "The coal's'll be good and white by the time we're ready."

He helped me get set-up and went back towards the house and got the Weber up and running in no time. While he was gone, I thought about how good it was to have some familiar company. It would have been nicer had it been Lisa or one of the other girls from Loyola, but it was more fun than doing all that work for nothing but myself, that's for sure.

So, we sat down and tossed our lines out. "You can smell the freshness coming off the water," he said. "I guess your tests were right on the money."

I nodded. "It's a totally different world than entertainment law. I may actually live past fifty now."

"You're lucky."

"Guess so," I said. "But I gave up everything I worked for at Loyola. I didn't drive my BMW to pick you up, you notice."

Grady smiled. "You always talked about getting that convertible." He turned to me. "Why'd you come out here to the beautiful Utah countryside to hide?"

"Like they say around here, I'm the river and the river is me."

"Your bumper sticker, right?"

I nodded and said, "I have to say that I felt like I was hiding in the shell of a man out on the West Coast, like I was a phony and an imposter. I just remember waking up one day and thinking . . . 'I don't like this. I don't like any of this at all.' These people. What am I supposed to do? I could walk away and not miss any of it. So I did."

"Just like that?"

"Just like that."

"I think I got something," he said.

I looked and saw his line was taut. "Looks like we'll have something to throw on the grill after all, doesn't it?" I joked.

"Don't you have anything in the house, or is this how you eat every night?"

"Sure," I said. "But not anything as good as what's probably on the other end of that line."

"That's comforting," he said. "You know, for a moment there, I was thinking we'd be out here for breakfast, lunch and dinner every day."

"Oh, no," I laughed. "Not at all."

It didn't take long for Grady to pull out his medium-sized trout. The fish seemed calm and didn't fuss much. It must not have known, I thought, that it was about to be eaten. As he did his best to get it off the hook, with the fish sliding on his lap and him tsk'ing the entire time, I noticed something peculiar. The fish was swollen in the middle.

"Wait a minute," I said. "I think that's a female and she's pregnant. We need to throw her back in."

Grady stopped fussing with it for a moment and squished the fish's middle with his first finger and thumb. "Nah," he said. "I think it's just fat." He squished it again. "Isn't the right time of year that fish get pregnant. They've got to be warm. This one's cold."

"That's not true. You know that. They can get pregnant whenever." Grady finally got the trout off the hook and placed it in the white plastic bucket. "There," he said. "Now we just need to catch a couple more."

I shook my head. "We're really only supposed to catch two fish each at any time," I said. "That's the regulations, at least."

"Oh, come on," he said. "Who cares about a bunch of dumb trout? We couldn't even catch anywhere near enough, one way or another, to make a difference."

"They make those rules to make sure the river doesn't get over-fished." I wiggled my line in hopes that I'd catch something before the conversation turned. "Just think if the one you caught was pregnant—how many fish did you just take out of the system, then?"

He cast his pole back in. "I don't think it's going to be a big deal. You really think that us fishing tonight—and maybe tomorrow night'd make all that much of a difference?"

"If you think of just us, then I don't. But the idea is to discourage everyone from going crazy. If everyone's got it in the back of their mind and most people end up respecting the river and the fish, then, the original intent of the law will be upheld."

Grady cocked an eyebrow. "Take the lawyer out of the courthouse, but you can't take the lawyer out of the man, can you?" He smiled. "Got me convinced."

I heard a splashing sound in the water. After I looked, though, it seemed it was only a small wave.

Then, a funny thing happened. Grady went on to pull out two more trout and a striped bass. The whole time, he was laughing and enjoying himself.

"Let's get to cooking some of this. I'm starving."

He resisted getting up and off the shore. "You go right ahead, kiddo. I'll keep reelin' 'em if you start cookin' 'em."

"I'm not doing all the slave labor," I said.

He put the handle of his pole in the holder and tightened the clamp. "I want to catch all the fish in the river by tomorrow."

"I couldn't find this place, this river, or your place on any of the maps on the net," Grady said as we cleaned the second trout.

"Really?"

"There's no Wabash River in Utah on either MapQuest or Google. It's weird. There's one in Tennessee, though."

"Huh."

"Yeah. And here we are, anyway."

"That's really strange," I said. "This river's been here forever. Definitely long before the internet."

"Do you have a map inside?" he asked.

I shook my head. "Nah. I don't bother."

"Well, we can always look it up on the computer later."

"No computer."

"What?" He was surprised enough to turn his head back. "You used to carry your PowerBook with you to the bar, man."

"I know, I know. But that was College," I said. "Guess I just got tired of that world after a while, you know?"

"I guess. But you still have a phone, or else I wouldn't be here, right?"

"Need a phone," I said. "I'd go crazy if I couldn't talk to people once in a while."

"But you can talk to people online just as easy?"

"I'd rather just stay outside and not get tied to a computer screen. I lost years of my life from just doing that, you know?"

Grady was done cleaning his fish, or so it looked. As he turned it over, we both spotted the unmistakable sac of eggs beneath the creature. "Looks like we're having caviar on the side tonight, eh?" With a nervous laugh, he wiped the eggs off the tabletop and back into the bucket. "There you dumb fucks go," he said to the fish in the bucket, who swam in little jerks as the eggs dropped on them. "Look at what mean old Grady did. I killed a pregnant trout and here's all your little babies." He screeched at them—imagining what they were thinking. "Oh, no. He killed all our unborn baby fish. Oh, what a monster."

Still laughing, he looked at me. I sure as hell didn't smile back. "You really need to stop that," I told him. "That's not cool at all."

"What? I'm just kidding. They don't know what's going on. They're just fish, Michael. They're just a bunch of stupid fish."

"I know that," I said.

He slapped me on the shoulder. Too hard. "When'd you get so damn sensitive, anyway?"

At that moment, my happiness at having Grady come visit me ended. I very much wanted him to go back to Los Angeles and work out all his problems by himself.

All that made me say probably the wrong thing. "When did *you* become so *in*-sensitive, man?"

Grady stared at me for a second. He finally realized I was not joking and was deadly serious. "Oh?" he said. "Is that how it's going to be then, old friend?" He clenched his jaw.

"I guess you're turning on me, too, now? Just like everyone else."

Before I could say another word, he grabbed the skinned trout in one hand, took the bucket in the other and marched down to the shore. I tried calling after him to stop, but he ignored me. "Stupid . . . fucking . . . Pinko . . . tree-hugging. . . chickenshit. . . stupid fish. . ." He mumbled just loud enough so I could hear what he was saying.

At the shore, he threw the dead pregnant trout as far out into the Wabash as he could.

"Stop!" I hollered and rushed towards the shoreline myself. "What are we going to eat?" It wasn't what I'd expected to say.

"I killed them for nothing!" His voice was half a yell and half a laugh. "Look, Michael! I'm just going to throw them right back in. You can put this in your dumb little reports. How's that sound?" He threw the white plastic bucket out as far as he could.

By some twist of fate, it landed bottom down on the water and did not sink. It bobbed a little on the current, which weren't particularly heavy.

"God damn it would you look at that!" Grady pointed at the floating bucket. "Can anything go right for me?"

I reached him by then; we only stood a couple of feet from each other. "Why're you so angry?" I asked. "Relax, man. It's no big deal. I didn't mean . . ."

"I really don't need this judgment from you, you know that? I dragged my ass all the way out to bumble-fuck nowhere to get away from the exact kind of treatment you've been giving me here all night long."

I protested. "I'm not judging you. You were just acting weird . . . different than I remember. You got so cruel out of nowhere." I don't think I helped matters any.

"You know what I think? I think you and your fish should just go to hell. And why don't you take Val with you. If you can get her face out of Juan's lap, that is, long enough for you to recognize her cheating ass."

He stepped into the river with both feet. His voice, changed then—it became softer and higher pitched. "You know what? You are right. I am a different person. A much different man than you knew at school."

"What're you doing?" He waded out almost to his waist. "Forget about the fish. I don't need the bucket."

Grady ignored me.

"It's too far out now!" I yelled after him. Something sunk in my gut. "Come back!"

Just as it looked as though he might have had the bucket, it drifted out further. He lowered himself down to his neck and swam out further for it.

I no longer wanted to cry out for him to return. He wanted to do what he was doing, I imagined. Grady wanted to blow off steam, and his antics, however curious, had to be just the last few months of repressed feelings coming out.

"I'm the river!" he yelled at the top of his lungs. "And the river is me!" I looked at him—both of his hands were over his head. He slipped underwater and I thought, finally, he'd completely lost it.

To my left, something dark splashed in the water close to shore. I immediately turned my head and squinted to try and see what it was. A finger-shaped fish had washed up too close to the shore and was dangerously close to drowning itself. I couldn't see its eyes because it'd flipped itself onto its back for some reason. It tried to wiggle free from several inky plumes of dark seaweed. For a moment, I pictured the pregnant trout come to thank me for defending it, although it'd been killed regardless. It understood.

Knowing I'd feel bad if I didn't try to help the fish, I leaned down and reached into the water to grab it. Just as my fingers neared, it jerked violently. Somehow the fish wrapped its hard, smooth body around my right forearm, squishing a piece of the seaweed between its body and my arm.

It pulled me, and with a blink, I found myself underwater; I was being pulled out to the middle of the river faster than I could ever swim. Water filled my lungs and none of my effort to counter-swim stopped the thing from pulling me. It was too strong. Immensely strong. It came to stop, however, it still held strong to my arm.

A thought came into my head at that moment: *Why had he yelled, "I am the river and the river is me" for? We hadn't been drinking anything at all, really.*

I tried my best to see, but it was not easy. Thankfully, it was a bright night and I'd been blessed with the starlight shining down through the water. Being a freshwater river saved my eyes and nose from stinging. Saltwater would have been a thousand times more painful and that much harder to see through.

With my three free limbs, I did my best to swim again. As I moved, more inky-black appendages found my arms and legs, curled around them and dragged me down twenty feet deeper. I saw the smooth body of what looked like a giant ray. The creature was long and thin and looked almost pounded-out into a blanket-like shape. Its surface was dark; yet, camouflaged in such a way that I imagined would blend perfectly in with the bottom of the river. On the right side, I followed its appendages from the edge of its body as they curled up and grabbed me. There were more appendages, too, but they reached out towards the underwater vegetation growing at the side of the riverbanks. I saw all of this in an instant.

I gagged. A reflex from swallowing too much water. My eyes opened as wide as they could and, as much as I tried, there was no stopping my body from jerking and spasming as it fought being drowned.

The appendages pulled me harder and farther and deeper to the bottom of the Wabash then. I was met with one large and probing black eye the size of a basketball cut in two, with an eyelid that blinked twice at my approach.

As fascinated and interested as I was at being face to face with such an alien creature, I couldn't help my body's reflexive jerks. I had to get air or I was as good as dead. The creature must have sensed it, too, because as soon as the thought entered my head, well, I was pushed upward and toward the surface of the river.

I gasped and coughed and tread and paddled. I tried to catch my breath and found it a lot of trouble.

Below me, the dark bottom of the Wabash slipped away downstream in a flash, leaving behind a brighter, sandier river floor. Splashing miserably, I tried to see if Grady was around. I couldn't see or hear him, and as the dark bottom of the Wabash swam away, I'd bet it took him with it to wherever it would next lie in wait. The bucket, too, I noticed, had gone.

I saw my home as I paddled. I tried to call out for Grady, but was too tired and too waterlogged. I took in the glistening barbecue and the lights in the lab room from inside the house. Only twenty minutes earlier we'd both stood on my porch. It felt like an impossibly long memory from the past.

With what little I had left, I swam to shore. Once I was safely out of the water, I turned on my back, coughed several times and looked up at the beautiful night sky and. . . well. . . I didn't cry. I didn't feel sorry for myself or for Grady. No. Instead, I walked my tail back to the house, went to my lab and grabbed a sample tube.

As I put the tube into the river, I wonder, what if anything, I'd tell people about what happened that night to Grady and myself. I wasn't sure, and there's a part of me that doubts what I saw, and thinks that maybe Grady just got pulled in by the undertow, and maybe I was suffering from a lack of oxygen or something. But my instincts tell me different—that there was something in the Wabash that took Grady and let me go. And then I remembered what Grady was yelling the last moment I saw him. And I know that what had happened was all too real.

I am the river and the river is me.

THE TENNATRICK

White ash fell like snow and Jen tasted smoke from the burn.

"Tell me what you saw," she asked Oswald, all the while keeping an eye on the flames creeping down the hill over his shoulder.

"Tennatrick," Oswald said. His brother and son stood quietly a few feet away.

"This guy have a first name?"

"No first name."

Behind Engine Three, Jen spotted someone else she recognized from the Fire Investigation Unit—Brian Riggs, her trainee. She waved him over before turning back to Oswald. "Who is he? A gang banger? Environmental activist?"

"Tennatrick's not a person."

She rubbed at a piece of ash burning her eye just as Brian made his way over. "How's it going?" He put out his hand.

"You have great timing," she said, taking her hand from her eye to shake Brian's. "I've got something." She turned back to Oswald. "You said you had a name for us? Tenna-what?"

"Tennatrick." Oswald pointed over her shoulder. "Up there. It started everything burning."

"You know this person?" Jen asked.

"No," Oswald said. "I was on fire duty. I was walking back to camp when I saw it."

The hot dry air settled in Jen's throat. "You say it looked like someone you recognized?"

Oswald looked toward the top of the mountainside and shook his head. "When the summer's get hot like this the Tennatrick digs up from the ground. Their oil starts the fires."

"Oh, come on. You think I'm stupid?"

A tunnel of flames exploded up on the hill—Jen ducked down and covered her head with her jacket. "Jesus!" she hollered. "Let's get moving."

Jen looked up to the towering wall of fire moving down the opposite side of the road. Three other police officers, a sheriff, and a canine hiked up nearby.

"How many acres are gone?" Jen asked. "Did Forestry Services give out any estimate?"

"Last I heard we were at about eight hundred acres." Brian kept his eyes locked on the fire. "Looks like it'll jump the line soon." A small tower of flame broke past the rail to their right. An aircraft flew overhead. "Air Ops are taking their final run."

The canine hurried past. "She's got something," someone said from behind. "Follow Cassie."

Cassie swerved left, then jigged sideways before she crested the hill and onto the high road. "Where'd she go?" Brian said.

"Bet we just got our suspect cornered. "Jen breathed heavier with each step.

Jen peeked over the top of the hill. "There's nobody up here," she said. "Where'd he go? This is a dead end."

"Maybe he made it down," Brian said.

Jen shook her head. "We would have seen him. The only way is up. And check out Cassie."

Cassie's nose pointed at a steep shill of mountain rising above the road. She growled.

"What's she barking at?" Jen swung her legs over the rail, and stood on the other side. She put her hand to her left side and got ready to withdraw her nine-millimeter.

"I don't see anything," Brian said. He looked behind them. "Where'd everyone else go?" He nudged Jen.

She looked back at him and he gestured down the hill. The officers and the sheriff looked up at them. One cupped his hands. "You better get back down here ASAP! You're going to get trapped."

Jen scanned the inferno. It grew as she watched. "Shit," she said. She turned to Cassie. "Come on, dog. Let's go."

The dog didn't register her command. Instead, Cassie growled and kept focused on the mountainside.

"Forget the dog," Brian said. "I mean, she knows what to do. Let's go."

"Right," Jen said and swung her legs back over the side. As she landed on the other side she spotted the fire line spread before them. The police officers furiously waved at them. "Go get us a line!" one shouted over his shoulder. "Quick!"

Two officers turned and ran.

"Situation's got real bad real quick," Jen said. "This is not looking good."

The fire rose, consuming ground cover. Jen felt the fire bake her cheeks despite standing thirty-feet away. "Get back up on the road," she said as she checked their footing. Dried vegetation littered the dirt. "This is all going to go up as fast as hell."

Brian scurried behind her and hurried onto the road. Jen watched the fire for a moment, knelt, spun round, and scaled back over the rail.

Brian knelt, too. "Something's up there, boss," he said. "Something big."

Jen crouched beside him. "Where? What do you see?"

A large, gleaming shadow descended from the mountainside above the road. Cassie stopped barking and back-stepped toward Jen and Brian. She whimpered.

From the corner of her eye Jen saw sparks in the air. Large spiral flames reached over the rails beside them.

The shiny shadow crept down the hill. "What is that thing?" Jen said.

"It's huge," Brian said. The animal reached the bottom and stood a few car lengths away. A long, sectioned head rose ten-feet high. Seven eyes glistened. Some were red, some were blue, while others were black.

It balanced on several black fin-like appendages, each with small pointed burrs at the tips. The SUV-sized oval body balanced gracefully on top of the fins. The creature shuddered and stretched its jaw; it spoke with several vocal clicks.

Tenna. Tenna. Tenna.

They both smelled the raw, bright oily stench of the Tennatrick's breath right before it lunged and snapped.

The Tennatrick's long neck jutted out toward Cassie. Fire reflected on the creature's skin; they could see every detail of the creature's horse-like head.

"This isn't happening," Jen said. "It's a hallucination from the smoke, right?"

Brian shook his head. "Sure," he said. "Whatever you say."

The animal made another clicking vocalization.

Trick. Trick. Trick. Trick.

"What is that noise?" Jen said. Despite standing in the midst of a burn, Jenn's veins felt filled with ice. Her right leg shook. She tried to make it stop but it kept wobbling. Use the adrenaline. Make it work.

"That sound?" Jen said. "What did that guy tell us they called it?"

"The Tennatrick," Brian said. "Something like that."

"Yeah," she said. "Something like that."

The Tennatrick inched towards Cassie and leaned back on two rear fins. Jen saw the Tennatrick's fins extended further and scooped Cassie. She yelped as the burrs punctured her body. The Tennatrick pulled the dog towards its head. The large gaping mouth reminded Jen of a pelican.

"Shoot it," Brian said. "Don't let it hurt Cassie!"

Jen swallowed. "I don't think that's a good idea."

"You don't know? Look at that thing."

She raised the site on her pistol, aimed squarely between the Tennatrick's eyes, and squeezed.

The gun recoiled and the Tennatrick squealed. A small red hole appeared between the creature's eyes. Black fluid spilled out and smoldered on the road.

"Shoot it again," Brian said. "Kill it."

The Tennatrick tossed Cassie to the side, shaking the dog from the end of its fin. Cassie landed against the railing with a yelp. Jen saw several large gashes.

"Okay," she said and squeezed off two more shots.

The Tennatrick screeched—there were more of its awful noises.

Jen spotted a hole just over the creature's mouth. It dripped more black oily blood. Then the hole closed. "It's like shooting into quicksand," she said. "It's not taking the hits."

Brian crouched behind her. "There's no way out," he said. "It's going to get us. Like it got Cassie." He looked over at the wounded dog.

Jen looked, too. Cassie didn't seem to be whimpering any longer. Smoke trailed from her wounds.

The ground moved. The Tennatrick stepped closer to them. It burrowed its fins in the ground like an ape resting on its knuckles.

They got a good look at it up close. The Tennatrick's head moved slowly from side to side. It watched them with its eyes, which seemed to change color from an oily greenish to a bright blue.

The voice came from the thing's throat in reedy bursts. Its breath stunk like old Sterno.

It swung at them with one of its fins. Jen hopped out of the way.

"Uh," Brian groaned.

She twisted around to see him lying on his back. A large triangular slice smoldered from the top part of his left thigh. She looked down—he looked down—they both screamed.

There was no blood.

Their eyes met. "Move!" he yelled.

She did. Just in time. She looked at her waist and saw the fin cut through the air in front of her. If she'd stuck around she would have been cut in half.

She raised her gun and looked right up into the Tennatrick's eye. She shot. The Tennatrick's oily eye turned into a black empty hole and it screeched.

Jen looked left and right and behind her. There was a break in the wall of fire. She leaned down to Brian. "Can you walk?"

"I don't know," he said back. He went to move his legs and threw his head back. Brian grit his teeth. "God damn. I don't think so."

The Tennatrick regained its ground, and stood on its back flippers so that it towered as high as the burning treetops. She knew she had only a moment, so Jen hurried behind Brian, grabbed him under his arms, and pulled him to his feet. He cried out, but he was still able to stand.

The Tennnatrick charged them as soon as it saw them move. Jen quickly pulled off two shots. Both vanished into the creature's hide like pins into a dashboard.

"I don't think it's doing any good," he said. "We better run." He limped backward.

"Where?"

He pointed behind them, towards the hill. The fire had slowed below, leaving a gap big enough for them to get through. "What if there's fire on the other side?" Jen asked. "We'll get cooked alive."

Brian stood, winced, said, "I'll take my chances," and turned tail.

"Shit!" Jen followed him further up the hill, but not before getting a good look at the Tennatrick. It recoiled when their eyes met and Jen thought it was about to whip out one of its flippers.

She ran and then heard the creature's sharp cries. The earth shook as the monster dropped down to all fours.

They reached the hills and ran as fast as they could. She wondered how he could be running with his wound and thought that either it wasn't as bad as she'd feared, or that his adrenaline had kicked in.

Fire surrounded them on both sides. Halfway up they had to put up their arms to shield themselves. The fires inched closer and closer with each step they took higher on the hill.

"I hear something," he said. "Listen."

Jen heard it, too. "Is that water or fire?"

"I think it's water."

She heard something rustle behind them that sounded like blowing leaves. She turned around. "The undergrowth is burning around us," she said. "Look."

Flames completely surrounded them. The fire had spread and chased them. Jen felt the skin on her hands and face bake. "This was a bad idea." She nodded to Brian. "What should we do now, huh?"

"I don't know." There was barely thirty square feet for them left to stand in.

"It might just be my imagination," she said. "But I think we're right at Santora Lake. There's a small waterfall and that's probably what we're hearing." She nodded at Brian. "It's now or never."

The fire closed in and the Tennatrick charged from behind the wall of flames. She jumped out of the way. As she jumped back, she saw Brian crouching just beneath the creature.

Jen yelled his name. As she did, the animal was on him. It moved quickly; Jen couldn't react quickly enough. In front of her, Brian's body lifted off the ground. She pointed her gun at the Tennatrick, but couldn't find a clear shot.

"Let him go!" she screamed. "Drop him!"

It was moving too fast—she'd hit Brian if she shot at the thing. She was sure of it.

Before she had another chance to do anything, The Tennatrick retreated into the flames holding Jim.

The Tennatrick's thin, insectoid arms grasped Jim as tight as anything he'd ever felt. He tried to wiggle and fight, but the animal had him. The animal looked him right in the eyes. He tried to turn his head to find Yanna, but he couldn't move. Another hand, or paw, or something, held his head tight. He heard her, though, screeching his name.

Jim looked up at the strange, awkward creature. He could smell the dirt of the earth still on it, despite them both being wet from the lake. He could feel its power: it held him harder and tighter than he could have ever imagined.

There was a sudden chill that seemed to come from his middle. He looked down to see a pinkish lip opening around his belly. "Oh, no," he mumbled and looked up at the sky, which, from his position, was ringed with fire. The smoke clouds seemed fitting—gray and colorless and neutral.

Jim's lights went out.

Jen looked up just as two halves of Brian flew out from the flames. She had to duck to avoid getting knocked out by his legs. They landed only a few feet from her. She could see the legs, twisted, his toes pointing at her—Jen noticed the soot coating the back of his innards and she thought about sandy feet at the beach.

Her saliva glands dried. A freezing, numb sensation worked its way up through her heels into the tips of her elbows. She couldn't quite register what she was looking at. He hadn't just been torn in half in front of her eyes by some animal, had he?

He had, and as much as it pained her, and she knew it'd be difficult later to get through, Jen knew she had to pull herself together and find a way out. *Don't turn right*, she thought. *Don't look at his face. You'll never forget it.*

From the flames, the Tennatrick charged directly at her, swinging its flippers and limbs, its head lowered, ready to do to her what it'd done to Brian.

Think!

Water. We're by the lake. It's just over to the right, past Brian's top half—

She stood and turned to face what she hoped was the water, careful not to look down at Brian's remains. and in only a moment Jen felt her feet fall out from under her. She dropped for ten seconds before she hit the lake.

From above she heard Brian. It got him. She felt freezing water all around her. It made the burns on her hands and forearms sting. Jen pushed her way up and out of the water. As she did she sensed something brush past her hip. *Probably a fish or plant or something,* she thought.

A thin layer of ash coated the top of the water and smoke drifted across the lake. She looked left and saw fifty-foot tall walls of fire soaring near the top of the hill.

She the Tennatrick through the flames. It spotted her, froze for a moment and backed fully into the inferno. It knows I'm down here.

To the right she spotted the creature once again between spits of fire. It raced around the ridge of the lake.

Jen looked around. Past the Tennatrick she saw a down slope that led to a short rocky beach. Past that the lake led right up to another steep slope. She spun round to find a flat rocky slab of what looked like granite jutting out of the water to form an island. It seemed completely isolated.

"Hope this thing doesn't like water." She swam back to it, keeping an eye on the creature's progress all the while.

The Tennatrick raced around the perimeter and kept watch on Jen. She saw it turn its head to her every few moments as it tracked her progress. The fire isn't burning it. It's running right through without anything happening to it. The flames lit the entire lake.

Jen turned and climbed up onto the granite slab rock island. *Hope that thing can't get here,* she thought. *Where the hell are the relief ops?* As she hauled herself up on the slab she pictured her gun. *Waterlogged. Useless unless I bash that thing's head in with the butt.*

She spun around and sat. Her chest felt like it was made of fiberglass. She covered her nose and mouth with the neck from her

T-shirt. It was wet and would serve as a filter, she hoped. Better than nothing.

Around the perimeter of the lake she spotted no sign of the Tennatrick. How long until this area burns itself out? Jen sat in the center of a burning inferno. *At least it can't burn in one place forever,* she thought.

The water on the lake looked still. The layer of ash on top made it look just like any other stretch of flat land.

She looked up to the spot from where she'd jumped. It was where she'd last seen Brian. *There is a waterfall here. This is the lake I was thinking of,* she thought. *The place I came hiking through a few years ago. We're in the Los Padros section here. I know it. Santoro Lake.*

Jen squinted to try to see Brian. She leaned back up against the rocks. She thought about her training and how much time and energy she'd put into her career. What can I say when they ask what happened? Her mind went blank for a moment. I can just say we pursued the suspect up the hill and got trapped by the fire. There was no way out. Nobody has to know about this monster thing. It was probably something else, anyway. Couldn't be real. Just couldn't.

Something moved across the lake. The Tennatrick peeked through the fire and spotted her on the rock island in the center. "You reading my thoughts?" she said. "I was just thinking how to explain you away."

Jen gulped. This thing's huge. What the hell is it? She reached for her gun. She coiled her hand around the butt, which made her feel a little better, even though she knew it probably wouldn't fire.

She looked behind her. She stood and checked out the area in back of the island. Water on all sides. At least fifty feet. It'd have to swim to get me.

She turned back around in time to see the Tennatrick approach the waterfront at the beach. The creature lowered a single fin to the water. It lowered its head at the same time.

The damn thing has fins, she thought. *Of course it's going to go into the water. Look at it.* She curled back up on her rock and watched the Tennatrick. *Okay. Where's there to go? Back in the water?*

Before she knew it she had slid back into the lake. *If that thing can swim, then that's it. I have to at least try to get out of here.* As the powdery ash on the top of the lake gathered at her neck and the chilly water seemed to seep right into her bones, something funny happened.

The Tennatrick snapped back from the water as if the water hurt. Fire coughed from its mouth. It screamed louder and angrier.

She could see something drip from the flipper it used to touch the lake. Black oily goo dropped to the sand and ignited on contact.

She backed herself up to the rock island, turned, put her palms on top and pushed. Her forearms shook from the exertion. *Am I that tired?* she thought and pushed up anyway. The whole time she kept her eyes on the Tennatrick. The creature bobbed its head up and down and seemed to be looking towards one side of the lake at something.

A second clicking voice came from somewhere else.

Toward the Tennatrick's right, fifty feet above, a second lighter colored Tennatrick peeked through the fire. It opened and closed its jaw, sucking the fire, which changed from bright red and orange into blue and then white as the creature consumed them.

Once it got its fill, the lighter Tennatrick walked onto the beach. The first Tennatrick twittered around and faced the new arrival.

Without hesitation, the second Tennatrick jumped on top of the first. It clamped its fins around the first, who tried shaking off her attacker.

Now's my chance, Jen thought. *While they're busy killing each other I can get the hell out of here.* But when she watched them a moment longer, she noticed the creatures weren't hurting each other.

A white round appendage dropped from the rear of the top Tennatrick. The appendage curled and hardened and found its way into an opening underneath its mate. As they worked their organs together a pinkish fluid dripped from the opening.

"For God's sake," Jen said. "Is that all they can think about at a time like this?"

But she couldn't look away.

The animal's humping got faster and faster and more intense, each thrust more violent than the last.

Finally, it stopped with four slow jerks inward and out. Its appendage slipped from her, flopping like a dead snake, dripping pink goo.

The top creature crawled off its mate and slowly lowered toward the sand. *Tired, aren't you, you son of a bitch? All that and it's over in five minutes. Guess some things are the same whether you're a person or a firebug.*

Jen kept still.

The darker Tennatrick crawled on top of the resting creature. At first Jen believed that, somehow, it might return the favor and drop its own appendage down. As soon as she saw the creature's jaw open she knew different.

Ripping mouthfuls of rubbery flesh from its mate, the Tennatrick spit them out onto the sand as fast as she'd ripped them off. The pieces smoldered and small flames jutted out in places.

"Good girl," Jen said. "You show him."

The wounds dripped the dark oily fluid, which sparked and flamed when spilled. It's what it must look like right before an engine ignites.

The Tennatrick tore several additional pieces from its mate. For its part, the other sounded no protest. It seemed to willingly accept its fate.

Now why would it do something like that? She wondered. *Why would it just accept being murdered like that?* And then she had an idea. *It's old. That's why it's lighter than the other one. It probably knows it's ready to die, I bet.*

Then the Tennatrick climbed off its mate, faced the opposite direction and walked backwards until its hind stood over the dying creature.

The Tennatrick looked out and spotted Jen. It opened its jaws, looked behind at its own rear and spread its fins outward. The back of its sectioned body split open slightly.

From the split at the back of the Tennatrick, a dark, obsidian egg slid out. The animal pushed and cried as the egg dropped onto the smoldering, torn flesh of the other.

A second egg slid out, although it seemed to only take half as long. The Tennatrick finished, stepped forward and lunged headfirst into the corpse, tearing out a piece of flesh, which she tossed on top of the eggs. She did this several times, each flap smoldering and smoking as she ripped them free.

The Tennatrick kept working until the ground seemed covered in black fluid and torn tissue. She chomped and pulled and rubbed the pieces on top of her eggs until the sparks turned into flames. Then the Tennatrick lugged bits and pieces of chaparral plants from the beach perimeter and added them to the fire.

The pile caught fire while the Tennatrick dropped down onto her hindquarters like a dog waiting for a snack. She watched the pyre raise and fall, all the while monitoring her eggs with the occasional prod.

Is she cooking them? Jen watched, fascinated with the ritual.

The mate's corpse smoldered. Deep within the dry, scorched, gray pile, the heavy seed-like shells cracked. Thick black fluid spilled out and sparked. Baby Tennatricks unfolded. *They look more like spiders when they're small,* Jen thought. They needed fires to splinter them. Nourished and pollinated by the fire, the newborns found their way from their own fire-split shells. They rose in the flickering firelight.

Ash from the burnt corpse blew across the lake towards Jen. She shielded her face with the neck of her wet shirt, but it was not enough to keep all the particles out. She gulped and did her best to suppress a tickle in her throat.

More ash sprinkled off the heap and landed on top of the already heavily soiled surface of the lake. In places, clumps of ash that became too heavy dropped down into the lake. She looked down and saw ash covering her pants, shirt and hands. Jen looked up through the heavy gray air. Most of the ash had blown onto the lake from the ridge over the beach. *Backwinds,* she thought. *The fire's moving downhill and all the air's sucking the ash up to the lake.* She looked over at the Tennatrick.

She couldn't see the babies. They'd vanished. The Tennatrick regarded Jen one last time before sliding back up over the hill.

Jen watched it disappear almost as quickly as she'd seen it first appear on the shore. The backwind from the fire blew harder and faster. The remains of the mate decomposed bit by bit and its ash blew across Santoro Lake.

Jen lowered her head, turned her back to the blowing ash and thought about climbing back into the lake. When she put her feet into the water, something spongy and hard bounced off them underwater. She pulled her feet up out of the water. It's the babies, she knew. But she was wrong.

"It's a fish," she said. "Just a fish." She looked at the large lower lip of the fish and the dark color. "Just a good old California trout." Then she thought for a moment. *If that fish is dead in here, then there's something really wrong with this water. Those fish are very hearty.* She curled back up onto the granite island. *Better if I just sit here and wait it out. The water's probably really toxic right now from all the ash.*

She shivered for long periods of time until finally, the first rays of the morning sun peeked out over the ridge from the same spot she'd last seen the Tennatrick.

As the dark night sky slowly turned into orange morning light, Jen heard a distant thumping sound. "Air Ops resuming," she said. "Only a matter of time until they find me." She thought about swimming through the lake, but it'd filled with dozens of trout.

Within the next hour, a small team of firemen crested the perimeter around the lake and she waved to them. Two paddled out to her in a small canoe. They asked her name and if she was all right. She nodded and they helped her sit because she found she had little strength left.

"Any word on Brian Riggs? And what the hell took you guys all night to get here? I can't be more than a mile from home base."

"We haven't found Brian," he said. "And the fire was too intense all night. We couldn't break through until just now. It's still raging on the north and eastern fronts."

"Oh?" Jen said. She wanted to say more, but none of it seemed real. She zoned out and stared at the dead fish all around the lake and felt empty and sad and that she was lucky she had survived.

"We should probably get you to an ICU and have you checked out for smoke inhalation and shock. You were in the elements all night."

"Okay," Jen said. "I think I could just use a little sleep is all." She heard her own voice as though she were a thousand miles away. Jen looked for the remains of the burned Tennatrick. There was nothing left other than a large indentation and a thick layer of ash. She saw no sign of the eggs or the babies. She pictured the Tennatrick digging itself back underground, leaving her with nothing but its myth until the next fires came. She'd be there, she knew, looking for it, listening for it, forever searching.

VAMPIRO

"No man's land," Sammy Avilla said as he looked out his window at the faraway peaks of the Sierra Nevada Mountains. *"La Tierra de Nadie.* Suicide Alley." They passed San Diego and rolled their converted pick-up through the outlying hills. Looking through the small window and into the back holding-pen area of the shell, Sammy imagined it filled with Mexicans. He turned to Danny Majo. "What's the Wall like?"

"The Wall goes into America twenty miles from the beach. And it's actually three walls. The first one's eight feet. There's another reinforced steel wall, climb-proofed, between us and Baja." Danny's grin cut through his heavily pockmarked face. "We're going right between them—throwing ourselves in with the illegals. Your arm still hurting from that shot?"

Sam nodded. "Hurts more now than when they gave it to me." He rubbed his left bicep. "Never had a headache this bad." Danny laughed. "Twenty-five? Shit. I got porn older than you." He pinched Sam's sore arm. "You're just hungry. We got to fatten you up. You in the mood for Mexican?"

He laughed. "After tonight, you'll never want to eat Mexican again!" He laughed and nodded up to the front of the pick-up to Solo, who was a few years older and a few inches taller than Sammy. "Right?"

Solo grunted and Sam couldn't see his eyes because big, silvery sunglasses that reflected the last rays of the pastel sunset camouflaged them.

"Lay off him." Von Sharp pointed back at Danny from the front passenger's seat. "This isn't a hazing. It's a job." Von was Danny's age, but was much better preserved.

Danny grabbed the headrest and pulled himself up to Von's ear. "This's more than a job. We get to go out there and bust a bunch of fuckheads, don't we?"

Von looked like he was going to kill Danny, who just smiled and jabbed Sammy. "Don't worry. I didn't mean you. You're not one of them. You're okay."

"I'm Latino, too." Sam felt his ears turning red. "So what?" Danny sat back and spewed more obnoxious laughter.

"You're not looking for a handout or to take from this country and not give back. Christ: you actually took the time to learn how to speak English. Not like them." Danny pounded his chest. "By the way: you're my guy now. I'll show your ass how this is going to work."

He wanted to say something back to Danny, something about self-hatred, but couldn't speak. He was dumbfounded.

Not yet, but maybe later he would.

A dull ache gnawed at the sides of his nose and the joints of his jaw—maybe the start of a sinus infection.

"Why do you want to be out here with us night people?" Danny asked.

"So I can make a difference for these people. Put an honest, good face to this." He stared at Danny. "That, and I can always go to the beach on my time off."

Danny laughed impossibly louder. "Oh, shit, kid, you're killing me. You're so clueless, my God. You ain't going to do anything except sleep when you get some free time."

"So this is the other side of San Diego. Calexico." Von gestured to the barren, dry landscape outside the pickup. "No steakhouses or fancy gas lamps out here. No baseball stadium. Just us between the walls."

"Yup." Sam said. "I've been out here before."

Danny cocked an eyebrow. "That so? Another slumming rich suburban kid who's probably part of the Aztlans. Want to take it all back for your people, don't you?"

"That's just a bunch of fear-mongers talking. Come on! That Mexican Nationalist stuff went out with rollerblades and Culture Club. I was here for science class at Cal State," Sam said. "Had us out here digging for rocks and plant life. Didn't get too close to the wall, though."

"You sure you just weren't out here smoking a little huh-huh trying to get inside little ol' Squirtin' Suzie's dress?"

Sam shook his head. "Nah, man," he said. "I'm a little more . . . romantic . . . than that."

"Bullshit!" Danny yelled. "You're just another pud-pullin', porn-downloadin' motherfucker. Just like everyone else."

"Not really." Sam said. "Just the opposite."

Danny's laugh morphed into a series of huffs. "What are you? A Jesus freak? Or a Mexican Jew? I mean: you've got light skin and freckles."

"I'm atheist and I'm Argentinean."

"An atheist from Argentina? Well, that's a new one." Danny thought for a moment. "You gave up on God just to protect the Mexicans, eh?"

"I never believed in Christ in the first place."

"Shit. Come on. What'd your parents teach you?"

"Nothing." Sam said. "I grew up with my grandparents."

Danny's mood changed. "That's good, though. You're in the right place. God can't help you out here."

The pickup pulled up to a small station outside the outer wall. Solo rolled down the window. "Greetings, Neil."

A pasty fellow with deep, dark circles under his eyes jerked up from the bottom of the station house. "Hey," he said to Solo.

"Sorry to interrupt your dinner," Solo said.

"No worries," Neil said. "It was cold anyway." He scanned the cab. "Who's the newbie?"

Neil stared right at Sammy and didn't blink. Sammy's gut tightened. *What the hell was he just doing eating off the floor? Something's really wrong here.*

"Got his papers?" Neil kept his eyes on Sammy, who thought his mind was being read.

Solo nodded and handed over a yellow sheet folded in threes. "Here."

Neil took it and handed it back.

"We good?" Danny asked.

"Been a slow night," Neil said.

"Just the way we like it. No one out here busting our balls."

Neil looked down at his feet and kicked at something, which reminded Sammy of someone kicking a dog. *He's sneaked his dog onto the base and wants to keep it quiet.*

The gate opened and Solo drove them down the sandy dune into No Man's Land.

Above the American side of the Wall, twenty-foot high work-lamps pooled grainy spotlights across the dunes and road. At the bottom of the hill they parked the pickup in one of the light pools so that it faced the Mexican side of the wall. As they got out, Sammy imagined the sandy highway stretching all the way to the ocean.

Von carried a small suitcase-sized metal box with FLIR stenciled on it, which Sammy knew stood for Forward Looking Infrared, which detected body heat. "I'll go set this thing up," Von said.

Danny and Sammy followed Solo to the pickup's shell. "Fuckin' Solo, man." Danny shook his head as he sized up his rather large co-worker. "More like Chewbacca, you big ape."

Solo opened the rear door of the cab where Sammy spotted three Berettas inside a lock box. *Why can't they let us just use rifles?* Sammy thought. His head was killing him and he tried to ignore it.

Von reached inside. "We'll just need these for right now," he said and clutched a pair of binoculars and shoved them at Sammy.

"So we're just going to watch the alley until we see something?" Sammy said.

"Right." Von handed a second pair to Solo.

Then Danny banged a hand on the back of Sammy's back.

"Welcome to the glamorous life." He walked past him and clicked his tongue. "Let's get a-peepin', fellas."

"What are those colorful boxes on the wall?"

Danny lowered his chin and smirked. "Coffins, man. Can't you read what's on them? *Muertes.* Used to be only on the Mexican side of the wall. Now those bleeding hearts are putting them up on our side, too."

Von pointed at the rocks about five hundred feet from them. "That's pretty much where a fence should be. Right at those boulders."

"Oh. Okay." Sam coughed a little and tried to stifle it away by swallowing. His throat was getting dry and the aches in his jaw and sinuses were worsening. "Anything to drink out here? Anyone have any Tylenol? Head's killing me."

"You're just hungry. Don't worry. We'll eat in a little bit." He sniffed the air. "I can almost smell it." He winked at Sammy. "It's almost like old, dried up cat piss, ain't it?" Danny took in a lungful. "Or a million unwashed scurrying bloodsuckers taking a piss on America."

Von returned and pointed at his watch. "It's after nine, you know. We've got a little bit until we'll see any action. Mind if I . . ."

"What? Go squeeze one out over a cactus bush?" Danny shrugged. "I don't care. Just don't ask me to take anything out that might get stuck in ya."

"That's not what I was going to say."

"I know what you were gonna say." Danny stepped away from the group and put his binoculars back up. "Now go away and fuck off." To emphasize the point, he gave Von the finger over his shoulder.

"Your mother."

Von sounded half-serious, to which Danny laughed. "I don't got a mother. Just like our Atheist Boy."

"We spotted one." Von hurried towards their pickup. He leaned in and nudged Danny, who'd fallen asleep on the shell's floor. "Come on!"

"I heard ya." Danny pushed up by grabbing the metal seat.

Watching from outside, Sam creaked his neck and shut his eyes. *Come on headache—go away,* he thought. *First day out and my body fails me.*

Von brushed by him. "You ready, kiddo?

"Yup."

"Look through your goggles." He pointed out a dune a few hundred feet from them.

Sammy spotted the tops of three illegal heads. They crouched down behind a north-side dune.

Solo rushed toward them. *God. He's running faster than I've ever seen anyone run before.* Solo had hopped over the dune so fast, Sammy was having trouble figuring out what had happened. The illegals vanished below the line of sight with Solo.

Behind Solo, Danny, and Von charged the dune.

How are they all running so fast?

He thought for a moment—tried to reason it out.

It's got to be the night vision. Playing tricks on things. Making them look faster. He took his eyes away and squinted.

Sam hurried to the dune.

What do I do now? What'd they say in training? Don't go in as a gang. If you see anything or anyone, call for backup. Don't act alone. What the hell are you guys doing?

Turning rank and sour, the air smelled worse than before. He couldn't place the scent.

They're playing a joke on me. They're just fucking with me. Hazing me. Breaking me in.

He hurried closer to the dune. He wanted to yell to them and let them know he was in on their shit. But he didn't. Just in case they weren't messing around.

Dry, rotten desert breeze filled his nose and sinuses. *It smelled like dirt and bad meat,* he thought. He licked his tongue across his back teeth, which felt like he had food stuck between them.

Sammy's head pounded, and all he wanted to do was to put his head down. *Maybe I am hungry. If I just had a cheeseburger, this headache might go away.*

He heard slurping from the ditch.

Sammy sniffled and mucous trickled from his inner nose to just outside his nostril. He wiped at it with his sleeve. Not the time to be getting sick.

He creaked his neck and shoulders, which did nothing to relieve the headache.

His teeth hurt. He tongued the front ones, convinced pieces of apple skin were lodged between them. He winced.

Damn it. Haven't been sensitive like that since I had braces. What the hell? To make sure it wasn't a fluke, he pushed his tongue towards his upper pallet and winced again.

Sam's stomach rumbled. Loud.

His palms and fingers went numb and his glands ached.

What's happening to me?

Sam inched closer, although he was seriously considering heading back to the shell to put his head down.

He kept walking instead.

Keep focused and forget the pain. Mind over matter.

He shut his eyes, took a breath and headed towards Danny, Von and Solo.

With each step, he saw more of someone's bent arm moving just over the ridge of the dune.

The gesture looked like they had to be digging. Or tearing. Or something. Around the dune, Sammy spotted dark shiny splotches.

Something deep and instinctual turned on inside him.

He raised his chin and took the last few steps that led him over the dune.

Sam saw Danny hunched over someone. Both bodies shook. His arms tore at the person under him. He heard more of the slurping noises.

"Danny?"

His teammate turned his head to the side.

His eyes are different.

Blood dripped from Danny's mouth, so he wiped it clean with the back of his hand. It appeared darker. *Because it's caked in blood.*

"Well, what'd you think we did out here? Give these poor little ol' folks lifts back across the border?"

His voice is different.

Sammy stood and re-processed what he was looking at in his mind until he felt his bottom lip trembling and the tops of his legs going weak.

Twenty feet south of Danny, Sammy spotted Von and Solo hunched over two other people. They didn't turn back to look at him.

But he did catch someone's eye.

A woman.

Her gaze met his—Sammy imagined he looked more scared than she did.

He turned back to Danny, who'd resumed his supper. Sammy talked to Danny's back. "We need to call for support. For backup. Like we're supposed to."

Danny laughed. That *fucking* laugh. "We saved the baby-maker for you, kiddo." He turned his head round. "Your teeth starting to hurt yet?"

Sam felt the sand on his cheek and above his eye. Pain cycled through his body in waves. "Kill me," he said as Danny leaned over him. "Hurts too much. Just do what you're going to do?"

Danny frowned. "Oh, no," he said. "You ain't getting off that easy, kiddo. Got something here that'll make you feel a gazillion times better."

He creaked his head to the side, motioning Von and Solo to drag the woman up towards Sam. "I'll take it from here," he said. "Gracias."

The woman faced Sam, and they looked each other in the eye. Danny dove down on the girl and jumped back up.

For a brief moment, it looked as though he hadn't done anything. But blood soon gushed from her throat.

"She's bleeding out, homey," Danny said. "You gonna let her die slow, or do you want to take care of her?" His voice lowered an octave. "You know you want to taste her."

"No," Sam said. "I'm not . . . like that."

Danny bent down, grabbed the woman's shoulders and lifted her. He dropped her in front of Sam. "Guess I gotta spoon feed her to ya, don't I?"

Her blood flowed into the sand and Sam could smell the minerals and sustenance—it made the ache in his head and body worsen. His lips and throat felt dry—his whole being felt dry.

Sammy needed her blood.

He managed to crawl a few inches. She'd closed her eyes, which made him a little more comfortable about doing what he had to.

"That's it." Danny hovered over him with his arms crossed. "Go on. Taste it." Von and Solo walked up beside Danny and watched Sammy. He could sense them lingering over him.

The girl's torn flesh stopped gushing. He clearly saw the wound, which was curiously luminescent. It reminded him of how the FLIR saw body heat, except that it was his eyes that were doing it and not some fancy technology.

Her complexion was young and burnt brown. Her jet-black hair was pulled back in a ponytail.

What am I doing? I came here to help people. I'm not a monster like this.

His neck went stiff and the pain inside his skull increased.

Do it, he thought. *She's already dead. Go along with it. They'll probably kill you if you don't. You can report them tomorrow.* But he didn't believe what he was thinking.

Sam wanted to drink—to eat.

He shook his head back and forth a few times on top of her wound, grazing it like a tentative lover.

Don't know if I can.

I don't know.

Licking at his teeth, he found they'd changed into sharp, pointed little things.

How did this happen to me?

He shut his eyes, opened wide, latched on, and sucked warm, milky blood onto his tongue. For a moment, his headache worsened. Then everything turned clear.

His body stopped hurting.

After the final drops bled out onto his tongue, Sammy rolled onto his back and looked up at the starry night. His headache was replaced by a drunken buzz. All he wanted was to sleep. Near him, he looked at the dried husk.

"You drained her nice. She's good and ready for America now." Danny peered down at him and Sam realized he'd cupped his hands between his knees. Danny pointed and smirked. "You're going to have to wait until you get home to squeeze one off, my friend, unless you want us to leave you out here. Your head feel better?" He put a hand out so that Sam could get up.

"Yeah."

"Good. But you ain't gonna want to be out in the open in a few hours when it gets light out. Now help me move her inside the shell."

Sammy found he had more energy and more strength than he'd ever had in his life. He picked up the woman's legs while Danny grabbed her under the armpits, and they lifted her.

"What's happened to me?"

"You're a *Vampiro* now, my friend. Spread the wealth." He walked backwards.

"I didn't want this."

"But you like it, don't you? Feels good." They moved

towards the shell. "Only bad thing is it tends to close your social circle a bit."

At the pick-up, Von and Solo lifted their prey into the shell. "You guys almost ready?" Von asked. "We got to get on the road soon. Sun'll be up in two hours. We got to make it back long before then."

Danny and Sammy lifted the woman up and into the shell. They laid her down next to the other members of her family. "So that's why there's no windows in the shell," Sammy observed. "Those people? They going to change? Like us?"

"Just in time for their asses to get processed and back in Mexico," Danny said. "If not, then . . ." he made a slicing motion across his own throat. "We'll have to take care of them."

"Then what? We just send them home with nothing?"

"Not with nothing." Danny smiled and touched his fangs with his tongue. "They'll have these."

"What about me? What do I do?"

"You guard the border. Make sure no one gets through. Grab the ones that do and throw them in the cab. Give them a little goody to bring back to Mexico. They can share with all their friends what America has to offer. They want to take from our country so bad and give it back to theirs, well, here's to them."

"Do we have to bite all of them? Turn them all into these things?" Sammy stepped away from the shell so that Von could shut the door.

"We change all of them. Make it an epidemic. Let 'em kill each other. Hell, they're going to, anyway. We might as well speed up the process."

"What if I don't want to do this?"

"Where else are you going to go to get what you need without getting caught? You going to go to your neighbor's house? Eat his kids?"

"No, but . . . I read that vampires can eat mice and birds and dogs and . . ."

Danny laughed. "You need human blood, my friend. There's not enough of what you need in mouse blood. You'll starve."

"I just wanted to give them some dignity."

Danny made a sour face. "This is better than selling oranges on the highway or begging for work at Home Depot, isn't it? Now their lives have a purpose."

"To kill more people?"

"They're not people," Danny said. "Not anymore. Not since they tried to suck us dry. Now those parasites can suck their own country dry."

"I just wanted to help people."

"These aren't people anymore, in case you haven't noticed. They're *Vampiro*. You're helping to save millions of Americans."

Sammy wakes up to sunlight burning his eyes as the pickup soars across the dark highway. He's hurting, but he's feeling better. The blood, Sammy knows. It's the blood.

Danny asks, "How's your arm, kid? Still hurt? It should. That's where we got ya."

"Got me?"

"Where they put the goods in you that gave you the taste, buddy—the taste for blood. You got to drink that all the time." That laugh. "You ain't ever going anywhere now, Homie. Trust me. It never ends. Things ain't ever gonna be the same."

X IS FOR XYX

I lost everything in a blink. My world came crashing down around me and left me living out of a small studio apartment in Hollywood. It was a long way from the Victorian house we shared back in Whistleville. We had a pair of dogs. We had our son, Tony, and he was even living out of the same bedroom I'd had growing up. I'm still very confused about how I made it from there to here in under a year. This much I know: It was all her idea. Her . . . Mercedes . . . the supposed love of my life. She was the one who wanted to move to the East coast. Then, when things hadn't panned out the way she'd wanted she insisted on moving us back to Los Angeles. "If we don't go back," she'd said, "you're going to lose me." I should have known better because I ended up losing her anyway. I think she'd planned things to turn out that way the entire time. I get little Tony on the weekends, but it's hard as hell transitioning to a single dad. I went into this whole thing thinking I was going to have a life partner. I never thought she'd leave.

The pills. Doctor Mark was treating my bipolar disorder with a healthy dose of Abilify when Mercedes dropped her divorce bomb on me. Those pills made it feel as though I had a pound of sand on my heart. When I mentioned that to Doctor Mark, he immediately pulled me off them. Turns out I was actually allergic. Mercedes didn't care. She just wanted the stupid pills to work immediately. The next batch ended up being better, but it was too late. She served me divorce papers and sent me packing.

That first night I crashed at my friend Mike's house. I'll never forget crouching on his floor, listening to Tom Petty's "Learning To Fly" while I watched my hot tears drop and disappear into his carpet. For his part, I'll say Mike didn't bother me. He was in the room, but kept to himself and let me have that moment. Learning to Fly, all right. Oh, and thank God for the Klonopin. That stuff got me through the darkest bottom of my life. I was able to go to work and function. Not that my stomach wasn't in knots, and not that my head wasn't in the clouds, because it was, but it was . . . livable. On the other hand, I was going through a bottle of Pepto-Bismol a day just to keep my guts in order.

So why is this all important? I'm not the first schmuck who'd gone through the hell of a divorce, after all. Better men than me had survived worse splits.

It's because the miserable feelings were too much for me and I was desperate to do something about it.

During the second night at Mike's house I found his gun. I knew where he hid it and I knew how to use it. Check One for the Boy Scouts: I'd actually learned something useful from them.

I sat on Mike's floor, Indian-style, and put his gun to my temple. Nothing mattered without Mercedes. She was my everything. Without her, I was worthless and weak. Might as well give in and take the easy way out, right?

Fuck it.

I pulled the trigger.

I saw a psychedelic spectrum of light. I saw everything turn red. I heard the noise of the gun, and something moist slapped against Mike' wall. I fell over.

Some time later, I woke up.

My head was spinning. I'd never felt so much pain in my entire life. There was an absolute mess around me: blood and pieces of flesh everywhere. What had I done? "Mike?" I called, absently. He didn't answer because he had a date that night.

To my right, the side where I'd shot myself, there was a pulsing mound of dark gray gristle on the carpet. I shut my eyes for a second to refocus them. When I opened them, I looked again. Something moved inside that pile of flesh. What was it?

Then I put my hand up to the side of my head and felt the wound. It stung so badly, and I cried out, my voice making a high-pitched, whimpering sound. Holy shit: I'd shot myself in the head and lived. I had to call 911. I had to go to a doctor. Even though I'd survived, I knew I'd probably bleed out. What was I doing looking at the chunks on the floor I'd blown out? I needed to be inside an emergency room or ICU.

But I had wanted to die, right? *Maybe, I thought, I could just go curl up in Mike's bath tub and let nature take its course. I'd bleed to death eventually. Mission accomplished. Sorry about the mess,*

brother, but understand I had to do this. *That's what I was thinking, at least. He'd get it. He wouldn't hold it against me.* Only thing was I didn't want him to have to clean up my mess . . . what an asshole I'd be just leaving all my blood and tissue all over his small living room. I should have done the job in his bathroom, where cleaning up such a gory mess would have been a whole lot easier. *Maybe, too, I should clean up after myself.* That was what I was thinking I should be doing. I stopped myself and went back and forth on whether or not to call for an ambulance. Did I want to live or die?

I put my hand back up to the wound. The blood was caked and dry—not at all fresh. What the hell? Wasn't I supposed to be bleeding? It was as if the wound had already clotted. I wasn't sure if that was good or bad. What was I going to do?

I thought of Mercedes and I wanted to die all over again. Of course I wanted to die, damn it all. I was in pain and suffering, with not only a concave hole to the side of my head, but a hole in my heart, as well. I tried to stand, but the pain and vertigo overtook me. I was able to get on all fours and crawled. It seemed like every single fiber of Mike's carpet was a mile deep. I kept going, telling myself I was going to rip the clot from the side of my head and let myself pour out into the tub once I got there. That was the plan, at least.

Each step hurt worse than the last. My head ached so badly, both inside and out. *How could I have messed up my own suicide? How could I have failed?* Then I thought: *Wait, why not just try again? Get the gun and press the trigger?* There was more than one bullet. When I turned around I couldn't even see the gun anywhere. All I saw was that nasty pile of my fleshy gristle right where I'd been sitting.

The Tom Petty CD was looping and it was on a song I wasn't familiar with. Didn't matter. I thought that, Jesus, he makes such depressing songs. They sound so light and airy, and then those lyrics are just murder. *Damn. Maybe if I'd been listening to some Guns N' Roses I wouldn't have tried to kill myself. Maybe if there was something angry instead of sad on the CD player . . .*

I made it past Mike's small kitchen. Despite the clot, I found I was leaking, but only a little bit. Meanwhile, I was staining the shit out of his rugs; Mike was going to have to explain this to the cops, and he'd probably move out from a place he'd worked hard to get. I felt like a selfish asshole, but still, what had to be done, had to be done, after all.

As I crawled, I thought of Mercedes. What was she going to think of me if she found out I tried to shoot myself? Probably very little, and I doubt she'd respect me for taking my own life. She didn't like weakness around her . . . it was like poison. She'd get pissed if I had the flu, saying she didn't want to have to 'take care' of anyone. Well, I'd taken care of myself, all right. Now I'd really done it.

Finally, I made it to the bathroom and forced myself forward through my agonizing pain. The cool, hard tile of the bathroom floor was different than the rug, and I had a harder time pulling myself along, but I did. I made it up to the bathtub and realized I was going to have to lug myself up and over if I intended on sitting inside. How the hell was I going to manage that? I had hardly any energy left, and I was fading fast.

I sucked in a breath and decided I'd just do it as quickly as I could. It would be the last time I'd have to really exert myself. Then I could lie inside the tub, fold my hands across my belly and bleed to death. Then all the misery would be over, wouldn't it? I couldn't wait.

Those moments were hard: I really had to fight the dizziness and pain to get myself inside the tub, but I managed it in the end. I was out of breath. I was hurting, totally spent, and ready to die. "Take that," I said to Mercedes, even though she wasn't there. "I'm stronger than you ever thought I could be." I put my right hand up to the side of my head and scratched at the clot. It wasn't as big as I'd remembered, which I found odd. The clot slipped right off my head. Fresh blood bled out and covered my fingertips. Then it dribbled out from the side of my head like a small stream. I passed my fingers through the blood and smiled. This was the end. This was peace. This was my eternity. I then passed out, cold.

My thoughts went black. I didn't dream. I just . . . went.

Squish. Squish.
I came to, slowly.
Squish. Squish.
My eyelids fluttered.

Oh, damn it, I thought. *Please tell me this is heaven or hell or somewhere other than Mike's bathroom. I'm supposed to be dead.*

Squish. Squish.

I looked over to where the sound was coming from and spotted another large piece of flesh right in the doorway of the bathroom. I hadn't remembered dropping any pieces of myself off. Looking down, I saw the brick-colored clot still on my lap.

My neck was stiff, but I managed to turn my head to the doorway again.

The thing moved. One side shrugged upward. Then it blinked. Was this the thing that had come from my head when I'd shot myself? Was this it? How was it moving and living?

I thought, *this is why you've always had migraines your whole life. You know, the ones that none of the strongest painkillers or head massages could fix? This is the reason. There was something in there with you . . . something growing . . . something different, and yet, the same.* A piece of me, that came from me, that had been cut free, was walking toward me.

This can't really be happening. You're dead and this is purgatory and you're just making all this up. You're not really here. Maybe you're in the ER now. Yeah. Mike found you and you're in the ER and you're just tripping on all the meds they've pumped you up with. It's got to be something like that, it's just got to be! None of this can be happening.

Then the thing moved forward and I could see its three chubby legs on each side. I was afraid, but then I thought: *This is me. This thing came from my head! How absurd! How insane! How utterly ridiculous!* Then it all clicked with me and I knew why I was seeing what I was seeing.

Dummy. You've blown out a chunk of your head. Of course you're having strange thoughts. Probably hit your optic nerve. You've probably triggered all sorts of weird memories that are now sloshing together and making you see this . . . thing, which, incidentally, is moving closer and closer to you, and it's watching you, and blinking, and crawling, and. . . and. . . and. . .

I put my hand to my head and found that there was no longer a chunk missing. It was sore and raw, like I'd skinned myself, but there was no hole. I'd expected to put my hand up there and feel the soft tissue of my brain, with little pieces of skull, like when you roll a boiled egg over your hand and you can feel the bits of shell left on top of the membrane. I didn't feel any such thing. Instead, it just felt like I'd taken a small hit. It was raw and sensitive, for sure, but that was it. How could it be? I'd pointed the barrel right at my head? Did it slip when I pulled the trigger? That had to be the reason.

The thing came closer, and it made a buzzing sound. It was calling to me. "Zzz."

My right eye was nearly swollen shut, which made sense. I'd seen boxers who'd gotten hit in the head the wrong way get their eyes swollen just like mine. My whole body was tingling, like it'd all gone to sleep. There was a throbbing going on inside my head, but it was better than it had been before. What the hell? I hadn't taken any painkillers. I looked around the tub and didn't see the bathtub full with blood as I had hoped. Jesus. I'd even fucked up killing myself. No wonder Mercedes was tired of me.

"Zzz."

It came closer, eyeing me, throbbing along on its little triplicate legs. When it got close, for some reason I felt compelled to put out my hand, palms facing the sky. It scurried faster, jumped onto my hand. It was lighter than I thought it would be. Then it ran the length of my arm until its face was nearly at my own. Not knowing what to do, I smiled. Just as I did, the thing clutched my upper arm. I felt six needle-like things poke into my arm, immediately injecting me with a warm fluid of some kind. I reached for the thing with my left hand, but halfway there, my arm just plopped down uselessly. The thing had injected me with something extremely powerful.

I felt an electric, spinning sensation run through me, almost as if I'd gotten the flu. Then the feeling numbed me. Last, it hit my brain and I'd found true love. I shut my eyes and opened my mouth. Every drink of alcohol, every illegal drug, every prescription mood altering pill could not compare at how instantly and fully I was transported into euphoria. I could sense everything. The tips of my toes felt amazing. My throat seemed clear. Even the wound at the side of my head felt distant and no longer hurt. You know what else didn't hurt? My feelings.

As I pictured Mercedes, I smiled. Who cared? Big deal. So what? There was a life before her and there would be a life after her, and it would be good. Those were the words that circled my brain.

It will be good. I will be fine so long as I have this thing...
this *thing* . . . this beautiful and wonderful thing that just happened to
appear after I tried shooting myself in the head.

My right eye didn't hurt, but it had swollen. I could
barely see out of it. The euphoria was so pleasant I had to shut
my eyes . . . close them . . . take it all in. I looked one last time at
the thing perched on my upper arm, smiled, and fell into bliss.

"Zzz." I heard its noise.

"I need to name you," I said to it as I drowsed. For some
reason I thought of Zyzzyx Road out on the trip to Las Vegas . . .
it always intrigued me . . . all those Xs and Ys in a name . . . and
I thought calling the little creature Xyx felt right.

"Goodnight, Xyx," I said.

It wasn't sleep that followed, but a kind of waking, sloppy
hallucination. First everything was green, like I was underwater
at the beach back on the east coast, in the sound. I tasted salt in
my mouth, too. That made way to a strong cinnamon flavor,
which was much more pleasant. Those only lasted for a few
brief moments. Soon I felt my mouth fill with a kind of metallic,
off-centered taste. My tongue went dry. I tried to open my eyes,
but couldn't. Then I tried to move, and found I could barely
move my limbs. Maybe Xyx was paralyzing me as though I
were a spider in its web. Maybe this was just the beginning and
it would harvest from me and eat from me until it exhausted
me and I died. Then again, Xyx had come from me. Xyx was my
baby, after all. It was helping me by injecting me and helping
me to ease my pain . . . both inside and out. Somehow I sensed it
knew what it was doing and why it was doing it. I had tried my
desperate act because I wanted to escape the overwhelming hell
I was feeling inside. It had worked, although not in the way I'd
thought it would. Xyx took all those horrendous feelings away.

What the hell was this thing? This Xyx? Had it always
lived inside of me? Had any of this truly and seriously happened
to me? It didn't make much sense, and I still felt that maybe I
was tripping out . . . and that maybe this was a fever dream
and I was really five miles away at Saint Joseph's Hospital
dreaming all of this. Despite my best efforts to stave it off, I
blacked everything out once again.

When I awoke I felt better. The darkness and the sadness that had so encompassed me was no longer present. I put my hand to my head to see if, indeed, there were still a wound. The area was sore and rough, but nothing at all like it had been. Xyx's healing juices had worked wonders. My body was stiff from sleeping in the tub and everything felt like pins and needles.

That was okay. My strength had returned. Everything was going to be all right. I just knew it. Then I thought about Mercedes. I really wanted to see her again. . . and not that I thought there was any chance of us finding one another again, but because I wanted her to see what she'd lost.

I got out of the tub and stood up. For sure, I was dizzy. I made my way over to the mirror and did a double take. The entire area where I'd shot myself in the head lacked any kind of pigment. It was pure white. What was I to do? How had that happened? I wasn't sure, but I did feel it once more and knew what it reminded me of: baby skin. I'd already healed.

Of course, I had to go to the bathroom, and did so. I finished up and walked out to Mike's living room. I wondered where Xyx would be.

At first I didn't see Xyx. That's because Xyx was taking up an entire corner of Mike's living room. He'd grown while I'd slept. He was taller than me, and he looked down at me from the ceiling. His eyes were warm and he blinked three times. Xyx looked like a giant moth, with each of his six arms crossed over one another in front of his body.

I smiled.

"We need to go somewhere," I said. "You up for a drive?"

With that Xyx folded down toward the ground and hobbled over toward me. He left behind a crispy shell. He'd molted. What remained was much smaller than his husk. In fact, as he moved toward me he seemed to lose a back section of his body, leaving only a cat-sized creature behind. That was all fine by me. He'd be easier to smuggle into my car.

All That Withers

As I drove Xyx toward Mercedes's North Hollywood apartment, I put a hand on his head. He was riding up front with me, on the passenger's seat. We got there a lot earlier than I'd thought and I'd parked the car out front. Mercedes had the locks changed on the place, but I knew she always left the back window open and I'd likely be able to push it up and get inside. I got out of the car, went to the passenger's side, put Xyx under my arm, and made my way through the metal gates, past the courtyard, and toward the back patios of the apartment buildings.

Once we were in back, I could tell Mercedes was not home: her minivan was not in its usual spot. I'd have plenty of time to get inside the apartment. I made my way up to the second story via her back steps and went to the rear window. It was wide open. I'd only need to undo two small latches that kept the screen in place. Once I did, I was able to remove the screen, bend down, place a leg inside, and slip into her apartment. I'd always warned her that she'd made it too easy for someone to infiltrate her ghetto house. She was careless. What did it matter? She never listened to me . . . called me a nag. Now she'd pay for it.

I was high. Xyx's potion gave me strength. I didn't care that I was now inside the place I'd been banished from. I didn't care that so much of my life still resided inside that apartment . . . my television . . . my movies . . . my computer . . . my artwork on the walls . . . none of it mattered. I found Xyx and Xyx made everything better. I wondered, as I stood inside my old home, how much longer Xyx's drug was going to work on me. What would it be like when I wasn't high? What would it be like to fall back into reality? I wasn't sure. Maybe I never would be able to go back to reality. What if the potion Xyx had injected me with had changed me permanently? Well, one could only hope.

I walked with Xyx into the living room and put him gently on the couch. I unwrapped him from his towel. "Do for her what you did for me," I said. "Show her when she comes."

I smiled.

Xyx wiggled on the couch. Then he jerked back and forth. His arms each shot outward, and were much longer than

I'd thought they would be. Each seemed five feet long as they unwrapped and unfolded. Once his legs were all the way out, they searched the couch, and then, the walls. Xyx pulled himself up and made his way to the far corner of the living room, near the windows. His legs stretched out as he attached himself to the walls of Mercedes's apartment. It reminded me of a giant, toxic kudzu. His arms stretched across the white ceiling. At their tips, small claws pointed downward. They glistened as though they were somehow salivating . . . maybe they knew what they were waiting for.

Xyx's body stretched out, too. He was leaner and I made eye contact with him.

"Yes," I said to Xyx. "She'll be home soon." I looked up at my monstrous creation . . . my horrific kin . . . and nodded. "Home . . . with . . . us."

SUNSET BEACH

Clive narrowed it down between an ice cream sandwich and a sherbet pop. "C'mon," his cousin Ray said. "You know you always get the ice cream sandwich. Why do you even waste our time?"

Ray was right, of course, and Clive happily took his selection from the vendor. The ice cream truck signaled the end of their day at the beach—his mother only gave him enough, and only allowed—a single treat. Supper would follow soon and she didn't want them to ruin their appetites.

Summer was Clive's favorite time of year. There was no school. People at the beach were happy. Kids weren't at school and parents weren't at work. It was perfect. His time was his own. He had so many memories of Sunset Beach, but his favorite was of his father pushing him on the swings. When he was on the beach, he often imagined his father was inside the sun, its warmth his smile shining down.

A ghastly smell like a fishing yard filled the area. From beneath the sand, long horizontal dark gray shafts broke through, rising as tall as beach umbrellas. One twitched.

"What the hell . . . ?" Clive looked at the things in horror. "Was there an earthquake or something?"

"They look like a bunch of giant sea snakes," said Ray. He cupped his mouth. "Smells worse than the dump. This is insane!"

The boys scanned the beach. Others stood near the shafts as if they were trying to figure out what they were, too. Many more regarded the oddities from the safety of their blankets or towels.

"They go right into the water." Clive pointed at the tideline.

A teenage boy in red trunks stood a few feet away. Clive tapped his shoulder and the teenager turned his head. "Where'd they come from? What are they? They're all around us."

Before the teenager could say anything, a girl holding a volleyball piped in. "They just came right out of the water, too," she said. "They slithered up like snakes."

A group of lifeguards hurried past.

"I don't know." Ray nodded. "What are these things?"

"We should get out of here before it gets too late," Clive said. People on the other side ran from the beach.

The ground shook and an incredibly loud snapping sound made them cover their ears. From their left the beach rose in the air, creating a wall of sand as high as two lifeguard stands. The sand wall stretched as far as they could see; its ends curved toward the water.

"We're trapped." Clive looked everywhere for an escape route, but couldn't see one. "We're all going to die. Is this the terrorists?" He had trouble catching his breath.

"Got to find a way to get out of here or we are going to die. No if's and's or but's about it," Ray said. "Got it?"

"Understood."

They went to the far side and searched for a gap. There was none. The beach crowd rushed about, to and fro, their faces twisted into pained expressions, frightened and confused. They all seemed to be wearing the same thought: How can this be happening? This can't be real. There's got to be a way to get out of here and be safe somehow. Somewhere. Some way.

People lucky enough to be on the other side of the sand walls fled.

There was no way for the boys to escape, though. Not that either Clive or Ray could see.

Large round clear balls rose from the water like massive alien eggs. There were several more visible over the large sandbar. Curled inside, black creatures with twitching exoskeletons. A scene was reflected on the surface of the balls—people on the other side of the sand wall ran. Clive wished he were with them instead of being trapped.

"What are those things? Monsters?" Clive's hands were shaking. He couldn't stop them. There was just no way what he was seeing was real. It had to be some elaborate joke. If only his father were there. Dad would know what to do—he'd know how to get them out of there.

Ray threw up his hands. "Dig!" he said. "We need to bury ourselves in the sand so that they can't see us."

Clive felt frightened. "I don't know."

"What's not to know? It's life or death. Do you have any other ideas? Do you have a plan?"

"No," Clive said. "I don't."

"Then dig."

The boys dropped to their knees and scooped up handfuls of sand.

A low-pitched cry filled the beach. Clive and Ray looked up. "What's that?" Clive said.

"Those things," Ray said. "We have to be fast."

Clive looked down at his small pile. "I don't know if mine's going to be ready in time," he said.

"You're smaller than me," Ray said. "Just keep going."

He did.

There was a second wretched sound, which made Clive cover his ears and grit his teeth. "God!"

Ray grabbed his wrists and shook him. "You have to keep digging. You have to hide or you're going to die. Do you understand?"

Nodding, Clive turned back to the small hole in front of him and dug.

Screams.

To their right, closer to the water, the clear round things had made it to the sand wall's crest. Two broke through the tops of their casings. Each released long, dark tentacle-shaped arms that drooped and slithered against the ground, leaving dark, oily streaks. They stood a head taller than the tallest person on the beach. Several eyes scanned their surroundings while fish-like mouths opened and closed.

"This is not good," Clive said. "Why can't Dad be here?"

"Dig!"

"What do you think I'm trying to do?"

The things were up and over the sand wall. Clive spotted one of their split feet squish an ice cream sandwich into the sand; close enough he made out the strawberry, vanilla and chocolate colors.

Ray said, "I'm done," and Clive looked over to see his cousin stretched out in the hole and covering himself with sand. Not deep enough to fully submerge his body, Ray looked like a mound. Clive prayed it'd be enough.

Sliding into his own hole, Clive pulled sand over and across his body. His heart beat faster than he'd thought possible.

A girl screamed and Clive craned his head backward, looking upside down at the scene. One of the things wrapped an arm around her torso while another cupped the top of her head. It squeezed and her forehead split. The thing lifted the top of her head off and tossed it down; sand stuck to the blood streaked hair. He looked back to where the rest of her stood with the thing. Its arm stirred inside her head, turning what was inside into soup. Some dripped over the sides and splattered on her shoulders. Her eyes were shut, thankfully, but her mouth was frozen in a painful grimace. Clive couldn't believe what he was witnessing.

Several more creatures raced over the sand wall and latched onto people. Clive hurried in pulling sand over himself. He had most of his body buried, while his head stuck out. *They'll see my head*, he thought. *They'll find me and kill me.*

Although his face was still more or less exposed, the rest of his body was completely covered. He craned his head up a bit and found Ray had very nearly disguised himself, too.

People screamed. Their cries made Clive wince. He wanted to cover his ears, but he was too scared to move his arms. He swore he could feel the things' heavy footfalls shaking the sand close by. Not wanting to risk discovery, he remained as still as possible.

He shut his eyes but still felt the sunshine baking across his face. Red splotches filled his eyelids.

This is the worst. I hope I get out of this alive. And Ray. . .

A shadow crossed over him. He couldn't believe it. The shadow stopped. He smelled something above him like a cross between dead fish and burning plastic. Clive knew it was one of the creatures. It looked at him, trying to figure out if he was alive or dead.

Hold your breath! Don't move. Don't breathe. Don't do anything. Just stay still. Think about Dad pushing you on the swings. Before the accident. See him smiling at you.

The smell became stronger. The shadow lingered.

Thank God Ray thought for us to cover up in sand. He might have just saved us.

A drop of fluid fell to his cheek. Was it the thing's drool? Sweat? Blood from one of the people it'd eaten? Some of their brain soup mix?

He heard a scream.

A familiar voice.

Ray.

They'd found him. Uncovered him.

No.

This isn't happening. Not real. Shut your eyes. It will all go away. It's a bad dream. Horrible dream. That's all. Not a big deal. It's like a movie. Or like when we played when we were kids. It's just more realistic, is all.

Ray hollered. Clive opened his eyes a bit and watched two things bear down where Ray had buried himself. Sand sprayed. Then blood. Then Ray whimpered. Green smoke billowed around the things. Ray was silent. The things stuck their long arms into his body and ate.

Clive kept still. His heart raced faster than he could keep track of and he really needed to pee, more than anything.

The stench from the thing was overwhelming, but he forgot about it when he heard Ray yell again. He'd heard Ray scream a thousand times, but it was always while they were playing and having fun, never while there was something serious happening. And there was most definitely, positively something serious going on.

Ray hollered and Clive wished he could take his hands and shield his ears from the noise but couldn't. The things would pounce on him if he made the slightest move.

The ground lifted. The area closed off from the sand walls rose upward, turning into a giant funnel of sand. Clive's stomach flittered. He tasted bile.

As he pushed himself up and out from his hiding place, Clive's limbs flailed automatically. People gathered near the middle of the giant funnel. The creatures each stirred their tentacles inside uncapped heads. Bright blood splashed into the sand, turning pink as it mixed in. Everyone else looked like giant dolls as they tried to keep their balance.

The funnel moved quickly to the right and Clive fell, landing between two dead people. The funnel jerked left and he fell onto his back. What was moving them?

Clive couldn't see anything but sky over the edges of the sand funnel. His belly felt like something dropped inside.

A woman with short dark hair graying at the temples locked eyes with him. She made to open her mouth, but as soon as she did, her eyelids closed. The top of her head came off like an upside down bowl shoved from a table. Clear fluid leaked out and poured over her face. Dark blood followed. A tentacle-arm stirred inside the cavity, its frilled, finned edges pulsing and sucking as it fed.

The funnel pitched like a giant carnival ride. Rolling onto his front, Clive put his arms up to break his fall. His forearms landed on a fresh, warm bloodstain. He pushed himself up and dropped backward. Strips of blood-soaked sand stuck to his forearms.

Those still alive mixed with the dead. Everyone flitted back and forth. He smelled the sand as it was shuffled around; its texture smooth on his fingertips. The indifferent sun beat down, warming Clive's face. He tried to think that if he just shut his eyes it would still be just another day at the beach. But he knew better.

The creatures moved around the funnel easily, their gestures graceful, sure and practiced. They balanced themselves against the gravity like airline stewardesses during heavy turbulence.

One muscular young man punched a creature. Its head jerked back as an unearthly howl pierced everyone's ears. The hero kept his fists high, but another creature slithered behind him, delivering a fatal slice to his crown. The top of his head flew down toward the sand like a Frisbee. His eyes were wide, shocked, and wet. Two tentacles stirred his pale brain into chunky pink stew.

Clive ran his fingers through the sand trying to gain a hold. One of the creatures hurried toward Clive. He thought about what he should do. The things surrounded him on both sides. He peered over the edge of the sand funnel and saw a massive gray eye watching him. It had a massive round face, like that of an octopus. Clive shivered. How could such a thing be?

He dodged the smaller creature's probing tentacles while the large eye followed him. He heard a rumbling sound coming from the middle of the funnel. The sand began to move around. Those who remained made a collective moan. The thing ran toward him again and nearly got its tentacles on him. He was grateful he was thin and fast and young because it didn't catch him.

Bodies flopped around him. They looked like rag dolls inside a washing machine. The sand whipped around and stuck to Clive's face. The funnel spun. The dead bodies were the first to go down into the mouth. They made swimming motions with their arms, unable to grasp anything. Clive saw rows upon rows of triangular teeth coated with saliva and sand.

Those not sucked into the thing's mouth tried to gain traction in the spinning sand. Clive did the same. He felt as though he had no breath left.

Overhead, he saw the giant eye squinting as it tracked him.

He looked back again and spotted two people fall into the vortex's opening. They both screamed, their mouths open, their limbs flailing. Clive couldn't believe what he was seeing—how could this be real? How could a beautiful summer afternoon turn into this?

How was he going to survive? He didn't know.

Three more dead bodies fell into the vortex. He watched the mouth close in on them, the teeth chewing them. One was bit in half. Another lost their lower section to the massive rows of timeworn teeth. Clive turned away. He couldn't stand watching any more. The smaller creature things kept busy pushing bodies into the mouth.

Clive had somehow found a way to both escape their notice, and hold on. He stuck his arms into the sand up to his elbow's, which held him away from the mouth. He looked for the creatures and for Ray, but Ray's body was nowhere to be found. The things were all over. He felt sick to his stomach while watching people get devoured. They didn't deserve to die like this. They had been having fun at the beach, just like he and Ray. What was this horrible thing, these horrible creatures that had invaded Sunset Beach? He didn't know, but he did realize he needed to get out of there as soon as possible. There's got to be a way. Think clearly. He couldn't let his emotions rule his actions. He knew he had to be logical about his next move. If he failed to do so, Clive realized he wouldn't survive.

And then the entire funnel turned sideways. Most of the dead bodies had already been consumed. Survivors scratched at the sand, trying to get a grip. Some fell from the top and dropped to the bottom of the vortex-like funnel, spinning inside the mouth of the gigantic creature. Clive pushed his body as close to the sand as he could. He felt heavy bodies fall on top of him. It felt like he was at the bottom of a dogpile. Hands grasped at him, threatening to pull him free from his position.

With the mouth tilted, he looked out and saw the ocean in front of him. The creature grew, rising as tall as the biggest building in town. Its smooth dark body stretched all the way across the beach and into the ocean. It looked like a giant gray whale with arms several city blocks long. Fins stretched out onto the sand of the beach. There were no other people left on the beach.

Clive imagined anyone who might have been lucky enough to escape being trapped by the funnel had likely fled to their cars. He had not been so lucky.

Looking down at the beach below, he realized he was floating seven stories high. He thought about jumping out anyway. He'd probably die from the impact, but it would be better and more dignified than getting eaten.

The monster moved its arms violently right to left. It was done with its meal. The top circumference of the funnel started to close. A God-awful smell encompassed everyone inside the funnel. The monster was digesting what it had eaten. It worked at closing its mouth around the rest of its meal. The monster was shaking them too fast. There was little they could do. Clive was lucky that he was near the edge of the mouth. He pulled his hand out from the sand as quickly as he could. He would have to take a chance and jump for it otherwise he would be swallowed inside the monster's orifice.

Screams became pleas. Pleas became moans, and moans were silenced, as the remaining people were sucked inside the creature's mouth. Clive pushed his way forward, his body aching, as every muscle protested his wishes to move forward. He had to live—he had to survive. He had too much to do with his life to die so young, and to die in such a way.

He pushed himself forward and looked over the lip of the vortex. He couldn't tell how high up he was. *It's now or never. Don't think about it. Just do it. There's no other way. Don't tense up. That's how you'll break bones. Don't you remember what they told you when you're getting your driver's license? That drunk drivers never got as hurt as the people they hit because they were loose? That has to be the way to do it.* And so he did.

Clive jumped out into the air, the vortex spinning behind him. He felt the air move behind him; the creature was trying to reclaim him. It had been swinging so quickly back-and-forth that it hadn't immediately realized he'd escaped.

He was not up as far as he'd thought. He hit the sand in a blink. Clive imagined he was higher than he'd been.

The wind was knocked out of him. For a moment, Clive couldn't move. Clive wondered if he'd broken anything on the way down. Had he managed to do himself in? But he was able to move his limbs and make his way to his feet. He was facing the ocean, so he had to find a way around the creature. He looked up and saw it towering above him. But the creature hadn't yet spotted him.

Good. I've got a running chance. I might make it to the pier. Or maybe I can get to the parking lot. There's a few gaps. Maybe there he'd find somebody there with a car that can get us out of here. He heard a sound unlike any he'd ever heard or imagined in his life. The entire beach shook from the noise. The creature's voice was unimaginably loud, with both low and high pitches drowned out any other sound, singing its otherworldly harmony.

Running with all he had, Clive took a chance and went for the parking lot. His chest felt like it was going to implode. His throat hurt and he tasted sand and salt water. His eyes never felt drier. He crossed the sand and made it to the grass, where, a few yards away, there were swing sets, slides, and seesaws. Clive realized he lost his sandals along the way. When his bare feet landed on the cement sidewalk, it hurt. He kept running anyway. He heard screaming behind him. The earth shook under his feet. Clive nearly lost his balance, but he managed to stay up right. He didn't know how far the monster could reach to grab him. He pictured it stretching to snag him once more, which motivated him to run as fast as possible. He didn't know if the creature needed to be in the water, or if it could survive on land for long. He didn't want to be the one to find out the hard way. He rushed toward the playground in front of him. He ran past the toys and then toward the building with the changing rooms and bathrooms. He did not look back, even as the entity screamed and shook the ground.

When will it stop? Please, God, get me out of here. He ran with all his might, his feet making rapid slapping sounds against the ground.

What about those things? The ones with the arms that were cutting people's heads open, and then eating their brains? Where did they go? I didn't see them disappear? Could they be chasing me?

Clive didn't see them anywhere. They had vanished almost at the same time the creature had been closing its mouth.

He faintly remembered seeing them slipping inside the sand, burying themselves. But what if that's true? Was his mind just playing tricks on him? Could they be lurking somewhere, waiting to snatch him, unsnap his head, and make a milkshake out of his brains? He looked quickly left to right but saw no sign of them. Maybe he'd gotten lucky. Extremely lucky.

When he made it to the parking lot he scoped the area. There didn't seem to be anybody anywhere near him. The sun was shining, and he was covered in sweat and sand. He didn't hear the creature behind him. Clive ran to the rear of the building that housed the bathrooms and changing rooms. He faced the parking lot. He felt a whole lot better with the building between him and the creature.

From his right, he spotted a gray Toyota Camry driving into the beach parking lot. It looked like one of his schoolteacher's cars: Ms. Wilson. She was the only one he knew in town who drove a hybrid. He wanted to warn her to leave, but he also wanted her to save him. He took several steps back to the edge of the building and looked back to the beach.

There was no sign of the creature. Save for a lumpy strange mass slithering back into the ocean. The beach itself looked untouched.

Clive hurried out into the road to meet the gray Toyota. The car stopped; he waved his arms. He wondered how he looked.

The car door opened. It wasn't Ms. Wilson, but Mr. Wilson, who exited the car.

"We've got to get out of here," Clive said.

Mr. Wilson asked: "What's wrong? What happened to you? Is everything alright?"

Clive said, "No. Nothing is alright. Something terrible has happened."

"What?"

"I can't explain," Clive said. "It's worse than anything I can ever say." Clive looked up and saw seagulls landing on the telephone poles. There were other cars beginning to pull into the parking lot. He wondered what people would do when they found out so many people were missing. How would anyone ever believe him? They'd think he'd gone crazy. If only Dad wasn't in that accident. He'd still be here to help me. He'd know what to say.

How would he be able to tell anybody what he'd just lived through? Even if they scoured the beach, he knew there'd be no evidence left of what had happened. Everyone would be reported missing, and there'd be no trace of anyone left behind.

Then he thought about it happening again. How would he be able to stop it? He pictured the dozens of people that he watched die in front of him only moments earlier, and he felt sick. He thought about his cousin, Ray. What would he tell his mother? His aunt? He'd have to tell the police something, wouldn't he? They'd wonder how he'd gone to a crowded beach and somehow been the only one there afterward. He wondered so many things. Clive fell to his knees, and then dropped into a sitting position. He rocked back and forth, and Mr. Wilson crouched down to comfort him. Clive shut his eyes and lifted his chin to the sun. How could the sun still shine? How could the world ever be normal again? How would he ever be able to live with what he'd seen? How would he be able to warn people about the thing lurking just offshore at Sunset Beach? The thing, he knew, that would one day return, larger, stronger, hungrier, and with no one ready for its wrath.

Summer would never be safe again.

I KNOW THIS WORLD

MAGIC

Lights blind me as I fall into endless abyss. The Gods work their magic on me. Chugga chugga chugga chugga: the sound of someone playing damped chords on a wicked distorted guitar surrounds me. This fourth dimension caresses my skin, bathes me and moves me down toward some bright and liquid place. I can't imagine what's next.

There's no pain anymore. All the discomfort and all the humiliations near the end of my life have vanished, the memories little drops of fluid archived inside my brain. You can't remember pain. You know that, right? Once it's gone, you can't really close your eyes and experience it again. Uh-uh. You'll be free and high and mighty and brand new. That's where I'm going: to be remade.

I hear echoes from my recent past hitting me like falling rain.

Do the right thing. Come on. Get off those things—those pills. They'll kill you. You've got God now and that's all you're going to need.

God? Is that what this is?

Big hands caressed my head and held me up. At first I shut my eyes so I could look inside. A fever stormed through and formed several painful pockets of hot fluid spread within my body. I felt the furthest from sexy. All systems "no." The dark cloud caught me and shook me like a cat that snared a big rat. My bones snapped and my veins stretched and cracked. It took its time with me, eating at me slowly until I was borderline insane. Borderline? Well: probably way over the line if it were anyone but me judging.

SPECIAL SAUCE

I taste the chemicals they pumped inside me, a lot like those blue popsicles I used to eat as a kid, but as if they were infused with liquid metal, too. Nothing can get rid of it. The one-of-a-kind medicine supposedly can get in there and crush the cells that aren't cooperating. But I feel like a piece of paper someone just dropped in the ocean. Only a matter of time until I'm totally saturated with salt water . . . my form will last for a little while once that happens . . . I'll be recognizable and someone could read what's written on me, but only until a wave comes . . . a wave big enough to overtake me and push me under, my delicate form turning to pieces, turning to strands, turning to fibers, turning to nothingness, assimilating and dissolving into the ocean.

Am I nothing now?

I am something.

More.

Can you hear what I'm saying? Feel the reverberations of my words broadcasting straight into your brain? Feel their weight and believe what they say. It's all I have left: this hope that somehow, some way, someone is catching these thought-casts.

Crinkling sounds and tingling feelings fill my body as my being remolds.

COSMOS

Before I fell I hovered in a starless heaven. Long, dark beings made from otherworld flesh lumbered, their giant eyes taking me in. They don't speak but I hear them inside. They tell me I am the punisher, the bringer of light that brings darkness, the one to deliver the unchosen from their flawed physical husks into this ethosphere, where they will be remade, reshaped, and beta-tested before being uploaded into some new fashion.

Our world failed. Plain and simple. The Gods sent messengers: A box that revealed and took those who weren't true; a boy who devoured brains, and another who ate the flesh, appeasing his lover. A young man whose left hand pulsed with pain and brought death to naïve masses. No one made the connection, but these were supposed to be a warning. Now it is much too late. The Dark Ones consumed our souls, their bellies pregnant.

Soon we will be born new.

OF UNKNOWN ORIGIN

No one knew how to treat my disease. Not really. They had their chemicals and their diets and their best intentions. It certainly looked like something they'd seen before, but they didn't realize that what they were dealing with was not from here. Shapeless organic black consumed me. So cruel. It left my eyes, ears, and mouth, but attacked my insides. Food felt impossible. Breathing hurt. Was this payback for the destruction I'd brought? Was the power in the palm of my hand so great it spilled over and infected me, like I'd been poisoned by some galactic nuclear runoff? Was there no cure? Even as the world burned and broke around them, the teams kept to their oaths and tried to save me. If only they knew it was pointless. Maybe it kept them from facing what was happening outside the walls of their hospital. Maybe it kept them from madness.

"Charles?" They'd call my name, expecting me to return, expecting me to respond to yesterday's title. I am nameless now, as I am shapeless.

The last thing I looked at was my hands. They'd created so much in such a short amount of time. For destruction and death is creating . . . allowing something new to be formed in its place from the broken down parts. Picture a cow in a slaughterhouse, it's final moments as it's brought to the automated knife. Its throat is cut, but the animal is too strong. Blood sprays forth in two jets, however, the wound is not fatal. It is led to a small black staging area, its floor layered in dry spongy gore. The beast cries and protests as a man slices its throat. This time the cow bleeds out, looking at the bottom of the man's jeans and worn down work boots as it dies. It does not immediately understand why it has been killed, but learns as its consciousness transitions from flesh to spirit. Its beautiful body will be deconstructed with blades, made into countless pieces. The parts will be cooked and ingested, digested, melted inside a vat of stomach acid. It will give life and energy before being expelled, its once gorgeous parts quickly reduced to filth, and then turning into dirt and soil from which new things will grow.

This last step is where I find myself. I've been expelled and am being reduced. From the dirt I will become, fresh things will be born.

Unimaginable pain overcomes every part of me. Numerous sounds and memories race through me. My life rewound and played back at random.

I am nothing.

Then I am everything once more.

Fresh water envelops me. Water? Could it be? Have I returned? I rise. My steps are unsure. Hot sun feels unreal. I reach the shore. My clothes are simple. My hair is long and fair. My left hand hurts and my palm itches. My hands are bigger and longer, as is the rest of me. I am like I was. I am different than I was. Taller. Stronger.

Buildings spread over the dunes. They seem made from sand and driftwood.

My feet touch the ground, but not as heavily as they once had.

I look upward and see a second moon.

As I approach the dunes the tendrils inch from my palm and lick the air for the first time.

I am not home.

I am home.

I know this world.

It will be mine.

FOREVER

You were right. There *is* more.

I found it hard to believe before arriving here, but there really are endless worlds of joy and rivers of love. Winds carry peaceful sounds of flowing water and laughter; light emanates from all you see. Flowers bloom. Everything one could want or need, and more than you might imagine. Voices whisper, telling me you're arriving soon, and that you'll need someone you love to help you through. That's me.

Our last day together was not frightening. We rode toward the town of Valhalla in upstate New York, and you and him held back your tears. Sweet fall air filled the long blue car. We passed more trees and lakes and hills than anywhere else we'd ever been together. You cared for me and brought me with you wherever you went since my tiny body fit in your hands. We lived all over the East Coast: New Jersey. Connecticut. Boston. You took me to New Orleans and Las Vegas and—my favorite place of all—California. Remember me jumping off that flat boat into the big lake with the tall sandy hills surrounding us? Getting back onto the boat proved too hard. He jumped in after me and lifted me back inside. I felt bad for scratching him, but that was the night we finally let him between us, so he probably thought it was worth it. That wasn't easy. Remember me sleeping between you and him on the bed? I always felt protective of you, because you protected me.

Here it is again, my turn being your guardian.

Don't be scared. You're going through a lot of pain right now. Blackness eats at your body. It hurts me to know you're hurting that way. Your loving soul doesn't deserve what's fallen on you. But like you always said: *We're not our bodies. We're what's inside.* It'll be over soon. Promise. You're going to feel your essence slipping away, then you'll feel, inside your gut, like you're on the longest and highest elevator ride of all time. We call it going on the *Lift*. Elevators always scared me so much, by the way. I don't miss those damn things. At all. Or airplane rides.

When you're riding the Lift, you'll remember lots of great moments. Most my memories are with you. The look on your face as you held me in the air the first night. The taste of the plastic seatbelt clicker in your new car. Apologies for that, but my teeth hurt so bad and there was nothing else for me to chew. Rain-soaked grass wet my paws when we lived on that busy street in California. Each smell at each house of our daily walk around the block plays inside my mind, and every inch we strolled is permanently imprinted on my brain. My memory rebuilt our walk here in *Forever*, and I have strolled it several times, but you're not here with me, so it's not complete. You will be soon. Can you smell the fountain close to where we lived in New Orleans? The warm concrete tickled my paws and the hot food always drove me crazy as it cooked underneath our little place on the second floor. Can you feel the cushy blankets when we stayed in the basement in New Jersey? The cold snow outside packed all the way up to my belly. Pure joy. It snows here, sometimes. You're going to love that.

You're probably surprised hearing me talk. It's true: We understood, and understand, everything. We're smarter than most people realize. All the fancy gadgets to talk and see the weather, but none can talk to us. Maybe that'll change with some future generation. Who knows? There are some who follow their instinct and *know*. You're one of them.

Your glories were my glories. The parties overflowed with people. The quiet times we watched the lighted picture box. Then the little boy came. Even though realizing my number one spot had to be relinquished, you have no idea the happiness that grew inside my heart. You deserved him and have been an amazing Mamma to him, as you were to me.

Sorry to say you won't see him again for a while. But we'll have lots of time together where you can discover Forever with me. Your pain will disappear. Your favorite places are here. Money doesn't matter. Only life. Yes, *life*. We go on. We build things here—places for souls to blossom. Our energy feeds the Big One. *God*. It's the most important work, yet, it doesn't feel like work. It's like when you're thirsty and you drink the best tasting water ever. That's how it seems. We gather and focus our thoughts on recreating someone's home from their childhood, their familiar streets, their favorite places, so when they arrive they are happy. We hear when they come, and we get little blips in our heads about them. When we gather together the blips collect together, too, and the places form between us. It's the neatest magic you've ever seen.

Of course, we cannot create people. That's forbidden.

Know, too, that your loved ones meet. They sense when

you approach the Lift. Those are amazing times and it's always exciting to bring people over. Most are terrified and can't believe it . . . Even the Believers.

When you come, you'll see. You're strong, and you'll adapt quickly.

Near the end of the Lift your world slips away and becomes *our* world. Your intuition changes. Your heart beats differently. Gravity lessens. Your body feels both bigger and smaller, because your flesh as you knew it fades, replaced and reborn from ageless cosmic luminescent matter. That's the best way to describe it. We look like our old selves, but we're not entirely physical in the ways we once were. It's weird to say, but we're better. We're not limited like before. No pain. No illness. No hunger. Just a state of restful being. Bliss.

I remember your hand on me, talking to me gently as the fire-medicine coursed through my body. Your man was there, too, keeping his feelings inside. That doctor's office floor faded from me, the edges blurring and darkening, your voice echoing heavily, until I smelled the distinctive pure air of Forever and pointed my nose toward where it came. My heart stopped beating. Pitch black surrounded me.

Was I scared?

Terrified, yes. This is it, life is over. I thought there would be nothing else and, within a few moments, that would be all: Goodbye, world. Goodbye.

I was wrong.

Only now does life begin. Our time before is only training for Forever. This, you must understand, is where things are truly realized.

You're coming now.

Please don't be scared; we're all here together to be with you. There're no tubes sticking out of you here, no pain or discomfort, no shame or sadness. It's okay to let go.

Good, just like that.

Feel your feet lighten, then your legs, then your belly, your heart, and your soul. You're being brought up toward the Lift. Someone's holding your hand as you slip away, his hot tears fall on your palm, as yours did mine during my last breaths. Smile for him, so he remembers when it's his turn. This moment . . . this *change* . . . will be okay, just like I smiled for you when I left. Your son knows your loss to him will be deep. The life and memories you gave him will never be forgotten and will shape the rest of his life: Showing him how to eat with a spoon. Leading him to walk. Your hugs. Your smile. Your laughter. Paddling down the river in a raft. Swimming with him in an Oregon lake. His successes. His losses. The passing of his father only a few years ago. You were there for him, his Momma, his joy, his inspiration . . . just like you were there for me. You will see him again, as you will soon see me.

Can you hear me? You've never heard this voice, but your heart will recognize the sound. Please come to my call, as I once followed yours.

You're so beautiful. Your heart beats through your skin and I hear the pleasant thump it makes. Your arms are outstretched and I'm running to your spirit. Look behind me and see those you've missed all come to greet you: Your mother. The father of your son holds flowers; he never stopped loving you. Your *Omi*, standing hands on her hips. Others I'm not familiar with. All have nothing but love to give.

Your arms feel the same as always: strong and tender. How I've missed you. We all have.

See? It's okay, isn't it?

Do you feel any pain now? Do you feel anything other than the fondness we all have for you? Isn't this wonderful? And this place you've made? The beach. We are bathed in golden light. It's where you go inside when you're sad, right? And now we're all together again here. And you're holding onto me so tight. And you're crying, and your tears are cool like a fall river. And you know me and you call out my name.

"Wolffie."

Welcome to Forever.

GAIA UNGAIA

The things that haunt us
Reappear
Reflecting Inside Our Eyes

We traipsed from the ocean and Brooke grasped my hand. My palms felt sticky inside hers as the salt water dried.

"This is the house where I grew up," she said. Her white tee-shirt clung to her, but she didn't seem self-conscious. She smiled. "I'm so glad you're able to see this house. It's a big part of who I am."

I couldn't help but imagine what growing up must have been like inside and around such a place. Long trees overhung the white house and its two-story frame. Curved, red wooden benches lined the side yards. She pulled me close and laughed.

Before we stepped inside, Brooke pointed to the sky.

"See those clouds?"

Bands of pink and red and blue stretched above us. It was as though someone painted them, capturing the most extraordinary light.

"I've never seen a storm so gorgeous," I said. "The clouds are moving in fast."

She nodded.

"I've been waiting a long time for this. You must be good luck."

We showered together and I barely glanced below her face. I shut my eyes two or three times and imagined what it'd be like if we were lovers. There'd be a time for us later, somewhere.

"Good to get all the ocean water off," I said. "I was feeling sticky."

Brooke soaped her face. "I don't mind the stickiness. I just don't want anyone to know where we've been."

"Really?"

"Sure," she said, washing her face. "Do you remember what month this is?"

"January."

"You've been living on the west coast too long. This is the east coast, where you're not supposed to be outside without wearing several layers. But there we were, in our bathing suits, swimming in the Atlantic just like it was August."

My temples throbbed with the first drizzles of rain.

"What's happening?" I asked.

We stood in her bedroom and dried. She'd put clean clothes out for both of us, laying them neatly across her bed.

"What are we going to see?" I asked.

"Something beyond ourselves. All the way through the world."

"The world?"

"Everything there is to see, we're going to see it."

We walked downstairs and there were small framed pictures at every step, but none had captured people. They all looked to be prints of paintings.

"Once I hit my late-twenties, everything changed," Brooke said. "Growing old is weird. At times, I feel like I'm still a teenager. It's like time stands still. Then I see myself in the mirror and have no idea who that person is. Everyone that was close to me years ago is now gone."

"Even your family?"

"They left all of this to me."

I wondered if they'd died. I tried to think of a way to find out more without sounding insensitive.

"Where are they?"

"They left."

At the bottom of the staircase, she turned and faced me and I smelled the peppermint from her shampoo.

"It's been up to me to take care of this house."

Behind her pretty round face, she hid something terrible. Maybe her folks had been killed, or there'd been some awful, unmentionable tragedy. Perhaps she kept the house exactly as they'd left it so she wouldn't forget them.

The living room centered around a large, fossilized tree stump. It'd been carved in such a way as to make it a chair. There were potted plants and flowers in vases everywhere. The far wall was painted edge-to-edge with a mural of people lingering in some woods. I pointed to it.

"What's that?"

"My mother was a painter."

"Was?"

"She stopped painting after we were born."

"That's too bad. It's great."

"You think so?"

"Absolutely."

There was a short table running alongside the wall closest to us. I recognized the white porcelain bowl where she'd put the seashells.

"We've been friends a really long time."

"We have," I said, nodding.

"I believed my memories and my gifts were locked away inside the rooms of this house. We tried to keep them safe, but the house becomes so empty at times. We all need other people, or else we disappear."

My heart beat steadily, as though sealed inside a small concrete tomb.

"I've only ever seen my parents when they're unearthed," she said. "Right now is going to be one of those times."

There was definitely a storm approaching. Ever since I was young, my sinuses ached whenever the barometer dropped. I suffered through allergy tests until the doctors figured out that the migraines were the result of atmospheric pressure changes. I tried to hold back a sneeze as my nose ran and my eyes watered. What I would have done for a serious painkiller . . . Instead, I worked my way through it—better than bowing out with a sack of ice over my eyes. I didn't want to miss whatever Brooke was about to unveil. I tried focusing on her, instead.

"Can you see it? The light's gotten dimmer. Things are going to change."

She had her thumbs on her sides, her head slightly cocked, and one hip jutted out a little, as if she were about to hitch a ride.

"The storm is coming," I said.

Our eyes met and she told me it was going to snow.

"Snow?"

"It's the middle of January, after all."

"It's too warm outside for it to snow."

A windy chill came through the door. Frosty air overtook the warm summer scents of sand and salt. The hairs in my nostrils froze stiff. Brooke seemed captivated with something outside the window as everything brightened.

I thought the sun had come out, but was wrong. Snow covered the sand. Several chunks of ice floated within the Atlantic.

"We're going to freeze," I said.

Brooke laughed.

"Don't worry. I'll make sure you're nice and warm. The house is prepared. Besides, we won't be here long."

The room turned colder; it was as though the whole place had been turned into the strongest of refrigerators. I crossed my arms.

"My mother made this," Brooke said, staring at the tree stump chair. Five roots stretched out and toward the floor, acting as legs. "Rings in the wood show you how old it was when it was made. A lot has changed since then. Sit. It's more comfortable than it looks."

"This isn't some kind of trap, though, right?"

"Gary, it's a chair. Don't worry about it. Trust me."

"I'm so cold. I don't know if I can even move."

"That will change before you know it."

"What's happening to the house, and outside?"

"We're making meaning, forcing the world around us to do what we want."

"You wanted it cold?"

"Yes."

"Why?"

"My father."

"I don't get it."

"He loves winter. It was his favorite time of year. He'll know that it's me."

"How do I play into this?"

"Energy, vibes: your desires. It will all become clear soon. Are you going to sit, or am I going to have to force you?"

I went to the chair and palmed the back. It'd been ingeniously carved, smoothed and rounded, and it was stained a dark rose color. The rings on the seat looked fresh, as if the tree were cut down only hours earlier, preserved perfectly. The illusion was remarkable.

"This thing's awfully amazing," I said. "So much detail."

"My mom did a good job. It's one of my favorite things in the world."

"Takes up a lot of room, though, doesn't it?"

"Sure does. That's a good thing, right?"

"You're probably on to something," I said. "I've been trying to make everything less cluttered in my apartment. It's so empty inside. There's hardly anything. Most of my books and pictures are digital. I have a small flat screen television and everything's wireless. My fridge is small. Even my bed."

"Why?"

"It gives me peace. I can focus on things. I grew up with a bunch of packrats. When I see piles, I start getting nervous."

"Some people find comfort being inside piles of things."

"It suffocates me."

"So, what do you think of my place, then?"

"There's a lot going on here," I said, looking around.

There seemed to be a tremendous amount of thought that'd gone into the placement of knickknacks and pictures and flowers.

"Feels like I'm in a really wonderful antique shop. Weird. I don't really feel all that cluttered in here, though. It all seems to work."

"Wonder why," Brooke said. "Many people feel smothered."

"This is different. Everything in here's spotless."

"You're right, you know. These are my family's things. I wanted them to be in perfect shape when they come."

I sat on the chair, which was much more comfortable than I'd imagined. The seat was flat, and yet, the perfect height and the perfect fit.

"Your family: they're coming tonight?"

Brooke smiled.

"You're dressed all in white, like a little girl going to a dinner."

"You, too," she said. "Only you're clothes are dark, like Daddy's."

A chill.

Was I wearing her father's clothes? Was he dead and had she dressed me up to look like him? Was this some sort of sick game? That would explain the lack of sexuality toward me. Was she turning me into her father?

The chair moved. I inched myself to the front of it.

"What the . . . ?"

It moved again, and again, as though the legs were stretching and wanting to shove me from its seat. When I stood, it stopped moving.

Brooke lowered her chin. Her eyes seemed to say: *Watch this.*

The cold air compressed inside of my chest and hurt my throat. My kneecaps shivered. I couldn't stop it from happening. Brooke was motionless, save for her eyes, which moved back and forth between the chair and me. The vanilla candle smells of the room were soon replaced with a lemony, fizzy-water aroma, not unlike a large vat of cold medicine.

"Are you okay?" she said.

"I think so. Ask me in a few minutes."

The sky opened, but not with brightness, or with sunlight, or with a flash; instead, everything darkened. Everything had become more visible, more hyper-real, as if the true characteristics of the world around us had been revealed. The reality I'd known — the way colors worked, the way my skin appeared — was only one small aspect of a bigger picture.

Brooke had peeled back some kind of ancient door.

"Are you still with me?"

Our eyes met in the new otherworld.

Brooke glowed. Barely visible beneath her skin, I could see her architecture: veins like little organic roadways, muscles like clouds, lungs like bodies of water, her brain like a cityscape at night exploding with millions of white bursts.

"You're here," she said.

"I am."

Through the window, the ocean waves unnaturally slowed.

Three shadowy figures approached from my peripheral and I startled. The room filled with a smell that reminded me very much like burnt popcorn.

One of the shadows reached out as they formed.

"Pop?" Brooke asked.

Her family: called from the beyond by their gifted daughter.

Shadows filled in as they gained color and substance, and before I knew it, the dark spots shrank completely away. There were areas that ultimately remained darkened, which wavered as her family stepped closer.

"It's us," Brooke's mother said. "Georgie's here, too, this time."

Brooke smiled to the slightly smaller figure behind them. Georgie hadn't formed as fully as his parents. His shape was quite different from theirs. Smaller and more squat, Georgie stepped toward his sister.

"Hello?" said a voice unlike any I'd ever heard.

"Hello." She went to him, putting a hand out.

His was not a hand that reached for her, but some sort of flattened appendage where a hand should be.

"B-Broooke," he said, as if he had three sets of vocal chords saying the same word, each with a different timbre and intonation.

"You are my brother," she said. "But you don't look like him anymore. What happened?"

Her father nodded and said, "Georgie's not doing so well lately. He hasn't believed in himself. We need you more than ever to come take care of him."

"This isn't the way things are supposed to happen," Brooke said. "We're going to have a nice visit and then go off somewhere new."

Her father looked to me, his eyes cutting right through mine.

"You've changed things by bringing something new to the equation."

"Peter's no bother," Brooke said. "He's one of the true ones."

When her father laughed, his head threw back a bit, and I could see through the dark spots inside his throat and through to the back of his neck, where his spine reached up and touched his skull; it shimmered and glistened with electric activity.

"Of course, he's no bother," her father said. "At least not to you."

"B-Brooke."

"This is not working for me," she said, throwing her arm down in defiance. "I can't even look at Georgie. You've let him turn on himself. He's gone disgusting. Aren't you supposed to be his parents and take care of him? How could you let him become this revolting?"

Her mother came forward. "Georgie looks fine. He's just sick."

Brooke bristled and said, "He's not fine at all. You've let him forget who he is and what he's capable of. You've let him turn into a creature from the deep, instead of a chosen soul. You should be ashamed of yourselves."

"He won't listen to us anymore," her father said. "We've tried everything, but he keeps calling for you over and over again. What are we supposed to do with him if he won't take our word for it?"

Brook turned her back to them. "I don't know. I don't want any part of this. I have to live my own life. I don't want to be chained to him just because he can't control his indulgences. It's not my fault he's lazy, and that you're lazy. It's your own fault. You need to come with us to help him. If you don't, he's going to die."

"We're already dead."

"No. We are alive. We stand together and we are alive."

Those were the words that stuck most in my head. How could these beings exist in such a form? How was Brooke channeling an alternate world where her missing parents visited? None of it made sense.

I recalled the many things we'd shared over the years: walks through the Boston Common during college, shows at the Globe Theater in Neville, awful relationships we'd both endured, crying on one another's shoulders. Never did we step forward with our relationship as lovers. Our friendship was something that neither of us wanted to forfeit. Of course, we were perfect for one another: Of absolute course. I knew I'd lose her friendship if we tried to progress, in the blink of an eye. What if it didn't work? What if we ended up hating one another? What if we found ourselves at odds, and at opposite sides of the spectrum? I'd never forgive myself.

We had gone forward; somewhere, somehow else, we had done just that.

Flashes of her kissing me sprinkled my thoughts: Brooke in her twenties, thirties, and then her forties. Each time she leaned in toward me, her eyes shut just a bit, ready to kiss my ever-nervous lips. The world changed around her. The backgrounds—all strangely familiar—flashed behind her as well. There was something unique about each one. Names popped into my head, flowing easily, as though they'd always been there and I'd somehow just unlocked them: Northvale,

Norwalk, Neville, Boston, New York City. Our first real date happened while she drove us into the city in her little red car, singing along in perfect pitch to every song on the radio. We stopped in the Village, where she tried on an amazing silver dress. Our lunch at a small sandwich shop. . .

She was not Brooke, but someone else. She was another name, another history, but she was the same woman.

Warmth spread over me. I saw our pets behind her in my mind: a black dog, a tan dog, a calico cat. I felt the heat for we had lived somewhere warm. Then the window behind her changed and held more details: the New England ocean side, train tracks, a stunning orange-red sunset. In a blink: back to the sands and warmth, back to the dry heat and desert.

I could sense everything, and it was all so familiar.

None of that life had I known before this moment.

I saw a boy with blond curls, laughing, pushing model trains. I saw a girl with strawberry blonde hair. I saw them older, more beautiful. I saw the boy leaning in to kiss me, because I was on a hospital bed and his eyes were wet, but he was still smiling. I saw Brooke behind him, not looking at me, not seeing me. And then everything faded.

I was back in her living room.

Where did it all lead?

"I'm sorry," Brooke said, "but I can't go with you to take care of him. I need to live for myself for a while longer, you know. I'm not ready to stop just yet."

Brooke sounded far beyond her years, sure of herself.

If it were me, I probably would have gone with them.

"You're my sister," Georgie cried. "You're supposed to be there for me."

"The best thing I can do is make you learn to dig yourself out on your own. I don't want you to be helpless."

"It's all his fault, I bet," he said, pointing at me, and his true face appeared. Dozens of large pots dotted his face, the round wedges under his eyes crusted with yellowish goo. "She'd rather be with him than with us."

There was nothing I could say. I could only hope he was right!

"I want to make my own world," Brooke said. "I want to do it on my own terms and in my own way. I don't want to be what you want me to be. I've got to find my own way."

"You've already done that," her mother said. "You never listened. You never agreed with any of our plans."

"Well, look how it turned out for you," Brooke said. "I wasn't right to follow the same darkness, the same negative energy, the same intent on hate that you did. I love you all, but there's nothing down that road but isolation and sickness. Just look at Georgie!"

"He's fine," her mother insisted.

"We've been through this already." Brooke shook her head. "Now there's nothing I can do at this point. You have to do it. So, I give you this gift, if you're ready. Come with me. Start over. I've found a way where we can do just that. We can start again and you will be with me, and Georgie will be all right, and we'll be fine, and you'll be here with me and Peter."

"I don't know if we can."

"All you have to do is say the word and it will happen. There is nothing you have to do other than to want something."

"Where did you learn how to do this?"

"I was born with it—my will, my strength, my foresight. The world is mine for changing and for making. The worlds beyond are ours for exploring."

"What will you have to give up?" her father said. "There is always a trade. There's always some terrible compromise."

Brooke's eyes filled; even with the strange luminescence, I could see her cry.

"I've already given up the one thing in this life that means the world to me."

Bluish tears rolled down her cheeks as she turned to me.

Again, in flashes, I saw what could have been between us—the things that should have been: our kisses, our lovemaking, our children, our long and wonderful future; gone in a flash, sacrificed so that she might rescue her family from their dark bind.

"Brooke," her father said, his voice shocked and saddened.

She wiped her tears and straightened.

"So there it all is," she said. Brooke looked at me, and I wanted to say so much, to tell her what I'd seen, but my thoughts would not let me open my mouth. How was I expected to do anything but stand there like an imbecile? She'd shown me every hope, dream, and fantasy I'd harbored, which she'd given up to them in hopes that they'd return.

Our world unearthed.

"You've given us your loss," her father said. "My beautiful, angel daughter . . . I'm sorry. How could I have known? We made mistakes. Things didn't go the way we wanted, things out of our control. We only wanted the best for you and Georgie."

"I know."

Georgie hobbled over and pointed his strange appendage at me. He squinted, and I recognized the similarities he'd shared with Brooke, the way his eyelids dropped. "I knew there was something with him! She's had a thing for him and he's the reason for all this nonsense. It's his fault!"

"He's what's going to get you out of this," Brooke said. "He's what I've sacrificed for you. If you'll take a step forward and admit what's happened, I can make all of this disappear."

"You're a witch," he said, his throat sounding scratchy, and his eyes were the ones that filled this time. "You're nothing but a manipulative tramp. You've never been on our side and now you come in here and you insult us."

"You're going to take him away from me," Brooke said.

"You said he's already been sacrificed. Make up your mind!"

"This will all go away if you say the word. If you open up, things will change, you will be free. The sacrifice—the trade—has already been made. If you deny me this, I will lose everything."

"This is why you called us, so you can have a boyfriend?"

"More than that," Brooke said. "In this life, I've given him up. I've lived alone, meager and unfulfilled, while you three have indulged. All you need to do is step forward, for me."

Her brother stepped back, his mouth moving a bit, but wordless for a moment.

"I don't want to forget again," he said. "I don't want to go through it again. It was too much! I like it here. Mom and Dad take care of me. We're fine. We're okay."

"We're not okay," her father said. "We're sick. We're so sick. We need to change this. We need to move forward. We can be brave."

"We'll forget all of this!" Georgie said. "It will all go away."

"Don't you want it to go away?" Brook said. She had never looked more hurt.

Her parents stepped in front of the boy.

"Everything we have will go away! It will all be lost . . ."

It was enough, I believe, that the two of them agreed. There were no words, and none needed to be said. Words can lie; hearts cannot. Their hearts believed.

Their hearts wanted the world.

"Wake up, sleepyhead," she said. Her name was not Brooke, I knew, but something else. "Time to get up." Her lips were on mine, as they'd been a million times.

The house, I recognized every bit of it.

Before I knew it, she was out of the room and I followed.

Voices and laughter filled the kitchen. Bright, warm sunlight permeated through every window. I went to look out and saw not the Atlantic, as I'd expected, but a large grassy yard stretching far toward a neighboring house. In the living room, next to the familiar wall once decorated by a mural of trees and forest, the wall with the bay window had been painted. I recognized the curve of the beach and the reef that stretched to the horizon, rendered expertly in paint.

"Good morning, Pete," her father said. "Sleep well?"

"I don't know," I said. "I had some really strange dreams."

He was not made from darkness.

Next to him, her mother was equally solid.

Georgie stared blankly at the television.

Mostly importantly, the woman most familiar. Her arms wrapped around me from behind and her chin rested on my shoulder. Her hair was not dark, but light, and not short, but long. There was no mistaking who she was, though. I'd recognize her anywhere.

"I'm glad we're all together," she said.

As I looked out the window, I saw a large front lawn, and two kids playing. I saw none of the darkness, but only light. The dreams I'd had were starting to fade, and the different, yet familiar people I'd met blended into the background.

Every time I sleep, I see her.

When it could be someone else, it is not.

The details may change, but we remain the same. Our world for the making. Our world for the planting, and growing, and walking. Our world . . . and always, always, with her.

> *The things that haunt us*
> *Reappear*
> *Reflecting Inside Our Eyes*

Perrollo's Ladder

Blood rained down onto the leaves of the trees and brush. A thousand *criaturas* were let loose from hell and rose to heaven. Instead of meeting embraces, they met the angels' swords in the sky. Many perished, their limbs and bodies tumbling and burning. Globes of fire lit the night. Ashes and embers settled to the ground, mixing with the mountain's topsoil, which was already saturated with their blood. This was how Ojo Mountain got its dark color, unique to those surrounding it. This is where those surviving *criaturas* remained and hid, unable to show their defeated faces in the underworld, and unable to move freely during daylight. In the darkness, if you look carefully, you might glimpse *criaturas* scurrying about the high, thin ledges, watching and wishing someone might summon them down.

Antonio visited Perrollo every Thursday. He'd walk from his small apartment on Huevo Road, leaving behind the strip malls, electronic billboards, and the never-ending noise of his life with the computer firm. He eagerly turned off his phone. Near the bottom of Ojo Mountain, Antonio always stopped for an ear of corn bathed in lime at his favorite pushcart vendors. No matter how many times he'd ask, Perrollo would always gently decline. "Next time I'm bringing one for you, too. They're delicious, satisfying, and cheap."

"Thank you, but no," Perrollo said. "There are only certain things that I can eat."

"Like what?" Antonio asked. "Mountain goats? Birds? It's so cold and there's nothing up here."

"I get by. Do you want to see the ladder?" Perrollo said.

"I do," Antonio said.

They walked through Perrollo's mountain cottage where he'd lived since school. Perrollo's occult projects filled every shelf, windowsill, and tabletop. Antonio glimpsed lanterns detailed with golden beads his friend claimed only shined in alien worlds, complex dioramas of heaven's streets,

and handmade books scored with symphonies Perrollo heard while he meditated.

Antonio spotted a picture of Perrollo and himself from high school. Perrollo had decorated the frame with castings of their school ring, each painted with bronze or silver shades. Antonio recalled Perrollo's voice from that era.

"The time has come for me to move from my parent's house in this valley, now that we're graduating," he'd said.

"I'll miss you," Antonio had said. "I'm sure you'll do wonderful at college."

"There's nothing for me there," Perrollo had said. "I'm only moving a mile away. On Ojo Mountain. I can be closer to the sky."

"There's no houses. No streets," Antonio had said.

Perrollo had smiled. "I'm going to build them."

Antonio peered over Perrollo's shoulder. "How long have we been coming back here and watching your ladder come together?"

"More years than a tree has rings." Perrollo grinned. He lifted a leg of his oversized white cotton pants upward in order to climb onto a rock ledge.

Antonio nodded. "We've always had that push to find out what made things work, didn't we? I embraced technology and betted everything it'd change the world. I get a hundred messages and hour and I've never felt more alone. You walked away from all that. You seem happier."

"Your answers are in the sky," Perrollo said and pointed up. "But you've always known that, haven't you?"

Barola's claws curled around the lip of Claudia's dresser. He watched her sleep. If Claudia woke she would not have believed there was a *criatura* such as Barola perched in her room. Five wiggling tendrils slithered out from Barola's mouth. They crawled along his bumpy face, eager with anticipation.

He remembered the night her parents conceived Claudia.

How her parents had prayed! They'd wanted a baby so badly, and he'd answered. Countless attempts didn't take. Barola followed their prayers, crawling down the mountainside. What else could he do? Barola lived to grant wishes.

As Fernando and Maria slept, Barola had perched on their dresser. Barola curled up next to Fernando and used the tendrils, prying within Fernando's belly. Their tips were coated with an anesthetic not unlike a mosquito's proboscis. Barola pushed downward inside Fernando's hanging pear-shaped sacks, where he'd suck the nectar. There were more direct routes, but Barola liked exploring, and wanted to take his time. On the end of one tongue, a small bulb inflated as Fernando's juice flowed inside. He'd keep it safe within his mouth.

Used to eating the small, bitter black snakes he found on the mountainside, Barola also chewed green leaves to stave his hunger when there were no snakes. Fernando ate heavy foods and marinated himself with beer and mescal until he fell asleep. The infused fats and fluids made a sweet, luxurious meal for Barola.

Fernando wouldn't notice the scars once Barola finished. Not only was Fernando's belly covered in hair, but the entry points were small and would cover over quickly. At worst, the man would feel itchy and might have a small stomachache for a day.

Once he'd had the man's magic nectar, Barola moved on to the best part: squeezing the juice inside Maria from the bulb. Fernando would sleep soundly beside them while Barola burrowed his head between Maria's legs, opened his mouth and his five tendrils made their way between her folds. The other tongues squeezed the bulb, oozing the essence deep within Maria.

They would have their child, and they wouldn't have the slightest idea, he knew, and that was the best part. They could go on living just as they had, and he could do the same. They'd just be missing a few precious ounces of Claudia. Barola liked cradling the swollen bulb using his other tongues as they swept across the inner walls of his cheeks. He blinked several times to freshen his sore, sand-swept eyes. Barola tried his best to remember the sleeping girl in the bed; he probably would never see her again. If their paths crossed later, Claudia would be grown, and she would likely need something from him. At the moment, though, she was blissfully unaware.

Ojo Mountain towered above them at the furthest part of Perrollo's backyard. The view always made Antonio dizzy. There were small trees and ledges and he wondered what sort of wildlife made such an inhospitable place home. Then he looked at Perrollo and knew they'd at least have to be just as stubborn, smart, and tireless as him. "You didn't ask me to help you build the ladder."

"These things," Perrollo said, "have to be started and ended with one set of hands, otherwise they won't work."

Antonio scurried up and over another small plateau. He found it challenging keeping pace with Perrollo. "What do you mean, it won't work?" Antonio asked. "It's just a ladder."

Perrollo shook his head. "Do you believe your old friend would spend all this time building something as simple and ordinary as a ladder? Why couldn't I just buy one?"

"I don't know. I just thought it was a challenge. A fun project for you to keep busy."

Perrollo shrugged, turned and hurried toward the ladder. He stepped closer and Antonio made out more details; Antonio could see its outline in the shadow. It looked higher. Finger holds were sanded into each rung. The ladder glistened from thousands of gems.

"I've always preferred night. The sun's gone down and the evening breeze arrives." Perrollo bent down and eyeballed the lower rungs. "I could really use a good glass," Perrollo said. "Filled with red wine."

"Sounds like a great plan." Antonio tried to catch Perrollo's eye, but couldn't.

"Yes," Perrollo said. "I've got the perfect bottle."

Perrollo rose, hurried past Antonio, and stumbled toward his hand made cottage. After Perrollo ducked safely inside, Antonio reached out and touched a rung.

Barola writhed onto Claudia's bed without waking her. His five skinny tongues slithered toward Claudia and penetrated her. *They make it so easy,* Barola thought. *Their ears*

are wide-open holes with no coverings. Their noses have two equally open holes. Their mouth might be shut, but their soft lips open with the slightest touch. He imagined what it might be like to kiss with such plump things on his face. His own mouth was thin, hard, and callous. Did theirs contain sensitive nerves, like he'd heard?

The girl's mouth parted as his tendril touched her lips, just as he'd expected. Electric sensations stretched from inside his mouth all the way to the tips of his claws. Barola tasted Claudia's exquisite, intoxicating flavor.

Barola felt his inner organs drink her essence, expanding like dry, brittle sponges dipped in a warm tub. His eyes glistened and his blood flowed smoothly for the first time in what felt like forever. Her vigor would be enough to last him several months.

He looked over her smooth face. The finest of wrinkles inched from the corner of her eye. Barola wondered how one so young could even have wrinkles.

Wrinkles?

Have I gone too far? Have I taken too much? Would she now be prematurely aged because of his greed and selfishness? Barola remembered what Vecelio would do to him. Barola could not suffer another eternity inside Vecelio's dark prison box. He twitched at the idea of being alone with his own thoughts and stench.

Barola pulled his tendrils from inside Claudia.

Because he hadn't slipped his probing tongues from her smoothly, Claudia stirred. Her eyelids fluttered and she sighed. Barola wanted to shush her but his lips could not form the right way to make the sound. Instead, he exhaled slightly so that he made what he thought would be a similar noise. It came out much more like a cat coughing up a hairball.

Claudia stretched; the back of her hand grazed Barola's scaly chest. He stiffened; frightened she'd open her eyes. Instead, she rolled on her side, her back to Barola. He stared at Claudia's scalp through the tiny slivers in her pitch-black hair. He wondered what her dreams were. Had he somehow changed her thoughts? Would she know? Would she be forever changed? He would never find out.

No wonder they wanted her, he thought. *So new. So fresh. So interesting.* His bottom claw twitched as Claudia's juices burned inside his veins. He couldn't stay, and so, Barola left her to her dreams and her life.

Claudia's essence would enable the ladder, and both he and Perrollo would benefit. He recalled Perrollo's recipe. "Essence drawn from an heir of the one who builds the ladder. One who is innocent and does not know the meanness of the world."

Barola understood as Perrollo had pointed to a passage inside the large book. "We need Claudia. Do this and the ladder will bring us rightfully home."

"Don't touch it," Perrollo said. "You're going to ruin everything."

Antonio stepped back, taking his hand with him. "I didn't mean . . ."

Perrollo made it over to him. "I should have told you." He lifted an uncorked, black-labeled bottle of wine and swigged. Perrollo handed Antonio the bottle.

"Okay," Antonio said. "Can you please tell me why this is a big deal?"

"I can use the ladder to fix my cottage's roof. I can use it to lie against the mountain and pick pears and oranges. Tonight? I can use it to call people from the sky."

Antonio squinted.

Perrollo said, "They talk to me. I hear them. They need me to invite them. Otherwise they're trapped."

"You sure it's not just the sunlight baking your brain inside your skull like an egg?" Antonio thought his friend might have been putting him on, or talking in some kind of intricate metaphor, which was not uncommon.

Perrollo said, "You know the story about this mountain? The blood of the underworld stains the dirt. The angels above sealed the gates. Tonight, I'm going to open the doorway."

"So the demons can get inside Heaven?" Antonio said.

"I don't believe in such primitive mythologies," Perrollo said. "Only what I've seen."

"Which is?"

"Lost souls live on this mountain," Perrollo said. "Many of them. They appear primitive and scared. They just need a helping hand."

Antonio said, "Shouldn't we call some organization or the government if that's the case? It could be scary. There could be diseases. They could be cannibals. Anything."

"They're none of those," Perrollo said. "They're the Enlightened Ones. There will soon be a whole new level of understanding and illumination. They've been waiting, just as we've been waiting. They are the missing ones in our history. When we feel spiritual voids, it is because they have not been there to guide us." Perrollo shut his eyes.

In the evening the mountain appeared different. The scraggly brush gave the area character during the day. Darkness camouflaged the brush, which slowed movement. The sharp sunbaked branch tips cut bluntly and quickly, and took much too long to heal. Barola still kept hurrying. It didn't matter to him. Someone called. How could he be so lucky? He'd just filled himself and finished his vampiric relationship with the family. A new one was about to begin, and how perfect that he had renewed energy and strength. Barola would be able to grant any kind of wish, even one of his own.

Barola peered up at the moon. *Maybe that's where I came from.* When he was younger, the other *criaturas* told him their story. Barola couldn't remember a time when he didn't live on the mountain. The older *criaturas* told him their race once fell from the sky. There was an older life they'd come from. One day they'd be called back to the sky. Until then, Barola was to remain hidden and listen for the prayers of the desperate. He'd only hear them if he was quiet and alone, and not too well-fed. He would answer the human's prayers. In return he'd gain nourishment from their golden sanguinity. Nothing more.

As he got older, many *criaturas* disappeared. He'd discovered several of their remains at different times. They'd all died the same way, their bodies shriveled and stiff. It'd looked like they'd tried digging themselves into the ground.

Just thinking of it frightened Barola. What else could he have done? They never came to him for help. They'd split up, afraid ganging might make them easier for the wrathful humans to spot.

Barola heard the call, much stronger than any before. Somehow the voice was coming not from the village, but impossibly, from the mountain itself. He recognized the voice.

Perrollo pointed toward the ladder, which had grown taller. Antonio had missed it. He didn't understand. He'd only looked away for a moment. "What is it doing?" he asked.

Perrollo said, "Reaching for the sky. Like I always said it would."

"I always thought you were exaggerating," Antonio said. "You weren't joking?"

"You didn't believe me when I told you things. Aren't you my friend?" Perrollo said.

"Of course. You have to admit that you do exaggerate things. They're like Bible stories. Like angels fighting in the clouds," Antonio said.

Perrollo wasn't smiling.

"You will find nothing I told you all these years was false. If anything I've left things out. These worlds are more fantastic than I can describe to you." Perrollo shook his head. "You'll see."

Just then, something large rustled behind the ladder. Antonio hopped backward. His arm shook. He had no weapons. Not even a stick. He thought it had to be a mountain lion; one so close could certainly gash them fatally. Perrollo was closest and Antonio raced through a thousand thoughts. How could he scare the mountain lion away? He reviewed conversations, websites, images hovered within blurry edges of his memory. *What should I do?*

Two big eyes caught the light and blinked.

The *criatura* stood only a few feet from them. Antonio tried to say something to warn Perrollo but couldn't find his voice.

Perrollo looked right at the *criatura*, seemingly unafraid.

He reached out a hand. "Come out from there," Perrollo said

The *criatura* was certainly not a mountain lion.

"Have you been here long, Barola?"

Antonio realized Barola was not human. The creature looked to him like a lizard standing on its hind legs. Barola spoke. "You have called for me." His mouth moved, although the words didn't seem to match the movements. "I am here to offer what little I can." His voice sounded hollow, as though he spoke through the inside sound hole of a flamenco guitar.

Antonio remained still, even though he wanted to run away from the *criatura*.

"Three things make the ladder work. You need to hear the call. That's why I've built my home as close to the sky as I could. Then there's the building of the ladder, of course. Last, we're sprinkling the ladder with Claudia's essence. Barola helped us."

The *criatura* opened his mouth and slid out his tongues, four of which cradled the fifth's bulb.

Perrollo finished the last of his wine with a sigh and offered the glass to Barola. The *criatura's* tongues squeezed the bulb. Clear fluid dripped from its bulb and filled Perrollo's glass.

The tongues squeezed one last drop and slid back inside Barola's mouth. "I only took just enough. She'll never feel it."

"Perfect." Perrollo took the wine glass filled with Claudia's essence to the ladder and dipped his fingers in the fluid. He painted the sides and rungs of the ladder with the essence. As his fingers grazed past, the coated areas glistened as though backlit from fireflies.

Antonio could not be sure, but he swore the ladder twitched from Perrollo's touch.

Antonio knew Perrollo's promises were real. The ladder would work.

"I've finished the ladder." Perrollo gestured to the still-growing structure. "You can go home."

Barola inched forward; he touched the ladder with one of his talons. "You have led the way."

"What am I supposed to do?" Antonio asked.

"You were invited to my home, and so, you are invited to come along with us," Perrollo said.

Antonio shook his head. "I don't know. Where would we go? Are we coming back?"

"All these questions! Life's too short to second-guess everything. You just need to trust that I would never steer you wrong."

"So there's no choice?"

"You can stay here and dream of what you see. Maybe one day your prayers will be answered and you'll be able to join us then. If there is anyone left to hear you, that is." Perrollo put a foot on the bottom rung and his hands on the sides. "You can simply stay here and watch. I bid you my best desire either way."

"I don't know," Antonio said. "This is all so sudden."

"You haven't been listening to me all these years." Both Perrollo's feet were on the ladder now.

Barola stood behind Perrollo. His mouth opened and

Antonio could see things moving around within. *My friend is going to die*, he thought. *That creature might kill him and there's nothing I can do to stop it.*

Antonio knew he was wrong. Barola was not going to kill Perrollo. He realized this because, during that moment, the sky opened. Rolling cloud planes hovered a few hundred feet beyond. The air smelled of the sweet mountain flowers mixed with the storm's broken electric ozone. The insects on the mountainside harmonized.

All manner of *criatura* gathered near Antonio. His face flushed as they crowded nearby. One being hunched in such a way that Antonio could only place it as some kind of upright dog. It shared the same sort of mottled, grayish fur, bare in patches, and dried to the root, as a coyote. Its black eyes glistened. Antonio saw his reflection on their curvature. The *criatura* matched his stare and opened its mouth, licking its skinny, gray lips with an even thinner, drier tongue. Its nib-like teeth chattered. Black stains dotted its otherwise pale, pink throat.

A scent not dissimilar to bleach overtook Antonio as another of the hidden beings slithered behind him. Feeling the weight of something peering over his shoulder, Antonio moved his head. A thin scaly face looked back, its eyes only inches away, hovering over his right shoulder. The head lingered and a hollow ticking sounded from the chamber if its mouth. A long neck stretched nearly to the ground, colored in rings of light browns and greens. If it'd coiled up, or leaned against a tree, Antonio imagined no one would give it a second thought, because it may have been a large piece from a dried old desert tree. As it moved, he was reminded of the coral snakes he'd seen on a television program as a child. One moment they were still, the next, they'd strike and deliver a deadly bite. This thing could end his life on a whim, he knew.

Others circled Perrollo. One looked very much like Barola, only taller and had missing one arm from below its left elbow.

A large white entity gracefully climbed down the mountain in back of them all. Each leg was only the thickness of a pencil, it seemed. Even so, the overall size rivaled the others. A slightly segmented body dangled between the dozen legs and eye tipped stems kept tabs on the goings on. This pale insect was followed by two more, each smaller than the one before.

"Now that we are all here," Perrollo said, "let's hurry."

Perrollo climbed the ladder and Barola followed.

Nothing inside Antonio made him want to join them. Everything inside him made him want to watch.

Something brushed past him. Other beings similar to Barola went to the ladder and climbed.

Thunder rumbled. The clouds darkened and rolled.

Perrollo arrived near the middle of the ladder. Barola stood underneath him. The other *criaturas* caught up.

Perrollo turned backward and his eyes met Antonio's. He didn't smile or nod. He just climbed another step. The ladder stretched higher than Antonio realized.

The clouds ahead of Perrollo parted. He hesitated before he climbed inside. The storm turned magnificent colors as he disappeared. Pinks turned into deep reds. Blacks turned into oranges. Veins of lightning danced through the thunderheads.

Maybe I should have gone, Antonio thought. *Maybe it's not too late.* He stepped forward and hurried toward the ladder. Above him the others had nearly vanished inside the clouds. He watched their feet disappear.

As each step brought him higher, Antonio remembered the warnings Perrollo had uttered.

And as Antonio put his first foot on the ladder he felt anything but brave. *Why am I doing this? Doesn't this go against everything I thought I wouldn't do? I always said I wouldn't follow Perrollo on his weird occult adventures.*

This was different. This was a ladder that reached inside heaven. How could that be frightening?

His entire body was on the ladder and he looked up, despite his thinking he shouldn't. The ladder stretched impossibly high until it touched the clouds. Antonio saw no sign of what might be keeping it upright. What? Was he supposed to have faith that it would hold him and stay upright?

This thing is as high as airplanes. Even higher. How the hell am I supposed to climb so high so quickly? How did Perrollo manage? It just physically doesn't seem possible that quickly.

A thought blanketed his mind.

The ladder helps. The ladder takes you and raises you toward the sky, if you are one of the chosen.

Perrollo's words.

Am I one? He thought for a moment while he climbed. He must have been. Not only had Perrollo invited him along, but Antonio had never settled down, either. He'd taken his jobs and cycled through his relationships. Commitments broke, if he even agreed to them in the first place. But he found himself, finally and absolutely, called to a higher place. Called by Perrollo. Called by the ladder.

Antonio looked up. *Doesn't seem too high yet.* The bottom of the clouds seemed a lifetime away.

Don't look down.

He did, despite himself. He was sorry he did because Antonio found himself much higher than he'd anticipated. He grabbed the sides of the ladder; the height made him dizzy. His hands were sweating and he very much wanted to rush back down the ladder. He could see the cottage and the town below.

Don't look down. Look up. Keep climbing. There's no turning back. He steeled himself, took a breath, and stretched his fingers for the next rung.

After Antonio reached halfway to the top, the heavy air made breathing difficult. He hung his head on a step. The world around him spun as though he'd drunk half a bottle of tequila. He clutched the sides. *Make it stop. Please don't let this happen. I'm too high on the ladder to fall without breaking something.*

Then the ladder shook. It was small at first, but he still felt it. He couldn't lift his head. The dizziness had bloomed into a horrid migraine. His eyes watered and fingers of bright acidic pain burrowed through his sinuses and behind his eyes.

Don't fall, whatever you do. Hang on.

He could only pray.

The ladder jostled. He felt like a plastic soldier on the end of a toy fire truck ladder. He crouched against it as hard as he could, but he was weakening by the second. The pain was too intense.

Then the ladder's movements became violent. He wished there was wind and rain so that that might explain why the ladder was moving, but there was nothing. He still heard the chorus of insects and still smelled the broken nighttime air.

His stomach hurt. To add to his misery, Antonio sensed what little strength remained sift away from his muscles. *I'm too high off the ground!*

Switching quickly to the right and the left, the ladder's

feet came loose, spraying small bombs of dirt. He imagined a toddler twisting the ladder like a straw in a bottle of warm milk and laughing at him. Then he pictured Perrollo doing so.

He heard something snapping. The ride intensified. The edges of the ladder spread apart. The ladder cracked and he felt the split coming from above. He still couldn't look up. There was too much movement. Antonio felt too weak and sick to fight.

Maybe if he just hung on long enough it would stop and he'd be able to calmly lower himself safely . . .

The rungs broke free. One smacked his nose and chin. The ones he held onto lost their weight and he felt air and gravity pull him.

He fell from the ladder as it exploded into pieces around him. *How will Perrollo get back?*

Antonio dropped. Hundreds of shredded pieces of the ladder fell around him. For a brief moment he felt nothing at all. His headache was gone. His stomach was not sour. His body felt just fine. Then pain flowed into every nook. He tried to raise his head to see how he'd fallen and found he was straight on his back. *Please don't let me be paralyzed,* he thought and wiggled his toes and back to make sure. Doing so nearly blinded him from pain.

The pieces of Perrollo's ladder continued to drop from the sky. Tiny splinters and half-pieces crashed everywhere throughout Perrollo's backyard.

Antonio felt the first rain drop on the middle of his left cheek. Quickly, there was more. The drizzle felt oily and warm as though infused with pollutants and acids. Then the rain pelted Antonio. Only it was not truly rain.

Antonio turned his hands over and found them coated with reddish, runny blood. *It has to be blood,* he thought. *What else could it be?*

He did his best to struggle to his side. The pain was excruciating. He'd had to have broken something, he was sure. A rib or three. His legs did work. He kicked and pushed his way through the dirt.

The blood rained down.

Antonio was coated and dripping, the fluid warm and fresh. The dirt muddied every bit of him. Blood showered him. He smelled hot, recently spilled organic minerals; he gagged.

Please let it stop, he thought. *Please. So much blood. Everywhere on everything. The mud soaked with blood.*

Antonio's eyes stung. He couldn't keep it from his mouth or nose. He wondered if Perrollo was dead.

Not dead. Just his body's gone. Changed. Distilled.

The downpour of blood lightened.

Perrollo's stories came back to him. The creatures from the underworld tried to rise, but were cut down at the gateways.

Cut down.

Perrollo.

The earth turned dark red, soaked with blood. The plants looked painted. The small furniture, the rocks, the steps, the wine bottle: every bit oozed with sanguine color. Perrollo's blood nourished the land where he'd worked and lived. His essence covered Antonio.

They had to have been killed, Antonio believed. How else could he explain the deluge of blood? How else to define the gruesome explosion? How else, unless there was another reason Antonio could not readily grasp? Had they actually been slaughtered, or had they crossed over, the Angels lowering their swords?

Antonio could not know for sure. Perrollo had been right about that, after all. He could only ask and hope for an answer.

He turned on his back. His body ached and stunk, his skin sticky from the quickly drying gore.

The clouds parted, showing the same clear sky as before they'd arrived. There was no trace of Perrollo, Barola, or the *criaturas*.

Antonio wondered what he would do next. Would he heal? How would he explain his condition? Where would he go to wash the blood from his body and clothes? He didn't know.

Ahead of him, though, when he blinked, he could still see Perrollo's ladder in his mind's eye. In that moment Antonio knew . . . knew exactly what he would have to do.

AFTERWORD

The Horror Writer's Association has some really cool programs for young writers, including a Mentor-Mentee program. Aspiring authors are matched with more experienced writers, professionals. Naturally, the young writer sometimes waits awhile to get assigned a pro. Occasionally, the match doesn't work, for a number of reasons. And that's okay, the head of the program tries another match. I've participated in the program for maybe twelve years. As an experienced writer, it is rewarding to watch a neophyte writer learn, apply new knowledge, gain confidence, and begin writing good stuff. I've had five mentees, each coming with widely varying degrees of experience and displaying different levels of talent. Some I worked with for a year or two, others for only a few months. Each one of the five matured and went on to publish professionally, which made me happy and proud.

That's how I met John, in the HWA Mentor-Mentee program. After being assigned, he wrote, introduced himself, told me his aspirations, and what he hoped I could help him accomplish. I knew from the start with the first piece of work I read that John had the right stuff. A characteristic that even now shows up in the stories of this collection. It is impossible to not get involved in a John Palisano story if you read the first page or so. He builds his stories around a compelling premise, not just some gory splatter display intended to shock or arouse. There is plenty of real emotion in a JP story, and from the beginning I could tell an adult intellect lay behind the words. Oh, he needed to focus and gain confidence, but that happened quickly enough. I think by the fifth or sixth story I read, we both knew John would soon be placing his work. I'm not positive, but I think he went on to revise and even place some of the earliest stories we worked on.

John is the only mentee that I've met and spent quite a bit of time with at conventions, readings, book signings. What a pleasure. As they say: John is a good guy, well-deserving of all the success his writing generates. We've read together at different conventions, been on panels, we both spoke/sang at a memorial for another young writer, Michael Louis Calvillo, who passed on before his time.

So it is indeed a pleasure to read this collection of compelling stories, each one a polished gem. I know that some of the work is autobiographical fiction, generated from real life. And that in itself is interesting, because the longer I write the more I believe everything we write is autobiographical. Another interesting observation, at least to me, is that several of these stories were from venues where John and I shared the table of contents. Which is especially satisfying for me.

With this afterword, I'd like to acknowledge my most accomplished HWA mentee, now a pro, and welcome my admired colleague, John Palisano.

—Gene O'Neill
Napa, California

All That WiThers

STORY
NOTES

"Happy Joe's Rest Stop"

Since I was a child, I've had a dream where I stood across from my father as a dark gulf opened between us. It grows until I can't see him anymore. In the dream, he's lost. That is the emotional hinge upon which Happy Joe's swings. On the surface, this seems like it could possibly be a standard monster attack story, and there are some fun action set pieces, but the Man in White Without A Face is pulling those images from our subconscious of what he thinks we'd be most afraid of. He underestimates the power from which fear might rally. As with so many of my stories, it begins and ends with a Dad and his son. This one took home the 2016 Bram Stoker Award for Excellence in Short Fiction.

"Splinterette"

This was written in Cupertino, California in a hotel room. The folks I was with wanted to go out. I looked at the big wooden desk with a view of the woods as a piece of heaven—a far greater temptation for me. They left me to it, and later that night when they returned I shared my Moleskine, filled to the end with this story and its accompanying drawings. A 2014 Finalist for the Bram Stoker Award for Excellence in Short Fiction.

"The Geminis"

For a time, I worked as a dog walker in the hills above Los Angeles. The section I was in was quiet, and trailed off into many undeveloped tracts high up. My overactive imagination went into overdrive. I felt eyes watching me. I heard ancient voices. I saw eyes peering out at me from slits in the sandstone. Rather than quit my job and drink myself into oblivion, I put these mind tricks into a story. I also was thinking about love's power, especially when it is new, and how it can, for a time, make our very frightening world feel tamed just enough for us to get through. A 2013 Finalist for the Bram Stoker Award for Excellence in Short Fiction.

"Available Light"

Originally titled "The Thing That Fell from The Sky", and beginning life as a rather long poem, this story tells the tale of two brothers, and of a family who are trying to keep their lives together despite some seriously strange hurdles. A 2012 Finalist for the Bram Stoker Award for Excellence in Short Fiction.

"Long Walk Home"

This one stressed me out a great deal while putting it down. I felt a creeping dread the entire time. My guts were tied up. Who knows if it translates into the story and to you, but it was certainly one of those tales that touched a nerve inside me. It felt all too real, as though the Sludge could be seen just over the horizon, ready to envelop us all.

"My Darkness Travels on Sunshine"

The photo-chemical process of motion picture filmmaking always fascinated me. Shooting on actual film is becoming a lost art, unfortunately. Organic molecules capturing light! It's real magic stuff. So here we wonder what if there were an emulsion that captured the opposite spectrum? What if a dark otherworld could be seen, captured and glimpsed in this way? This one was inspired by S. T. Joshi's magnificent *Black Wings* anthologies.

"The Haven"

This was a breakthrough piece for me. It began, as many of my works, in a dream, in which I found myself in high school again, the walls made of sticky flesh. Despite my best efforts, I kept getting stuck to it. I woke thinking it was a neat idea: a place covered in living flesh. I flipped it around and played with some symbols and settled on a man-child stuck inside a house covered in his mother's ever creeping flesh. Metaphoric and symbolic, it stands as a personal favorite.

"To the Stars That Fooled You"

Growing up, I'd often head into New York City with my dad as he went to work at CBS. Most of the time it'd be during the day. I'd hang with him a little bit, but more often, I'd head right down to Greenwich Village and just explore. One of my favorite things to do was to check out the record shops. Just browsing, you'd hear amazing music over the store PA. Once in a while, my Dad would stay overnight in the City. We never stayed at the Chelsea, but I made it there many times, and met some amazing characters. I love the original wave of punk, and thought I'd play up a fantasy that maybe an infamous incident wasn't driven by drugs or madness, but by something else entirely. The title plays on fame and that the starlight we see is probably from stars that died long ago.

"Mother You Can Watch"

Christopher Conlon put together an amazing poetry collection centered around Hitchcock films. I chose *Psycho*. An easy, obvious choice, but I did my best to flip it around and really get into the weird sexuality between mother and son.

"Outlaws of Hill County"

The Longfellow! One of my favorite creatures. It hides by blending into trees like a pitch-black praying mantis, and preys on kids on Halloween by sucking their souls out through their fingertips. Its name is a fun literally nod, even if it doesn't make total sense. The world here is as rich as anything I've ever created at novel length. Probably my most reprinted story at this point.

"Welcome to the Jungle"

This was written as an absolute hoot. Living in Hollywood, I know folks who will go to insane lengths to get their SAG cards and an IMDB credit. I love them for it, but also know of some who've gotten into scary situations while answering casting calls. Luckily, they escaped unharmed. Mostly. In the story, we also get to meet a really awful creature named Red, who lives in a basement, which are very rare in Los Angeles. Never a good sign. Of course, there are some really fun Guns n' Roses nods along the way.

"Wings for Wheels"

I've been a lifelong Springsteen fan. There were pilgrimages to his shows by me, my friends, and family throughout my life. So when I found out I'd be a part of tribute anthology, I flipped. The only hard part? Making "Thunder Road" scary. That song is like *Grease* meets John Steinbeck. I found the key to the story in the line about the boys having ghosts in their eyes. At the time, I was married to a Jersey Girl from just outside Asbury Park, so we made a few pilgrimages down that way and I took a lot of mental notes. I love the story, and there are subtle nods to other Bruce songs throughout. The music I made for the trailer to the book was questioned by Bruce's people to make sure it wasn't an actual Springsteen track. It wasn't. Just a very realistic simulation. That was a great compliment.

"Secret Sea"

The premise for this one: What if someone turning into the undead remembered? What if their minds weren't blank, primal slates? What if it hurt like hell? And what if the person who found out that secret tried to weigh them down so that they floated in a secret sea of the undead until they drowned? And say that didn't quite do the job.

"Eternal Valley"

Taking place in early America as a young family makes their way out west in order to help their young child recover in a warmer, less severe environment, the story is a sort of prequel to the next story in the collection, "Curious Banks of the Wabash River", as it shows the creature in the water from that story seventy years earlier. It also flips the expectation of a monster in a lake being there to hurt. What if it were there to heal?

"The Curious Banks of the Wabash River"

This story has always been one of my favorites because of the characters. This place seems so damn real to me, although I've never been there or seen anything like it. The mythology returns to me and draws my story mind there often. I'm glad it's finally being read with this collection.

"The Tennatrick"

What if the California wildfires are not being started by drought or arson? What if there are large creatures whose very life cycle depends upon fire? That was the idea behind The Tennatrick. Sometimes accused of being over the top in its action, which was intentionally cartoonish. Why? Because the entire conceit seemed fun and outrageous, so I wanted to make a big monster story on the page, complete with a heroine that should have been dead any number of times.

"Vampiro"

For a short time, I had a friend who hated himself. Like the boss in this story, he was Latino, but hated being so. He spoke about it all the time. But then? If someone else was ever critical, he'd go nuts. I thought that'd be an interesting thing to explore: cultural self-hate. That, and I thought it'd be fun to play with the No Man's Land area right near the border of the United States and Mexico, which if you've ever been, is eerie and quiet in the worst way. Of course, I thought it'd be a great place to find meals for vampires and get rid of the bodies of people caught between two countries—lost on one side, unwanted on the other, with official resources spread too thin to deal with the situation. Who'd know or care if they were done in by the elements or the stray, self-loathing vampire?

"X is for Xyx"

Darkness brought this story out of me. I barely remember writing during that period of my life. It was one of the first complete stories I completed right after my divorce. To say I was in a deep emotional hole would be putting it mildly. I suffered near-crippling anxiety non-stop for a few years. Thankfully, that has been surmounted, and all that remains are the writings I made to channel it all outward. There are some tough passages concerning depression and suicide. It's an honest reflection of a person struggling to make sense of life through grief.

"Sunset Beach"

For a short time, *Famous Monsters* had an online fiction magazine. It being *Famous Monsters*, I wanted to make a big monster story. What better place than a sunny beachfront with a nearly escapable monster?

"I Know This World"

I first met Michael Louis Calvillo in Toronto at a World Horror Convention. We became fast friends; he, his wife Michelle, and Benjamin Kane Ethridge. There were many cliques and we were these young outcasts. We three talked about the amazing day when we'd be published by the big five New York publishers and would gain entry into those elusive circles. Mike gave me a copy of his book, which blew me away. We lost Mike at a very young age to cancer, and there is not a day that goes by that I don't think of him, his stories, or our many conversations. I was beyond honored to be asked to participate in a special edition of his first novel. I did my best to make an afterworld to his story . . . one I hope like crazy Mike would dig.

"Forever"

We always hear about how fast life is. One never knows when we'll be counting down the hours, and we will be crossing over into the great unknown. Sometimes there are special people waiting to greet us on the other side. . . people who have meant a lot to us. . . a soul that will help us transition and adjust. There's one soul here who greets our narrator who meant more to her than any person during her life.

"Gaia Ungaia"

Probably the most explanatory of my stories when it comes to unravelling the mythology and other-verse that runs through several of my stories ("Perrollo's Ladder", "I Know This World", "Available Light", "The Geminis", *Nerves*). It literally means: earth-unearthed. Our world turned upside-down and inside out. There are keys to other stories in here that unlock them. Of course, there are more secrets just as the answers to the first questions are given.

"Perrollo's Ladder"

Another rich and metaphoric story. How fun to play with the idea that the old spiritual story device of building a ladder to get to heaven actually has the opposite effect. Perrollo is very passionate and driven and totally convinced this is a benign and wonderful way to attain a lofty spiritual place. Too bad it rains hell. Literally. I think there's a lot more to this story, and even though it stops, it sure feels like it can keep going. This is also tied into the world of my novel *Nerves*, through the ladder and through the completely sickening and nasty Criaturas, one of whom plays a vital role in the *Nerves* universe.

About the Author

John Palisano's nonfiction has appeared in *Fangoria* and *Dark Discoveries* magazines. He has been nominated for the Bram Stoker Award three times, and won once for his short fiction.

He had a pair of books with Samhain Publishing, *Dust of the Dead*, and *Ghost Heart*. His novel *Nerves* was published through Bad Moon Books. *Night of 1,000 Beasts* is coming soon. He has edited the anthologies *Scales & Tales* and *Unnatural Tales of the Jackalope*.

John's short stories have appeared in anthologies from Darkhouse, PS Publishing, Darkscribe, The Lovecraft eZine, Horror Library, DarkFuse, Bizarro Pulp, Written Backwards, Dark Continents, and others.

Say 'hello' at *www.JohnPalisano.com*, his Amazon Author Page, *www.amazon.com/author/johnpalisano*, or on social media such as Facebook, *www.facebook.com/johnpalisano*, and Twitter, *www.twitter.com/johnpalisano*.

All That Withers